ROAD TO PARADISE

Paullina Simons was born in Leningrad and emigrated to the United States in 1973. She lives close to New York with her husband and four children. Go to her website, www.paullinasimons.com, for more information about her novels.

Visit www.AuthorTracker.co.uk for exclusive updates on Paullina Simons.

By the same author

Tully
Red Leaves
Eleven Hours
The Bronze Horseman
Tatiana and Alexander
The Summer Garden
The Girl in Times Square

ROAD TO PARADISE

HARPER

...ns *Publishers*
... Palace Road
Hammersmith, London W6 8JB

www.harpercollins.co.uk

This paperback edition 2008
1

First published in Great Britain by
HarperCollins*Publishers* 2007

The extract from "I walked the boulevard" is reprinted from
COMPLETE POEMS 1904-1962, by E.E. Cummings, edited by
George J. Firmage, by permission of W.W. Norton & Company.
Copyright © 1991 by the Trustees for the E.E. Cummings Trust and
George James Firmage.

Paullina Simons asserts her right to
be identified as the author of this work.

A CIP catalogue record for this book is
available from the British Library

ISBN: 978 0 00 724158 3

Typeset in Goudy by Palimpsest Book Production Limited,
Grangemouth, Stirlingshire

Printed and bound in Great Britain by Clays Ltd, St Ives plc

Mixed Sources
Product group from well-managed
forests and other controlled sources
www.fsc.org   Cert no. SW-COC-1806
© 1996 Forest Stewardship Council

FSC is a non-profit international organisation established
to promote the responsible management of the world's forests.
Products carrying the FSC label are independently certified
to assure consumers that they come from forests that are managed
to meet the social, economic and ecological needs
of present and future generations.

Find out more about HarperCollins and the environment at
www.harpercollins.co.uk/green

*For my husband's mother, Elaine Ryan, from
the time she was twenty, a mother first*

Earth's crammed with heaven,
And every common bush afire with God;
But only he who sees, takes off his shoes

ELIZABETH BARRETT BROWNING

And all my former life is seen
A crazy drowsy beautiful and utterly
appalling dream

ALEXANDER BLOK

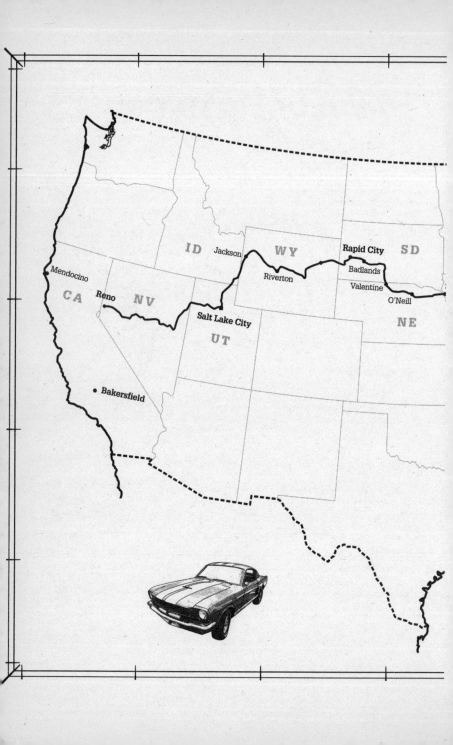

Road to Paradise

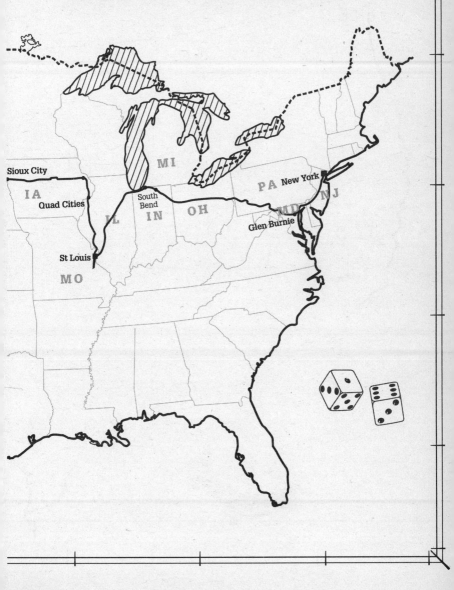

PROLOGUE
"MOTEL"

Do what you like, Shelby Sloane, the bartered bride had said to me, smiling like an enigma, just remember: all roads lead to where you stand.

Back then I said, what does *that* mean?

This morning I knew. It was the morning of the third day I had been trapped in a room, two miles from the main drag of the Reno strip in a place called "Motel."

I stood alone, broke, and in Reno.

There is one road that leads to Reno from the east—Interstate 80, and in Salt Lake City, Utah, 569 miles away, there is a bellman at a four-star hotel who, when asked if there is perhaps a more scenic route than the mind-numbing Interstate, blinks at me his contempt in the sunshine before slowly saying, "In *Nevada?*"

But there *is* another road in Nevada that takes you almost there: U.S. 50, the loneliest road in America.

Reno is in the high desert valley, 4500 feet above sea level, but the highway climbs into the mountains before twisting down the black unlit slopes to the washbasin where the lights are. The town itself is one street, Virginia, running in a straight line between the mountain passes.

On Virginia stands the Eldorado and the Circus Circus; the Romantic Sensations Club; Horseshoe, the 24-hr pawn shop ("nothing refused!"); the Wild Orchid Club ("Hustler's All-new Girls!"); Heidi's Family Restaurant; Adult Bookstore ("Under New Management: More Variety!"); Limericks Pub&Grill (*Once a young lass from Mamaroneck/Decided to go on a trek* . . .); Arch Discount Liquors; Adults Only Cabaret (Filipino waitresses in Island outfits); St. Francis Hotel; Ho-Hum Motel; Pioneer and Premier Jewelry&Loan; "Thunderbolt: Buy Here! Pay Here! We buy Clean Cars and Trucks!"; Adventure Inn: Exotic Theme Rooms *and* Wedding Chapel; a billboard asking, "Is Purity and Truth of Devotion to Jesus Central to your Life?" and "Motel."

That's where I am.

"Motel" is a beige, drab two-story structure with rusted landings built around a cement square courtyard that serves both as a parking lot and a deck for the swimming pool. The cars are parked in stalls around the pool right behind the lounge chairs. Not my car, because that's vanished, but other people's cars, sure.

I was waiting for the girl in the mini-skirt to come back. She wasn't supposed to have left in the first place, so waiting for her was rather like waiting for the unscheduled train to run over the car stalled on the tracks. I came back for her, and she had disappeared. Along with my car. The note she left me could have been written in hieroglyphs. "Shel, where are you? I thought you were coming back. Guess not. I've gone to look for you. Here's hoping I find you." Two kisses followed by two hugs, as if we were sophomores in junior high passing notes back and forth. She had taken her things.

I was half-hoping the "Motel" manager would throw me out, seeing that I had no money and couldn't pay for the room, but he said with a smile and a wink, "Room's bought and paid for till the twentieth, dahrlin'." As I walked away I was tempted to ask the twentieth of what, but didn't.

The first day I didn't get that upset. I felt it was penance. I hadn't done what I was supposed to; it was only right she didn't do what she was supposed to.

The second day I spent foaming in righteous, purifying fury. I was eighteen, stopping for a day in Reno, on my way even farther west, to help out a fellow pilgrim I met along the way, and look what I got for my troubles. I whiled away the hours compulsively shredding into tinier and tinier strips fashion magazines, an old newspaper, informational brochures on Reno, and gambling tips, then strewing them all over the room. "TOURIST ATTRACTIONS!" "PLACES TO EAT!" "THINGS TO DO!" all sawdust on the floor.

Paradise, California, Butte County, Sierra Nevada Mountains, Tall Pines, Blue Skies, Paradise Pines, Lovelock and Golden Nugget days. Paradise Ridge was inhabited by the Maidu Indians who lived there ten thousand years before white man came. In Magalia, near Paradise, gold was found in 1859. The Magalia Nugget is world renowned, weighing fifty-four pounds, of which forty-nine ounces is pure gold. And my stagecoach of life had stopped in Paradise, near Magalia, on its way out west. It was summer of 1981.

Days in an empty room while outside was full of rain.

Rain, in Reno, in August!

The first day I ate the musty, half-eaten candy bars the girl had kindly left behind and an open bag of potato chips. The second day I finished a bag of peanuts and tortilla chips so stale they tasted like shoe laces, but I ate them anyway and was grateful. I drank water from the tap.

Inside me was detritus from weeks on the open road. The stop sign near Valparaiso, Indiana. The Sand Hills of Nebraska. The Great Divide in Wyoming that, I thought then, split my life into the before and after. Silly me. Yesterday Paradise. Today Reno. Like still frames. Here is Shelby driving her Shelby—the car dreams are made of. I have a picture; it must have happened. Here is the flat road before me. Here are the Pomeranians. Here is the sunset in St. Louis. Here's the Ohio, the Mississippi, the Missouri, the Black Hills, the Yellow Dunes, the casinos and the slot machines, and Interior, South Dakota, with Floyd, that sad, tattooed boy.

Do what you like.

Indeed.

When we spotted her a second time, we couldn't believe it was

3

the same gal. I slowed down, we looked. Can it be? we said. It is. Should we stop? No, no. No hitchhikers. But she waved to us; recognized us. Look, it's fate, I said. What are the chances of running into the same girl in different states, hundreds of miles apart. I don't believe in fate, said my friend Gina. Come on, I said. You gotta believe in something. What *do* you believe in?

Not fate, said Gina, pointing. And not her.

I cajoled. We'll give her a lift down the road. When it stops being convenient, we'll let her off. I saw her in the rearview mirror running toward us. Running and waving. That frame is on every page in my helpless head. Seeing her get closer and closer. This is what I keep coming back to: I should have kept going.

If only I hadn't gotten that damn, cursed, awful, hateful, hated car. How I loved that car. Where was it?

At night I paced like a caged tiger, growling under my breath, choking on my frustration. I couldn't sleep, couldn't lie down, couldn't watch TV, couldn't sit still, couldn't think, couldn't breathe. Night was senseless; day was worse.

During the day, I prayed for night to come. But at night I barricaded the front door with two chairs and a dresser; I chained and locked it, and locked the window looking out onto the open landing. I didn't turn on the TV because I wanted to hear every footstep coming close, but every footstep coming close made my heart rip out of my chest. Now that the others were gone, I thought at any moment "they'd" be coming for me; a few days ago there were three of us and today only I was left. Otherwise how to explain my car's vanishing, my friends' vanishing?

On the third day of rain, I thought I was losing my mind. I couldn't recall the farms of Iowa anymore, or when we crossed the Mississippi. I couldn't remember if I'd graduated, the last name of my good friend Marc, my home phone number. I didn't know what to do. The girls were gone, my car was gone, my money was gone, phone numbers had left my head, and a man at the reception desk was smiling at me with his filthy grin saying, "Stay as long as you like, dahrlin'."

On the third morning I slept. I had nothing to eat and nowhere to go. I didn't know where relief was going to come from, and I couldn't allow a single thought without doubling over in fear and despair. Perhaps my hitchhiker was wrong and the Eastern spiritualists right. You *should* train yourself to let go of all passions. Train yourself to let go of all earthly things, detach yourself from life.

Think only not to think.

Will only not to will.

Feel only not to feel.

God have pity on me, I was crying in my self-pity, on my knees in front of one bed, then the other, my forehead sunk into musty blankets.

Help me. Help me. Please. Why hadn't I insisted she tell me what the fourteenth station of the cross was? She told me that no prayer asked in faith could remain unanswered at the fourteenth station; and when I asked what it was, she became coy. "You'll have to learn one to thirteen first," she said. Where was I supposed to learn this? On U.S. 83 in South Dakota? In the Badlands? From junkyard Floyd? Besides, back then I was curious but fundamentally indifferent. And why not? I was young, the sun was shining, my car was fast like a jet, and on the radio, one way or another, it was paradise by the dashboard light every night for the local girls. I should've insisted she tell me, because now, when the only thing that remained true was that I was still eighteen, I didn't know where to turn.

Maybe that Gideon's Bible in the musty drawer would shed some light on the fourteen stations, but no. I was by the side of the bed, kneeling in the paper shrapnel, my fingers sightlessly tracing the words I didn't and couldn't understand, closing the Book, opening it to a random page, sticking my finger into a paragraph, struggling to focus. This is what I got:

Lift up thy hands, which hang down, and thy feeble knees.

I got up and climbed into bed. It was still raining hard. How could I stand one more day in here, waiting, listening through the curtains for the steps of the one who was coming to kill me? I didn't know what time it was. It felt early, though I couldn't be sure because the night before in my helpless terrors, I'd smashed the alarm clock with the heel of one of my newly-bought summer sandals. This morning was so dark and gray, it could've been after dusk, or before sunrise. It just was, without dimension.

Suddenly there was a knock on the door. Not the tentative knock of an illegal immigrant asking to clean my room, but the insistent, demanding knock of a man's fisted knuckles. I jumped out of bed and hid in the closet.

"Police. Open up."

I threw on some clothes and peeked through the hole in the curtain. I moved furniture out of the way and opened up. Two cops in different uniforms stood outside on the second-floor landing.

"Shelby Sloane?"

"Who wants to know?"

One flashed his badge. "Detective Yeomans. Paradise Police Department."

The other flashed his badge. "Detective Johnson, Reno Police Department."

"Do you have anything to eat?" I asked.

"What? No. Are you Shelby?"

I felt like falling down. Nodding, I held on to the door handle. I said nothing; they said nothing.

"We found out what happened to your car."

"Did you." It was not a question. It was as if I already knew. I wanted to say, well, took you long enough to find a car of which only a single one—mine—was made in the year 1966. One car, and it's taken the police departments in two cities three days to find it. Good job.

"I'm real hungry. Is the phone working?"

"How would we know if your phone's working?" said Yeomans from Paradise. "Where did you call from when you reported the car missing?"

"I don't know."

The two cops exchanged an awkward look, then cleared their throats.

"Look, we came to see you on a matter of some urgency."

"About my car?"

"Uh, not quite," said Yeomans. "We need you to come with us. We'd *like* you to come with us."

"Am I under arrest?"

"Did you do anything to cause yourself to be under arrest?"

"No."

"Then no."

"Do I have the right to remain silent?"

"You always have that right."

I chose not to exercise it. "Is something wrong?"

They nodded.

I fought for words. "Is the car in Paradise?"

"No."

That surprised me. I thought it might be.

"It's here in Reno. Well," Johnson amended. "Moran's junk shop is here in Reno. Moran is now under federal indictment."

"Has there been"—I couldn't get the words out—"Has there been an . . . accident?"

"Not with the car. But . . . Look, put your shoes on and come with us." Yeomans from Paradise looked me over. "Wear something warm. It's cold out."

I didn't want to put on my shoes. I became not hungry, not thirsty. I barely moved, dragging my feet, bending low, pretending to look for them under the unmade bed, except there was no under the bed, and I knew it; the shoes were in the closet, but I didn't want to go get them. I couldn't find anything except the inappropriate clock-smashing heels. Three-inch stilettos with jeans and a sweatshirt. I moved like a sleeping bear through molasses.

I felt Yeomans staring at my back.

How I got the sandals on, I don't know. Perhaps Johnson helped me. How I got into the patrol car, I don't know. It wasn't a Reno black-and-white. It was a Paradise black-and-white. So they'd come all the way from there. I felt like I was still on the floor,

7

looking under the boarded-up bed, not for my sandals this time but for my lost life.

"Are we going to stop at Moran's? Get my car?" I asked in my faux calm voice. We were driving down Virginia.

"Unfortunately he doesn't have your car anymore," said Johnson. "I'm sorry about that. And no, we're not going there."

I was waiting for the rain to let up. We drove slowly, pushing through the wave of oncoming morning rush-hour gambling traffic. She must have taken my car and sold it to Moran's, the title and registration being conveniently in the glove compartment, and he, who was not allowed to buy cars without checking the identity of the seller, wanted it so bad—and who wouldn't?—he took it from her anyway, and then, belatedly realizing he was in a deepload of trouble, dismembered my car for parts, while she pocketed the money and split.

Moran's Auto Salvage, in the middle of an ocean of grass, nested on a sloping bank, just a rusted trailer listing limply, its side wheels missing. It was surrounded by junk cars. We didn't even slow down as we passed.

"How much did he pay for the car?"

"He said a thousand."

A thousand! Oh, the gall. The insult. Of him, of her. The pit inside my stomach was a gorge deep.

It was raining, raining. The window in the back was open and the rain was coming in sideways, onto my lap, my seat, the floor of the police vehicle. I didn't care, they didn't care. Eventually, they got cold and I rolled up the window.

"How in heaven's name did you get yourself into this sordid mess?" said Johnson from Reno.

I pressed my face against the damp glass. It was an eternity through the mountain passes and the strawberry fields back to Paradise.

ONE
THE CAR

1

Topless Imponderables

My former friend Gina came up to me when I was changing after track. I was sitting on the bench, still damp from the shower, bent over my knees, rummaging through my sportsbag for a clean bra. All I had on was underwear. Suddenly she was in front of me, pacing, fidgeting a little, obscuring. "Hey, Sloane."

All my friends called me Sloane instead of Shelby. My *friends*.

"Whazzup." I didn't even look up. Though I was surprised, and wanted to.

"Can you believe we're graduating?" she said, false-brightly. "I still think of myself as twelve, don't you, and this summer's going to be great, isn't it? I'm thinking of getting a job at Dairy Barn again, I meet so many people, and Eddie, my boyfriend—remember him?—he dropped out. Did you know?"

"Uh—no." I resumed rummaging.

"Well, he went back to California. His mom's sick, so he went to be with her. He'll graduate with an equivalency diploma; he says it's just as good, and anyway he says he doesn't need a piece of paper to be a success, he's very smart, well, I don't have to tell you, you know." She paused. I said nothing.

"I watched you out there today, that was amazing, did you run the 440 in fifty-seven seconds?"

That made me look up. "You watched me? Why?"

"Why? You were incredible, that's why. Remember when we first started to train, you couldn't run the two-mile in seventeen minutes? What's your time now?"

I stared calmly at her. "Time's five to five and I've got to get home."

"Oh, yes. Ha ha."

Ha ha? She was small and busty, and slightly plump in the stomach. She had long, straight light-brown hair, and used to have a terrible nervous habit of plucking out her eyebrows and eyelashes. When she ran out of hair, she'd pluck the hairs from her scalp. She wore tight jeans and high heels. She wore no underwear. She used to be my best friend.

But that was a while ago.

"I don't want to keep you," she said, "but while you're getting dressed, can I talk to you?"

"Go ahead." I gave up on the stupid bra; the one I'd worn running was damp, and I suspected I hadn't brought another. Damn.

My palms pressed against my breasts, I stood in front of her.

"Look how skinny you got, Sloane," Gina said. "You must be training a lot."

If I didn't run I'd be prone to child-bearing hips, but I was always running. I said nothing.

"I heard you were going to California after graduation."

"You heard that, did you? So?"

"Are you or aren't you?"

"What's it to you?"

"Well, if you are, I was wondering if you'd like some company." She continued before I had a chance to vigorously shake my head. Actually, she continued *as* I was vigorously shaking my head. "I'd split the expenses with you." She saw my head spinning from side to side like a pendulum on coke. "And we could share the driving," she offered. "We'd get there in three days if we did that. How many miles is it? Like a thousand?"

"Three thousand to where *I'm* going," I said coolly.

12

She tried to whistle. "Long way. Well, like I said, I'd help drive, split the gas, and the hotels, you know, it'd be cheaper."

I was quiet. "You know what's cheaper?" I said. "Taking the bus. If you take the Greyhound, it's only a few hundred bucks."

Gina hemmed and hawed. Finally she said she was scared of buses. Then admitted her mother was scared of buses. I didn't like buses much myself, but I really wasn't interested in her or her mother's opinion of the Greyhound.

"Look, I really gotta go. Emma's waiting." Opting for no damp bra, just a T-shirt, breasts poking out, hair wet, jeans barely buttoned, I grabbed my stuff.

She followed me, clutching my arm, but when I gave her a long look, let go. "Promise you'll think about it?" she said, stepping back. "Just think about it, that's all. It'll be easier and faster for you. It'll be better. And we won't have to talk much—if you don't want. We can just listen to eight-tracks."

Damn Emma. Damn car. Damn ideas. I vowed to just tell her no. Sorry, *Geeena*, I thought about it, and I don't think it's a good idea.

I was wary of her and her intentions. I was wary of her the way some people are of otters. Or leopard seals.

Gina is so ethnic-sounding, like Larchmont. Larchmont may be pretentious, but there is nothing pretentious about Gina.

In the statistics for the most popular names in the last twenty years, Gina has appeared in the top fifty every year. Gina, when she heard this, said, "Groovy!" And flung back her hair. All the boys think Gina is Italian, but there's not an ounce of Italian blood in her. She just has an ethnic name. I don't know why this bothers me, except perhaps because every time we went to the amusement park or the beach and the boys would hear her name, their smile would get bigger and they'd drawl, "Ohhhh, you're Eyetalian . . ." as if being Italian endowed her with some special gifts, gifts I clearly did not possess. You know what wasn't lost on me? Their expressions. "Geeeeeena," they'd call, and every time they did, my irritation quotient twisted up.

I, on the other hand, can only wish I had an anachronistic or ethnic name. Instead mine is just androgynous. Mine isn't a name, it's a last name. I'm epicene. Not one thing, not the other.

Whatever it is, you can be sure that not once, not a single time, not when high on Ferris wheels, or dancing in clubs or swimming in the Sound, has any boy ever drawled out my name, with their eyes widening. "Shelbeeeeeee . . ."

Shelby. This is who I am. Here is my name. I am Shelby.

Gina approached me again the following day. "Are you still thinking?"

"It's only been a day!"

"Soon summer'll be over."

"It's barely June."

"I gotta know. I gotta know if I need to make other plans."

"Okay. I think you should make other plans."

"Come on, Sloane."

Sloane! "If you need to know now, my answer is no 'cause I haven't thought about it."

"But we're graduating in two weeks!"

"I know when we're graduating."

She lowered her voice. "I gotta make tracks. I gotta get to some place called Bakersfield. I just have to. Don't ask, okay?"

"Um—okay." Like I'd ask.

"I have to know soon," she said, beseechingly. "Because if we're going, we have to make a plan."

It was as if she had said a magic word. It was better than *please*. My whole face softened. "*Plan?*" I loved plans. I liked to think of myself as a planner.

"Yes. I have to tell my boyfriend when I'm arriving."

Frowning, I stepped away from her. "That's the sum total of your plan? Notifying other people?"

She didn't know what I meant, and frowned, too. I really had to get to my Urban Public Policy class. "What else is there?"

14

I said nothing. What else *was* there?

"What? Going cross country? Oh, please." She waved her hand dismissively. "We get in the car. We go."

"What about gas?"

"When we run out, we get some."

"I posit that when we run out, it will be too late."

"So we'll get some before. Shel, I'm telling you, you're overthinking this."

Ugh. I shook my head. Underthinking, clearly. "I'm not headed to Bakersfield."

Gina blinked at me. Her blue eyes were slightly too close together, and when she stared, it made her seem vacant and crosseyed. Perhaps I was being less than totally kind since she *was* pretty, and all the boys thought so. She was no slouch in the looks department, looked after herself and wore tight jeans, there was just something slightly blank about her eyes when they stared.

"I gotta go. Look, even if I agree to do this," I said, pressing my books to my chest like palms to my breasts, "you're going to have to take a bus to Bakersfield. I can drop you off in San Francisco, but then you're on your own."

"You want me to take a bus?" Gina said as if I were asking her to eat pig slops.

I moved to go. She caught up with me. "Listen," she said. "Please say yes. I won't be able to go without you." She lowered her voice. "I *really* need to get to Bakersfield as soon as poss. And Mom won't let me go unless I go with you."

"Your mother won't let you go? What are you, five?"

"That's what mothers do, Shelby," said Gina, pompously. "They care what happens to you."

God! What she didn't say was, you'd know that, Shelby, if you *had* a mother.

2

Emma

I was raised in a souped-up boarding house near Mamaroneck, New York, a four-star boarding house, which is akin to saying a sirloin burger. It's still a burger. Actually, the house I lived in was in Larchmont, next town over, but I enjoy saying Mamaroneck, because it has the word Mama in it, and I don't like telling people I come from Larchmont, as it carries with it a superior tag I don't much care for. You have to have a French accent to pronounce it properly. Larsh-*MOH*. People who don't know won't understand, but people who know raise their eyebrows and say, "Oh, *Larchmont*. Wow." It is for them I say I live near Mamaroneck. Nobody ever raises their eyebrows at that. It's suburban-sounding, not French-sounding, unpretentious, not posh—all the things you can't say about Larchmont, a cosmopolitan, sophisticated, old-world European city in the middle of parochial, provincial suburban America. The streets are winding and canopied, the houses Tudor, compact and esoteric, with square rooms, hardwood floors and tiny kitchens, a town where the Christmas lights get strung up for December down Main Street and twinkle merrily in the snow. Many houses are for rent, and there is one particular furnished Tudor, off Bridge Street, on a *cul-de-sac* (even that's French) where Emma and I live in three small rooms above the garage that stands on a driveway overhung by enormous trees that drip sap in the spring and fall, staining my running shoes. We live there for free, but the way washing machines and vacuum cleaners live for free. In exchange for our rooms, we maintain the house. Mostly Emma does this. I help out on the weekends.

I live with Emma. Her last name is Blair. And mine is Sloane. These things I know.

Now for all the things I don't know. I don't know who Emma is, why I live with her or who she is to me. When I was a child, I used to call her Aunt Emma, but then I grew up. Always, since then, she has been just Emma.

I also know this. And I only found out because Gina's friend, the ridiculous and bug-eyed Agnes Tuscadero, eavesdropped on her parents' very private kitchen conversation late one night a few years ago. Apparently my father, Jed Sloane, while married to my mother, took up with a woman who they *think* was named Emma, who might or might not have been my mother's sister/aunt/best friend. So the reason I don't have a mother is because of Emma. My mother split, leaving me with Dad and his new mistress/lover/fling. Agnes's parents gossiped and Agnes told Gina who told me that my mother left a letter saying, *I know all you ever wanted was your smokes and your drinks and your whore. Well now you can have them. My life and everything in it was a complete waste of time.* My mother wrote that, I presume, sometime before she left me.

I don't know where this letter is, and believe me, that's not for the lack of looking. Every crevice of every drawer in our two rooms and a living room, I have scraped through, searching for it, wanting to see her handwriting, and her name. Haven't found it—yet.

Now, I don't know what my mother looked like, but I know what Emma looks like, and I find it surprising, to put it euphemistically, that any man would leave home for a woman like Emma, who, with her thick ankles, square low-heeled shoes, gray stiff helmet of hair, and matronly dresses, couldn't engender passion in a rutting stud dog, much less a male human being. She simply seems too Puritan for love of any kind.

What's interesting, in a purely academic way, of course, is that my father also left. I assume it was soon after my mother, because I don't remember him. What's odd is I do remember her, like a pale ghost with warm arms. He left and then died somewhere on the road. That's all Emma told me, wanted to tell me; that's all I asked, wanted to ask.

Agnes told Gina who told me *he* did not leave a letter. Jed Sloane left, died, and left me with "the whore."

And she raised me.

Who was my father?

Who was my mother?

And if Emma is no good, and my father left her, why am I still with her?

More important, why is she still with me?

Does she feel guilt over me? Do I ask this of her when we're cleaning the bathrooms of the French U.N. diplomats?

Emma, my father left; why did you stay?

My mother left; why did you stay?

Can you answer me as we wax the floors and cut up onions?

If they all went away, walked away, why didn't you walk away?

I could not fathom what her answers might be.

Eventually I began to feel that the time for questions had *sort* of passed; nonetheless, I felt that every day I had to tread carefully, to make sure I walked around the gullet where the fragments of answers had fallen.

Question: irretrievably fallen?

But I have this to add in conclusion. My friend from across the road, Debbie, had been spending a lot of time with us this year. She had two parents, a mother, a father, three brothers, a Beagle; her mother was home with the kids, her dad worked as a manager at the Larchmont hardware store. And yet Debbie, who had a whole family plus pet, was over with petless me and Emma; why? She helped us in the evening, watched TV, and though she lived across the street, would often ask if she could stay over. Emma always said yes. Just yes. No less, no more. Yes.

A few months ago, Debbie finally told me that her father was sick. Our neighbor, Ralphie, was driving him every week to the hospital. Turned out his liver was shot. He needed a transplant in a hurry but couldn't get one despite having a wife, four kids and no job: he was a drunk, and no one gave fresh liver to alcoholics. So he would drink, scream at his wife and kids, and be sick. When he was sober, Ralphie drove him to the hospital for kidney dialysis and tests. Debbie's dad was a drunk for twenty years. Ralphie drove him to the hospital for his last two months. One day Debbie's dad didn't come home from the hospital, and Debbie's mom took Debbie and the one brother who was still home and left, possibly for Florida. I missed them when they went. They had seemed like such a nice family.

Emma and I get up at six, prepare the house for morning, work silently. I make the coffee, she empties the dishwasher, we wipe down counters, I take out the trash. My bus comes at seven-thirty. Emma speaks then. "Do you have what you need?"

And I speak, too. "Yes."

I took typing, so I could have one actual skill when I graduated. I got a D-minus. I do my homework during my free period because at home there's too much to do. After track I take the late bus and help Emma with dinner, with clean-up, with laundry. Our work is done by eight. The Lambiels like us because we're quiet, and they're quiet. The husband is a diplomat and the wife a flight attendant; she's never home, and he drinks the whole time she's away. Their only child, Jeanne, a blonde all-that, went to our school for about five minutes, but then, feeling rather ignored by the people she held in such contempt, transferred to a private school for children of foreign diplomats. Certainly when I'm in her house, she doesn't speak to me. Sometimes she says, "Shell-BEEEE, get us some pop cooorn, *s'il vous plaît*."

Okay, so the French chick who can barely speak English drawls out my name like the boys at the ice-cream parlor when she wants me to fetch and carry. Nice.

Six days a week, three hours a day, I run. Our meets are Saturday afternoons. On Sundays, our day of rest, Emma and I cook for the week for us and the Lambiels so all we have to do Monday to Friday is heat stuff up.

If people ask, I say I'm a Christian because Christianity is the one religion where you don't have to do anything to still be a member. I like that, and since I don't want to say I'm nothing, I call myself a Christian.

I have never been inside a place of worship of any kind.

I have never had outside work. Emma's been giving me a little money for helping her. I've saved five dollars a week for as long as I can remember, and last I looked, my bank account had $2400 in it. My one continued expense has been my running shoes—new ones every three months. Emma pays half. My few leftover bucks go frivolously on hair gel, mascara and lipgloss, Milky Ways and Love's Baby Soft.

Two weeks ago, Jeanne Lambiel was caught by her father stealing twenty dollars from his wallet when she wanted to go out with her passé French friends. He screamed at her for half the night; the whole neighborhood heard him. Why would you steal from me, he kept yelling. Why? You have thirteen million in your trust fund! And Jeanne said calmly, "Yes, but, Papa, I needed not thirteen million but twenty bucks."

I got away from Emma and the Lambiels by running. I've been cross country and track and field from the time I was ten. I run the mile and the two-mile. Once I ran the mile so fast I had to go to the hospital. They thought I was dying. So much for go all out, try your best, do your best, stop at nothing. Give 110 percent. Well, I gave 110 percent and it almost killed me. So you can just imagine the kind of life lesson I took away from that: a little less than your best, Shelby Sloane—that will have to be good enough.

3

The Gift

On my eighteenth birthday in May of 1981, which happened this year to fall on a Saturday, Emma said, unduly excited (Emma never got even duly excited about things), "Come outside with me. I want to show you something."

I followed her down the stairs and out. In the sap-covered driveway on this Saturday May day, parked behind the Lambiels' government-issue Mercedes, stood a little yellow Mustang. I say little, but to me, it seemed gargantuan like a house, like an airplane hangar. A bright yellow hangar. It had two black stripes running over the roof and hood. It looked both classic and stunning, as if I knew anything about Mustangs. Except we once saw a documentary on them a few years back, and I might have mentioned that it looked like a cool-cat car, but what did I know, I was thirteen at the time, and Emma had been half asleep.

I stood silently, staring.

"It's for you." She coughed. "You like it?" She looked alternately exquisitely excited and morbidly uncomfortable. I think she might have been uncomfortable about being so excited. "I wanted to get you something special. You know—for your eighteenth."

"You bought me a *car?*"

"Not just a car, Shel. A 1966 *Shelby* Mustang!"

21

I was dumbstruck.

"Go ask your friends tonight about a Shelby Mustang. They'll tell you."

What it cost her I have no idea; when I asked, she wouldn't say. She was very proud of it. "Engine's clean," she kept repeating. "V-8 350 horsepower. Transmission's good. No rust." And then laughed like she was joking. "After he took my check, I slept in the car overnight, until the check cleared the next morning. I was afraid to let anyone else get their hands on it."

"Emma . . ."

"You don't understand. He was the original owner. He had three of them for sale, the other two were fifty percent more expensive and they sold while I was still deciding on this one. I think the only reason it was cheaper and unbought was the color. Back then, he had it painted special because it was his personal racing car. Honestly, there was a very good chance I might not get it." She clapped her hands. "But it was fate! It was meant to be. A Shelby Mustang for Shelby. I mean, come on."

I had not seen Emma this animated since—

The dealer who sold it to her, she said, was a born-again Christian. "So I knew he wouldn't sell me a lemon."

"Why?" In a daze, I walked around the car. This couldn't possibly be mine! I asked what he had been before he became born-again. "Maybe he's a car thief, out on parole? The other day I read in the paper that a murderer on death-row became born-again."

"Don't they all become born-again on death-row?" returned an unfazed Emma. She didn't know what the man had been, "but he asked me to pray in the car with him after he took my money."

"Wow." I peered in. It was all black inside. It had a wood wheel. The backseat was the size of a Matchbox car. It could fit a deck of cards and a GI Joe if they squished. But the two front bucket seats were roomy, and shiny.

"All vinyl foam seating. And air conditioning!" Emma said. "Go ahead, open the door."

I shook my head, patting the hood instead. I touched the glass, the windshield wipers. I left my hands on the hood. "Emma," I said. "I don't know what to say. It's very . . ." I struggled. "Yellow."

"Yes! Summer yellow it's called. The car can go up to 136.7 miles per hour."

"Is that because of the yellow?"

"Shelby."

"Driving 136 miles an hour, is that something you'd like to see me do?"

"I'm just saying."

I peered inside at the controls. "Guess no FM stereo in '66."

She straightened up from unbridled to frowning in 1/60 of a second. "No, and don't you dare touch anything in this car. It's a classic. There were only 1200 hard-top Shelbys made in '66, and only one in this color. Only *one*, do you understand? You can't change a single thing in it."

"I know. Like I would."

She opened the door on the passenger side and got in. More reluctantly than a frightened virgin going to her marriage bed, I got in on the driver's side. I touched the wheel like it was hot. I tried not to breathe. It was impossible! I couldn't wait to tell my friend Marc, the car freak. He'd die. *Die*. He might actually ask me out now.

"Did you?" My hands clutched the wheel.

"Did I what?"

"Pray with him?"

"I did. I prayed: Dear God, please don't let this car be a lemon."

Emma laughed, and I laughed. This had been the most she'd said to me, well, ever.

I had been taking driver's ed classes in high school; now that I had turned eighteen, I could take the road test for a full license. I had learned how to drive on a four-speed manual; this one was a six. It was hard; I didn't know what I was doing, and painfully ground the gears every time I shifted up. Emma didn't mind even that.

I took her for a ride. We drove through Larchmont with the

windows down; she told me Ford only made four convertibles in 1966, and they were out of her price range. "I don't want a convertible," I said. "This is perfect." The day was cool and breezy, in the low sixties, and it smelled like spring. When you're young that means something. You always notice when the air smells like summer is coming, because it's everybody's favorite part of the year. For a kid, summer is a time of possibilities, even when you stay home and do nothing.

I felt conspicuous, like a streaker at the Oscars. The car was so ridiculously yellow, the hood blinded me with its brightness. I took Emma for ice cream in Mamaroneck on Boston Post Road. We both had lemon sherbet, in honor of the Shelby. We had four people say something to us in the parking lot. And *everybody* stared.

"Thanks, Emma. Really. Thanks a lot."

"Happy birthday."

I had a Shelby Mustang!

I wasn't sure, though, what I was supposed to do with it.

Why would Emma get me a car?

Me, Shelby, who'd hardly ever been out of Larchmont, barely out of Westchester County, a dozen times to New York City, a handful of daytrips to Connecticut, once to Pennsylvania Dutch Country, once to New Jersey Six Flags Great Adventure amusement park, once on a senior trip to Washington DC, why did this Shelby need a car? Ninety-nine percent of my life, I had never been more than twenty miles from the town where I was born.

"Emma," I said when a few days had passed, "it's very generous of you. But why did you buy me a car?"

"I don't understand the question. Isn't it self-evident?"

"Well," I said, trying to appear thoughtful at first, "no." In case that sounded too abrupt, added, "I don't go anywhere."

"Yes," said Emma. "And now you can."

I took her for ice cream again a quarter mile down the street. I wondered if this was what she meant.

Days passed, I got my license, June came, the weather got warmer.

I drove myself to high school once or twice and parked in the lot for seniors. I'll tell you this: for the boys, a yellow Mustang is the equivalent of the name *Geeeena*. The boys *loved* my car, and the girls were jealous. "Nice 'Stang," they all murmured, eyes widening, an inviting smile on their faces. The football jocks, the runners, the basketball players, the debate team, all in unison now, "Niiiiiice 'Stang."

Tony Bergamino, the captain of the football team, had a tall, blonde gazelle-like girlfriend. Covetously, I used to watch them kissing in the halls between periods. Even he noticed, with a big smile and a thumbs up. "Nice!" He might as well have been checking me out. He, who usually stepped over me like a gnat on his path, smiled at my car, which is the same thing as smiling at me, and said, "Nice car, Shelbeeee."

My friend Marc hyperventilated for two weeks. "You don't deserve this car. You know nothing about cars. You can't drive. You've never been out of your house. It's another proof that there's no divine justice in the world. The universe is a cruel place." Marc, brooding and always dressed in black, bow-legged, Afro-haired, wearing a permanent air of studied artistic indifference, couldn't stop talking about my car. He sat at the lunchroom table and, over a tuna hero with extra mayo, said, "You ask why Emma got you a car? Shelby Sloane, have you considered the possibility that she got you a car because she wants you to *go*?"

During the few fights Emma and I had had, I kept saying, soon I'll be grown up and you won't be able to keep me under your thumb anymore. I'll be outta here. Won't like that, will you? Well, here it was, me all grown up, but did I have some place to go that required a car?

How many times can two people have an argument where one person says, "Just you wait till I'm eighteen. I'm leaving here, and

I'm never—do you hear me?—*never* coming back. Then what are you going to do, huh? What are you going to do with your life?" This is what I used to say to Emma when I was angry at her rules, her inordinate strictness, her guidelines, and her unsophisticated ways. And my favorite of all, "You're not my mother. You can't tell me what to do."

How many times can a person hear *this* spit out before she starts to believe it? Yes, she knows they were angry words, and yes, Shelby always says she didn't mean them, but why is it, whenever she gets mad, this hurtful thing comes out of her mouth?

I started watching Emma while she dusted, started wanting to ask her things. I'd mumble I really didn't need such a present.

Marc thought it was hilarious.

"You're eighteen, and she's telling you like a stewardess at the end of a very long flight: Take your stuff and get the hell out."

I regretted ever having had a crush on him, him and his thick mop of chocolate curly hair and his questions about his sexuality— just a *fantastic* trick for getting girls. Thank God, I was smart enough to stay almost completely away. I don't count the night his mother was out and we drank her beer, too much of it, and he said, "I think I might be gay." I fell for it for five minutes, let him test his possible gayness out on me, then his mother came home, so the result remained inconclusive, that is to say uncon-summated, at least with me.

In that early June week, when I should have been dreaming about the prom and graduation, limos and dresses and flowers, I had fevered dreams instead about a tiger ripping apart a much larger lion with his teeth. In my other, even more frightening dream I ran into Emma at the local dollar store. She said, Shelby, I can't talk too long because I've got a lot to do. I don't have time to get into it with you. And then she went about her dollar-store business, cold, unfriendly, cut off.

After that dream I couldn't talk to her about anything. I was overthinking it. That had always been my problem. I was an over-thinker and an underdoer. *So* convenient, that. Didn't someone say that no decision was worse than a bad decision? Not me. I'd never say that.

The radius of my life up to this point had been only a few miles, and I was terrified by what lay beyond my open window, its deep and abiding mystery.

One night I decided to test Emma. We were done with our work and were sitting on the couch between commercials. It was a weeknight, and I was staying in. I said, "Emma, where did you say my mother lives?"

"Your *what?*" That got her attention.

"My mother," I said calmly. "Didn't you once tell me she lived in a town in California? Montecito? Manzanita? Monte Carlo?"

"I never said," Emma said slowly, "your mother went to California."

"You did. What was it? Mesa Vista? Mokelumme? Monte Cristo? When I was five, you said she was sick and she went to some town in California to get better."

"I don't remember saying that. *How* do you remember this?"

"It's just the kind of stuff you remember." Montesano? Minnesota? Mira Loma?

"I don't think I said it." Emma shook her head. "It's possible I said it, but, Shelby, I was talking to a *five*-year-old. You asked me when your mother was coming back. What was I supposed to say? I just said something to make you feel better. Like she was far away and couldn't leave. But honestly . . ."

Commercial ended; we went back to watching "Dynasty".

That night, I pulled out a map of the United States. After thirty minutes of carefully combing the fourth largest state in the union, I gave up. Maricopa? Mission Viejo? Mira Flores?

"I don't think it's a town," Emma continued the next day, as if she knew I'd been looking, thinking about it. "I thought she went to have a rest at a mental hospital. Like Bellevue. Or Menninger in Kansas."

"What was the name of the mental hospital?"

"Shel, I don't know. I wasn't serious."

"You know she went somewhere."

"I don't know."

"You told me a name back then. I know you did. Did she have family from there? Why am I so sure it begins with an M? That it has four syllables?"

"I don't know."

"Mariposa? Minnelusa? Miramonte?"

She rubbed her eyes, as if she were tired of me. The commercial ended, "Dallas" came back on, and Emma had no time to respond. Nor did she respond during the next commercial. And then "Dallas" was over and she got up and said, "I'm going to bed. Goodnight."

"I thought maybe that's why you got me a car," I said after her. "So I could go visit my sick mother at the Montezuma mental hospital."

Emma turned around. "I got you a car," she said, "so you could be free. You kept saying you wanted to be. So now you are. I don't know where your mother is. I never knew."

"I'm not going to be gone long," I said. "Just a few weeks. Maybe two."

"Two weeks? Takes longer than that to drive there and back."

"Nah. I'll be quick. Maybe two and a half. I'll be back by the middle of July. You'll be okay for a couple of weeks, won't you?"

"I'll be okay," said Emma. "But two and a half weeks to where? And starting when?"

I bought a map of California from the Rand McNally store in New York City. I put my finger on the letter M in the town index, and went down, mouthing the names to myself one by one, from Mabel to Mystic, and then back again from Mystic to Mabel.

The third time through, at two in the morning, I found it.

Mendocino.

Men-doh-SEE-no.

Mendocino!

I couldn't sleep until Emma woke up at five.

"Mendocino!" I exclaimed later, like an operatic clap.

She gazed at me through bleary, blinking eyes, as if she'd

just woken up. "You have your notebooks, your running stuff?"

"Emma, Mendocino! Isn't that right?"

"I think so," she said. "That sounds almost right. Do you have your lunch, or are you going to buy one in school?"

"I'll buy one in school. It is, it is right. It feels right."

"Good. You want some eggs before you go?"

I had eggs. I had orange juice.

Mendocino=Missing Mother.

Emma! I wanted to yell. But yelling's not our style, unless I'm angry. But how could I be angry? Marc told me Emma could have spent as much as $5000 (though I told him that was *impossible*) on my car so I could go find my mother. It had been so long since I'd seen her. She might be wondering how I'd been.

I laid out the map of the United States on the floor of my room and studied it like the periodic table. I measured my route with a ruler as I used to in Miss Keller's class, with an X-axis and a Y-axis and plot points along the way. I measured the miles in days and inches. I used physics (time and distance), geometry (points along the X-axis) and earth science (weather conditions in July) to determine my course. I used my seventh-grade social studies to help me with geography. My trouble was: seventh grade was a *really* long time ago. I thought after Pennsylvania came Kansas, then Nevada, then California. I took earth science in ninth grade, and geometry in tenth, but physics was a senior year subject, and afraid of flunking I opted out of the physics program, and so was stuck with the most rudimentary knowledge of the space-time continuum. As in: how long *does* it take to travel 3000 miles? Oh, but the Shelby Mustang can fly at 136.7 mph! The *Kitty Hawk* didn't go that fast. Twenty-two hours. I could be there and back in two days. Sweet. Three if I dogged it.

Utah's time and distance didn't even make it into my calculations. I don't have to go through Utah to get to California, I said to myself, and dismissed it. I lost interest in geometry and physics somewhere before crossing the Mississippi.

What became clear to me was this: with my flagrant and obvious limitations, I don't know what I was thinking, planning to go by myself. After Iowa, I had no strategy for the rest of the country. And I like to nap in the afternoons. How could I nap if I was the only one driving? With so many skillsets clearly missing, a vague half of the western country appearing to me monolithically when I slept—snow and yellow flowers between two vast bodies of water—I was on a rack of doubt.

Which was precisely why when Gina approached my breasts in the locker room and offered to go with me, to split the costs and share the driving and the fear, I did not say no right away. Anxiety danced in me, but summer danced in me, too. I was eighteen, out of high school, and had a 1966 stock-car racing Mustang with black Le Mans stripes. And Gina didn't. Though she had had other things that I know meant a lot to her. Boyfriends, and things.

Gina and I were like sisters in kindergarten. She lived on Summer Street, a short walk away, and had a stay-at-home mom, a working dad, a grandma living with them, and a sister she didn't get along with, but still—an actual sister.

Her mother didn't mind that we used to play mostly at her house; she said she didn't like the endless parade of strangers through mine. I don't know quite what she meant by that. Strangers didn't parade through our rooms above a garage. So there we were, tight and inseparable, and suddenly, just like that, out of the blue, for no good reason, almost to spite me, my bestest bud Gina becomes friends with the mousy, gossipy Agnes Tuscadero, whom I didn't like to begin with but after the revelations at the Tuscaderos' idle-talk kitchen table, I hated like Jews hate Hitler. Gina said we could all be friends. She didn't understand why the three of us could not *all* be friends. So we feebly played together, got together, walked into town, went to Larchmont beach, talked about being grounded, getting freedom, lying to our parents, and suddenly, just like that, out of the blue, for no good reason, it occurred to me it wasn't Agnes who was the third wheel.

30

Marc said Gina was not a serious person, that she was too light-weight for me. I deserved a better, more profound friend. Like him.

Gina maintained we were all still friends. Every Saturday she kept inviting me out, to the beach, to Rye Playland. "Come on, the more the merrier." She wouldn't take my no for an answer, though it was the only answer she kept getting. Except once. A year ago June she invited me out to a club with her new boyfriend Eddie. "Come out with us, please? I really want you to meet him. I want him to meet all my best friends. You'll love him. He is *so* funny."

"What about Agnes?" I said glumly.

"She's not as funny." Agnes apparently was grounded. I couldn't believe I agreed to go as Agnes's pathetic mid-day Friday, after-thought replacement. But I went.

Eddie *was* pretty funny.

Then Agnes wasn't grounded anymore, and Gina cold-turkey stopped asking me to go places with her. Nearly the entire senior year had cruised by and we had barely spoken till the afternoon in the locker room.

Gina and I weren't such strangers once, but there is something so personal about traveling in a car with someone. So intimate. Sharing the minutes of your day, your *every* minute for days, maybe weeks, with another human being. I couldn't understand why in the world she'd want to come with me. But the thought of traveling alone was not entirely pleasant. Tension was inherent in both scenarios. On the one hand, Gina, but on the other, terror *and* alone! It was like that Valentine's Day Hallmark card for fools: "BEING WITH YOU IS ALMOST LIKE BEING WITH SOMEONE." Now that was sentiment I responded to. What was better: Gina or violent dread?

"I'm thinking, I'm thinking," I told her when she accosted me again in the hall.

"Well, I have to know soon."

"Why?"

"What do you mean why? I have to pack, no? I have to tell my mother. I have to get ready, too."

"Look, if I agree to do this, you have to agree to take a bus the last leg of your trip. I'm not driving to Bakersfield."

"You sure about that?" Gina said, and before I could respond, quickly added, "How close is Bakersfield to Mendocino?" a wide smile on her not really Italian face.

About me. First, all the things I'm not. I am not objectively beautiful. I have found very few people who are; is that fair to say? On the bell curve, I fall somewhere near the top of the downward creep toward homeliness, though perhaps more like a drop than a creep first thing in the morning when I don't wear mascara or lipgloss, but I bet not even Christy Worsoe, the homecoming queen, looks good then. I can be thought of as plain in my unadorned state, but Emma, who has no obligation to make me feel better about myself, says I look cute when I crawl out for Saturday morning French toast with ricotta cheese before track, all sleepy and punk-haired, and because she says this, I don't feel as homely as I might. There is nothing wrong with my face, but there is nothing extra right with it, either.

Other things about me. I don't function well at night. I'm a morning person. I deeply believe that in that two-word, sea-like panoply of "morning person" are veiled a thousand tributaries, big and small, which comprise the essence of a human being. I have tested this divide on my friends Marc and Debbie and Tracy, on Emma too, and found it to be true. I get up and function best early in the day. I clean my room, get my work and schoolbooks together, make sure my sneakers are dry and my clothes ready for track. I take a shower, I eat breakfast. I have a list of things to do before the bus comes, and I do them all. My brain works. I get things out of the freezer for dinner, I make coffee for Emma, I check the boiler to make sure the pilot light is on so that the Lambiels have hot water. We once had a big problem with that, and it became my responsibility to check, and I never forget. I go to school. My library books are returned on time, I don't indulge in compulsive behavior when I have things to do. I don't leave my schoolwork until the last minute. I don't put down my library books and then forget where I put them. I don't squander the little money I have. I help out. When Emma and I are working an evening for the diplomats, I stay until the work is done. I always say, is there anything else I can do? and, what can I do to help?

If Emma wants me to iron, I iron. I don't like ironing, and once I burned a silk shirt and the top of my hand and still have the scar to prove it (the blouse needed to be thrown out), but I iron anyway.

I don't cut corners. If I am told to run seven miles to prepare for tomorrow's 440-meter race, I run seven miles, even if I think it's excessive. I don't get so obsessed in watching TV/reading/knitting/washing the car/cleaning that I forget what time it is. That's the major part of it, I think—I, as a morning person, always keep track of time. I know when it's time to go to school, and when it's time to clean, and when it's time to read, and to rest, and to ask Emma why she has taken care of me for thirteen years (though there's never been a good time to ask that, so I haven't). We sometimes stay up and watch a late movie on a Saturday night, but rarely. Once, in 1978, we stayed up for "Towering Inferno" because I wanted to see how it ended. It ended at two, and I've never forgotten the feeling of having to drag my sorry ass out of bed four hours later. I sometimes read late, in my bed, but when I see it's eleven-thirty, I put the book down and go to sleep so I won't feel like a zombie the next day. I hate feeling like a zombie. I hate that feeling, because it's not me. It's not who I am, zombie-like on Sundays because I couldn't put down *The Reincarnation of Peter Proud*. I don't like myself when I lose track of time, so to like myself more, I put down the book and go to sleep.

Now take my friend Marc. Marc doesn't know the definition of the word "time." He does stay up till two, three, sometimes all night, and then I don't see him in school the next day. He is constantly on the verge of failing, making up work, being late with assignments, copying my notes between classes, rushing, dropping things, forgetting things. Oh, does he forget things. Even things that are important to him. He likes to paint; you'd think he'd remember to bring along the tools of his craft, like his brushes and oils. But no. I can't tell you how many times he doesn't have his notebooks, or his chalks, or his special coal pencil. He is ridiculous and knows it, doesn't like himself but can't help it. His mind is on a thousand things at once, and he can't remember where he has to be, or what he has to do. Things fall away. And when he's up, he wants to stay up. And when he's asleep, he wants to stay asleep. He says: "Whatever I'm doing, I want to continue doing."

"But what about the things you *have* to be doing?"

"Not so much for those, Sloane."

We are quite uncertain about his future at college. He and I are both worried and frankly not optimistic. Fortunately he's going to New Rochelle, just five miles away, and will commute, so if he flunks out, he'll still be in his own bed.

Things don't get away from me.

Guess what kind of person Gina is?

"Four hundred and seventy miles," I said to Gina in the hall as we walked from Health to English. "From Bakersfield to Mendocino."

"Well, how would I get there?"

I said nothing. I was providing the use of my outrageous wheels all the way across the country. I wanted to suggest the use of a Greyhound bus all the way across the country. Or perhaps an airplane ticket. I said nothing, hoping she would see reason all by herself, but she spent two or three minutes until the bell rang heartily complaining, after which I said, "Gina, you'll have to get on a bus. It's just a few hours."

"If it's a few hours, why can't you drive me?"

"I'm being metaphorical about the few hours. It's incredibly out of my way."

"Just a few miles."

"Four hundred and seventy few miles to be exact. And I don't know why I have to point out the obvious, but you do realize I have to drive back to Mendocino? That's two extra days for me. You're staying in Bakersfield, but I'm actually driving back."

"I'm not staying in Bakersfield," she said, sounding defensive. "I'm coming back here. With him."

"With who?"

"With Eddie, of course. Who do you think I'm going to Bakersfield for?"

I said nothing. Really, there are times in your life when it's better to say nothing. This was one of them.

Gina's blue eyes stared at me for a second longer than I was comfortable with, and then ran to class.

My hands itched all through English, I couldn't hold a pen. What I wanted to say was, are you kidding me? I'm not bringing you *and* him back to New York. I'm not spending a week with him *and* you in my car. You might as well ask me to start speaking French or type sixty words a minute. It ain't happenin'. *Mais non. Jamais. Jamais.*

Instead of talking about this, the important thing, Gina and I had an arithmetic lesson. An elementary physics lesson. A time and distance lesson. We took minutes, divided them into hours and siphoned miles through time, and time through miles, taking 470 of them, which was almost 480, dividing them by 60 minutes, and concluding with 8 hours without stops, *each way*, but after 30 minutes of this, Gina still couldn't grasp what 60 minutes had to do with how fast the car was traveling, as if time and distance were in no way related. She didn't understand why my 350 horse-power Mustang, traveling at nearly 137 miles per hour, couldn't get from Mendocino to Bakersfield and back in 55 minutes. While explaining it to her, I could barely understand it myself, and it certainly didn't help me to understand the most important thing—

was she really expecting me to bring her and Eddie back to New York? *Jamais!*

The preparations were monumental. Maybe it was because I'd never been anywhere. Or because I was a planner and couldn't plan for two weeks I couldn't foresee in my pedestrian imagination. I didn't want Emma to know I was having trouble because I didn't want her to say, if you can't pack and plan for a little trip, how are you going to pack for college? I wanted to reply to her unasked question that it's a lot easier to pack *all* your stuff than to selectively pack some of it. Like, how am I supposed to know what I'm going to wear in Nevada, on an indefinite tomorrow? Is the temperature the same in Nevada as in Larchmont? "Probably a touch warmer," said Emma.

Are there mosquitoes? "There are mosquitoes everywhere."

"Really, everywhere? But there's no water in Nevada. Aren't mosquitoes swamp creatures?"

"Well, then, you've answered your own question."

"No water?" said Gina when she heard. "What about Lake Tahoe?"

"What do you know about Lake Tahoe, Reed?" exclaimed Marc. He called all the girls by their last name. Took the sex right out of them. And mine stuck. This took place during lunch.

"Nothing," Gina defended. "Except Fredo Corleone was killed on it, and it was in Nevada."

"Oh, *Fredo* Corleone. Well, then, absolutely. Better bring repellant."

Did it get cold at night? No one knew, not even Gina; that part wasn't in "The Godfather."

Was it windy? We decided it was. We packed some breakers.

Do I bring hairspray? Extra underwear? Warm socks?

"I don't think it's ever a bad idea to pack extra underwear and socks," said Emma. "But you don't wear hairspray here; why would you start there?"

36

Maybe I was going to be a different person there.

Challengingly I bought hairspray.

Are hotel rooms warm or cold? Do they give you towels? Extra blankets? Sometimes I get cold at night.

"In the summer?"

We circled the horses around to the original question. Did it get cold at night and are hotel rooms warm or cold?

"Does it get cold at night where?" said Marc. "In Nevada? You'll blow through the state in four hours. What about South Dakota? Iowa? Utah? Wyoming? Why don't you care if it gets cold there?"

What did Utah have to do with my business, and should I bring my favorite pillow?

Should I bring a camera, my Kodak Instamatic? Or will Emma lend me her Polaroid, and what's better, the top-notch quality of my Instamatic, or the stick-it-in-the-darkroom-of-a-partially-closed-drawer quality of the Polaroid?

Should I bring books to read?

"Do you plan to be doing much reading while you're driving?" Marc asked. He asked this slowly to convey what he really thought of my question.

"Aren't you all Walden Pondy," I said, shoving him. "Go sketch something while I do all the work."

He was sitting in my room doing nothing. He sketched me packing.

"Perhaps a book for a rainy day?" I asked. Why did I always sound so defensive, even with my friends?

"You won't be driving in the rain, then?"

Should I bring cash?

"Yes, Sloane," said Marc even more slowly, the wretch. "You should bring some money. After all, you might need gas."

I threw my pillow at him, knocking the coal pencils out of his hands.

"I *mean*," I said, "cash or Travelers' checks? And if I bring cash, where do I stash it? Do I hide it?"

"Hide it from who? Gina?"

"Well, I don't know. Can I trust her?"

"Can she trust *you*?" said Marc, and I didn't have a pillow left to throw.

"One more comment like this, and you'll have to walk home."

"Where are you going to hide your money from her in your little Shelby car? How hard would you have to hide it before she a, realizes what you're doing and b, takes it personally?"

I sighed. "You're exasperating."

"*I'm* exasperating?" He went back to sketching.

"How much money will I need? Do I bring more than I need? Or just enough? And what if I run out? How will I get more? I have no credit card, and who'd give me one anyway? I have no job."

Marc got up and handed me his drawing. "I'm going home," he said, wearily. "I'm glad I'm broke, and can't go, and don't have your problems."

After he left, I wished he could come with us. He'd drawn me like a brown flurry in the middle of a messy room, with greenbacks flying in the air. I taped it to my wall, as I figured things out.

By my estimation we would be gone fifteen days and fourteen nights. We needed gas for 6000 miles. But what if it was 6500? And what if on uphill slopes, the Mustang's gas mileage dipped from twenty-three miles per gallon to twenty?

"So?" said Marc when I called to discuss the imponderables. "On downhill slopes, mileage will be twenty-six. You better hope it'll all even out."

But that's the whole thing right there. What if it didn't even out? What if Gina twisted my arm and I had to drive her 480 miles to Bakersfield, go north to Mendocino and then head back south again to pick her up? *Pas possible!* How did I calculate for that kind of unknown?

The hotel room. Fifteen nights. But what if it turned out to be sixteen? What if it took me a few extra days to locate the woman who gave birth to me? What if Gina wanted to spend a few extra days in Eddie's stellar company?

"So? Sleep in the car," Marc said, in a "Freebird" voice that said it would be the height of adventure to sleep in the car because you ran out of money.

I calculated fifty dollars a night for a motel for sixteen nights. But what if it was sixty dollars? And what about room tax?

"Yes, room tax is different in every state," Marc said. "And parking? And what if you lose your room key and have to pay ten bucks for a new one? I don't think you're planning enough, Sloane."

I agreed. Food. Did we *have* to eat three times a day? Plus water for the drive. Maybe an adult beverage, once, twice, in a bar somewhere?

"Yes, good, plan for a drunken binge," said Marc. "But what about a cover charge?"

The car will need an oil change.

"Every 3000 miles. Your car, maybe more often. And incidentals?"

"I budgeted for them. Like what?"

"Well, I don't know. That's why they're called incidentals."

I thought about it. "You mean like nail polish?"

"Yes, that's exactly what came to *my* mind. And acetone. And aspirin."

"Forget it. I'll live with a headache." I bit my nails to eschew the incidentals.

"A flat tire?"

"Okay, I'll bring an extra forty dollars."

"What if you hit a deer and get another flat tire?"

"Why would I hit a deer?"

"Sloane, I don't know why you do many of the things you do."

"Shut up."

I calculated. Hotel: seventeen days at sixty bucks a day. Gas: 7000 miles at twenty miles a gallon at a buck twenty-five. I factored in three cans of oil, another pair of windshield wipers, jumper cables, a tire jack, a poncho. Plus: enough cash for three daily squares, ice cream seven times, two daily Cokes, a daily coffee.

Also: six adult beverages, forty bucks for a flat tire, another fifty bucks for just in case, and twenty dollars for a gift for Emma. I added it up. I divided by me and Gina.

It came out to $1700. Each. Plus a gift for Emma, so my share was $1720!!!

Perhaps it was a blessing Gina was coming with me. When I told her how much her share was, she didn't pause, didn't blink. "That's all? Hmm. I thought it was going to be more. But I'm going to bring an extra hundred for clothes, because I love clothes, and another hundred just to be on the safe side." She sounded almost like a morning person. So clear-headed. I applauded her cautiousness and followed her example. Gina said she worked in a Dairy Barn for two years, saved a little. She was a saver, too! Was I wrong about her?

I took all my money out of the bank—or what was left of it after new running shoes and a prom dress and paying for a quarter of the prom limo I was sharing with my friends Marc, Cindy, and Jessica.

Emma offered me an extra $300.

"No, Em. You already did plenty." I tried to think of what she'd done. "You got me a car!" I said brightly, hoping she'd notice.

She didn't. "Take it," she said sensibly, and then—nonsensically, "*Believe* me, you'll need it."

More? Less?

"No, no, I'll be fine. I planned it all out." Then I remembered. What about shampoo, conditioner?

"Hotels give you that." Emma paused. "Maybe not conditioner." She paused again. "Maybe not motels."

"Maybe not motels what? Not give you shampoo or conditioner?"

"Either."

"Oh."

Hotels were going to be too expensive. Which led me back to my question: how much shampoo, how much conditioner? A bottle of "Gee Your Hair Smells Terrific" usually lasted a month. I decided

40

to bring two of each, just to be on the safe side. Emma paid for those.

Gina and I didn't get together for an inventory before we left. We should have, and wanted to, but I was busy, and she was busy. I went to four parties, there was a graduation, a senior picnic, a prom, packing, planning. We didn't have time. We didn't make time.

I did make some time for Tony Bergamino, though. Rather, he made time for me. He came up to me after the prom, told me he thought I looked good and danced well. "Gee, thanks." If I were a peacock, I would've opened up my tail.

"I heard you were driving to California."

"How'd you hear?"

"What d'you mean? Everybody heard."

I tried not to smile. Tony Bergamino heard I was going to California! I was a ten-inch red balloon with twelve inches' worth of helium under his unprecedented attention.

"You taking Gina with you?"

"I'm not *taking* her with me. We're going together. We're sharing the costs."

"Of course. She's a firecracker. I didn't know you two were friends."

"Yeah, used to be . . . friends."

"Must have been a long time ago." He glanced at me funny, like he knew things.

"It was."

He shuffled his feet. Someone called for him (perhaps his lover, Gazelle?).

"Well, good luck. Have a great trip."

"Thanks. You too." Oh, idiot! And he smiled at me like I was an idiot.

And then, because he *was* a peacock, he opened up his tail. "Feel like getting together before you go? There's this great place down the coast, in Newport. We could drive." He hemmed. "Maybe *I* could drive?" he asked sheepishly, shining down at me his football-jocky, legs-apart smile.

41

Hallelujah!

Hallelujah, hallelujah!

"Yeah, sure, you can drive. If you want to. When would we go?"

We went overnight, right before the end. Newport possibly was a nice town. Beachy. White. Quaint, with ships and sails. I heard it was by the sea, by the sea, by the beautiful sea . . . but the place we stayed was inland.

"Emma," I said the evening before I was leaving. "Tell me about my dad."

It took me thirteen years to ask this question. I thought at first she didn't hear me. You know, when your own voice is just an echo, and you start to doubt whether you spoke at all; start to doubt whether you *are* at all because the largest, loudest questions in your head are never answered.

She was so quiet. She was listening to the answers on "Jeopardy." *The largest of the Great Lakes for 10,000.* Apparently it was Lake Superior.

When they went to commercial, she turned the volume down. "You really want to know?" She sounded pained. But no matter how tense her words, her hands were composed and on her lap, threaded together. "He got into a bar fight. It went terribly wrong and he killed a man. The prosecution said he didn't use equal force. The dead man used a bottle on your father, but your father used a bat. The bottle was broken, though, jagged edges everywhere. Your father clearly felt threatened. No matter. The man he killed was a local and well-liked, and your father was a journeyman, just passing through. He was convicted of first-degree manslaughter and went to prison for ten years. He got sick in there and died. They said pneumonia. But it could've been from his congestive heart failure. He always had a bad heart." She stood, picked up her empty teacup with a steady hand.

I didn't know what to say. "How come you never told me?"

"You never asked. I told you your daddy had died. I thought that was enough. I didn't want to upset you. You were always so sensitive. I thought when you were ready you would ask."

"How come we never visited him in prison?"

"He was too far. He was tried and convicted in California. I didn't want to take you on the bus. I was saving up my money for us to fly, but then he up and died." She stood in front of me, still holding her teacup, her gray hair set in curlers, her houserobe clean and smelling of detergent.

"What was he doing in California?"

Emma didn't answer at first, rubbing her cup. "I reckon," she said at last, "the same thing you're about to do."

She was right. I hadn't been ready, and was still not ready. Only when she had fallen silent did I catch the hook between the lines: *your father went to find your mother and he ended up dying in prison. And now you're going.*

Straining hard to be grown-up, but staring hard to glean her reaction, I asked, "You think my mother is still alive?" I was hoping she'd say, no, Shel, she's long dead. Don't go anywhere. Please. Stay here.

I wanted her to say it.

"How would I know, Shelby?" she said. "Perhaps."

Perhaps, perhaps, perhaps. What does one say to that?

"Where's the letter she wrote him before she left?"

"What letter?" Puzzled at first, suddenly she frowned. Her neutral gaze darkened. "Oh my God. Have you been believing vicious gossip all these years? What's wrong with you? Why are you so eager to make up things about your life? What, life isn't hard enough?"

Life was hard enough. "*Am* I making it up?" I mouthed.

"What do you think is going on around here?" Emma clunked her cup down! "Who do you think I am? Who do you think has been raising you all these years?"

I didn't answer, but she glared at me as if expecting an answer. So finally I said, "I thought my father left my mother to be with you. So she left."

Gasping and falling speechless Emma straightened, her usually kind and casual eyes flushed with incomprehension. "I simply don't understand who you are. Shelby, your father didn't leave your mother. Your mother left him. And for your information, I am not your father's slutty mistress. I am his sister."

I sucked in my breath. "You are?" I was dumbfounded. "How can that be?" I stammered after minutes of silent shame. "You—you—have different last names."

"So, expert on names? We had one mother. Your father was ten years younger than me."

"You are my *aunt?*" This could not have been said with more incredulity than if I had said, *you are a man?*

"Why do you think you called me Aunt Emma?"

"I was just a kid then," I muttered.

"Yes, and with more sense than now, after twelve years of school. When your father set out to look for your mother, he said he'd be back in two weeks. I agreed to watch over you. Two weeks turned out to be thirteen years. He left you with me because there was nowhere else for you to go."

I was ashamed and ashen. Humiliation sometimes turns into a parade of pride. It did so with me. To cover up, I said, "Well, why didn't you ever tell me?"

"You called me Aunt Emma!" she nearly yelled.

"Just a name," I doggedly repeated.

She shook her head. "Yes. Just a name of your daddy's sister." She was breathing heavily, gathering her thoughts. "Does it benefit you to talk down your life? To make it up out of damaged cloth? Did you ever ask yourself why a jilted and abandoned woman would raise her ex-lover's wayward, ungrateful and preposterous child?" I asked myself this a thousand times a day.

"Because that's you, Shelby," Emma continued. "Preposterous and ungrateful. You've been spinning and believing these lies about yourself, but it's not to make yourself feel better. It was always to make yourself feel worse."

I had nothing to say after that.

Neither did she.

"I'm leaving tomorrow," I said. "And I'm not coming back till I find my mother."

"Good," she said. "By all means, I beg of you, do keep open the questions of youth. As if they're the important thing." She turned to go. "That's what your father said, too, by the way. But perhaps you'll need your mother's name, if you're going to be looking for her, and all." She fell silent and waited.

Why was she waiting? As if she were holding her breath for me to choose to stay or choose to go. But she gave me a car! I had to go.

I had to.

"What was her name?" I asked, defiantly.

Emma lifted her teacup off the table, her gray face tight, her gray eyes sober. "Lorna Moor."

Lorna Moor!

My mother hadn't left a letter. But she did send a postcard. Emma showed it to me. It had daffodils on a Main Street and beyond them cliffs and a hard-breaking ocean. *Mendocino, California*, the card's location read, and in small sloppy handwriting, "*Say hi to Shelby.*"

This is how you move toward the rest of your life: sometimes by repetition and, sometimes, by revolution.

TWO
MARY'S LAND

1

The Pomeranians

It was a beautiful late June morning when I set off. I got to Gina's house around nine. It had taken longer than expected to pack up and get out. I had told Gina to be ready at eight. I think I milled around for a few extra minutes to see if Emma would say something to me. What, no words of wisdom? She said, "Do you have what you need?"

And I said, "Yes."

"You don't." She brought something out from my bedroom. "You forgot this." She was holding my pillow with the pink cotton jersey cover. "You know how you don't like to sleep without it."

She was right, I didn't like to sleep without my pillow. "I don't want to take it, Emma," I said. "I'm afraid I'm going to forget it in a motel room. I'd rather have it waiting for me when I come back."

Emma laid it down on the kitchen table. "Okay."

Absurdly I kept feeling my cash, all of it in one large manila folder. It made me feel vulnerable carrying it like that; one snatch, the whole trip over. I should have bought a purse. But what was I going to do, carry $2000 in my purse to the convenience stores to get a Coke? But now what to do with it? Leave it in the glove compartment? I opted for the bottom of my suitcase, all except twenty bucks in the back of my shorts for drinks and things.

Emma gave me a pat with a little squeeze. "Be well," she said. "Be good." She didn't even say be careful. Personally I would've thought that was a prerequisite, but what do I know. Perhaps a mother would've said it.

At Gina's house, her mother, Kathy Reed, was fussing over her like ... well, like a mother whose eldest daughter was taking an unprecedented trek across the country. Morning, evening, Kathy Reed was always exceptionally coiffed and this morning was no exception. Made up and in a soft-knit skirt, she carried Gina's suitcase to the car herself, stepping across the lawn in her beige three-inch heels. "Shelby! I haven't seen you in ages." She hugged me, smiled. "How've you been?"

"Very good, Mrs. Reed," I said, but she was already walking back to the house to fetch another bag. I hoped it would fit in my trunk.

Gina's grandmother was there, too, hobbling on her cane, muttering, trying to dispense advice. "Bring a jacket. You'll get cold." "Bring a book. Shelby, did you bring a book?" "Bring *all* the telephone numbers in case of emergency."

All telephone numbers? I mouthed to Gina. Like *all* telephone numbers? She laughed.

"Bring quarters." The dogs were barking, the cat was underfoot.

I kept my distance from the goings-on; to me Gina didn't look ready to go, and I didn't want to be in her way. I kept glancing at my watch, hoping that would give somebody a sense of urgency. We needed to get through New Jersey and Pennsylvania today, stop somewhere in Ohio. That was 500 miles away, but we could do it if we left immediately, hit only a little traffic going through New York City, maintained 50 mph on I-78 west, and kept the stops to a minimum. One for gas, one for drinks ...

"Remember, don't eat any of the cannoli," I overheard Mrs. Reed instructing. "My sister loves these. She can't get them in Baltimore."

I came out of my geographical reverie, narrowed my eyes. Suddenly I was paying attention. Mrs. Reed might as well have slapped her hands together at the end of my nose.

"Um," I said, aptly. "Um, excuse me, your *sister?*"

"Yes, you know Flo, Shelby," said Mrs. Reed. "Gina's aunt. You've met her many times at Christmas. She lives in Baltimore."

"Of course. I like her very much. *Does* she . . . live in Baltimore? When did she move there?" I thought Flo lived right around the corner. Didn't all aunts?

"Well, Kathy, actually, *near* Baltimore," the mother-in-law, propped by her cane, corrected her daughter-in-law about the whereabouts of her daughter-in-law's sister. "Near the airport."

"Scottie," said Mrs. Reed impatiently, "Glen Burnie is still considered Baltimore."

"Well, it's really its own little town. Probably better to say *near* Baltimore . . ."

I cleared my throat, trying to catch Gina's eye and anybody's attention. "Gina?"

Gina said nothing, busying herself with looking through her bag, muttering, "I hope I have everything . . ."

"Now, Gina, remember . . ."

"Wait, wait," I cut in. "What does Baltimore have to do with us? We're not going to Baltimore."

"Not going to Baltimore?" said Mrs. Reed. "Then how are you going to get the Pomeranians to Aunt Flo if you're not going to Baltimore?"

"The whatteranians?"

Gina was still studiously ascertaining if her bag was ready for travel. We were standing on the brick path near the front lawn, the birds were chirping and she was solemnly bent over, rummaging for hair clips. That's when I noticed the barking cage. It was pointed out to me by Gina's mother and grandmother, the latter with her cane, that was now a canine pointer-outer.

"Gina!" That was Mrs. Reed, not me. "You told me Shelby was all right with it. You told me you spoke to her!"

"I was going to, Mom, but we got so busy, and went away to Mystic, and it slipped my mind. Sorry, Sloane. Sorry, Mom."

"But you told me you spoke to her!"

"Sorry, Mom. Sorry, Sloane. I thought you wouldn't mind. I thought it was on our way. Isn't it?"

This coming from a girl who thought Bakersfield and Mendocino were neighboring towns, separated by a mere 500 miles! What was I supposed to do? The dogs were anxiously looking up through the bars of their crate.

Mrs. Reed rolled her eyes in exasperation. "Shelby, I hope you don't mind. My Rosie had puppies recently and I promised two of them to Flo. And it's a little on the way, isn't it?" She said this sheepishly, beseechingly, as if she was pretty sure it might not be *quite* on the way, but perhaps I wouldn't notice.

"I think it's a little out of the way," I said, sounding like such a stickler. "I'm sure it won't be too bad."

Mrs. Reed smiled warmly. "I'm pleased. My sister was sick last Christmas and hasn't seen the girls. Or you. She'll be very happy."

"We can stay with Aunt Flo and it won't cost us," said Gina, trying to organize her half-dozen pairs of sandals into a small shopping bag. "That's good, right? We save a little money. And she loves cannolis."

"Who doesn't?" I grumbled. Baltimore! I showed them my back so they wouldn't see me grind my teeth together. Surreptitiously, I flapped open the map. Sure enough, Baltimore was a miserable 200-mile detour south when we were heading west. Well, not anymore. Now we were heading south.

"Come on, Sloane," Gina said, coming up to the car. "It's just an adventure. I know it's not on your list."

"No, no, it's fine. It's going to add a day to the trip, get us to California later, but that's okay, I guess. One day won't hurt us. I'll adjust it on my calendar. I don't mind."

When I folded the map and turned around, Gina's mother had her hands on Gina's shoulders and was dispensing more advice. "Now remember, don't stop for anyone. Do you hear?"

"I hear."

"Do you promise?"

"I promise."

"Shelby, you promise? Be safe."

"Yes, of course, Mrs. Reed. I would never."

"Oh, you don't have to worry about Shelby, Mom." Gina laughed. "You know there's no one less likely in the world to pick up a hitchhiker than her."

"I know. That's why I'm letting you go with her," said Mrs. Reed. "And don't lose your money. And have breakfast every day. Don't forget to drink fluids on the road. And lock the car when you stop to go to the potty." I blinked. Did she use the word potty to an eighteen-year-old?

"I will." "I won't." "I will." "I won't." "I will."

"Don't talk to strangers. Don't even look at them."

"I won't."

While still holding on to Gina's shoulders, Mrs. Reed turned her head to me. "And, Shelby, when the tank is half full, gas up. No reason to wait till it's empty."

"We will, Mrs. Reed." She was preaching to the converted.

"No, no, not we. *You.* Don't let Gina touch the gas. The fumes will give her a fierce headache. Gina, when Shelby gasses up, you run to the bathroom, okay?"

"Okay, Mom."

"Don't stay near the pumps. Don't inhale." She turned to me. "And remember, she's allergic to peanuts. So no peanuts."

"No peanuts, got it. What about peanut butter?" When I saw her face, I said, all teeth, "Just kidding?"

She calmly continued. "Shelby, she's also allergic to bees and wasps. She'll swell up something awful if she's stung. Don't drive around country roads with the windows open. Just stay on the Interstate. We have such a good system of highways in this country. I heard someone made it from New York to California in three days!"

"Probably without diverting to Baltimore," I muttered, almost inaudibly.

"Be safe," she said firmly, after a sideways glance. "Don't speed. Keep to the speed limit. It's fifty-five. I don't care what kind of car you have. And don't pass trucks on the right. Let the trucks pass. They win all ties. And avoid aggressive drivers. Shelby, okay?"

"Okay, Mrs. Reed."

"How long have you had your license?"

"My student license for a year. My full license just since this month."

"Okay. You'll do well to be careful on the road. You're a new driver. Don't drive at night. When it starts to get dark, stop. Have dinner, then stop for the night. No reason to keep going like maniacs. You're not running to a fire. Better safe than sorry. Remember the story of the tortoise and the hare?"

Did she mean running *from* a fire? I thought it best not to ask. And didn't she just say someone made it from New York to California in *three* days? Was that the tortoise or the hare?

At no point did Gina say, Mom, we have to go. She just stood there, with her mother's arms on her shoulders, listening and nodding. After Mrs. Reed appeared to be done by having fallen silent, Gina said she was going to make one last "potty" break and disappeared inside. I was left with the two Mrs. Reeds standing looking me up and down. There was nothing to me this morning. I was wearing jean shorts with silver studs on the pockets the shape of roses and a beige Aerosmith T-shirt. My hair was clean, so were my teeth. I barely had on any makeup. Really, nothing to see here, folks. Yet they examined me, perused me. Mulled, like I was an indecent painting they thought was overpriced. "Shelby, you'll take good care of our Gina, right?" finally said the younger Mrs. Reed.

I had no idea what that meant. I hadn't taken care of anything my whole life. I couldn't get a one-eyed frog to last through winter. Naturally I said, "Yes, of course, Mrs. Reed. But Gina and I are friends. We look out for each other."

"You're her keeper now, Shelby," Mrs. Reed continued as if I hadn't spoken. "You know I've always thought of you as her older sister."

"Absolutely. Me, too. Well, actually, she's ten months older, but I know what you mean. And you know sisters, they take care of each other."

"She's in good hands. I know you'll watch out for her. I've always liked you. You really don't mind taking the dogs to Baltimore, do you?" She offered me fifty dollars for my trouble. I have a hard time saying no when people offer me money (it happens so rarely) and I didn't say no then.

"And Molly promises she'll be no trouble."

Dumbly I said, *Molly?* The time was nearing eleven. I was too afraid to look at my watch. I ripped it off my wrist and threw it in the backseat, as if removing the time counter from my person allowed me the illusion of control, as in, if I don't know what time it is, then it's not really that late, is it?

Gina returned. Behind her trailed a grumpy, barely awoken, unbrushed young girl. *Molly*, Gina's sister! I hadn't seen her in two years, and since then, she'd sprung things on her body, like boobs and hips. Back when I knew Gina's sister, she was a kid. Now she was twelve and unrecognizable. Cheerfully, to balance her sister's sulky pre-teen face, Gina said, "My mom wanted my sister to come along, too."

"Gina, don't lie," said Molly. "You invited me."

Flushed, Gina glared at her sister and to me said, "I thought it'd be fun, don't you think?"

"Is she coming with you all the way to Bakersfield?" I asked, not so carefully.

"Shh! Don't be silly. No, no," Gina quickly said, not looking at me.

Molly, as it turned out, was even less prepared than Gina. She had gone to get her toothbrush, a book to read (though she didn't look like the type that read books; that read *period*), her rather large cassette player, *and* her makeup. What else did a twelve-year-old bring to her aunt's? What else was there? Miniature golf clubs? She said she had to sit in the front. "I get dizzy in the back."

Gina agreed! Gina was going to sit in the back?

I shook my head. "Molly, do you know how to read a map?"

"Yes," she said defiantly.

"Oh, good. Because I don't know where your aunt lives, so you'll have to direct me out of New York, all right?"

"I can't read in the car. It makes me dizzy," said Molly.

"I see." I nodded. "Perhaps best to sit in the back, then."

"I can't sit in the back. It makes me dizzy. Besides, backseat's too small."

"Well, that's perfect, because you're small, too."

"No, I can't."

"Moll, give Sloane a break, will you?" said Gina with hostility. I suddenly remembered that Gina hated Molly. They never got along. Gina said Molly was spoiled and selfish. Why in the world would she invite her with us to Baltimore? Like children, we stared at Molly, and then pleadingly at Molly's mother, who pointed a finger at her daughter. "You've got one second to get in the back or march right upstairs, young lady."

Mrs. Reed's words made no impression on Molly other than to cause a hysterical fit, during which she stormed off upstairs screaming she wasn't going "Anywhere!" Mrs. Reed soothingly followed. I, for lack of anything to do, other than feel like a dumb ass, brushed my hair. My hair is thin and easy-care, and takes no time at all to brush out. I keep it fairly short for running. I brushed for fifteen minutes. Everyone by this time had left the lawn: the cane-carrying grandmother had gone inside, and Gina had forgotten "one more lipgloss." Only me and the Pomeranians remained. They had stopped barking and were whimpering now. I knew how they felt.

It was noon. Taking out my spiral notebook, I adjusted my schedule, wrote down the mileage from Larchmont to Glen Burnie (about 250 miles, measured by my pin-point scientific thumb), noted the time, the starting mileage . . .

By about twelve-thirty, when I had pulled out all of my thin, light, straight as a pin, easy-care-for hair and was debating picking up Gina's eyelash-tearing habit, a wet-faced Molly reappeared on the grass, mollified. She would sit in the back, "like a good girl," and would get a hundred dollars for her trouble.

"Ready?" I said to Gina, through my teeth. Molly and the mutts were squeezed in the back. "How about if I drive this leg, and you take the next?"

"What do you mean, take the next?" said Mrs. Reed, leaning in to kiss her daughter goodbye. "Gina doesn't know how to drive."

We were on the New England Thruway, and I was yelling. Me, yelling. "You don't know how to drive? Gina, you told me you had your license! You told me you'd share the driving!"

"I know, I know," Gina said guiltily. "I'm sorry. I did have my permit, just like you."

"So what happened? You still have it?"

"Well, no. You know how we're not supposed to drive at night. In April, I had a little mishap. Drove at night, very slightly teeny bit buzzed. Got stopped. Hence, no license."

"Oh." I brightened. "But you do know how to drive, then?"

"No. This wasn't this past April, but a year ago April. I hadn't even started my driver's ed. Sorry, Sloane."

"Unbelievable. But I kept saying how we would share the driving!"

"I know. I thought you meant that metaphorically."

"*Metaphorically*? How do you mean something like that metaphorically?"

From the back the twelve-year-old pulled off one of the headphones on the recently released and all the rage Sony Walkman. "Oh, shut up, already. I can't hear Journey."

I lowered my voice. "Why didn't you tell me this?"

"I thought you wouldn't let me come if I told you," said Gina.

She was right. I wouldn't have. I had been hoping she'd drive in the afternoons so I could nap, and now that was out the window; I'd have to readjust my schedule that I'd so carefully written up. But she had disarmed me with her honesty, because I wasn't used to it. I let it go. What choice did I have? Turn around and bring her back home? After all, I had calculated my expenses for two.

Besides, who was *I* to lecture Gina on honesty and forthrightness?

We drove a little while in silence.

Well, silence if by silence I mean two squabbling orange furballs and a snoring adolescent with earphones that blasted "Don't Stop Believin'" to everyone in the car (how in the world could she sleep to that?).

"So we're off," Gina said. "Are you excited?"

"Sure," I said.

"I'm so excited! I like your car," she added, as we approached New York City.

"Goes fast, don't it?" We were moving at a clip of about twelve miles per hour.

It was two in the afternoon.

By five, we were still in New York City, having gone four miles in three hours (construction and two accidents), but on the plus side, it looked as if by sundown we *might* get to the Battery Tunnel (about forty miles from my house). Still more than 200 miles from our destination of Glen Burnie. And 3200 miles from Mendocino. Gina suddenly seemed a little less excited. We had long eaten all the cannolis.

Molly woke up and asked if we were there yet. I told her I didn't know what she meant by there, but if she meant downtown New York, then yes, we were. After whining in disbelief for twenty minutes, she announced she was thirsty. Then she was hungry. She had to make a stop. "And the dogs certainly do. Gina, you're supposed to be responsible for them."

"They're fine." She hadn't even looked back at the dogs to check. She was wearing tight jean shorts and a blue-striped sleeveless tunic, and was humming along to the radio.

The gas tank was half empty. But we were in the tunnel now. And in Brooklyn, I wasn't about to get off anywhere. I'd never find my way back to the BQE. And now look. The Verrazano Bridge was rising up out of the water in front of me, and it was five-thirty at night! "I hope Aunt Flo isn't going to get upset about our late arrival."

"She's expecting us for dinner," Molly said from the back. "And I'm thirsty."

"It'll have to be a late dinner," I shot right back. "Because it's dinnertime now, and we're 200 miles from her house."

Was this how I'd been planning my first day of freedom? My frustration tasted like metal in my mouth.

"I know this is a little slower than we'd hoped, Sloane," said Gina, "but it's okay, it's all part of it."

"Part of what?"

"Did you girls know," said Gina, "that there is one letter of the alphabet that does not appear in any of the states' names. Which—"

"Z!" yelled Molly from the back.

"No, and don't shout," said Gina. "Sloane?"

"I'm not playing," I said. "Q?"

"Yes, very good. Q is correct."

"Where does Z appear?"

"The Ozarks," said Molly.

"The Ozarks are not a state, Molly."

"Missouri, then."

"Missouri has no Z." Gina rolled her eyes.

Molly mouthed it to herself a few times and then exclaimed, "Arizona!"

"Very good. It wasn't a question, but very good."

I glanced at Gina as we were pulling off on Victory Boulevard in Staten Island. "How do you know this?"

She shrugged. "I know a few things."

"What letter doesn't appear in any of the states? That's knowing a few things?"

She was philosophical. "And a few things more."

"When did you learn all this?"

"Dad loves trivia. And he's so competitive and critical, I had to read up on things."

59

"He's supposed to be critical," said Molly. "He's Dad."

"No, he's right," said Gina. "I'm going to be a teacher. I have to be smart." She adjusted the straps of her black bra.

We got gas at a gunky rest-stop; I pumped while Gina walked the dogs; we were back on the road by six-thirty. As we were getting on the expressway, I noticed a young, barely clad lad with a guitar on his back standing by the side of the road with his thumb out. Gina rolled down the window, stuck her head out, and yelled, "Need a ride, cowboy?"

"Gina!" I pulled her back in.

She waved, blew him a kiss. "Maybe next time, huh?" she shouted.

"What are you doing? We agreed!"

"I'm just joking, Sloane," she said pretend-solemnly. "Just having fun." She smiled. "He was cute, though."

"He could be Robert Redford, we're not picking anyone up, okay?"

"Oh, come on, you wouldn't pick up Robert Redford?"

She was right, so I shut up until we got to Goethals Bridge forty-five minutes later and crossed into New Jersey when it was nearing seven o'clock. The sun was hazy in the sky, the noxious industry around us.

One of the passing trucks beeped his jolting loud horn and gave me the thumbs up, which I didn't understand. We turned up the radio. BBBBBennie and the Jets were plugging us kids into the faithless.

"Are we almost there?" asked Molly again.

"No."

"Are we almost there?"

"No."

"Are we almost there?"

"No."

We drove like this for two interminable New Jersey exits.

"Gina, Molly wears a lot of makeup for a twelve-year-old."

"I'm gonna be thirteen soon," said Molly, "and what's it to you?"

"I'm just saying," I continued to Gina.

Gina shrugged. "Who does it hurt?"

"She is twelve."

"Thirteen soon!"

"How soon?"

"May."

"Thirteen in eleven months?" I shook my head. "Like I was saying."

"I'm thirsty."

"I'm really getting hungry."

"I think I need to make another stop."

"No way am I stopping again. No stopping till Aunt Flo's."

"Are we there yet?"

"Stop it!"

"I think the dogs have to go again."

I glanced at Gina. "You sure you don't want to take your sister and the dogs to California with us? Come on. It'll be fun."

Gina snorted.

"I'll go with you guys to California," Molly said brightly. "This *is* fun."

Now it was my turn to snort.

"You should feed her, Sloane," Gina said. "Did you know that if the stomach doesn't produce a new layer of mucus every fourteen days, its digestive juices will cause it to digest itself?"

From the back came Molly's revolted screeching. "Hmm," I said, stepping on the gas. "So the good news is, only thirteen days to go."

I watched Molly's warpainted face in the rearview mirror when she wasn't bent over the crate playing with the dogs. She was such a kid, yet the makeup made her look seven, eight years older. She wasn't *my* sister, and I couldn't quite articulate what I felt, but what I felt was this. Why did a twelve-year-old need to look older? Why did a twelve-year-old need cherry-red lipstick, the brightness of which Debbie from Dallas would shy away from? Come on, Sloane, I chided myself. Stop being so old.

"The New Jersey Turnpike is arguably the dullest stretch of land in all of America," I said.

"Do you know that studies have shown," Gina said, "that more accidents with people falling asleep at the wheel happen on the Jersey Turnpike than anywhere else in the country?"

"Really?"

Gina shrugged. "I don't know," she admitted. "But if it isn't true, it should be."

Molly piped up once more. "Hey, Shelby, we haven't seen you in a long time. Where you been?"

"I've been around."

"Not around our house."

"No." I trailed off. I didn't really know what to say. And Gina interestingly didn't say anything. What *do* you say? What did Gina say to her mother when her "sister" Shelby had disappeared as if vaporized? I didn't like Gina's silence on the subject. She was usually so chirpy. But both her mouth and hands had tensed. She seemed to be almost actively not responding to her sister's question. We just stopped being friends, that's all, I wanted to say, but didn't. Things change, you know? You'll find out soon enough, Molly. Don't forget your extra layer of black eyeliner.

Finally! Two hours later, Delaware Memorial Bridge and a wide rushing river; it was the first pretty we'd seen.

"Did you know that the Hudson becomes the Delaware?" asked Gina. "It flows from St. Lawrence in Canada, and then turns into this river."

"Really?" She was so geographical, this Gina.

"Are we there yet?"

We were there an hour and a half later, at almost eleven.

Aunt Flo, hectored by Gina's mother, had called the police, alerting them of a mysterious disappearance of a bright yellow Mustang, three "children" inside it (this is how a frantic Mrs. Reed described us to the police officer who came to retrieve us from the Maryland phone booth from which we called for directions) and two small, "*very* expensive" dogs. While Gina was on the phone with her mother (telling her to calm down or "the trip will be ruined for sure, Mom!"), Aunt Flo could not understand why it took *me* so long to go two hundred miles. The Maryland state trooper who helped us find the house was nonchalant. "Hit some traffic, did you?" he said.

"Yes, and it hit back." I poked Gina's arm, still holding on to maternal telecommunication. "I hope it's not a harbinger of things to come, going 200 miles in fourteen hours on the road."

Barely listening, she poked me back. "We weren't on the road fourteen hours, and you know it damn well *is* a harbinger of things to come. Mom, I have to go." Pause. "Yes, of course, we'll be careful. No, of course, I haven't pumped any gas. No, of course we haven't picked up any hitchhikers." She winked at me.

Aunt Flo, who looked like a carbon copy of Gina's grandmother Scottie, to whom she was not remotely related, kept berating before salutations. "There was nothing we could do," Gina endlessly repeated. "We. Were. Stuck. In. Traffic. Remember Shelby, Aunt Flo? Say hello, Shelby."

"Hello, Shelby," I said.

Aunt Flo barely nodded my way. "Where are my cannolis, Shelby?" and then without a breath, "But why would you go through New York City? That's your number one mistake right there."

So after eleven hours of driving, before being fed or shown our rooms, or given a drink, we parried another fifteen minutes of post-mortem critique about all the wrong roads we took to get to Glen Burnie, Maryland.

I lay in bed that night, my hands under my head, staring at the ceiling. If Marc were here, he wouldn't stop taunting until Wyoming. He'd say it was definitely my fault. What was I doing in a car with a girl who made my hands anxious and my brain malfunction, a girl who brought her odd sister to be a buffer between us, a girl who could not drive? I hoped Gina could read a map. I missed my comfy pink-roses bed.

Lorna Moor.

My mother's name filled my insides with an ache like freezing, but all around that aching was a peculiar sort of heat. Emma was related to me. Emma was my *aunt*. By blood. I was her niece by blood. I had a connection to her. She had a connection to my father. That's why she didn't leave, and in Glen Burnie, Maryland, with the planes sounding like they were landing on the roof of our house, that knowledge made me feel better.

Still, my first day of travel had turned out to have in it nothing I wanted, or had prepared for, or planned. I took out my spiral notebook from my duffel and looked over my schedule. We weren't in Ohio. We weren't west. We hadn't gone 500 miles. On the plus side, the lodging was free. Recalling Gina's little trivia diversions made me smile a bit, but otherwise, I couldn't relax, or even look forward to tomorrow. But I knew what would make me relax: checking off the items on the agenda for today. Didn't forget anything. Left on time. Headed in the right direction. Did not get lost. Oh well . . .

I made a list for tomorrow. That did make me feel better. Number one: Leave no later than nine. I couldn't make any more plans as I'd left my maps and atlas in the car, and also because I had fallen asleep.

2

The Vedantists

Number one in my plan was out the window at nine-thirty because no one had woken up, not Gina, not Molly, and almost not me.

"How long are we planning to stay?" I asked Gina, when she finally tumbled out of her room around eleven.

"At least a week," said Aunt Flo, who overheard. "Haven't seen my darlings in years."

"Yes, yes, of course. And I hope we have a nice visit." A week! "It's just that . . ." I became tongue-tied. What was there to do in Baltimore for a week? And I had a mission! I had to get to Mendocino. I'd rather spend a week looking for my mother than be here in Glen Burnie. Not wanting to be impolite, I stared at Gina until she said something, about ten minutes later.

"Shelby has to get to California, Aunt Flo. Mom told you. We'll leave Molly here, but Shel can't stay that long. She has to be back to get ready for college. And me, too."

"Yes, so true!" I piped up. "I told Emma I'd be getting back in a few weeks. Plus Gina has to get to—"

"Shh!" Gina interrupted, glaring.

"What's the hurry?" said Aunt Flo. "It's supposed to be a fun trip. An adventure. Stay a few days, relax. Then you can drive your sister back, so she doesn't have to take a bus home."

"Aunt Flo!" That was Gina. "We're not driving Molly back.

Mom and I agreed. We're going cross country. We're not commuting back and forth along the Eastern seaboard." Way to go, Gina. But to me she said, "She's right. What's the rush?"

No, no rush. In one day I was going to chew off my own skin, piece by piece, beginning with my hands.

"You're right to go," Marc had said. "This is the only time in your life to take a trip like this, Shelby. Once you start college, you'll have to work during the summer. You'll be an intern. And then you'll have a job in the city. When you have a real job, you'll have an apartment, bills, a dog. And then even *you* might find a husband—and then forget everything. Once the kids come, you'll never willingly get in the car again." Marc talked of these things as if he knew. "I *do* know," he said indignantly. "My older sister has four kids. You should see her. You won't believe she's a member of our species." He drew her bent over the corn bread; the corn bread a happy yellow, and she all in gray. Later, when he showed me the picture, I said, don't show it to your sister, but he told me she had had it enlarged and framed.

Gina and I went downtown to Harborplace Mall, looked around, flirted with some boys, bought nothing. The following day we went to the town pools. That was okay, even though we took Molly with us. We also took Molly to Burger King and to see "Raiders of the Lost Ark." That night I lay fretting, and when I woke up, it was another day. In Glen Burnie. Close to the factories and the Camden Yards and the airport; just another drab neighborhood, familiar enough and bland, but how was staying in a small house with a large yard helping me get to California on my road to self-discovery? I took my Folgers instant coffee outside.

The backyard was home to dozens of Flo's dogs, small and smaller, running around, yapping. It was the yapping that got to me. I wasn't used to the cacophony. My inner life was quiet, so too my life with Emma. Sometimes my friends were loud, but they were loud temporarily, and then I went home, retreating into quiet again. I liked to listen to music, but quietly, even rock. When Emma and I cleaned or cooked, the house was quiet. Sometimes

Emma would put something classical on. I enjoyed that; but this? A constant high-pitched, grating yelping? My point isn't that it was unpleasant. Undeniably it was. My point is this: someone had chosen this voluntarily; a green backyard with trees and ungroomed flowers, filled with a running mass of barking fecal matter. I then realized. Flo couldn't hear them. After an hour outside, I couldn't hear them either. The house was under the path of planes landing at BWI airport four blocks away. Every five to seven minutes a deafening roar in the clouds muted any dog mewling which seemed like Bach's cello concertos by comparison.

"Girls, why don't you do something? Why are you sitting around? It's a beautiful day. Drive down to Annapolis, see the harbor. There's so much to do around here."

"We were thinking of leaving to do something," I said.

Gina kicked me under the table. Aunt Flo said, "Yes, yes, good. There's an afternoon game today, why don't you go? The Orioles are playing the Yankees."

My interest in baseball was only slightly below that of cleaning a yard full of dog poop. And that, at least, would take less time. Besides, we didn't budget for ballgame tickets. But Gina wanted to go, though she also had no interest in baseball. "Come on, we'll get some bleacher tickets, they're cheap."

Aunt Flo picked up the shovel scooper. "I have to keep at it, otherwise they overrun me."

"Really?" I said, neutrally.

"Oh, yes, yes. I have to clean the yard four to six times a day. Well, just imagine—twenty-four dogs, pooping at least three times each. Some as many as six."

"I *can't* imagine."

Gina kicked me again.

"Twenty-four dogs, really? That's a lot." Nodding, muttering, I turned my head away so I wouldn't have to watch a heavy-set, middle-aged woman spending her brilliant summer morning cleaning dog poo. If man is the dog's master, then why was she picking up their poo and not the other way around? I got up to say we *really* had to be going. But how do you say this to someone who is fecally engaged? I waited. She was at it a long time. I went into the house, got my things together, my toothbrush, my shoes.

"Come on, let's go," Gina said, coming into my bedroom. "She'll give us money for the ballgame."

"Why do you want to go to a stupid ballgame?"

"You don't understand anything. Bleachers are full of single guys. Jocks. Sports lovers." She grinned. "Nothing they like better than two goils interested in baseball." She threw back her hair.

"Are you kidding?"

"Not at all."

"But we're not interested in baseball!"

"And they'll know this how?"

"Gina! Don't you have to be in Bakersfield?"

"Shh!" There was just us two in the room.

"Why do you keep telling me to shh," I exclaimed, "every time I say the word Bakersfield?"

"Because no one knows I'm going there. I told them I was just going with you for the ride. That you wanted some company. This is what friends do. That's why they think there's no hurry."

What could I do but shake my incredulous head? "I thought you wanted to get to"—I waved my hand around—"as soon as possible? To get to him?"

"Why do you keep referring to Eddie as him?" she asked, her blue eyes narrowing.

"As opposed to what?"

"As opposed to Eddie."

"He's not here," I said, taking out my spiral notebook and my Bic pen. "I can refer to someone in the pronoun form when he's not here. It's not rude."

"It's weird is what it is."

Oh, that's not the weird thing, I thought, writing down: *Number 1: Must leave, must go, must get going!* "Besides," I said, "why do you say, *keep* referring to him, as if we talk about him non-stop?"

"Yes, okay, you're right, you win, you can have the last word."

"Fine, you can have the last word. So when we go out cruising for boy toys, is your twelve-year-old sister coming with us?"

"She can if she wants," said Gina. But even Molly refused. We went by ourselves. Gina turned up the radio real loud, and the only discussion we had was about whether or not the Nazis in "Raiders" had been destroyed when they opened the Ark of the Covenant because the Ark was not to be a tool in human hands. Gina maintained it could have been opened and looked at by the good guys.

"Gina, you think if Indy opened that Ark, he wouldn't have gone up in flames?"

"No, I don't think he would've."

"He most certainly would. Why did he tell Marion to close her eyes, to not look? They only made it because they didn't look!"

"You're wrong. He told her just in case, not because they couldn't look."

"You're so wrong."

"No, you're wrong."

I think the Yankees lost. They could've won. It was hard to tell sitting a mile away in the bleachers. Men hit a small ball with a stick, ran about, then the game was over. Everyone around us had too much beer and was therefore unappetizing to Gina.

As we were returning to Aunt Flo's house, I told Gina we had to leave tomorrow.

"Okay," she said.

It took us another two days to get out.

Aunt Flo, to help us, I hope, told Gina and me that Aunt Betty, whom Gina hadn't seen in years and who loved Gina and liked me, too, lived near Toledo which was on the way. "Why don't you stay with her, save yourselves some money? I'll call her while you're getting ready."

I didn't want to say that I'd been ready for days. "On the way to *where*?" I cut in.

"To California."

"Toledo is on the way to California?" Once more I wished I had a clearer idea of what the U.S. looked like. An adult woman was saying to me Toledo was on the way; what was I going to do? Say excuse me while I skeptically check the map, because I don't believe you; check the map in front of you, just to prove you wrong? So I said nothing, thereby, with my ignorant silence, tacitly agreeing that Aunt Betty was "near" Toledo.

"Shelby, why do you always look like you know best?" Aunt Flo threw open the map. "Look. Toledo is right off Interstate 80, and you have to take I-80 to California, don't you?"

Well, now I definitely couldn't even *glance* at the map in front of her. "Of course, you're right," I agreed. "I got confused in my head."

"Oh, we'd love to, Aunt Flo," said Gina. "What a great idea. Aunt Betty's wonderful. Molly, you want to come with us?"

I widened my eyes. Gina did not (would not?) return my gaze. Wow. Gina *really* didn't want to be alone in the car with me. By some miracle, Molly declined. She said she didn't like Aunt Betty's companion, Uncle Ned. "He makes me feel weird," she said. "He *is* weird. A *starer*." She made a yuk sound.

Visibly disappointed, Gina tried to convince her. "He's not so bad. He's quiet."

"Yes," said Molly. "A quiet *starer*. Nothing worse. So, good luck with that."

Finally around noon of the nth day, sunny, possibly a Wednesday, though it could've been Friday, I screeched out of the driveway, going from nought to 136.7 in three seconds.

"How can your aunt live in that house with so many yapping animals?" I finally asked, after the radio was the only sound in our car for twenty minutes.

"You know what I think?" Gina said casually, tossing her hair about. "I think you're not a dog person. You don't like dogs."

What was she talking about? I loved dogs. I just didn't love them in my brand new beautiful yellow car on my all-vinyl black

70

seat, barking for 200 miles, needing to go "potty". I liked my dogs bigger. And farther away. I liked dogs the way dog people like children.

"You have to give them a chance," Gina continued, putting on peach lipgloss. She was wearing a white tube top and jean shorts today. "Dogs are wonderful. And therapeutic. Did you know they bring terriers to terminally ill patients in hospitals to comfort them?"

"What? And who's they?"

"Like my mother said, you should keep an open mind, Sloane. You're narrow-minded. You're not open to other ideas."

"Open to ideas about dogs?"

"No. Dogs *as* an idea. An ideal of affection and comfort." What was she talking about? Why did she sound annoyed? I had driven her mother's dogs, hadn't I? It wasn't enough for me to drive them, I was supposed to love them, too?

She put on the radio to drown out the barking silence.

David Soul beseeched me not to give up on us but then Mac Davis begged me not to get hooked on him and Toni Tennille wished things to be done to her one more time. Woof, woof.

Finally I had to know. "So what's with the dogs? That's new. Your mom, Aunt Flo. I don't remember them being like that."

"Aunt Betty, too," said Gina. "All the sisters got into dogs. They breed them, sell them."

"Really?"

"What's wrong with that?"

"Nothing, nothing at all." I coughed. "It takes time, though. And what about Hathayoga? Your mom was obsessed with that. She was so into . . ." I tried to remember the name. ". . . Swami Maharishi?"

"You mean Baba Muktananda?"

"That's it."

"My mother's moved on from Baba," said Gina. "She and all my aunts."

"From Baba to dogs?"

"She keeps busy, makes a little money." Gina turned her face away from me to the passenger window. "Dogs are kind and loving, gentle creatures." When Mrs. Reed had discovered Eastern spiritualism, she spent four Christmases in a row trying to convert me. *Get in touch with your inner Chakra, Shelby. You are one with everything, and everything is one with you.* I kept telling her I could not be converted because that would imply a *verting. I'm just trying to open your eyes, Shelby, open your eyes to the truth that's out there.* I listened politely, ate turkey at her house, and opened my Christmas presents.

We were going rather slow on Liberty Street, with strip malls all around, stopping at every light. I didn't care, I was so happy to be on the road again. *Number 1: Leave Glen Burnie at 9 a.m. Number 2: Gas up, buy Cokes, potato chips. Number 3: Keep conversation with Gina light. Number 4: Drive 500 miles to Toledo, OH.* According to the map, in one and a half inches we would be near the Appalachian Trail and then the Pennsylvania Turnpike would take us north to I-80. Mrs. Reed and her three sisters had been into the reality of yoga and the oneness of the swami so seriously, they even persuaded their brother, a classics professor at University of Connecticut, to come with them to the Ashram, their upstate monistic Upanishad retreat. How many miles had we gone on Liberty Street, ten? It was one in the afternoon. Gina had taken off her sandals and put her bare feet up on the windshield.

"What happened with the yoga?"

Gina sounded reluctant. "Nothing. The dogs have replaced Baba."

"Why?"

Looking away into the passenger window, Gina said, "Aunt Ethel killed herself."

"She *did?*" I tried to keep the wheel straight. It wasn't easy.

Gina shrugged. She still wasn't looking at me. "It was called a car accident. But we knew. A clear blue day, no drugs, no alcohol, no heart attack, and she'd been depressed for years. Really depressed. The Ashram didn't help one bit."

"No, of course not," I muttered, clutching the wheel. "I'm really sorry. I didn't know."

"How could you not know? Agnes told everybody."

"I make it a point," I said, "to immediately stop listening to anything that's begins with the word *Agnes*."

As we drove past the bars and the tattoo parlors, I thought about Aunt Ethel. She was beautiful, soft-spoken and loving. "Her poor kids."

"They're okay. Daughter is grown. The son has a year left of high school."

"What about the husband?"

"My mother thinks he's the reason my aunt killed herself."

I clutched the wheel tighter. I remembered him, with his overgrown beard and intense eyes. He never quite fit in the family celebrations. "What's he doing now?" I asked carefully.

"I don't know. We don't see him anymore. He never liked our family."

That was true. He always seemed like an outsider. I had thought Aunt Ethel was the only one he actually liked. He looked at her fondly when he said her name. "*Ethel.*" Yet I also remember feeling there was something slightly creepy about him, the way he stared at me longer than appropriate, the way he tried to engage me in conversation, and how, once, after Ethel and Mrs. Reed were done regaling me with the consciousness of the yogic vision and the attainment of the Moksha, he recited Donne's poetry to me. *I will not look upon the quickening sun/but straight her beauty to my sense shall run/the air shall note her soft, the fire, most pure/waters suggest her clear, and the earth sure.*

I had been hoping he was talking about Ethel, beautiful for an aunt, and said nothing, embarrassed under his gaze. I was relieved when I didn't see him at Easter.

How gravely Gina and I had grown apart, that not a rumor, a rustle had blown my way, not even from scandalous Agnes. "When did your aunt die?" We used to talk about everything. Every day. Not a day would go by without Gina knowing every minute of my life and me knowing every minute of hers.

"A year this November."

This made me sad, made me think about things I didn't want to think about—reminders of the past I wanted put away. Here I was, leaving home for parts unknown and still couldn't leave them behind. Gina and I used to babysit for Jules and Jim, Aunt Ethel's kids. Ethel would feed us dinner, and then she and her husband would go out to the movies. They had a beautiful house on the water in Rye. They had a boat, their own slip, eighty feet of private beach, a membership to the yacht club, and both the elementary school and Rye Playland were within walking distance. To Gina and me they had seemed to live an enchanted life, but I guess it was more like enchanter's nightshade. Beautiful on the outside, poison underneath.

"My mom couldn't forgive the Vedantists for not bringing my aunt any peace or comfort," said Gina, "when she needed peace and comfort most. See what I mean about religion?"

I didn't see what she meant, but I did finally begin to notice that nearly every road we crossed was named Divine Way, Mary's Way, Cross Way, Holy Road, Holy Family Road, Trinity Drive, Spirit Way. And on every corner rose a church, sandwiched between tattoo parlors and a Jack in the Box. Or were the tattoo parlors sandwiched between the churches? The only thing I noticed about the one church remotely near us in Larchmont was that on Monday each week, the bulletin board in the front would change its inspirational message. "JESUS IS THE ANSWER." "JESUS IS THE ANSWER TO EVERY QUESTION."

"Gina, look at all the churches. I've never seen anything like it. Have you?"

"Well, there aren't any churches on the Jersey Turnpike. So no. But I wouldn't have noticed even these had you not mentioned them. I don't notice things like that."

"Hmm. Hard to miss."

Gina must have been thinking troubling things, difficult things—her eyes were unseeing. "What a weird life it must be around here," she finally said, coming out of her reverie. "What do you think these people do all the time?"

"Well, judging from the road, get tattoos and go to church."

She laughed. "I'd die if I lived here. Absolutely die."

I stopped at a light. The road was called St. John's Path. A white church on one corner, a white church on the other. We waited. There were no more strip malls or Burger Kings. Now, beyond the white spires were rolling fields of green, shivering trees, and sunshine.

"Did you know," Gina said, "that 57 percent of all people who get tattoos regret them later in life? And that number goes up to 71 percent for women. More men get them, but more women regret them. And tattoos for females are on the rise. Like smoking. Apparently it's the next trend. Women getting tattooed. Interesting, eh?"

"Yeah, very." I was only half-listening, trying to figure out a mathematical riddle on the white board.

$$1 \text{ Cross}$$
$$+ 3 \text{ Nails}$$
$$= 4 \text{ Given}$$

I was stuck on the numbers. One plus three did equal four, but what did it have to do with *Given*? I couldn't decipher the meaning. Gina glanced at it and instantly said, oh how stupid. It took me another shameful mile to figure it out. Then *I* felt stupid. And resented her, like it was her fault. But numbers sometimes confuse me. I can't see past them. *RUL8*? Master's Ministry proclaimed I was, but they were praying I wasn't 2L8.

"I'm a good person, I have nothing to be forgiven for," Gina said. "I'm so beyond that."

Didn't Emma once tell me, when I was preening, that just as you're about to put yourself on a pedestal for being good, the devil knocks you down with pride right back where you belong. I kept quiet.

Chapel View, Chapel Lane, Chapel Hill. Freedom.

3

The Black Truck

The road wound through the fields. We rolled down the windows, turned up the music, the wind blowing through our hair. The Climax Blues Band yelled that we couldn't get it right, and Kiki Dee croaked that she had the music in her. It was on Liberty Road, past Freedom, when the Blockheads were hitting us with their rhythm stick and I was flying, showing off my Shelby GT 350 to the blue skies, that I suddenly had to slam on the brakes for a black truck ahead of us.

"God, it's crawling," I said. In reality, though, it was probably doing forty. Gina groaned, I groaned. We continued singing, but it was one thing to sing and speed but another to sing at the top of your lungs, slam on your brakes, then dawdle along almost at walking pace.

The medium-sized, four-wheel utility truck in front of us was from the coal mines. Not painted black, but dirty black, covered with tar-like nicotine, its *two* smokestacks emitting black plumes. What was happening inside that it needed two smokestacks? Not only was it dilly-dallying as if on the way to execution, but it couldn't stay in its lane. It kept rolling out to oncoming traffic. There was no traffic, but that was beside the point. It was a menace. We stopped singing.

"What's wrong with him?" I asked.

"Maybe he's drunk."

"It's Wednesday morning."

"What, people can't get drunk on a Wednesday? And it's not Wednesday morning. It's Tuesday afternoon."

We passed a billboard, huge black letters on white board. "WILL THE ROAD YOU'RE ON LEAD YOU TO ME?"

"Did you know that reading billboards is responsible for eleven percent of all vehicular accidents?" stated Gina.

"Is that so?" But I wasn't paying much attention to her or the billboards. I was entirely focused on the increasingly erratic truck. The driver could've fallen asleep at the wheel. I gave him plenty of room. No reason to tailgate; a good safe distance is what he obviously needed. We were two car lengths behind.

He had a bumper sticker on the back tail—everyone was so clever in this neck of the woods with their little aphorisms—I speeded up so I could read it: "I DO ME . . . YOU DO YOU."

"Oh, ain't he the comedian." Gina laughed. "It's supposed to be *I do you, you do me*."

"He frightens me."

"Ha," she said. "I like him better already. He says leave me the hell alone and let me tend to my business. That's priceless."

"Yes, but what business could he possibly have that he's weaving all over the road like that?"

"So slow down. Give him some room."

"Any more room, and I'll be in another state."

"Maybe he'll turn soon."

"Turn where?" The empty country road stretched between fields and forests.

"Wait, what's he doing?" Gina said.

At first it looked like he was turning, but he wasn't. He was stopping. Suddenly and without preamble, his coal-tar vehicle zigzagged to a halt in the middle of the road right in front of us. We had no choice but to stop, too. Like for a school bus. Maybe he was in trouble. I didn't know, didn't want to know and didn't want to be any part of his trouble. I didn't want to help him. What if

77

he had run out of gas? What if his door opened and he asked us for a ride to the nearest gas station? My insides filled with liquid nitrogen. No way! No rides to weaving strangers driving black trucks.

The passenger door flung open. There was shouting, and suddenly a girl was propelled from the truck onto the grassy edge. She didn't hop out, she fell yelling, "You bastard! Hey, give me my stuff!" A hobo bag flew through the air, landing heavily on the grass. A man's hand reached for the door, pulled it violently shut and the truck peeled away, leaving smoking tire tracks on the pavement, black fumes piping furiously out of the stacks. He drove fast now, and straight.

"Asshole!" the girl yelled after him, getting up, dusting herself off. She didn't seem to be hurt, though I was trying not to look too closely. I put the 'Stang in gear and accelerated, not like the truck—in anger—but in fear. The girl stood, picked up her bag, turned to us, smiled, and stuck out her hitching thumb. She waved with the other hand. She was young, heavily made up, wearing not summer-in-the-city shorts, but a white mini-skirt, a small electric-blue halter and lots of flashy costume jewelry. We passed her slowly, pretending like we didn't even notice her, la-dee-dah. I whispered, "Gina, roll up your window."

"Why are you whispering?" But before she could turn the crank, the girl called out. "Hey, come on, be Good Samaritans, help a sister in need, will ya? Give me a ride."

Gina shook her head, I stared straight ahead without acknowledging her, and as we passed, the girl's hitching thumb morphed into the middle finger to our departing yellow Mustang. "Thank you!" she yelled. I stepped on it, catching her in the rearview mirror walking uphill in high-heeled wedge sandals and her spicy blue halter.

"Who wears sandals like that?" I asked.

"Who wears a skirt like that?"

We drove in silence.

"We couldn't pick her up," I said.

"Of course we couldn't." Gina glanced at me askance. "What are you even *talking* about? We made a deal."

"That's what I'm saying."

"Shelby, did you *want* to pick her up?"

"Slightly less than I want to be scalped," I returned. The ridiculous part was I now had to stop and look at a map to see where we needed to turn to get on Penn Pike, but I couldn't stop. I was afraid the girl might pursue me and force me to explain how I promised I wouldn't pick up hitchhikers, not even a girl my age shoved roughly out of a black truck by angry hands.

I was going eighty on a local road, through fields with mountains up ahead, past abandoned gas stations.

"What's wrong with you?" Gina asked.

"Nothing."

"Why are you driving like a maniac?"

Silence again.

"We did the right thing, didn't we?" I asked.

"About what? Can you stop for a sec and check the map? I don't see the turnpike signs anywhere."

We did see another billboard, this one from the American Board of Proctology: GIVING SOMEONE THE FINGER DOESN'T HAVE TO BE A BAD THING.

"I mean, that girl could've been trouble, right?" I said.

"Oh, her. Why are you still talking about her?"

We turned up the music. Diana Ross plaintively wanted to know if we knew where we were going to. Gina plaintively wanted to know when she was going to be fed. Having lost my sense of how far we'd come, whether we even were still in Maryland, I made a series of rights and lefts hoping the zigzag would eventually lead me to the toll road that transsected the entire state of Pennsylvania, as per Rand-McNally road atlas. Past a meandering town of antique stores and law firms we drove, past a deserted little town with not even a sandwich place for us to hang our hats, and, still hungry, we left the churches and the placards behind, the girl, too, and drove through the Appalachian Trail, sunlit and hazy, covered with a silken green and gold canopy. I pointed out a street sign that said *Applachian Road*. "You'd think that since they live here, they'd know how to spell it." We chuckled at that, and then again at a sign that stated without punctuation: SHARP CURVES PEDESTRIANS 4 MILES.

For four miles we looked for these pedestrians with sharp curves. Liberty Street had long since become Appalachian Trail with the tall filtering trees looking almost yellow with their light green sparklings. After the trail was Hagerstown. The shops along the way seemed too dinky for us. Finally, our long-awaited toll road! With a shopping center and a Subway sandwich place.

At the table I stared blankly at the open map. Gina wanted to know if Toledo was in Pennsylvania. I glared at her over my tuna sandwich. "Toledo is not in Pennsylvania. It's in Ohio. Everybody knows that. God, Gina." Why was I so suddenly annoyed?

She shrugged, unperturbed, fixing her hair and applying lipgloss *before* eating.

"Did you say you were going to school to become a teacher?" I asked disapprovingly. "How are you going to teach little kids if you don't know something like that?"

"The reason I don't know it," Gina said patiently, eating her Cheddar and Swiss on rye, "is because we weren't taught it. And the reason my kids won't know it, is because I won't teach it."

"But isn't this something we need to know? Where things are?" I pointed to the state of Pennsylvania. "Look. I want to show you." For some reason Gina had unreasonably irritated me with her torpid unhelpfulness. I flipped open my spiral, started to write down how far we'd come. I estimated it to be barely sixty miles. And it was nearing three in the afternoon. How in the world was I going to drive another 420 miles to Toledo? When I said this to Gina, I could tell by her glazed-over eyes she thought it was a rhetorical question she had no intention of answering. Her attitude seemed to be: I sit in the passenger seat, you drive, you get me to Eddie. For my part, I sing, pretend to stare at a map, look out the window and give you a little bit of money.

"Gina, you have to help me. I can't do this on my own. I'm going to get lost."

"Why would you get lost?" She sounded frankly puzzled. "You just looked at the map."

"Yes, but so did you!"

"Yes, but I'm not driving."

"What does that have to do with anything?"

"Look, I'm hopeless at maps. It's just how it is."

"I'm not very good either," I retorted, "but I still have to look, still have to figure things out."

"So figure it out."

I crumpled up the map like a soiled tissue. I didn't finish my sandwich. "Ready?" I jumped up and left the table without even glancing back to see if she was coming.

Was it ridiculous for me to be this ticked off? We were not yet in Pennsylvania, the state *next* to New York! My original plan had been to cross the George Washington Bridge at ten a.m., drive on I-80 for two hours and be in Pennsylvania for lunch by noon. So how was it more than a week later and we still weren't there?

I had lots of reasons to be simmering. It wasn't the geographical ignorance that was irking me; after all, I was no Henry Stanley myself. What was getting to me was the supreme geographical *indifference*. Not just, I don't know where I'm going, but I don't care.

In the parking lot, the sunshine beating down, stomach half-full, the Interstate up ahead, things bubbled up and spilled over. Molly, Aunt Flo, too long in Glen Burnie, the prickly sadness about lost closeness.

"Look," I said, whirling to Gina on the sidewalk. "This was a really bad idea. You clearly don't want to be here, don't want to do this. I don't blame you. Why don't I drop you off at the nearest Greyhound station and you can take the bus back home. You'll be there by tonight. Or go to Bakersfield. Do whatever you want. Just . . ."

"*What?*"

"You heard me."

"Sloane, come on . . ."

"Gina, I am *not* your chauffeur, while you sit in my car with your eyes closed and act like Molly."

"I'm not that bad, am I?"

"Almost! You see me struggling and yet you refuse to help me out by looking at the map."

"You wouldn't stop the car! How is that fair?"

"You've got absolutely no shame for deceiving me. We're going to see *your* stupid aunt in Toledo and you won't even help me figure out where we're going!"

"We're going to see my stupid aunt, as you put it, because we stay with her for free. Your little spiral notebook likes that, don't it?"

"I'm not your hired driver, Gina. You want to get to Eddie? Take a bus. Or fly. Call him from Bakersfield airport, ask him to come pick you up. But I can't do this anymore."

"Shelby, we've been on the road five minutes . . ."

"Yes, and doesn't it feel like five centuries?"

"I'm sorry, okay?" She waved her hand dismissively, not remotely sorry. "I'll look at the map, if you want. Jeez, I didn't realize it meant that much to you."

"You know what means that much to me? You pulling your weight. You helping me out. You sharing in this. I'm not your mother."

"Okay," she said, quietly now. "I thought you had things under control, you and your written-down plans."

"Leave my plans out of it," I snapped, looking around for a phone booth. "Yellow Pages will tell us where a bus station is."

"Sloane, come on. I said I'd try to do better."

"What is this try? Yeah, and I'll *try* to put the gas into the tank, and I'll try to put the car into first, and I'll try not to turn the map upside down when I look for your aunt's house. What's with the try?"

We went on like this for a few more minutes. But the bubble had burst; deflated I knew I could not take her to the bus. I also knew three other things.

One, I did not have enough money to get to California without her.

Two, I was hoping a little bit she would talk me into driving her to Bakersfield.

And three—I couldn't do this by myself. When I got out to pump gas, I made Gina get out with me, her mother's imprecations notwithstanding. Not so much for company, but because I couldn't get out of the car without some man, young, old, white, black, Hispanic, hassling me. Saying hello from his car. Smiling, coming over to see if I needed help. Now I'm no beauty. I'm either somebody's type or I'm not. That's not the point. And maybe they were coming over for Gina. Cute little Geeeeena, her shorts and blouses always tighter than mine, her breasts bigger. All these things, true. But that's not why they sauntered over. I started bringing Gina out of the car only *after* I realized that every time I went to get a can of Coke, male strangers were giving me the eye. I knew, if I put Gina on that bus, my own trip would be over. For a number of good and not very good reasons, I wouldn't be able to continue. Fear—but justified or unjustified? Real or imagined paranoia? My bravado was big, but some of my vexation was at myself, a thin thread of self-hatred for not being braver, the kind of girl who could pull into a gas station and get out of her car without worrying that some man was going to be casing her from ten yards away, hiding in the camouflage of Pepsi bottles and potato chips. But it was hardwired; I didn't feel safe, and Gina made me feel only marginally safer. Still, even a few degrees of confidence was better than not being able to pump my own gas for 3000 miles. This is one of the reasons the bus felt unsafe to me, to Gina, to Gina's mother, to Emma. This is one of the reasons a car was better. It allowed a measure of control, no matter how illusory, and I thrived on control. You could lock the car. You could hide in it. You could speed away. They'd have to catch me first on my canary Pegasus.

I sighed. She sighed. She apologized. I apologized. We hugged, awkwardly. Hugged for the first time in almost two years, and drove out to the Interstate. She asked if I wanted a piece of gum and even unwrapped it for me. "Are we going to put it behind us?" she asked, and I wanted to say with a falling heart, *put what behind us*, but instead said *yes*, hoping she was talking about the argument we just had. She opened the atlas, and asked where we were, and when we saw we were near Emmaville (Emmaville!) she found it in the atlas.

The scenery had changed dramatically from Maryland to Pennsylvania. Where Maryland was rustic and rolling, Pennsylvania was all about the green-covered Alleghenys. Every five minutes on the Interstate there was a warning sign for falling rock. WATCH OUT FOR FALLING ROCK. What were we supposed to do about that? Swerve out of the way down the rocky ravine? The highway curved and angled, and every once in a while ascended so high it seemed like I could see half of southwestern Pennsylvania and a little bit further. I kept saying the mountains were pretty, and, in response, Gina regaled me with Pennsylvania trivia.

"Did you know the Pennsylvania state insect is the firefly?"

"Gina, do you remember how you couldn't pronounce firefly when you were a kid?"

"No."

"You called it *flierfly*."

"Did I? I don't remember."

"You did." I trailed off. "It was so cute."

"Well, fine," she said. "The state insect is the flierfly. And did you know that George Washington's only surrender was in Pennsylvania, in Fort Necessity?"

"George Washington surrendered? Aren't the mountains pretty?"

"On July 4, 1754, to the French."

"I don't understand. How can you know so much about Pennsylvania, but not know where Pennsylvania is?"

"I'm going to be a teacher. And what does one have to do with the other?"

I was tired. It was my usual afternoon exhaustion. This Penn Turnpike wasn't dull like Jersey, flat and straight, but it didn't matter; even the high vistas through the Alleghenys couldn't keep me from drifting off to sleep. The next rest area wasn't for twenty-seven miles, and there is nothing more debilitating than trying to drive when your eyes are gluing shut. It's worse than falling asleep in math class. Worse than falling asleep during final exams, or oral exams, or at the movies on a first date (more accurate to say *one and only* date) with someone you really like, worse even than falling asleep on the couch after having too much to drink with your friends. There is a different component that enters into falling asleep on a gently curving road through the mountains doing seventy. You're going to die, my brain kept yelling at me. You're going to die. Wake up. You will never get anywhere. You will not go to college, see your mother, get married, have a life. You will have nothing. You will be dead. Wake up!

It didn't work. I opened the window, gulped the hot air, banged the wheel, turned up the music, tried talking except I couldn't string two words together.

"What's the matter with you?" asked Gina.

I couldn't explain. I tried chewing gum, one stick after the other; I had a wad of gum twenty sticks big in my mouth. That helped as long as I was chewing; trouble was, I wanted to be sleeping. An excruciating twenty-three *more* miles passed before I finally pulled into the rest area.

"What are we doing?"

"Sorry, I have to close my eyes for a sec." I parked in the large lot away from other cars. I rolled down the window and tilted back my head.

"But it's the middle of the day!"

"Yes. I can't explain. It's just—" I fell asleep nearly instantly, couldn't even finish the sentence. Not even fear of death could snap me awake.

"Sloane!" Gina's voice sounded alarmed.

I opened my eyes. Rolling up her window, Gina was shaking me awake, pointing to the black tar-truck in the parking lot, not twenty feet away. The driver, a fat man with tattoos on his neck and shoulders, was yelling something, gesturing to the backseat, and giving us, or something behind us, the finger. I almost wanted to turn around to make sure his girl wasn't in the backseat.

"You got the witch in the back with you?" he yelled. At least I hope he yelled *witch*. "Tell her I'm not done with her! Not by a long shot!" He screeched away, rough-looking and sweaty, erratic on the exit; he nearly hit a sedan pulling into the lot as he was pulling out. After we'd watched him weaving through the service road onto the Interstate, Gina rolled down her window and yelled, "Screw you, mister! Go to hell where you belong!"

"Oh, very good, Gina. And brave."

Gina turned to me. "Awake now?"

"You betcha," I said, rubbing my eyes. "Jeez, what was his problem?"

"Dunno. I guess he thought that girl was with us."

I didn't want to tell Gina I was glad I wasn't alone. The man, big, angry, with a red bandana on his head, looked like the poster boy for public service announcements exhorting you never, but *never* to talk to strangers. I slowly got on the road, not wanting to catch up with him. But sure enough, in seven miles, doing eighty to his sixty, his "I DO ME, YOU DO YOU" coal contraption loomed ahead, and when he saw us smoking him on the left, he gave us the finger once more. Gina gave him two fingers of her own, and gesticulated wildly, pretending to be furious, silently mouthing things through the glass. She rolled down her window, and with the eighty mph wind whipping through her hair yelled for real: "Good luck trying to catch *us*, buddy!"

"You're crazy; stop it! You're going to get us into serious trouble."

"What's he gonna do? Race?" Gina rolled up her window. "I can't believe that chick got into the truck with him."

"She must be brave to hitchhike." I said it wistfully, as in, I wish I were brave, not, I wish I could hitchhike.

"Brave? You mean stupid, dontcha?"

"Maybe." I thought. "But she doesn't have a car like us." I patted my wheel as if she were a silky kitty.

"She could have taken a bus," said Gina.

What, to be safe? I said nothing, but I was thinking that perhaps the girl who could get into a truck with a man who looked like that would probably not be the kind of girl who'd be afraid of taking a little bus.

Gina settled into her seat and closed her eyes. "I think that's why you were upset before. At Subway."

"Why?"

"I can't believe I'm saying this, but I think you think we should've helped her out. Given her a ride."

I didn't say anything.

"I hope you know by that crazy guy, just how many kinds of wrong that would've been."

I didn't say anything.

After another 200 miles of turnpike speeding, I gave up any hope of getting to Toledo by nightfall. Scratch the last item on my list. It was ten at night and we were just nearing Cleveland. "Have you got anything to say about Cleveland?" I was exhausted.

"Yes!" said Gina, all sparkly. "Cleveland was the first city in the world to be lit by electricity. Back in 1879."

"Hmm. Looks like they're all out today." It was dark in the distance and unlit. "How far to Toledo?" I asked the tollbooth operator.

"A hundred and twenty miles," she replied.

Too many miles. We'd already traveled 454. Ten minutes later, we had ourselves a spare room in Motel 6, right off the Interstate. It was on the second floor, had two double beds, an old TV, and a broken air conditioner. It smelled only vaguely of other people. The sheets were white and starchy, not soft and pink like those Emma had bought me for my thirteenth birthday. It was our first motel room, well below budget at forty-five dollars, which pleased me. Gina was in the shower singing "By the Banks of the Ohio" and "Fifteen Miles on the Erie Canal" as I was laying out my clothes for tomorrow and brushing my teeth. I had intended to turn on the TV, but I liked the sound of Gina's happy soprano voice, *I've got a mule and her name is Sal*, and the din of the shower through the open door, *fifteen miles on the Erie Canal* . . . I lay down on the bed, the lights on, *git up here, mule, here comes a lock.* I was going to write a list for tomorrow and think about my mother . . . *we'll make Rome 'bout six o'clock* . . . but all I could think about was that girl and why didn't we stop. Oh, we couldn't, no, we couldn't, but if that were so, why did I have her young face, her short skirt and hitching hands in front of my eyes, her lilting voice in my head as the last things I saw and heard before I fell asleep? *One more trip and back we'll go, right back home to Buffalo* . . .

Come on, help out a sister in need . . .

THREE
ON THE ERIE CANAL

1

Ned

The next bright morning I drove like the tail winds were in my hair. At a hundred miles an hour I was the fastest horse on the road. I had trucks honking at me the entire way. There was no one faster on the road than me and my sweet yellow Mustang. We passed two cop cars, but I blew by so fast, they didn't see me.

The music was loud, and Gina and I were singing. *O Mary don't you weep, don't you mourn, O Mary, don't you weep, don't you mourn* . . . We opened the windows for a sec, but I was going too fast, we couldn't catch our breath. We had slept well, eaten McDonald's for breakfast, the sun was shining, not a cloud in the sky, and all was good, better than yesterday, and the days before that. My heart was light.

We punctuated the 120 miles by screaming every song on the radio at the top of our lungs. Our rendition of REO Speedwagon's "Keep on Lovin' You" would've brought down the house had there been a house to be brought down.

The Interstate through the northern part of Ohio is just a straight wide road amid a flat lot of nothing. Ohio didn't impress. But going faster than a single engine plane did. Gina cheerfully compared and contrasted the Jersey Pike, the Penn Pike, and the Ohio Pike. We concluded that Penn Pike was best but only because of the unfair advantage of Pennsylvania's mountains. Pennsylvania's beauty was more dramatic than Maryland's but it wasn't more beautiful. For some reason I had really liked the sloping, cozy back roads of Maryland. Gina wasn't crazy about either.

We got to Toledo around noon and hungry. I asked Gina for her aunt's address. It took her a while to find it; she said we might have to stop for directions. I didn't disagree. I'm not a guy, I have no problem asking, but stopping on an Interstate *was* a little problematic. It's not like the information founts are working by the side of the road in little booths. When I asked to see the address, Gina demurred.

Turns out it was a good thing we didn't push on straight till morning the night before, because Toledo's being farther north and west than we had expected was the *least* of my concerns.

"Three Oaks, Michigan?" I gasped when I looked at the address Aunt Flo had written down. "Three Oaks, *Michigan*? Are you kidding me?"

"Well, that's what it says."

I ripped the piece of paper away from her and stared at the words again. "What does Michigan have to do with Toledo? Does Michigan even border Ohio? Isn't Indiana the next state over?"

"I don't know," she said, wrinkling her little nose in a guilt squint. "I think so." She blinked her blue eyes at me and grinned. "Want to check the map?"

"Someone is going to have to. Why would your Glen Burnie aunt tell you your Toledo aunt lived in Toledo if she doesn't live in Toledo?"

"She didn't say she lived in Toledo. She said she lived *near* Toledo."

"Is Michigan, two states away, really near Toledo?" I flipped open my notebook.

Gina snatched it away. "Look, Miss Spiral, let's get Burger King and get on with it. You know we're going to have to go see Aunt Betty no matter what. She's waiting for us. No use bitching and moaning. And it'll save us at least fifty bucks in hotels." She smiled. "Depending on how long we stay."

When we had food in our hands, Gina called the number on the scrap of paper. "Aunt Betty is so happy we're coming!" she said when she got off the phone.

"Oh, yeah? Did you tell her she lives in Michigan, not Ohio? That'll wipe the smile off her face."

Gina laughed. "Sloane, you're so funny. So what? It's nothing. Michigan, Ohio, what's the difference? We take the road we're on . . ."

"I-80?"

"I think so. We take it to Route 12, just a few miles west from here, and then take 12 a few miles north, and then we make a left, and it's right there. Can't miss it. She said from here it shouldn't take us more than an hour."

"Famous last words." I unfolded my big map so I could find this Route 12. Oh, yes. So close. Just half a jump to the left, half a step to the right. Let's do the time warp again . . . "Tell me, explain to me, how near Toledo means near Lake Michigan," I grumbled, biting into my burger and fishing out a handful of fries. We were leaning over the hood of the 'Stang. "Tell me. Toledo is on Lake Erie. Tell me how Lake Michigan is near Lake Erie."

"Aren't they adjacent lakes?" Gina said helpfully.

"They're Great Lakes! One lake is bigger than the Black Sea. The other is bigger than the Gulf of Mexico."

"Come on, that's not really true," said Gina, helping me fold the map, her mouth full of fries and fish. "The Gulf of Mexico is the largest gulf in the world. And the Black Sea—"

"Gina, I don't want to hear it." I was getting tetchy again. "One giant lake, another giant lake, a rinky-dink town that doesn't even rate atlas mention, that's not *next* to Toledo, Ohio!"

"All right, all right. Can we go? She's waiting."

"*Not* next to it. You have to tell your Aunt Flo that, Gina, when you see her."

"I will. It'll be the first thing I tell her. Now come on."

After we found Route 12 and got off, *and* drove twenty miles, we were told we were going the wrong way. "You're going south," the tollbooth guy said when we finally capitulated and asked. "You have to head north. Just head on up for ten or fifteen miles. Three Oaks is right before the bend. Watch for it. If the road turns, you've already missed it. You'll be in New Buffalo."

"So we won't know until we've missed it?" I said accusingly, pulling away. "Gee, I wonder why it's called Three Oaks?" I revved the car into second. "I'm sure it's ironically named. It's probably a booming town."

Of course we missed it; missing it was built into the directions. When the road turned, a sign genially informed us that we were now leaving Three Oaks township (no less!) and counseling us to drive safely. We turned around. A little elementary school on the corner, a gas station, a bar. No sidewalks.

Michigan wasn't what I expected. Perhaps my mind was poisoned by my perception of Detroit. I imagined all Michigan, like Flint—built up, industrial, a sort of bleaker Elizabeth, New Jersey, which is as bleak as apocalypse, all smokestacks and black electric-wire factories. It wasn't anything like that where we were. This was all driving country, no towns, no strip malls. Silos, fields, curving country roads with little ramshackle delis built into the shoulder like bushes.

The aunt's house wasn't actually in Three Oaks, but on the outskirts, off a dirt road, marked not by a number but by a stone dog on the rusted mailbox. Next to it was a broken-down limp trailer with one end inside a small rotted-out barn where there was a cow and a goat.

Aunt Betty was waiting for us out on the dirt driveway. She was tall and thin, with watchful, perpetually moist brown platters for eyes. Her mouth was slightly ajar, as if she was about to say something, yet didn't. She did quietly lament our tardy arrival as she and Ned had already eaten lunch and weren't making another meal until sundown; was that all right with us?

"I don't know," said Gina. "What time does sun set around here, Aunt Betty?"

She showed us to our room, hurrying past the kitchen. The

house was not as neatly kept as Aunt Flo's—it was dusty, piled with years of layers of stuff. Ned was sitting at the kitchen table so immersed in a newspaper, he barely looked up.

"Hi, Ned," said Gina.

He said nothing, just raised his hand in a wave.

"Come on," said Aunt Betty. "I only have the one guest room. You don't mind sharing a bed, do you? You used to all the time when you were small."

Gina and I said nothing. Perhaps she did mind. If only we could put Molly between us, maybe that would be better.

Adolescent Molly may've been right about Ned. He gave me the willies, sitting there lumpen, his great blubber-belly hanging over his belt. Each time he turned a page of his newspaper, a frightening shower of dandruff snowed from his sparse, greasy comb-over onto his light blue T-shirt.

Later when he left the table and the paper open, I glanced over to see what had happened in the world that was so fascinating. A 500-pound woman had died and was two months in the deep freeze while waiting to be cremated. There was some issue about who was going to pay for the "highly involved" process of cremating a body 200 pounds over the allowable weight of 300. The son was indigent, and the coroner's office, the hospital, and the morgue remained in bitter disagreement about who *had* to pay for it. I saw the date of the story: April, 1974. Ned couldn't tear himself away from a news story seven years old.

After "Wheel of Fortune," when I was faint with hunger, Betty gave us food, but not before she showed us the backyard with pens for her dogs. She cooed over them, fussed, fed them (fed *them*!). Then us, then Ned. He was last, after the dogs and the guests.

"Sloane," Gina said to me quietly, "honestly, don't let it slip how you feel about small furry pooches. Even Hitler liked dogs."

"Yes," I barked. "Preferred dogs to children. Quite the paragon of canine-loving virtue, that Adolf."

Gina tutted and turned to Aunt Betty. "Aunt Betty, is there somewhere fun to go around here?"

"Fun like where?"

"I don't know. That's why I'm asking."

"No, that's why *I'm* asking. What kind of fun are you talking about?" She narrowed her eyes. "There's a bowling alley in South Bend. It's about forty miles away. But that's a college town. It can get real rowdy there. Real rowdy. There's an outlet mall in Michigan City. It's closed by now. You can go there tomorrow."

"We'll need to be on our way tomorrow, Aunt Betty," said Gina. "I'm just asking for tonight. Anywhere to go to in Three Oaks tonight?"

Betty's eyes remained narrowed. "What kind of fun you talkin' about?" She looked at Ned, dutifully drinking his beer, not looking up from his news page. He was re-reading the story about the obese woman. "Boy fun?"

Gina shook her head. "Not boy fun. I have a boyfriend. We're getting married soon."

"You *are?*" I whispered.

"Shh."

"What about your friend, here?"

"I can't vouch for Shelby," Gina said. "Can I, Sloane? Vouch for you?" She was turned to Aunt Betty when she addressed me. "We were looking for a bar or something. To get a quick drink."

"No bar you'd want to go to. Girls don't go to bars around here. Not good girls anyway."

Some small measure of sense and her aunt's Calvinist expression kept Gina from saying, "Who says we're good girls, anyway?"

"You don't want to be going into no bars around here."

"Okay, gotcha."

"You're my sister's kid," said Aunt Betty. "I don't care if you're forty-seven, you ain't givin' up no pooty while you stayin' in my house."

Pooty? Gina stifled a groan. "Allrighty, then. Well, Aunt Betty, we're feeling kind of tired. I think we'll have a shower and head on to bed. Get up nice and early tomorrow, set out. Thanks for dinner. Goodnight."

"We're going to bed?" I whispered. It was nine in the evening!

She pulled me to our room. I told Gina I'd been there a thousand times, when a woman who was not my mother kept me from going out, from having fun.

"So what'd you do?"

"Nothing. I stayed in."

"Fool. I just lied to my mother." Gina was looking in her suitcase for clothes. "I told her I was sleeping over a girlfriend's house. She never checked. She wanted to trust me, and as long as I didn't get caught, I knew I'd be okay." We giggled at the gullibility of mothers and Emmas trying to keep their girls from having fun. "Well, don't just stand there. What are you doing, pulling out a book? Hurry, go have a shower, get dressed."

"For bed?"

Gina grinned. "Whatever you want to call it, girlfriend. Just put on some 'pooty' clothes."

"We're going out?"

"Of course. What do you think? I didn't let my mother tell me what to do, you think I'm going to let my mother's enfeebled sister do it?"

"But she said no!"

"Oh, well, better tuck ourselves in, then." She snorted. "Come on. We're not going to walk out her front door."

"How are we going to get to the car in the driveway?"

Gina pointed to the window.

"We're going to sneak out the window like cats?"

"Cats on the prowl. What, you've never done it?"

"My window was on the second floor above a garage. So—no."

"Chicken. I would've built a ladder in the trees."

"Yes, I suppose you would've." After showering, she put on her jeans, and a cute beige top that came with cleavage. I didn't have a beige top that came with cleavage, but I had runner's legs. So after showering I put on a mini-skirt and high heels. We spent extra time on our makeup. Gina was *really* taking time with hers. Three different eyeliners, two shadows, mucho blusho.

"Gina . . . um. What about Eddie?"

"What about him?"

I watched her apply another coat of black mascara. "Must be some fun you're thinking of having with four coats of Great Lash. Didn't you just say you're going to California to marry your boyfriend?"

"Fiancé. He asked me to marry him before he left." She waved the mascara wand, licked her lips. "I love Eddie. He's the only one I want. But he's been up to no good."

"How do you know?" And is that how it worked?

"Oh, he confessed. He didn't like having the burden of his wrongdoing on his conscience. To make himself feel better, he told me."

My throat went kind of numb. I said, "Told you . . ."

"His little thing with Teresa. You know Teresa, the county slut? God. He justified it, as he justifies everything, by saying it was my fault. After all, he said, I had a boyfriend I refused to break up with when we first got together."

"Huh," I said carefully, throat less numb. She did actually have a boyfriend she refused to break up with when she and Eddie first got together. He was the tallest jock in school. Eddie was short.

"I know. But I was in love with Eddie, and he knew it. Still am. I just didn't know how to break it off with John."

"So how'd you break it off?"

"Don't you know anything? Agnes isn't doing her job. I didn't. He broke up with me. So then Eddie and I were supposed to be exclusive, but now he's gone back to Bakersfield and I know there's a girl there he used to, like, date."

"How do you know?"

"He told me. He doesn't like to keep that stuff to himself."

"Really?" I wasn't looking at her, and she wasn't looking at me.

"They're sitting by streams, on rocks, picking flowers, reciting poetry or some shit. When we talk he tells me they're hypothetically talking of what it might be like to be married. After all, that's what they talked about when they were twelve."

I didn't know what to say. "Does he know you're coming?"

She nodded. "I called him before I left, told him I'm on my way. He said, please come as soon as you can. Please. Save me from myself. I think I may *accidentally* end up marrying her."

I blinked.

"I don't want to talk about it any more with you," Gina said. "All I'm saying is, he hasn't been good. And he doesn't have to know about tonight. Come on, let's go. Let's get us some real rowdy." She smiled. "How do I look?"

"Great," I said. "But the dogs are outside. They'll start barking. They'll hear my car."

"The dogs are already barking." Gina winked. She messed up the bed and put towels and pillows under the sheets to make it appear as if two sleeping forms were underneath. "I'm sure my aunt's out by now. It's eleven; way past her bedtime. Don't worry. They're both none too swift. Ready?"

Dolled up, done up, I hitched my mini-skirt, adjusted my tube top, made sure money and ID were in my pocket, and crawled out the window into the side yard littered with broken lumber. We tip-toed our way to the car; of course the tiny dogs, mistaking themselves for German Shepherds, snarled like we were about to rob the house.

I put the car into neutral and released the handbrake. In her heels, Gina helped me back it out the drive, I started it on the road, and we drove off, giggling like kids. "Why are you wearing underwear?" she said in the car on the way to South Bend. "I'm not."

"I know."

"Come on. Trust me, you feel completely different without underwear. Like anything's possible."

"Oh, I'm sure," I said. "But my skirt's too short. I'll get arrested for indecent exposure."

Gina said her mission was to make out with a cute college guy. She'd never had a college guy. She wanted to test if that thing they said about men and women was true.

"What thing is that?"

"That when a woman wakes up she can say to herself, today I will get laid. And have it be true. But when a man wakes up, he can say, I may never get laid again. And have that also be true."

I laughed. I hoped it was true. We were wearing shiny lipstick, and had on lots of drugstore perfume, Coty and Jean Naté. Gina's jeans were tighter than my skirt, but that was only because I was thinner. Too much running, though not since being on the road. Felt weird not running every day.

In South Bend, we cruised the noisy strip of bars, looking for a boisterous place where the patrons were neatly dressed and young. Gina didn't want to go to Vickie's ("Only girls there") or McCormick's or Corby's ("The Irish get too drunk and pass out"). We debated between Linebacker Lounge and Library Irish Pub. She wanted the former, I the latter.

"Are you joking?" she said. "*Library* Pub? You want them to talk to you about Hardy and Yeats? Or do you want them to look like linebackers? That's really the question here."

"I want them to be able to speak."

"That's the *only* thing they'll be able to do at Library Pub," Gina returned.

"I would like," I said, "a better class of boy."

We had to play rock, paper, scissors to decide. We played best of three. I won. "If only all decisions were that easy," said Gina, as we pulled into the Library parking lot.

"What do you mean? That's how we used to decide everything."

"*Everything*, Sloane?"

Two preppy, clean-cut guys walking inside saw us getting out of our car and whistled. "Nice 'Stang, girls!" And I, Shelby, smiled, because it was *my* Shelby. I may have kept my underwear on, but I had a nice 'Stang.

"That was *so* easy," Gina whispered to me, as they were walking up to us. "Maybe you were right about this place."

"Yeah, the car's a stud magnet," I whispered back. "Even with bookworms."

The car, the mini-skirt, Gina's moniker and panty-free manner combined with two or seven Sloe Gin fizzes was enough to hook us up with two sophomores from Indiana State, English majors and on the lacrosse team. The music was too loud, we couldn't talk. We just sipped our drinks, smiled, and stood close. They kept leaning toward us to hear the words we weren't saying, like, "You come here often?" and "Yes, I'll have another drink. And another." I laughed too much and too loud, which is what I do when I get a little tipsy, and thought everything they said and didn't say was so funny. And every time my boy spoke, I touched his arm. Alive and Kicking were holding on a little bit tighter, baby, and Blondie was dancing very close cuz it was rapture time.

Gina and I didn't get back to Three Oaks until her goal was more fully accomplished than even she had expected, and since I didn't have a goal, I was quite surprised by the turn of events. So, at four in the morning when we climbed into our room, sneaking in like thieves into the den, we felt as if we'd run a marathon, or aced the SATs, or perhaps come in first and second in our class. Giggling, inebriated, and relaxed, Gina barely threw off her clothes before climbing into bed, and though I was also drunk, I folded my clothes, put them away, and got out my outfit for the morning, my notebook as well, but in bed I asked how in heaven's name I was supposed to drive tomorrow, and Gina, nearly unconscious, muttered, let's stay a few more days. I tried to remember my mother, whether the cover charge had been more or less than I'd budgeted for, and to count up how much money we'd spent so far. Had I paid for any of the drinks? I think I ordered bacon potato skins and buffalo wings, and tipped the waitress, maybe bought one drink. Thirty bucks, forty? But a song of freedom kept whirling in my head for the happy road day, *won't you help me sing . . . redemption songs. Redemption songs.*

2

The Chihuahuas

We woke up at noon! Which was so not like me, and for some reason noon and sobriety didn't make me feel as great about the previous night as last call, intoxication and songs of freedom had. I'd had a bad dream. And, who *were* those guys we'd been with?

"Who cares?" Gina said, stretching, rolling over. "We were like men last night. We came, we took what we wanted, we left. Wasn't it awesome?"

My heavy skull cracking and my mouth parched, I said, "Yeah. Totally." I wasn't used to drinking, I was dehydrated. My dream had been so creepy and real, I didn't know how I had continued sleeping. I sat up in bed and looked around. Everything in the room seemed to be in place. Our two suitcases, our makeup. Maybe we could ask Aunt Betty to let us do a wash today. "Did you get his name?"

"Todd."

"Hmm." I licked my lips, touched my face. Did I forget to take off my makeup? Yuk. "Mine said he was Todd, too."

We stared at each other for the briefest of moments. "So?" Gina pulled open the curtain to glance outside. "So maybe they lied about their names, What, you think guys'd care if *we* lied about our names? If I said my name was Kathleen, you think they'd care? Look, a beautiful day again. And so hot, too. Want

to go swimming? And tonight we can go back to South Bend."
She winked naughtily. "We'll try the Linebacker Lounge this time."

"Swimming?" I was still stuck on the boys and the dream.
"Swimming where?"

"Uh—Lake Michigan?"

"Oh." We were stretched out in bed. "But we didn't lie, did
we?" I said. "We could've, but we didn't. We wanted them to know
us."

I didn't tell Gina my bad vision of trouble: I had woken in the
blue of night, and there, in our room, in the chair by the door,
sat Ned, watching us, his scalp flaking, his belly overflowing, eyes
slow-blinking.

We threw on clothes and went to the kitchen, where Aunt
Betty eyeballed us like we were stale cheese. Ned sat at the corner
table, reading the newspaper. He didn't look up. Betty said the
dogs had barked at four in the morning and woken her. "They
never bark in the middle of the night." Cleverly, we said nothing.
She asked why we slept so late when we went to bed so early.
Again, a simple shrug sufficed for reply. But at that moment Ned
looked up from his early 70s newspaper, and gave me a slow blink.

I got scared, then. Perhaps, after all, nothing in the night had
been a dream. When I quickly looked away from him, I saw Aunt
Betty staring at me with those doe moist eyes, now wary, and
considerably cooled.

As she was sliding me some unfriendly toast and burnt bitter
coffee, she asked if we wouldn't mind taking two of her home-
grown Chihuahuas to a very good customer a few miles away. She
said the pups had been born eight weeks earlier and the woman's
young sons were dying for them. They'd been inspected and paid
for so all we had to do was deliver them, a quick in and out drop-
off thing.

"See, Sloane," said Gina, sipping her coffee as if it were champagne, "there are some people in this world who like dogs."

I ignored her, pushing my cup away. "Aunt Betty, did you tell
the woman," I asked, "that whether or not her sons get the puppies

at eight weeks or eight years, the Chihuahuas are going to look exactly the same?"

"Excuse me?" She remained humorless, and then turning to Gina said, "Please, niece? A favor to me?"

Gina looked at me with a friendly open shrug, as in, why not? I wasn't reluctant, just silent. "Aunt Betty, we'll be glad to, right, Sloane? But I haven't seen you for so long, we wanted to stay a few more days, go to the mall, swim in the lake. Is that okay?"

Betty shook her head. It wasn't *okay*?

"I'll give you 200 dollars to deliver the dogs today."

That's when I perked up, that's when my cement-head morphed upward into swamp-head. "Two hundred dollars?"

Gina generously offered to split it with me.

"Oh, you will, will you?" I returned. "Well, why not, after all, you'll be doing half the driving."

"Shut up. Aunt Betty, we'd love to, but please, can we go tomorrow?"

Vehemently, Aunt Betty shook her head. "You have to leave today." Suddenly 200 dollars became a hefty chunk of change to drive two rodents a couple of miles down the road. I became suspicious. "Hang on a sec," I said, my turn to narrow my eyes, furrow my eyebrows. "Where exactly are we going?"

"De Soto."

"Ah, well, De Soto." I got up to swill my coffee into the sink. It splashed and left a terrible mess. Not one to leave a mess behind, I cleaned it while saying, "And where might this De Soto be?"

"I have the address," said Aunt Betty. "It's just down 55-South. It won't be any trouble. It's on the way for you, girls."

How many places were "on our way?" How could everything be on our way? Every single thing? What kind of coordinates did our way have? It zigged down and zagged up, it meandered on country roads, on Erie Canal, then curved around a bend—South Bend—and a lake, two Great Lakes even, and now was jutting on 55-South. South! Did anyone realize we were heading *west*? Everything between New York and California, point A and point

B was on the way. Everything between the coasts was on the way. From Canada to New Orleans was on the way.

I went to get my map. Aunt Betty also disappeared, emerging a few moments later with cash in hand. "Are you girls packed, ready?"

"Ready? Aunt Betty, we just got up. We haven't even showered!"

Betty frowned. "Why would you need to shower again? I heard you showering at nine last night."

Without a blink, Gina said, "Always like to start my day with a shower, Aunt Betty. Sort of like brushing my teeth."

"Well, no use wasting my water. I got a well around here, it runs dry on hot days like this. Why don't you two get going. You can be done by evening."

Well, at least De Soto was close enough to get to by evening, though by the hurried way Betty was shepherding us out, maybe *this* evening was optimistic. "I can't find it on the map, Aunt Betty," I said. "Show me."

She declined. "I'm terrible at reading maps," she said. "But I have the address." Betty handed me a scrap of paper and a donut. Everything was on a scrap of paper. "You best get going. You wanna get there before dark. The Kirkebys live in the country, no lights anywhere; will be hard to read the street signs." Before I could protest, she stuffed four fifties into my hand. "Here. You look like you need the money."

"Do I?" What can I do never to look like that again? Is it my Levi's shorts? Or my plain white blouse? Is it the Dr. Scholls on my feet? Or the two-dollar Great Lash mascara that was caking from last night? I didn't carry a purse, but did my eight-cylinder, 350 horsepower stock car that cost someone a second mortgage give my financial status away? What was it about me that made me look impoverished to a pale woman with slow speech and a mute man that *almost never* looked up from his newspaper?

Money in hand, sugar from the donut sticking to my fingers, I opened up the piece of paper like it was a fortune cookie: "YOU

WILL BE RICH." "YOU HAVE MANY GIFTS." "1809 Chariot Way, De Soto, MO."

"MO?" I muttered. "Gina, what state is MO?"

"Dunno. Montana?"

"Not Montana!" That was Aunt Betty. "Where would I get a customer from Montana?"

"Is it here? Is it Michigan?"

"I don't know what you mean," said Betty, collecting the toast plates. "*This* isn't Michigan. Flo always gets it wrong. It's Indiana. We're right on the border. Listen, don't get yourself in a twist. You have the money. Go." And then she added, "Need directions?"

Puzzled I stared at her; clear-eyed and judgmental she stared back. Where had I heard that before, seen that before? *Need Directions?* I saw it like a billboard in front of my eyes. "Yes," I said. "Where's De Soto?"

"St. Louis," Aunt Betty exclaimed. "Just a few miles south on I-55. Why don't you go and get ready. It's getting late."

Near St. Louis. A few miles south. On I-55. Carefully, folding my map, I said, "Is *that* on the way to California?"

"Of course!" replied Aunt Betty. "Don't you know what St. Louis is called? 'The Gateway to the West.' What do you think the St. Louis Arch was built for?"

I straightened up and shook my head. "Aunt Betty, I don't think St. Louis is that close. We were planning to stay on I-80."

"What, two hundred isn't enough?" she said. "Shaking me down for more money, Shel?"

"What?" I exclaimed. "No, of course not, like I would, no, but . . . now that you mention it . . ."

"Sloane!" That was Gina.

"No, no, niece, she's right." Aunt Betty smiled ruefully. "That's fine. I'll give you a hundred more. Will *that* cover it?" She stared at me meaningfully. "And here's some water for the road."

We're leaving? But I hadn't planned my route yet, hadn't written things down in order—

Within thirty minutes we were flasked, packed, dogged-up, and shown the door. Betty did not allow us to shower.

"Goodbye!" She waved, disappearing into her broken-down trailer with the cow and the goat. "Was so good to see you, girls. Gina, I'll tell your mother we had a nice visit. Be careful, you two!"

"Wow," I said as we drove out onto the main road. "Wow."

"Wow what?"

"Huh. Nothing. Strange is all." I turned around to glance at the Chihuahuas in the crate taking up most of the backseat. What odd-looking dogs.

"What's strange?" Gina opened the map.

"Don't even pretend. Put that map away," I said. "You didn't get the feeling she was trying to get rid of us?"

Gina looked up. "No. She's just efficient. Doesn't like nonsense."

"Yeah, that must be it."

"Do you know where you're going?" Gina put the map away.

"Haven't you heard? St. Louis."

We left that moment, not a few days later, like I planned, like Gina wanted. We were hurried out in the middle of an afternoon. I could've said no to the dogs, to the money, and didn't. I could've said no to many things, and didn't. Like I keep saying, sometimes, life alters by increments and sometimes by insurrection.

3

Two Todds

Route 12 was rural. Stretching through the strip of trees that flanked Lake Michigan, the countryside stopped being pretty, became utilitarian. But to me, where Aunt Betty lived looked like not a bad place for kids to grow up. There was nothing to do, but there were fields and forests. The kids could have adventures. In Larchmont you always had to be careful. Look both ways, don't jaywalk. Not much adventure. Here, the kids just ran with the dogs. And the goats.

"Is Ned your aunt's husband?"

"I don't think so," replied Gina. "I think they met up in a rest home Betty had been living in, recuperating."

"Recuperating from what?"

"I don't know. Life's little stresses. She gets stressed out easily." Gina chuckled. "You saw Ned."

"You could say I saw Ned."

"What?"

"Nothing. What was he recuperating from?"

"Well, I don't know. He's had some problems."

"You don't say. What kind of problems?"

Gina raised her eyebrows. "*Mental* problems."

"Oh."

"But I don't really know."

"Why don't you ask Agnes? She'll tell you."

"How would Agnes know about Ned?"

"Agnes often speaks of things she knows absolutely nothing about."

"You think?" said Gina, with a breath, then another. "But sometimes Agnes speaks of things she knows something about. No?"

After the briefest of pauses, I said, "No. Tell me about Ned." See, this is when we needed Molly! No wonder Gina had brought her. If it wasn't for crazy Ned, she'd still be with us.

"Once I overheard my mom say he was out on parole."

"Parole?" My head jerked. "For what?"

Gina hesitated. "Look, he was falsely accused. He didn't mean any harm. But some young girl, about fourteen, who'd run away, claimed Ned took her into his home where he was living with his mother and wouldn't let her go. Kept her there like a slave or something. I mean, that's preposterous, isn't it?"

My heart was in my stomach. "Gina," I said, because I couldn't keep quiet, "why would you go visit your aunt when the man she's with has accusations like that hanging over him?"

"He was innocent! They're just accusations. He was living with his mother, for God's sake. The girl should've just told his mother on him, if she didn't want to stay. He probably thought he was being hospitable. It was all a big misunderstanding. He makes Betty happy."

"Was he arrested?"

"Arrested, tried, convicted, but the charges were dismissed on appeal. Why the sudden interest in Ned, Sloane? You've seen him before at the house."

I didn't remember him. I barely remembered Betty, I'd seen her only a couple of times. She'd always been silent and watchful.

"You really think Aunt Betty shepherding us out with such exquisite haste was because of the dogs?" I asked skeptically.

"Why else?"

"Oh, Gina."

"Oh, Gina what?"

Clearly she didn't want to talk about it. In front of us rose an enormous concrete structure that looked like the nuclear power plant at Three Mile Island. Instead of talking about why she would agree to stay in the secluded home of a convicted child assailant, we had a nice long discussion on whether Three Mile Island was in Pennsylvania or Michigan—like right in front of us. Gina kept saying, "Can't you see this isn't an island?"

"People who live on an island don't know it's an island!"

"Oh, Jesus. It's in Pennsylvania!"

I retreated. "Tell me this doesn't look exactly *like* Three Mile Island." The near-nuclear-reactor-meltdown accident happened just a year or two ago. It was still fresh in my paranoid mind. We'd never seen a nuclear power plant before; we gawked, we rubber-necked at a stone tank. Adjacent to it was Lighthouse Place, an outlet mall. That made us laugh.

Ladies will shop even under the volcano, we said. Girls must shop. Were we two of those girls? Should we stop? Shop? I'd taken an aspirin for my head, was tired and didn't feel like driving. I wished Gina could drive so I could close my eyes. "If we stop," I said, "we'll be forced to buy things. Do we need things?"

"We might. We won't know till we stop."

"But do we really *need* things?" I wanted to look into my note-book at the list of my expenses.

"I think we do."

"Like what?"

"I don't know yet," she said cheerily. "We'll know when we shop."

"I'm tired."

"I'm hungry."

"We just ate."

"Toast doesn't count. I'm hungry for something else."

"Like a pair of jeans?"

Gina beamed.

"I didn't budget for a nuclear shopping spree." I allowed twenty dollars for a gift for Emma, that was all. Aside from some flat tire money. Was I really willing to spend it now on a bathing suit I didn't need?

"We just made some extra," said Gina, "but the question is, do we want to be girls who shop under a nuclear cloud?"

We giggled; we thought we would like to be those girls. Okay, I said, pulling into the mall parking lot, we'll shop, but let's look at a map first.

Gina groaned.

We spread the map out onto the steaming hood, too hot to touch. "Go ahead, tell me. How far is St. Louis?"

She looked, not too close. "About six inches."

"How many miles is that?"

"I don't—"

"Look at the legend!" I was too hot to stand in the parking lot.

"Hard to tell. Maybe seventy miles. Eighty?"

"Maybe we shouldn't stop."

"Of course we should. Besides, we're already stopped."

I started to protest; she raised her eyebrows and gave me a look that said I wasn't being adventurous enough.

"Come on, we made some extra. Let's go spend it."

"What, all 300 dollars? Get out!"

She pulled on me. The reactor noisily emitted a plume of white smoke. She pulled me again, by the wrist, toward the walking mall. "We'll be in St. Louis in about three hours. It's fine. First we'll swim, though."

"You mean, first we'll shop?"

"Yes, then cool off in the water. Let's go."

It was three in the afternoon, the worst time for me to drive, I was so low-energy. The alcohol had sucked the oxygen out of my veins. "Okay, let's go," I said, allowing myself to be pulled. To the left of us was a road with four churches in a row, like last night's bars. Another religious experience, Gina said, wondering out loud if church was a good place to meet guys. "Nice choir-singing boys. Maybe we should stay till Sunday."

"As a Buddhist are you even allowed to go to church?" I said,

111

glancing at the white sign outside the Prince of Peace Lutheran church. "TWO GREAT TRUTHS: 1. THERE IS A GOD. 2. YOU ARE NOT HIM."

"You're a fool," said Gina. "The Christians allow everyone in."

"Even Buddhists?"

"You think they discriminate? They don't care. We were Jehovah's Witnesses for five minutes, and we still went to a Catholic church once on Christmas. It was the Jehovahs that got mad."

"Huh." I was dull like bouillon.

"That's when my mom stopped being a Jehovah. She liked Christmas too much."

"Are they mutually exclusive, those two things?"

"Jehovah's Witnesses don't celebrate Christmas. Don't you know anything?"

"Nothing," I said. "But the French Jewish family who lived in our house celebrated Christmas."

"Are Jews and Christmas mutually exclusive?" asked Gina and we laughed. We turned to each other, and she took my hand for a moment. "Three Jewish families on our block have a tree and exchange presents," she said. "They tell my mother, why should Christians have all the fun?"

Lazily we moseyed through the deserted outlet mall, bought a horrific hot dog, looked inside Ralph Lauren, BCBG, where we asked the shopkeeper how many miles it was to Indiana. She looked confused, said, you *are* in Indiana. I shook my head, said, no, no, you're mistaken, we're in Michigan City, and she said, "Yes. Michigan City, Indiana."

"Oh."

Then she told us our ready-to-emit radioactive fumes nuclear reactor was nothing more than a cooling tower for a regular Indiana power company generator. We lost interest in shopping after that. It was only fun when we thought we were being risk-takers, living life on the edge. "How long do you think to St. Louis from here?" I asked the BCBG cashier, as I was giving her money for my new white shorts. "A few hours, right?"

"St. Louis, Missouri? Try eight hours. It's about 400 miles from here. Probably longer, what with the rush-hour traffic near Chicago."

Eight hours! It couldn't be! Mealy-mouthed, I said, "You said, St. Louis, Missouri. Is there perhaps another St. Louis? Somewhere in Michigan, maybe?"

Dejected we walked back to the car. "Some map reader you are," Gina criticized.

"Yes, and your help was invaluable," I snapped. "*Now* what are we going to do? We're never going to find that house in the dark. Aunt Betty said."

"Let's try."

"Try what? We couldn't figure out the mileage on a *map* in broad daylight!" I wanted to get on the highway and drive until I hit the ocean on the other side. Just stay on one straight road. Gas? Right there. Food? Right there. Lodging? There, too. Everything, anything right at my fingertips. I wouldn't even need a map.

We let the dogs out on a patch of grass. They were panting, rat-like, sniffing dandelions. Did rats pant? It was hot, it was four p.m. There was no way we could arrive at a stranger's doorstep at midnight. Resigned to a night on the road, we decided to take the dogs and ourselves swimming. We would take the gateway to the west from St. Louis to get to California. Aunt Betty said. We each picked up a mutt and headed toward the car.

In the parking lot, with Chihuahuas in our hands, we passed a group of guys getting out of a pick-up truck. I instantly recognized one of them as the "Todd" I'd been with last night. "Todd!" I called, to get his attention. Hey! Look in my direction. Nudging Gina, I motioned toward them, about ten yards away. "Todd!" Gina said to her own "Todd", but louder. No one looked up. They were laughing, talking among themselves. They glanced peripherally at us, as in, we're five guys, none of us is named Todd, and there are two chicks with dogs in our path. I waved, and they waved back, said something to each other, laughed heartily, passed us and walked on. Gina and I stopped walking. I looked at her, stupefied.

"What?" she said. "They were with their friends."

"They were." And last night was dark, and we were dressed differently, and so were they. It was loud; there was Sloe gin. But still. The following day, in broad daylight, a young, well-groomed, smart young man, who not twelve hours earlier had Biblical parts of him inside Biblical parts of me, passed me in a parking lot and didn't recognize me. He didn't know who I was. We could've shaken hands last night. I could have served him a drink. I could've sold him gum at the local gas station, and he would've walked by me slower today, he would've paused for the briefest moment to say, gee, you look familiar. Don't I know you from somewhere? Oh, yeah. Wrigley's Juicy Fruit. Todd didn't do any of that. No young man and young woman could have been more intimate, and yet, he passed me in an outlet mall and didn't know me. I wasn't even a stain on his memory like he was on mine.

"Unbelievable."

"I know," said Gina. "But look, we agreed to take the dogs. We took her money. Spent some of it. We can't go back now."

After a moment's silence at the gasping realization of how far Gina's thoughts had been from mine, I said, "No, of course. We have no choice. Let's go."

I cared less about the dogs now, about St. Louis. My heart began to hurt a little bit.

Slowly I started up the car, and we rolled on.

"I'll give you my share of the $300," Gina said, "if that'll make you feel better."

That wasn't what was making me feel bad.

"Gina, doesn't it bother you that they didn't recognize us?"

"Couldn't care less. Hey, turn here. We'll go swimming."

Reluctantly, I turned into a deserted National Dunes Park; in the car, like ferrets in a sack, we changed into our bathing suits and set off for the beach. The only thing that saved the dogs from immersion was the 126-foot, 80-degree incline sand dune that neither Gina nor I could climb while holding them. And what saved us from swimming after we struggled up Mount Baldy like Edmund Hillary and his Tonto was that the lake was another half a mile of sand away. We stood asthmatically at the crest of the dune. Lake Michigan didn't look like any lake I'd ever seen—it was like an ocean with white sand.

"Did you know that Lake Michigan is our largest lake?" said Gina. "It's the only Great Lake entirely within U.S. borders. It's got 1100 cubic miles of water in it."

"What I would give for a pint of that water right now." I was so hot.

"You and the Chihuahuas. Imagine how thirsty they are."

"Maybe it's best we didn't bring them. What if they couldn't swim?"

"All animals can swim," said Gina. "Even cows can swim."

That made me laugh. She always somehow managed that, to say something supremely silly.

We slid down 130 feet on our butts back to the parking lot. Sandy, hot and exhausted, though we'd done nothing all day, we got back to the car, and while the crazy dogs were running around the pine needles chased by Gina, I examined the map, trying to get my bearings, control things. I had been looking just at the road to St. Louis, but when I traced the road from St. Louis to California, I quickly realized we had a bigger problem than driving a few extra hundred miles south. The Interstate out of St. Louis west to California was I-70, but when I-70 got to the middle of Utah, it just sort of dissipated. Broke into a dozen little pieces that became other roads that headed north and south, but not west to the Pacific coast, not west to Mendocino.

"I knew it," I said to Gina when she returned, panting. "I may know nothing, but I knew we had to stay on I-80. From the beginning I said so. George Washington Bridge to San Francisco, that was my planned route. But no. We had to go *all* the way to Maryland, and come *all* the way back, and now we have to go *all* the way to St. Louis and come *all* the way back. We have to make an 800-mile detour. Eight hundred miles!" I shook my head. "This is crazy. Why, oh why, did I agree to something this stupid? Plus two days' time driving to De Soto!" My voice was so high, I sounded like somebody's exasperated parent, trying to explain why mumsie couldn't just drop everything and buy her darling a pony. We can't. We can't. We can't. "It'll cost us more than 300 bucks and we'll lose two days. That's if we find this little De Soto. It's in St. Louis, the way New Jersey is *near* New York."

But it was impotent rage. I couldn't go back to Aunt Betty's, and I knew it.

Gina looked composed and unconcerned; she rubbed my arm, said shh, tried to use a soothing voice, as if she were now the mumsie, and I was the unreasonable tot demanding a pony. "It's fine," she said. "We'll be okay. So we'll go to St. Louis? What's a couple of days in the scheme of things? I've never been to St. Louis. Don't you want to see the Arch? We can go all the way to the top. Did you know it's the world's tallest man-made monument, at 630 feet?"

I was so tired. I wished Gina, all perky and bubbly, could drive so I could sleep. If horses were wishes.

FOUR

THE LIGHT AT
PICNIC MARSH

1

Candy

We got back on the road around five. It was time to start thinking about dinner, and we hadn't gone but *ten* miles from Aunt Betty's house, our sum total for the day. I couldn't believe I told Emma I'd be back in two and a half weeks. I must've been delusional.

"Hey, you want a Blue Jay pumpkin? Look, they're only a quarter."

"No."

"Look at the name of the town." Gina laughed. "Valparaiso. Isn't that funny?"

I didn't know what was *so* funny.

"We're in *Indiana*. You've got Joe's Bar and Grill, and you've got Tony's Car Repair next to Pump's On Restaurant, next to Tasty Taco, in *Valparaiso?*"

"So?"

"You don't think Tasty Taco is a little too hoi-polloi for Valparaiso?"

"No. I just think the people who named the town came from Chile."

"I think, Miss Literal," Gina said, "somebody's lost her funny bone."

"Completely," I agreed. "I'm cranky like a child."

I glanced over at Gina sitting there, whistling a tune, a smile on her face. *And then he'll settle down* . . . Eddie was planning to marry someone else and she was whistling. *In some quiet little town* . . . If my boyfriend were planning to marry someone else, I sure wouldn't be whistling. Perhaps she didn't care. But then why was she riding shotgun across the continent and the Great Divide to stop him? Either you care or you don't, but what's with the whistling? I pulled her hair. "You're not worried?" I asked.

"'Bout what?"

"Anything."

"I'm not worried 'bout nothin'," said Gina, wiping her head and humming. *You know he'll always keep moving* . . .

We passed a little brown sign that said "Picnic Area at Great Marsh State Park." *That* made me laugh.

"Oh, *now* she's amused." *You know he's never gonna stop moving* . . .

"Because it's funny. First of all, why in the world would anyone have a state park in a *marsh*? That's first. And second, why would you want to have a picnic there?"

"Not as funny as Valparaiso."

"Funnier."

"Don't think so."

"Yes."

"No."

Suddenly we fell mute as if the power had just gone out. Up ahead on Dunes Highway near Fremont, at the traffic light, on the right-hand side of the road across from the Great Marsh Picnic Grounds, with her thumb in the air was the girl from the black truck in Maryland. She must've recognized our car because she smiled at us and waved happily.

Gina and I blinked, not believing our eyes.

"Oh my God," I said. "Is that the same—"

"Holy shit. Shh. Think so."

"Why are you saying shh? It *can't* be."

"Well, look!"

"It *can't* be!" I exclaimed.

"It most certainly is."

120

"God, what do we do?"

"I don't know. Holy shit. Can you turn somewhere?"

"Turn where!" We were on U.S. 12, with the lake on the right and the marsh picnic grounds on the left, and nowhere to turn. The railroad yards and the steel mills were up ahead. The headquarters of U.S. Steel were up ahead. And so was she. I don't know what loomed larger. The light was turning red; I was forced to slow down and come to a stop. Right next to her. Her thumb still out, she came closer, staring expectantly into our passenger window.

"What do we do!" That was me, in a deathly whisper. I was flabbergasted, blinking furiously, as if hoping that she, like the haunting by Ned, would evaporate. I mean, it *couldn't* be her. Not here, it just couldn't be. *We* weren't meant to be here; why was she? We had passed her in another life, days ago on a local road four states away; what wind blew her here? What wind blew us here? "What do we do, Gina . . ."

"Nothing." Gina turned to me. "What are you talking about? Nothing. Look straight ahead, like when the homeless in the city come to wash our windshield. Look away. Ignore her. The light's gonna change soon."

"Gina . . ." I couldn't look away. I was staring at the girl outside the window. Her smile was broad, like me she was chewing gum, smiling like Gina (who was no longer even faintly smiling). She looked so young, and she opened her hands at us, as if to say, "*Well?*" standing in her little blue skirt, skinny, her hair all weird. In her hands she held a shopping bag. What I was seeing was a cataclysmic coincidence, against all probabilities, impossible in a rational world, in a statistical world, in a world ruled by my plan.

"It's fate, Gina Reed," I said.

"Are you kidding me?"

"No." I looked at the girl again. "It's a supernatural event."

"You know what we do when the gods show us what they have in store for us?" Gina said. "We snub our noses at them, and do something else, just to shake things up, to make it less boring."

"You're not curious?"

"No! I'm non-curious. I'm the anti-curious. I'm negatively curious."

"Come on. We're giving the stupid rats a ride. Why do the dogs rate a Shelby, but not the girl? Open your door."

"No! Are you out of your mind?"

"You know she isn't headed to St. Louis."

"How do you know where she's headed?" Gina exclaimed. "*We're* not supposed to be headed to St. Louis."

"True. Look, we'll give her a ride to I-80, drop her off at the first rest stop, no harm, no foul. It's just a few miles. I'm dying to find out how she got here. Look at her. She's a kid. She could be your sister. That's Molly out there."

"No."

I got some energy back. The light was still red, and she was outside our car with her hands open. "Gina, it's a miracle."

"No, it isn't. A miracle is a good thing."

"It's like magic!"

"Yes, black magic."

"We forgot all about her, and yet here she is, hitching on Route 12 on the Great Lake. At our red traffic light. She is the extraordinary. She is the unexpected. Let's give her a ride." The light finally turned green. The sedan behind honked to speed us on.

"Please, no," said Gina. "Sloane, keep going. We're doing well, we're friends again, don't ruin it, don't spoil it."

My heart squeezed. I almost sped up, if only the pull of the unknown weren't so great, the pull of something I didn't understand, but wanted to. This wasn't in my spiral notebook. It could never be. This was no random event. And if this wasn't, then the black truck wasn't. And if the black truck wasn't random, then nothing in the world was random. I had felt so bad back then for being such a chicken, for not letting her in. How often did you get a second chance? "I'm not going to spoil it. Come on. I traipsed around the country for your aunts and your dogs. What's the big deal? You said so yourself. It's just for a few miles. To the Interstate.

Let's help her out. Or some horrible guy in a black truck is going to pick her up. Is that what you want?"

"I don't care!" Gina shook her head. "It's a terrible mistake. We made a pact. We promised each other. No pick-ups."

"Where's the harm?"

"We made a pact," she repeated doggedly. The cars kept honking.

"Well, I know, but I was talking about sweaty men with tattoos. This is to help a girl like us. What do you think *she's* going to do? Come on."

"I'm asking you, please no."

But I wasn't listening anymore. I crossed through the light and pulled onto the shoulder, rolling down my window, sticking my arm out, waving her on, honking twice. I saw her in the rearview mirror, running toward the car. Not quite running, but skipping, like skipping from happiness. A big smile split her face, her shopping bag, her hobo bag flapping.

"Open your door, Gina," I said quietly.

"I can't believe you're doing this. I can't believe *you* are picking up a hitchhiker. But then again, what's a pact to you, right?" She huffed out and flipped forward her seat. The hot summer air swooshed in, and the girl fell in, hips first, then bags, then legs, all teeth, beaming, and said, "Thanks, you're a Godsend." Gina slammed the door shout.

I turned to the girl and didn't know what to say.

She was one peculiar duck up close. She had short spiky hair bleached in punk strands of hot pink and jet black, some standing up, some falling to her neck. She wore thick, black eye-makeup and red glossy lipstick. The makeup was so heavy, I thought it was perhaps to disguise how young she was. Rings perforated her ears from the lobe to the top cartilage. Her body was weighted down with costume jewelry: red, white, and blue stars and stripes, copper bangles, silver hearts. Around her neck hung chains of all lengths, rings adorned fingers and wrists, three bracelets circled each bare ankle, and her tongue was spiked by a small silver ball. Under her short halter, even the bellybutton of her flat stomach was pierced.

I'd never seen that before, except in pictures of African girls in *National Geographic*. She clanged as she sat and breathed; one part or another of her jangled like wind chimes. She had tattoos of flowers on her bare shoulders, and just the top of a red heart showed saucily at the edge of her pink top. Her skin was white as if her body had never been touched by the sun. Her voice was throaty. I rubbernecked her the way I had rubbernecked the nuclear power reactor. More. I couldn't look away.

She smiled widely showing all her teeth; the silver ball twittered. "Like my noise?" She shook her head to ring herself like a bell.

"Looks painful," I said, "but good," then lower, "good in a painful sort of way."

"So," she drawled, "second time's the charm, eh?"

Embarrassed that she remembered us so well gaping at her predicament before deciding to keep going, I turned red.

"Don't worry 'bout a thing." She stuck out her hand. Her brown eyes were merry. "I'm Candy. Nice to meet ya." She popped a gum bubble. I shook her little hand and said I was Shelby. "Love it," she said. "Shall BE?"

"No. SHELL-bee."

"I'm Gina," said Gina. "Sloane, are you going to drive or you going to sit here all day?" Slowly I moved on. "So where are you headed?"

"I'm just along for the ride," the girl replied. "Thanks, Ginashelby." She sat back, a relaxed smile on her face. "Is there anything to eat? I'm starved."

"Nothing in the car." That Gina.

"Gina, give her the potato chips from yesterday."

"Oh, I love potato chips from yesterday!" She flicked her gum out of Gina's window.

Gina, glaring at me, passed her the open bag.

"We can give you a ride to the Interstate," Gina said. "Is that okay?"

"That's okay," the girl said, her mouth full. "But where are you two headed?"

"We have a little errand further south. But we have no problem taking you to I-80."

I love how Gina talked about I-80 like she knew where it was. "Um, Gina," I asked, "how long, you think, till I-80? In your estimation?"

She gave me a shut-up stare and turned back to the girl sitting behind her. I angled my rearview mirror so I could see her better. I was open-mouthed at the whole thing; it was taking me a while to figure out what to say, to float down from the hot balloon of the shock of her in my car.

"What kind of car is this?" Candy asked. "It's cute. A little cramped in the back."

"It's a 1966 Shelby Mustang," I said, tail opening.

"Oh, it's named after you! Love it."

"So, will I-80 be okay?" Gina persisted.

"I think I-80 is in like ten miles," Candy said quietly. She was a little too soft-spoken and throaty, I had to turn the music way down to hear her. "Where are you gals going after that?"

"Really far south. To St. Louis."

"Oh," she said, licking out the salt from the bottom of the potato chip bag, "I'll take a ride with you to St. Louis. Man, these were good. Got any more?"

"No," Gina said slowly, turning to face the front and folding her arms on her chest. She kept glaring at me, in a bug-eyed meaningful way until I finally sighed.

"Candy," I said, "we can't take you to St. Louis because it's really far and we're not getting there till tomorrow. How about we let you off when we stop for food, okay?"

She didn't say anything. She was leaning down to glance into the pet carrier, and her taken aback, slightly puzzled face told me she wasn't sure what she was looking at. She stuck her finger into the cage. "What are these?" One of them stopped barking long enough to nip her finger.

"Chihuahuas. Keep your hands away," said Gina. "They bite."

"No kidding." She laid her hands primly on her lap. "But you still didn't tell me what they are."

"Um—dogs?"

"*Those* are dogs?" She was a composed girl, not a fidgeter. Her hands and body remained still. Carefully, she moved the crate away so it wouldn't touch her. Gina turned the music back up. The Stones were helping us on our way through our busy dying day.

We didn't know what to say, and she was quiet. It was rush hour, and Route 12 dragged on like Jersey Turnpike. Once we got to the Interstate, things weren't any better. Eight lanes in all directions were full up. It took us forty-five tense minutes to crawl a few miles, just slow enough to see a billboard that said, "GO AHEAD, KEEP USING MY NAME IN VAIN. I'LL MAKE RUSH HOUR LONGER."

Oh God!

Candy sat in the back, her shopping bag under her feet, her hands on top of her small tote in her lap, and stared serenely out the window.

"So—Candy. Is that your real name?" asked Gina, making conversation.

"As opposed to what?"

"I don't know." Gina shrugged. "A nickname, I suppose."

She laughed. "Yes, my real name is Candyloo."

"Be funny if your last name was Cane." Gina chuckled.

"It is Cane," Candy said calmly.

"Your name is Candy Cane?"

"Yup."

"You're yanking my chain."

"Why would I?"

Gina opened wide her eyes. "Allrighty." And then, because she couldn't let it go, she said, "Your mother named you Candy?"

"Yeah. What'd your mother name you?"

"Gina."

"Allrighty."

"So, Candy, we're dying to know," I asked, changing the subject, "how did you get from Baltimore to here?"

"I don't know what you mean," she said. "I was never in Baltimore."

"We don't know what *you* mean," said Gina. "The first time we saw you was when you fell off that truck in Baltimore."

"Oh, that." Candy shook her head. "I'm not a turnip. I didn't fall off that truck. But that wasn't Baltimore. It was near Thurmont. Maybe Hagerstown."

"Not the point. How'd you get from there to here?"

"Same way you did. Rode on four wheels."

"To Michigan City?"

"Yup."

"But why Michigan City?"

"I go where the ride brings me," she said. "It brought me here. Lucky for me, because the scumguy who threw me out in Thurmont kept my clothes. I went to the outlet mall to buy some new stuff. Got some neato things. Wanna see?"

"No, thank you." Was she at Lighthouse Place when we were? "What outlet mall? The one by the power plant?"

"What power plant?"

"That huge cement tower," said Gina. "Don't tell me you didn't see it, the concrete thing that hogged the sky and blocked the horizon?"

"Didn't see it."

I took my eyes off the road, I turned around, Gina turned around. Candy stared at us blankly. "I didn't see it," she repeated. "Was it near the street with the Prince of Peace church?"

I swirled back to watch the road before I crashed and burned.

When something new and alive comes into your life, it becomes hard to concentrate on the old things. The new thing commands all your attention. Whether it be a frog, a fly in the kitchen, a new diplomat with his family or a jangling, brightly-lit hitchhiker, it commands you to itself. So it was that Candy took my focus off the road, off the map, off the Interstate, even off dinner. I stopped paying attention to the gas gauge (though clearly it needed paying attention to), to the signs on

127

the road for gas-food-lodging, to Gina's frowning. I forgot about the dogs.

"So what were you doing at the Great *Marsh* Picnic Grounds?"

"Ride dropped me off." She rummaged in her bag for another stick of gum and then chewed loudly. "The *marsh* is not the funny thing," she said. "But it's in a place called Climax Forest." She twittered. "Now *that's* funny."

AC/DC were rocking my car, telling me she was the best damn woman they'd ever seen. Then, after they shook me all night long, Queen bit the dust, and Alice Cooper told me school was out, as if I hadn't known. Gina and I hummed, we sang; Candy sat serenely, looking out the window. Not a muscle moved on her in response to either Kiss or the Bee Gees.

"Candy, how come you're not singing?"

"Dunno. Dunno any of the songs."

"You don't know 'Stayin' Alive?'"

"Nope."

"'I Was Made for Lovin' You?'"

She shook her head.

"Blondie's 'Call Me?' How could you not know 'Call Me?' It's been number one for like thirty weeks straight," said Gina.

"Don't listen to the radio."

"What about 'Hotel California?'"

"What about it?"

Gina and I didn't know what to say. A girl who looked to be our age never heard of "Hotel California?"

"You don't know any of those songs? Not one?"

She shrugged. "I don't listen to the radio," she repeated slowly, as in, which part of I don't listen to the radio don't you understand?

"How old are you?" Gina asked.

"Eighteen."

"So what about when you were a kid? Didn't you listen to the radio then?"

"Nope."

"What about the Beatles? The Stones? The Monkees?"

"Don't know 'em, I'm afraid. Sorry."

"So where'd you go to school?"

"School?"

"Yeah," said Gina, "you know, a building where you go and learn things."

"Oh, yeah. Haven't been to school in years. Hate school."

"You dropped out?" We didn't know anyone who had dropped out. We were impressed. It was scary cool.

"I just stopped going."

"Yes," said Gina. "That's called dropping out."

"Okay, then."

"So where'd you live before you got on the road? Where are your folks from?"

"My folks?" She smiled dryly. "I don't know where they're from. They live in Huntington."

"Where's that?"

"West Virginia. On the banks of the Ohio."

"Oh. Like the song."

"Yup, just like that."

"So how old were you when you dropped out?"

"Thirteen."

"*How* old?" Then we fell silent.

"I hated school," she spat.

"What did your parents say?"

"Dunno. Didn't ask 'em."

Gina turned around. "Come on. They must have noticed you weren't taking the school bus in the morning."

"Well," said Candy, less bubbly, less bright, "my dad didn't know, 'cause he wasn't living with us. And my mom hated school herself and didn't care if I went or not."

"So what did you do when you dropped out?"

"Nothin'. Just hung out. Worked. Made money."

Worked at thirteen? "Didn't listen to music, though."

"No. Look, a Burger King. Can we stop? I'm starved."

2

The Price of Stamps

We stopped in Mokena, still on I-80. Food came to twelve dollars. I asked Candy for four. She said she didn't have any money, she spent her last thirty bucks buying clothes at the radioactive mall. ("By the way," she said, "did you know cockroaches can survive a nuclear explosion? They can live without their head for a week.")

I didn't know that and I also didn't know what to do.

Gina came up to me as I was getting the napkins and straws, whispering in a hiss, "I refuse to pay for her food!"

"All right, fine," I said. "I'll pay for it. But we're at Burger King, not the Four Seasons. Let's just . . . just give me *your* share, will you?"

Candy, despite being stick thin, ate like a ravenous child. She swallowed the burger and the fries, finished her Coke, and said, "I'm still starved. Are you going to finish that?" pointing to the hamburger still in my mouth. I gave her two dollars and she went to buy more burgers.

"Shelby, what the *hell* are we going to do?"

"What?" I was watching Candy in line. A man in front of her turned and started talking to her. She smiled. He smiled back. Why was he smiling at her like that? And the man behind pointed to her patchwork bag and told her it was open. She closed it, thanked him, smiled at him, too. He smiled back. He leaned in, made a joke, she laughed. She had a good laugh. Hearty.

"You told her we'd let her off when we got food. Let's leave her here."

"Gina, it's eight at night."

"So, Miss Talking Clock?"

I chewed my nails. I never chew my nails, so that told me a few things. "We have to get a room anyway."

"Get a room *anyway*? Are you out of your mind? She is a total stranger! Also she can't pay her share."

"So?" I stopped eating. "The dogs can't pay their share either. And as I recall, at the rest stop on I-95, Molly bought a coffee, which she wasn't supposed to drink, a sticky bun, fried chicken, a biscuit, ice cream and potato chips. I don't recall you pitching a fit that Molly wasn't paying her way."

Gina took a breath. "My mother gave me money for Molly. And are you comparing *my* sister with a *total* stranger?"

"I'm just saying. And your mother gave *you* money for Molly? Then how come *I* paid for half her food? She didn't give *me* any money for Molly."

Candy came back, sat down. Warily we watched her wolf her cheeseburger. When she drank her Coke, she said the syrup in it was good, and the soda was fizzy, not flat. She approved the temperature of the burger and the crispness of the fries. While we were complaining about the six dollars she was costing us, she ate, commenting with every bite how good it was.

Gina cleared her throat. "Candy, can I ask you, um . . . what do you plan to do without any money?"

"I dunno. What do I need money for?"

"To eat, to sleep."

"When I need money, I'll get some." She grinned, her mouth full.

"How far are you headed? And please don't say where the ride takes me."

She clapped her hands. "It'd be great if I could ride on with you, girls," she said. "Wherever you're headed."

We stopped eating. I put up a false shield of indifference to

131

parry the daggers coming at me from Gina's eyes. I milled words through my brain but couldn't get any out. Gina turned to Candy. "Look, we're *very* tightly budgeted. We didn't bring enough for you."

And Candy said, "Enough what?"

Gina stumbled. "Money."

Candy waved her hand, the one that still had half a burger in it. "Oh, don't worry 'bout that."

Gina glanced at me for support. But I'm terrible talking to other people about paying their share, so I let her flail on her own. "We brought barely enough for us. That's it. No extra."

"All right. But gas and motels you have to pay for, regardless of me."

But what about food? "How about breakfast, lunch, and dinner, plus drinks and snacks?" Gina said.

"What, you didn't bring any for a rainy day?" Candy smiled at me. "You look like you're a planner, Shelby."

"But this isn't a rainy day!" cut in Gina. "A rainy day is when your car breaks down and you have to get it fixed. A rainy day is when you run out of gas and need to pay to get the car towed. A rainy day is an accident." We both knocked wood.

Candy watched us puzzled. "What are you knocking wood for?"

"For luck. We can't feed another person."

"We really did budget very carefully, Candy," I said apologetically.

"How do you budget for a rainy day?" the girl asked, knocking on the table. "But this table isn't wood, it's, like, plastic or something. And why would knocking on wood bring you luck?"

"Oh, never mind!"

Candy brightened. "Look at it this way, you've knocked wood, so chances are good there will be no rain. And then you'll have plenty."

"But what if there is?"

"But you've knocked on wood."

"Stop."

"Well, then, we'll cross that bridge when we come to it."

We?

"Candy, we don't know you. You can't be frivolous with our money," said Gina.

"Feeding another person is being frivolous with your money?"

It did seem peevish to be cheap about a few bucks. And we were going to be letting her off soon.

"What are you so worried about?" she said breezily, tapping on the formica. "You have money now, don't you? I have no money at all, and I don't look as worried as you. You have to learn to relax. Instead of all this knocking, have you tried concentrating on something positive? Away from anxious thoughts?"

Plan ahead. Organize. Make a to do list. Plan for the future. Be careful. Don't overspend. This is what I knew. Assume horrible things are going to happen and plan accordingly. But I didn't plan for this gal who didn't have a penny. What would Marc say? You brought forty dollars for a flat tire, Shelby. Didn't you bring a thousand for an unexpected guest?

"Look, I started out prepared, too," Candy said in her throaty, lively manner. "But then I got thrown off a truck like a turnip." She laughed. "Didn't expect that."

I wanted to say that perhaps getting into that truck in the first place was her mistake right there, but didn't.

"Girls, don't look so tense," she said. "I found you guys, didn't I?"

When we got outside and let the dogs run, she stretched, raising high her arms, her little skirt riding up; she smelled the air (in Mokena, off the Interstate!) and smiled. She wondered if there was a river up close, maybe the Mississippi, because she could smell fresh water. She asked if we had any lip balm (like we would give the things we put on our lips to a stranger!). "Three hundred and fifty miles to St. Louis? It's nothing. Let's go, girls." She was so upbeat. I didn't know how to tell her to find another ride at a Burger King travel stop. I asked if she knew how to drive. She looked at me like I'd asked if she peed standing up. "No, of course

133

not," I muttered, sighing. "Why would anyone traveling on the highway know how to drive?" I got behind the wheel. We'd gone barely sixty miles the entire day. I said I was going to push on I-55 South till we got to Normal, Illinois. Then we'd stop. Normal. Nice name for a town.

On the way, I found out a few things about Candy. The girl had never watched TV. Didn't know any prime time shows. She knew no nursery rhymes or popular songs, had not read *Separate Peace* or *Ordinary People*, never saw "Rocky" or "Star Wars," could not recall a single quote from Shakespeare, had no idea how far California was from Maryland ("Far?"). Could not play any road games such as naming states or capitals (except Iowa and Des Moines). Could not name a single make of any car on the road (everything was a Cadillac).

She didn't know how much a stamp was. How much milk was. That was not a school thing. That was a something else thing.

Candy, as it turned out, had only one math skill, but she knew it cold—truck drivers covered 800 miles a day. Therefore the only thing stopping *us* from going 800 miles a day was will. I tried to explain it was probably 800 miles in a twenty-four-hour period, but she insisted it was "a day," and that was it.

We asked again where she was headed and again she demurred, telling us she had some business to take care of a few miles down the road. But I had learned from Aunt Flo and Aunt Betty, that "a few miles" was code, for very very very far from where I was at the moment and completely out of the way. I didn't pursue it. I was going to let her off in St. Louis and that was that. Beyond that, I didn't care. It had gotten dark and was very hot out. The dogs were panting in the back, the AC wasn't working great. Candy asked where we were headed after St. Louis. Gina said she was going to Bakersfield to hook up with her boyfriend. She didn't say she was going to keep her boyfriend from "accidentally" marrying someone else. "Bakersfield?" exclaimed Candy from between the seats. "Isn't that in . . ."

"California."

"California!" She looked so happy in my dark rearview mirror. "What about you, Shelby? Are you going to hook up with *your* boyfriend?"

I told her I was going to find my mother.

"You lost your mother? Or," she asked, with her funny little smirk and a poke at my shoulder, "did she lose you?"

"Neither," I said, failing to be non-defensive. "Why would my mother lose me? We lost touch, that's all."

"Gotcha. So she's expecting you?"

"How would I know?"

"You didn't call her to say you're coming?"

I didn't say anything. I hadn't called Lorna Moor in Mendocino. How hard could it be to find a Lorna Moor in a village of 500 people?

"Oh, a surprise!" Candy clapped her hands. "I hope your mom loves surprises. I know I do."

I frowned, stopped talking, resumed sulking, turned up the music.

Reaching over between the seats, she turned the music down. "Tell me more about the mother," she said. So, speaking into the darkness of the car, I related for the first time the truth I had so recently learned.

"Get *out*! Emma is your father's *sister*?" Gina exclaimed. "Since when?"

"Apparently since always." I shrugged as if it were no big deal. Fucking Agnes.

"How come you didn't tell me? How come I was the last to know?"

"Well, no," I said. "*I* was the last to know."

"So let me understand," Candy said. "Your mother left your father, your father went to the big house, and your aunt took care of you?" When I told her that was right, she thought a moment. "This aunt of yours," she said, "is one decent person."

I had never thought of her that way. "Is she?" The words flapped in the air like clothes on a line.

135

"So what have *you* been doing?" asked Gina. "Okay, you didn't go to school, and we know you didn't watch TV."

"Well, no, no TV." She paused. "My mother thought I'd be better off at a halfway house, so I got sent there."

"Halfway house?"

"Yeah. It's like an orphanage for kids with parents."

Ah. That was worthy of conversation. The curiosity, the interest would make the road fly by. But to my disappointment Candy didn't want to say any more. I could see Gina, less curious than me, wanted to say things, but couldn't, and didn't. The first and most important of which was: you can't come with us all the way to California. That isn't what Shelby and I planned. That isn't what we want. Where can we let you out so that we don't feel guilt and you're relatively safe? Your safety is not our responsibility. We don't assume duty for you just because we're giving you a ride. What Gina said grumpily instead was, "What kind of mother names her child Candy?"

"A mother with a sense of humor?" offered Candy. She tapped me on the shoulder. "Shelby, why are you looking for your mother?"

"Haven't seen her in a few years," I said. "Wanted to have a visit before I went off to college." When Candy didn't say anything, I pressed on. I said I thought there was a scale in life, a scale that measured the half a dozen in one hand (me) and six in the other (California). I wanted to find my mother to ask her just how tipped that scale had been.

Candy pursed her lips and then laughed softly. "Shelby, darling," she drawled in her hoarse bubble-gum voice. "What if you discover that you weren't even on the scales? What if the answer you're looking for isn't the answer you want? You need her to say, yes, luv, you wuz six in one hand and California wuz half a dozen in the other. I could've stayed with you, I just chose to go. But have you considered the possibility she might tell you there was nothing in the hand where you were supposed to be?"

I exhaled. Gina exhaled. "Well, no," I stammered, "I guess I didn't . . ."

Candy put her hands together and bowed her head. "You forgot to ask yourself this most important question."

"Like you know the most important question," I snapped. "You don't even know how much a stamp is."

"Is the price of stamps the most important question?" She shrugged. "What if the answer you get is not the answer you want? You forgot to ask yourself if what you want is truth or comfort. They're two different things." Candy shook her spiked head. "I'd think it over before I plunged head first into Mendocino."

I could hardly let her out on the shoulder of the highway because she spoke up, could I? I fixed the rearview so I wouldn't see her anymore in the reflection of the passing cars. I turned up the music. Thank God for the road. I could pretend to concentrate on it.

She began talking about the Mississippi with Gina. Gina was so good at that, talking about meaningless stuff to avoid talking about the real stuff. Candy asked why the river was muddy. Gina liked that; it brought out the teacher in her. She lectured that the Missouri was cold and crystal clear, flowing from the Montana lakes, but mixing with the warm, muddy Mississippi gave the combined river its decidedly brown look. Candy laughed and commented pithily how nine parts chocolate and one part shit was still shit. Gina disagreed with this assessment of the mighty Mississippi and so it went. Candy, who hadn't *heard* of *Huckleberry Finn* (let alone read it) asked to be told Huck's story. "We have time," she said, her head leaning back. "And then I'll tell you a story." I wanted to tell her not to block my rearview mirror but couldn't do it without sounding churlish, so I said nothing, wondering *when* we were going to get to Normal.

The storytelling flagged, then stopped; Candy had fallen asleep, curled up against the dog crate. It was ten p.m.

"What do we do?" Gina whispered. "Do we get a room?"

"Where do you suggest we sleep?"

"Well, I know . . . but what about—" She pointed to the back.

"Do you want to tell her to get out?" I almost wished Gina would insist.

"I feel bad," Gina whispered. "She's sort of cute. Like a baby."

I felt less inclined to think of her this way after she, ignorant on all subjects, opened her mouth, and in twenty seconds spoke the kind of truth to power I had spent eighteen cold years avoiding. I had just pretended to assume Lorna Moor would be overjoyed I had forgiven her, had come looking for her. That she would be guilt-ridden, receptive, apologetic. So I was contemplating letting off the tattooed hitchhiker with a belly ring before we got a room. Waking her up by repeatedly calling her name louder and louder, I said, when she finally lifted herself into a sitting position, "Hey, listen, we kinda have to stop for the night. You mind if we let you off at the next rest stop?"

She said nothing. Not yes, not no, just sat there, and let my words hang in the stale air.

"Oh, what the hell," I said. "Fine. But we'll drop you off tomorrow in St. Louis."

She said nothing.

If she was trouble, I figured we'd be dead already. "Tomorrow. In St. Louis," I repeated.

We found a Comfort Inn for $37 (well below budget!), and were given a room on the first floor with two double beds. I parked my car right outside the door, and Gina quipped that if I could, I'd sleep with it. Candy used the bathroom first, showered, washed her underwear and hung it out to dry on the shower rod.

"What?" Gina said to me quietly. "She couldn't buy an extra pair at the place she bought that slutty skirt?"

"Maybe they don't sell underwear in places like that."

She put on a bra and new underwear, then knelt down in front of the bed. I thought she was looking for something, but she closed her eyes and then crawled under the covers, and with a little sigh was asleep, with all the lights on, the water from the bathroom running, the front door still open, us bringing things in and out, dogs barking, the radio going. Just asleep. I wanted to check inside her hobo, but she was clutching it like a stuffed animal.

Gina and I took the dogs for a walk to talk about her. The night was stifling hot in Normal, Illinois. No cool salty breezes from the Long Island Sound like in Larchmont. "She is *so* weird!" Gina exclaimed.

"I know. Did you see her kneeling?"

"What was *that* all about? What do you propose we do with her?"

I tapped on the car. "Wanna hop in, take our stuff, and take off? We'll leave her a couple of bucks by the bedside." I giggled.

"Seriously, though," said Gina.

"Well, I don't know, do I?"

"This was your great idea. Are you really going to let her off in St. Louis?"

"I guess."

Gina was quiet. "I don't want her going with us to California."

"God, no, never! St. Louis, I said."

"Promise? I *really* don't want to spend another night with her. She creeps me out."

I hemmed and hawed. I didn't want to promise, just in case Gina accused me again of my word not being good. "We have to go back up to I-80 anyway."

"Why would she come with us all the way south to St. Louis," Gina wondered, "if she needs to stay on I-80 herself?"

I agreed it was weird.

"You see what I mean? You gotta talk to her. You gotta set her straight."

"Why should I talk to her? What can I do?"

"This was your bright idea."

Back in the room, Candy was curled up on her side, hands under her cheek, blankets pulled to her neck, sweetly sleeping. I sighed. Gina sighed.

I, terrified of the unknown, had invited the unknown into my car! But she was just a kid, like Molly, except sweet, and slept like a baby who'd found her crib, peaceful, not stirring, not making a sound. We crated the dogs, and together got into the other bed. I was impressed by how peaceful this chick looked as she slept. I couldn't stop staring. Gina turned off the lights and we lay in the dark, just the air conditioner humming, dripping water onto the stained carpet. No noise from our hitchhiker. Well, sure. She'd taken off her baubles and beads and laid them on the bedside. "How do you figure she can sleep like this?" I whispered to Gina. "She doesn't have a car, doesn't have a penny, has almost no clothes, is wholly dependent on the kindness of strangers, and has no idea how she's going to get ten miles from here, yet sleeps like that."

"Ignorance is bliss," said Gina. "Did you see? She knows nothing."

"I know! Amazing, isn't it?"

We stopped talking. We were tired. But I was thinking—perhaps Candy was ignorant, and didn't go to high school and hadn't read *Huck Finn*, but how come in thirty seconds of hearing about my mother, she asked the question I, with all my high school diplomas and Scholastic Aptitude Tests never even thought of? How come they didn't ask me this on the SAT analogies: Mother is to Shelby as Candy is to wealth. Really far away.

3

Comfort

I couldn't sleep. The unfaded imprint of Candy's hands on my life's quest was causing havoc inside me. I crawled out of bed, opened the door and in my T-shirt and sleeping shorts, tip-toed barefoot on the paved walkway down the row of motel doors and called Emma collect from the public phone outside the ice machine. We had crossed one time zone. I thought it was only midnight in Larchmont. But when Emma picked up the phone and accepted the charges, she said, "My God, what's wrong? Are you all right?"

"I'm fine," I said. "Why do you ask?"

"Because it's two in the morning, Shelby," said Emma. "I figured you wouldn't be calling unless you were dead." I had calculated the time zone one hour in the wrong direction. "Shelby," said Emma, "I hope you're better with directions than you are with time. Because driving west and not east might cause a slight delay."

Emma was joking! If she only knew.

"I just ... wanted to say hi," I said. We chatted for a few minutes. She asked me how the money was holding out, how the car handled, if I was eating enough, because sometimes I forgot to eat, how Gina and I were getting along, if we were in any trouble. And then I said, "Emma, please tell me, why did my mother leave my father?"

"Oh, child. I don't know," she said. "You called all the way from Illinois to ask me this?"

"That's what I'm thinking about in Normal."

"I don't know why she left," she said sincerely. "I didn't know your mom very well. She was closed up. Perhaps she was disappointed."

"With what?"

"With your dad, maybe. With her life."

"But she must have loved him to marry him, right?"

Emma was quiet. "They never actually had a wedding."

"They *eloped*?"

A prolonged cough.

"They went to *Vegas*?"

A weigh-your-words silence followed. "Shel, hon, don't be upset. They were never married."

When I hung up the phone, I was so sorry I called. Why did it make a difference to me? So he never gave Lorna Moor a ring. So what. They were boyfriend and girlfriend. Like Eddie and Gina. Eddie hangs around, has a little fun, goes to clubs, has a few drinks. Gina gets knocked up, and suddenly she's home with a squaller and he's still in bars. And then Gina runs off, and now Eddie's home with a squaller. And he still goes to bars—and look what happened.

Candy's words sprang once more to my ears, rasping in the chirping night. I realized that I had called Emma wanting one answer, got another, one I emphatically did not want, and now was stuck with it, but I had never asked myself the Candy question, and I should have. What answer did I want, truth or comfort?

I had wanted comfort.

FIVE

THE ROAD TO ST. LOUIS

1

A Little Buddha

In the morning, I couldn't wake up; bricks were on my head. When I finally craned my head from the pillow, I saw that the dogs were gone, the girls were gone. For one brief moment, through the haze of sleep, it felt as if they had never been on this trip with me. I was alone, and fleetingly, I was not afraid.

I found them outside near the 'Stang. Gina was unwrapping a cherry Blowpop, her breakfast, I assumed, and perching on the hood of my car, legs crossed, hair in long braids to keep the heat from her head, smiling like a school girl, chatting to—

Well, chatting to Candy. She, too, was sitting cross-legged on top of the car, sucking a lollipop in the sunshine. Hair spiked, eyes caked with black makeup and adorned with cheap jewelry, she wore a barely-there jean skirt and a backless thin yellow halter, which displayed her flower-power tattoos to good effect. More Alice Cooper than schoolgirl. A Sex Pistols Lolita, part of the punk movement, and a symbol of rebellion, except, of course, that this schoolgirl had never heard of the Sex Pistols or the punk rebellion. This was the kind of girl your mother, if you had one, would pull you away from on the street, whispering vehemently, "Stay away from the likes of her, do you hear me?"

It took me an hour to shower and clear out. I bought some aspirin, chewed it like one of Truman Capote's crippled killers, and began driving again. It was lunchtime. What was happening to me? I, who always went to bed at ten and got up at six, was now sleeping till noon. I had been replaced by a pod zombie.

"I kind of like her," Gina whispered to me before we got in the car. "I can't believe I'm saying it, but I do. She's so sweet and dumb. It's endearing. We had a fun time talking while you slept."

Ignorance of physics was preoccupying bliss. Trying to figure out how many hours went into 220 miles if we kept a speed of 70 miles an hour took us nearly 70 miles. But what if we stopped? What if we had to gas up? What if we went 68 miles an hour for 47 minutes and 75 miles an hour for 54 minutes?

Candy took my mind off physics for a stretch of the Interstate between Normal and Lincoln. She was so sunny. Her lipstick wasn't as heavy, and she smiled all the time, even tried to bounce along to "Hot Child in the City." Sitting up and looking pretty.

"Candy, come on, tell us, where are you headed?"

"Paradise." She was still bopping.

Ah. She responded to direct questions.

"Paradise, where is that?"

"Somewhere in California. North of I-80, though."

"Oh, *California*, really, what do you know?" said Gina, widening her eyes at me. "So you're going to California."

"Yes. To a place called Paradise. But I'm pretty sure there's a place called Paradise everywhere. Don't you think, Gina?"

She was uncanny, this Candy. It was as if she had already figured out that Gina was a triviaphile. Appealing to Gina's trivially investigative nature, Candy sent my braided friend into a flurry of atlas activity that occupied her from Normal to Lincoln.

"So, what's in Paradise?" I asked Candy in the meantime.

"Nothin'. Just some loose ends."

"Are you staying there?"

"Yuck," she replied. "Not for a second longer than necessary."

"Are you in a hurry to get there?"

"Well," she said carefully, "let's say I'm not *not* in a hurry."

"Illinois has a Paradise!" Gina exclaimed.

"Of course it does," said Candy.

The ratio of trucks to cars on the Interstate was ten to one; they were flanking and passing us. Candy was lowered on the backseat, Gina stuck in the atlas looking for Paradise in Missouri and Montana.

"Gina," Candy said, after some time had passed, "you can stop looking now. Trust me when I tell you there's a Paradise in every state."

"How do you know?"

"Because man names things."

"What?"

Candy shrugged. "Gina, a version of Jane, female of John, Christ's apostle."

"Whose apostle?" Gina was stunned. I was stunned. Did she just say *Christ*? She seemed to be the kind of girl who wouldn't know who Christ was, much less use a word like apostle.

"What about Shelby?" I almost held my breath: like maybe my name was a version of one of Christ's apostles also.

"Shall Be. Not formed yet."

"Who's not formed? Shelby?" Gina laughed.

But I said nothing, constantly feeling my own hunger for things I had not found and didn't know how to look for. My mouth opened a little bit, then closed again. Interestingly Candy said nothing. Then, quietly she added, "A name is much more than a way to set you apart from me."

"Candy, forgive me for saying," said Gina, "but I think more than my name tells you apart from me."

"That's true. And you're forgiven," said Candy, continuing. "A name reveals the very essence of the thing. To name a thing is to show the value God gave it. It's the capacity to bless God. Hence . . . Paradise in every state."

Dumbfounded we did not speak again until Candy said, "Maryland. *Mary's* Land."

We waited. She said nothing. Then: "Virginia. The Holy Virgin."

We said nothing. She said, "Florida."

"I also can recite the names of states," said Gina. "Indiana. Ohio. Tennessee."

"Florida comes from a Spanish phrase meaning *Pascua de Florida*," said Candy. "*Paskha* is the Orthodox word for Easter. Florida is flowers. Feast of the Flowers, meaning Easter."

How did a girl who knew nothing and read nothing know this? Candy was scooted down on the seat again. "Gina, come on, look away from South Dakota for a sec, talk to me instead," she drawled. "Eddie and Gina. Gina and Eddie." She shook her head. "So why did he go to California and leave you in New York?"

Gina, looking away from South Dakota for a moment and forgetting that it was dangerous to tell Candy things, said, "He didn't leave me in New York. I was in school."

"And he?"

"He dropped out. Like you."

"At thirteen?"

"No, he just didn't graduate high school. Eddie," Gina said proudly, "is a genius, and school bores him." She began tracing the list of names again.

"Hmm." Candy leant forward between the seats. "How does he know he's a genius?"

"He took an IQ test and was tested at 169. Aha, yes! Paradise in South Dakota."

"Hey!" Candy said happily, "maybe I'm a genius, too. School bores the shit out of *me*."

"He was *tested*," Gina declared loftily, flipping the atlas page to Tennessee.

"But that's not *why* he's a genius, is it? He didn't become a genius *because* he was tested, right? That's what I'm saying. Maybe I'm a genius, and just don't know it."

"Yeah, maybe," said Gina. "Highly likely, in fact."

"Well, why'd he go to California and leave you behind if he's so smart?" Candy wanted to know. "You're pretty, guys must be beating down doors to get to you. Why would he leave you?"

Don't do it, Gina, I mouthed, but Gina, smiling happily after being told she was pretty, opened her entire heart and told Candy that he left to go visit his mother, that he was going to follow Gina to the teaching college in upstate New York where she was going in the fall, but while visiting his mother, he had hooked up with an old girlfriend. Gina said Eddie had become confused and was thinking of marrying this girl.

"He was confused so he thought he'd marry her?" Candy repeated dumbly. "Is confusion grounds for marriage?"

Now Gina was confused.

"I thought you called him your fiancé?"

"I did. He is. We're going to get married. Not yet; after I graduate college, but that's our plan."

"But if he's going to marry this other chick, why are you going to California?"

"To stop him from making a foolish mistake, obviously," Gina said. "He doesn't love her. He loves me. He just gets confused sometimes. Doesn't he, Sloane?"

I didn't even glance at Gina, but Candy stared at both of us from the back, from one head to the other, and slowly said, "Why would Shelby know if your boyfriend Eddie sometimes gets confused about who he wants to marry?"

"No, not marry, just . . . Eddie likes the girls, doesn't he, Sloane?"

"I don't know," I said, staring straight ahead. Soon I'd need directional help. From who, though? They were both hopeless. I'd have to pull over. I was deliberately avoiding Candy's eyes staring narrowly at me in the rearview mirror. "Gina, open to Illinois," I said, "and tell me where we are."

We were near Sherman.

"The thick is plottening," Candy drawled. "I find you both *fascinating.* You been friends a long time?"

"We were good friends once," Gina said.

"I just bet." Candy sat back against the black vinyl, smiling. "Oh, yes." She closed her eyes, but not before giving me a glance through the looking glass.

"Candy, can I ask you," I said, desperately trying to change the subject, "why do you drop low like that?"

"Like what?"

"Well, like now. You're practically lying on the dog crate. Why?"

"Just trying to get comfortable."

"On the dog crate?" But she wasn't getting comfortable. She dropped down like a helmeted head in a trench. Last night when it was dark, after fine dining at Burger King, she sat up between the seats and never lowered herself. Perhaps she didn't need to get comfortable then.

Being in a small car on the Interstate, driving to St. Louis surrounded by trucks keeping to a steady fifty-five, knowing you're not headed in the right direction, trapped and hot, hungry and frustrated—why, there's nothing like it. We chattered idly, whiling away the miles. I kept checking the clock, the mileage. How much farther could this St. Louis be? We stopped a couple of times to eat, gas up and walk the dogs, but it was a seemingly endless, stifling afternoon confined in a car with the AC failing.

"It's broiling," complained Gina.

"Well, it *is* summer," said Candy.

"Oh, doesn't she sound like a little Buddha," snapped Gina, irritable like a rusted crank.

"Please, anything but a Buddha."

Gina perked up, provoked. "You got something against Buddha?"

"Nope."

"Come on, cough up."

"Nothing." She was nonchalant.

"Then why don't you want to be a Buddha?"

"I don't want to be many things. I don't want to be a Chihuahua, either."

"Gina was a Buddhist," I said, stirring things.

Poking me, Gina said, "I was not a Buddhist. I believed in his teachings. Still do."

"Do you?" I glanced at her skeptically. "What about . . ."

"Ah, yes," said Candy, casually sitting up. "The wisdom of the Vedantic Brahmans: strive to achieve nothingness."

"What did you just say?" I mumbled.

"I don't know what you're talking about," said Gina. "Not nothingness at all."

"What's the highest attainment in Buddhism?" Candy asked.

"Nirvana," Gina replied.

"Right. The non-answer to every question. Nirvana is a state of not being. Not something, not nothing, not anything. Just— not being. Not joy or sorrow, life or death. Not glory. Nothing."

"Satisfaction," said Gina, frowning. "Peace."

"Nope. Those are feelings. States of being. Nirvana is a state of *not* feeling and not being."

I blinked uncomprehendingly. Gina frowned at me and shook her head at Candy, who laughed.

"You're working for the ultimate detachment," Candy continued. "Work on detaching yourself from all earthly things. Am I right, Gina?"

"You're wrong."

"Don't commit, don't engage, don't ask, don't seek. Think only for the purpose of stopping all thought. Feel only to numb yourself so you feel nothing. Will with all your will to achieve no will at all, so that your will suffocates and dies. Speak with words free of meaning so that you communicate nothing. Oh, and the good news! You don't even have to be human to achieve this. You can be a chair. Or a sloth. Or a tree trunk. Your humanity is non-essential and not required. As Buddha said on his death bed: remember, brethren, death is present in all things. Work out your own salvation diligently. In other words, diligently work for nothing." Candy sat back, her arms crossed, and smiled.

"What the hell," said Gina, "are you talking about? That isn't what we learned at all."

"No? What *did* you learn at the Ashram?"

"How do you know I went to the Ashram?"

"Don't all Eastern spiritualists?"

We got distracted by a honking truck. Candy scooted down into the seat. The truck honked, Candy went down. The driver of the twenty-four wheeler looked inside the 'Stang and gave me the thumbs up, honked again.

"They're just honking because they like my car, Candy," I said carefully.

Candy didn't say anything.

"Candy?"

"Yes?"

"Why are you hiding? And don't give me that crap about getting more comfortable. A pretzel is more comfortable than you."

Her eyes were closed. She was lying down on the seat, her legs in the well, her hands on the dog cage. The truck had passed, and so had the conversation. But not for Gina, whose hair was up. "At the Ashram, we meditated. We ate good food, did yoga, achieved serenity, took walks, tried to put things in perspective. It was beautiful. You know anything about that?"

"I know something about that, yes." Candy raised herself up, leaned forward. "Did they teach you that all craving was bad? All wishing needed to be stamped out?"

"Not at all! They taught us not to care about earthly things."

"Exactly. The earthly self is bad. Material things are bad. Beauty is meaningless. The outer world is meaningless. The inner world, your inner Chakra, needs to be purged until all want, all desire are gone from it. Only when your soul is empty can you achieve the perfect void. Total emptiness is the goal. No?"

"That's not true!"

"Nirvana is not the goal?" Candy asked, all innocence.

"And what does your god of hitchhikers and the homeless teach you?" Gina said with sharp irritation.

"Rejoice always," replied Candy. "That's one. Pick up hitch-hikers off the road. Give them drink. Give them food. Give freely, because you have been given freely. Don't worry about what you eat and what you wear. Pray without ceasing. Be good. Have love. Value your earthly life. Be. And be not afraid."

That last thing got inside me—I had spent my life being afraid. "Who says this?" I asked.

"Jesus," Candy said simply.

Gina laughed. "What the hell do *you* freakin' know about Jesus? You haven't read a book in your entire life!"

"Clearly I might've read one book," said Candy, twinkling. "At least about Buddhism."

Unpleasant silence fell in our little car.

"You don't know anything about Buddha," Gina said eventually. "Nothing. You dropped out of school."

"Oh, I didn't know public schools taught about Buddha. Maybe I should've stayed."

"You should've, yes!"

Candy fell back on the seat and rubbed a Chihuahua's nose. He promptly bit her, but she didn't take her finger away, still cooing to the two of them through the cage. "Hello, little Cheewahwah. Do you want to open a little hospital for lions and tigers and mice to prove you're not a canine but a superior being, oh, yes? Or are you reconciled with your canine Mokshu?"

Were we near St. Louis? God, I fervently hoped so. After passing Chatham, I asked Gina to look it up, but she was too riled and didn't. "I want potato chips," Candy whined. "I want an ice cream. I want some milk. I want potato chips most of all. Can we stop for French fries? Any potato will do."

When we stopped, Gina said to me, as we were walking the dogs and giving Candy a few bucks for potato chips and Coke, "*When* are you going to let her off? Because I don't like her one little bit."

"Come on," I said dryly. "I thought she was so sweet and ignorant."

"That's right. She knows nothing."

"Then why's she getting under your skin?" Candy was thoroughly amusing *me*. This is what I knew—I couldn't take my eyes off her, hitched up on a picnic table, looking around, smiling, her skirt inappropriately short, her pink and ebony tresses glimmering, her red mouth shimmering, eating from a bag of potato chips clutched in her little fist.

We passed the hours on the road to St. Louis this way. This is the thing: sometimes you want to confess, share intimacies, divulge confidences. Sometimes you want to talk about real things, with meaning. But the time to do that is around a fire, or late at night in bed. I wanted to ask Candy many questions about her life, and how she knew so much about Buddha, but darkness is usually a prerequisite for midnight confessions. Yet the miles are stretched long, even in daylight. You have to talk about something. So you talk about words, because *words* have meaning. You use *words* to talk about words. You listen to *words* on the radio, you look at *words* on the signs. Litchfield. Staunton. Hamel.

"Did you know that the longest word in the English language is forty-five letters?" Gina said, having long ago abandoned her quest for Paradise, and her defense of Buddha with whom, in any case, she had parted ways after her aunt died, though she didn't tell Candy that.

"Really?" This was said utterly devoid of interest. "Is it anti-disestablishmentarianism?" Accompanied by a chuckle and a gulp of Coke.

"No. That's a measly twenty-eight letters. Are you ready?"

"Candy, you have to humor her."

"I'm ready," said Candy.

"It's pneumonoultramicroscopicsilicovolcanokoniosis."

"I lied. I wasn't ready. What?" Candy was laughing.

Gina said, "It's a lung disease that affects miners."

"Is your father a miner?" asked Candy.

"No, he makes metal fixtures."

We turned up the music, and Captain and Tennille assured us that love, love would keep them together.

A little later Gina asked: "Why don't you tell us your story, Candy?"

154

"Okay. Here. Here's my story. After Judas died and went to hell, he was sad, and remorseful and filled with shame. He was in a deep hole, and he was cold. He spent a long time like that with his thoughts and his regret, then looked up and saw very high above him, a small patch of light. He contemplated this light, thought about it for maybe a thousand years. Then he grabbed on to the sides and began to climb, but he kept slipping and falling back to the bottom. It was a very difficult task. Finally, when he was almost at the very top, he slipped and fell back to the bottom again and spent many more years with his shame and regret. After many attempts and many failures, he eventually managed to claw his way out. He crawled into a small, dimly-lit room, in which stood a table. Around this table sat twelve men. Jesus looked at Judas, and said, 'Well, Judas, at last you're here. We couldn't begin until you came.'"

Candy leaned back against the seat.

I wasn't laughing anymore, troubled by the bleakness of what she had just told us. There was something in it that frightened me. It was a terrible story, for sure, but I didn't quite know why. Gina was more direct. "What the hell does it mean? We wanted something personal."

"How do you know it wasn't personal?"

"I didn't understand a word of it," Gina declared. "What's the point?"

Candy smiled. "You didn't ask for a point. You asked for a story. Someday it might have meaning for you. Then again, it might not."

The road became more congested, less open. The fields had gone, there was rush-hour traffic, factories near the river, industrial blight. Candy remained permanently down on the seat. She looked squeezed up, with her legs one way, her torso another, trying to fit around the dog cage and the Chihuahuas that she, as best she could, was trying to ignore. "Gina, we're going to have to figure out where we're going," I said. "Look at the map and tell me where to go."

Reluctantly, Gina opened the atlas.

From the back Candy said, "Gina, did you know that cockroaches can navigate perfectly when they're deaf and blind?"

"And how exactly does that apply here?" snapped Gina, pretending to search the map of Missouri.

Slyly, Candy smiled. "Navigate. Perfectly. When deaf and blind."

I knew that Gina fervently wished she were more adept at map reading just to prove her superiority to the creature in the back who never finished junior high. The only problem was, Gina's intense desire to appear smarter than Candy was in no way related to her actual geographical competence. She could not find De Soto on the map. We had to pull into a gas station, and I was the one who had to struggle to find the little town fifty miles south of St. Louis, near a road that led to a road that could be the road we were looking for. The trucks kept honking at my car. It was blisteringly hot, we were sweaty and tired, and Gina kept whispering as I struggled with the pump, "Are you going to let her off or not?"

"Here? In a gas station?"

"She's *really* starting to get on my nerves."

2

A Full Bladder

We got to the Kirkebys' after eight. As if on the Oregon Trail, we moved our wagon west across the Missouri River and past the Gateway Arch, all man-made 630 sunlit feet of it, at which we barely glanced, down the floral, verdant, watery winding river trail of Lewis and Clark ("Who?" said Candy), south into the sloping, overhanging, sun-infused hills, expansive, rolling fields to the horizon, trees the brightest green, the lowering sun gilding all. I had imagined it to be flat, burnt-out, but it was neither. Everything was surprising me these days. Nothing was as I had expected or imagined it to be.

Nancy Kirkeby was strong and tall, a blonde, good-looking friendly woman, who came out to the drive and shook our hands, even Candy's, though she did say, "*Candy*? What kind of a mother would name you that, child?"

Nancy oohed and aahed over the dogs, ushered us in, carrying the cage, said her boys were having a nap, but would soon wake up and be happy.

"What kind of a mother lets her children nap at nine in the evening?" whispered Candy, but I shushed her.

The two boys were on the floor of their parents' bedroom, a sunlit western room, on top of casually thrown-down blankets, fully clothed and snoring. Their mother stood over them, smiled and said, "Pumpkins, wake up, look what I got."

There was much grateful excitement. We were asked to stay. Nancy's husband came in from the shed, introduced himself briefly as Ken Kirkeby, then disappeared until supper. They fed us Sloppy Joes, rolls, cheese, macaroni, some leftover stew. Candy ate like she hadn't been fed in months, complimented the food, and talked non-stop to the boys about dogs, the farm and cats, even school(!). It was ten-thirty by the time Nancy served hot chocolate and ice cream, then invited us to sleep over and start out in the morning. Exhausted, I readily agreed, welcoming the chance not to pay another thirty-seven bucks for a room it would take us an hour to find, since the Kirkebys lived in the middle of nowhere.

The open lands were vast and had smelled so good in the setting sun. The family sure looked like there was nowhere else they would rather be. Even I, for five minutes, became enamored of their life, imagining myself getting a house like this, raising chickens, taking care of things, having food late when unexpected and uninvited guests came to my door bearing not one but two Chihuahuas, and seeing the sun set from up high. Nancy gave us linens and blankets, extra pillows and a double bed with space on the floor for the third person. Candy took the floor. No one protested. "Well, I'm turning in," Nancy said. "You girls, not too much noise. Ken and I have to be up at sunrise tomorrow."

"Oh. What are you doing tomorrow?" I asked.

"Nothing." She laughed. "We're up at that time every tomorrow," she said, waving a cheery goodnight.

I had long been asleep, or thought I had, but in the middle of the night I had to use the bathroom. I didn't know where it was, so I stumbled down the hall, bleary-eyed, looking for a half-open door or a dim light. I found both. When I pushed open the door I saw it was not a bathroom but a guestroom with a bed and a chair. In this brown leather chair sat Ken Kirkeby, and on the floor, between his legs, was Candy, her head lowered into his pulled-down sleeping shorts.

"Oh, excuse me," I muttered apologetically, backing out and hitting my foot on the doorjamb, stumbling, possibly even yelping. "Excuse me . . ." My eyes to the carpet, I fumbled for the door handle. Oh God. Yet the bladder was desperately full. Still, I couldn't risk any more discoveries in this farmhouse. Rushing back to the bedroom, holding on to the walls, I leapt into bed onto a sleeping Gina. "Wake up!" I hissed. She didn't stir. "Gina!"

Grumbling, she pushed me off and turned away. I climbed back on top of her, straddling her and shaking her urgently. "Gina! Wake up! Mayday, I tell you."

Her eyes still closed, feebly she tried to detach me. "Sloane, are you crazy? Get off!" she muttered.

"No. Gina, I'm telling you for the last time—"

I broke off, hearing shuffling footsteps outside, doors opening, a sleepy female voice making a loud gasp, a man's voice making a loud gasp, followed by apologetic muffles. I swirled off Gina, plopped next to her and pulled the covers over our heads. "Gina! For God's sake! Will you wake up?"

My whispering appeal wasn't what finally woke Gina. It was the sudden yelling coming from the hall, the guttural fury of a woman's voice. Under the blanket, Gina was finally awake. "Sloane, why are you suffocating me?"

"Oh, we are so f—"

Unholy screaming coming from the corridor stopped me, ear-splitting banging, footsteps running, the sound of something wooden being hurled against a wall, followed by a man's contrite voice. Pulling the blanket off our heads, Gina lay breathing in deeply, staring at me, as we listened. I could make out only every other word. "SWINE! Gibberish, gibberish, gibberish— BASTARD! Gibberish, gibberish, gibberish, BITCH!" Oh, and then a whole phrase: "GET THE FUCK OUT OF MY HOUSE!"

"Who is she yelling at?" whispered Gina, and then she had her answer when our door burst open and a panting mad blonde woman in a house robe stood in the hall light. "Get the FUCK out of my house!"

Gina and I jumped out of bed. Nancy disappeared. "God," I said, "I *really* have to go to the bathroom."

"Better not ask, Sloane. What's wrong with her?"

"Better not ask, Gina."

We stuffed our clothes and toothbrushes into our duffel bags, hearing Nancy somewhere in the house screaming at her husband, his quiet baritone in reply. The dogs were barking as if the house were getting robbed. I hoped we had everything but didn't think this was the time for a thorough inspection; the wife was so angry, yelling so loudly, I was afraid the shotgun in the living room was going to come off the wall before we had a chance to get into the car.

Throwing on our Dr. Scholls, Gina and I grabbed our bags, Candy's bag and, hurrying, saying nothing, clop-clopped like mares down the hardwood-floor hall. Here was the bathroom! Right at the end of the corridor. I just hadn't walked far enough. Damn. My body twitched from my urinary discomfort. "Gina, I'm going to pee my pants," I whispered. "You think I have a sec to run in?"

"No! Let's go. Where's Candy?"

"Don't know."

"Hurry. Where's the door?"

I gave the bathroom a longing last glance, and in the kitchen, Nancy was waiting for us, out of breath, red in the face.

"Thank you," I mewled. "Everything was delicious—"

The woman flung open the back door and shoved me roughly into Gina and outside, slamming the door so hard behind us that one of the glass panes shattered and fell. The dogs continued to bark.

We ran across the pebbled yard to our car, me fumbling for the keys.

Candy was standing by the passenger door. "Did you get my bag?"

I threw her hobo bag at her.

"What's going on?" cried Gina. "What the fuck happened?"

"Just get in the car," I said. "We have to get the hell out of here, that's what happened."

160

Candy was already in. But Gina was still reluctant, standing for a moment, looking at the house, so peaceful in the dark rural fields, just the windows bright with light, shadows walking back and forth, throwing up fretful hands, following one another.

It was three in the morning, the pitch black, rural road unlit, and I drove in a hurry, taking the turns too fast. Where were we headed? Toward a crash, that's where. The downhill lane was winding, and I was having trouble navigating with my shaking hands. There was depthless silence in the car. Candy sat in the back, pressed tightly against the window. Maybe she was hoping I'd forget she was there. Gina didn't forget, though.

"Would someone *please* tell me what happened?"

"Candy?" I said. "You want to take that one?"

"No, not really."

What was I going to do? It was the middle of the night, and I had to either drive or fight; I couldn't do both on De Soto's hilly roads, I'd go right into a ditch. Slowing down, I steadied my foot on the gas. I meandered, my brights on. "I want to find the highway," I said. "I just want to find somewhere we can stop. I can't keep doing this."

We found a small shopping area, all locked up, and I pulled into the parking lot, idling the car. I couldn't wait another second. I ran to the bushes with the driver door still open, and Gina calling out.

"Sloane, what are you doing, for God's sake? Come back! We can't stop here. We'll get mugged. Or worse."

"Everyone's sleeping," I snapped when I returned, turning on the overhead and opening the atlas. "Where are we?" Wasn't that the eternal question? I couldn't see the map, couldn't fix my eyes on it. I whirled around to Candy. "What's wrong with you? Tell me, do you want to get us all killed?"

She said nothing, just pursed her lips—contritely?

"Would someone please, *please* tell me what's going on?" Gina was almost beside herself.

I rolled down my window. "Don't shout," I said. The night was warm and still. What if someone heard, came into the lot? I did not feel safe, and longed for the sun to come up.

At last Candy put Gina out of her misery and related the whole sorry tale. Stunned Gina laughed, then kept repeating Oh my God until I told her to shut up. Candy said nothing, Gina and I stared hard at each other in the dark.

"Girls, why are you hyperventilating? He gave me money." She produced a fifty-dollar bill and waved it around. "Next breakfast and motel on me."

We turned to her aghast. "He gave you *money?*"

"Yes. He knew I didn't have any."

"Help me out with this," said Gina, "because I'm having trouble here. Did he give it to you before or after?"

"Before. There was no after. His wife walked in. Shelby's little stumbling woke her up."

"Oh, now it's *my* fault!"

"No, I'm just saying."

"Candy, the wife could've killed us!"

"Don't be so melodramatic. Why would she kill us? For giving her husband a little head? Someone had to. She wasn't."

"He *told* you?"

"Nope. Man passes by his wife in a narrow corridor without touching her, don't take much to figure he ain't getting *any.*"

"Oh, okay, Dr. Dropout Psychologist," Gina snapped. "Few things more I love than hearing your theories on marriage at four in the morning."

My neck was aching and I rested my disgusted head on the wheel. "Gina, stop speaking to her. She's not getting it."

"*I* get it," Candy said. "*You* don't get it. I didn't approach him. He approached me. I'm not the guardian of his marriage; he is. For a moment we had a free exchange between two consenting adults. I gave him something he desperately wanted. And now *I* have fifty bucks. You girls have been making me feel bad about being broke and all. Now I can make a contribution. So quit griping."

162

"And this is how you contribute? By nearly getting us killed?" Gina's voice boomed through the open windows into the quiet parking lot.

"And there I was," I said, "worried about letting you off on the big, mean Interstate, when obviously you know quite well how to take care of yourself."

Her saying nothing, her *not* promising not to do it again, was noted by me, even at this late hour.

It was still so long till sunrise. We sat in the car, I put my head back, closed my eyes. Sleep was impossible. What was Gina thinking about? What was Candy thinking about? Come to that, what was I thinking about?

"I'm not meant to be perfect, girls," Candy said at last. Was that a semblance of an apology? And why did I need an apology? She didn't go down on me. I wasn't the one married to Ken. Who was I to be so righteous?

"Not perfect is about right, isn't it?" Gina said, holier-than-thou.

I found this to be ironic, considering what she and I had been doing not forty-eight hours earlier with men as unknown to us as Ken Kirkeby was to Candy. We did more with them for free than she did for fifty bucks, and all we got for our trouble was them passing us by on the street. I bet this man would remember Candy.

I didn't know what to do. I felt unprepared, out of control. I thought I had been meant to stop for this girl, to help her. But what if . . . what if I was meant to keep going, and didn't? What if this was a life lesson of an entirely different kind?

3

The Least of Candy

We stayed in the car till dawn. I never did get a second of sleep. When I knew McDonald's was open for breakfast, we got going. It took us a long while to make our way back to I-55. With eyes turned away from the St. Louis Arch, we crossed the mighty muddy Mississippi and began driving north again, to get back to the Interstate that might eventually, maybe not soon, but eventually lead us to the end of our journey. I wanted so much to be done with this part.

My eyes felt full of sand, and I know my judgment was impaired like a drunk's is impaired, but why did it seem like ditching Candy was the only way out? Just let her off at the next rest stop and never think about her again. I was sensing a heap of trouble. As soon as we were back on 1-55 we stopped for breakfast and gas. Gina asked to speak to me a sec and dragged me to a tight corner between the bathrooms and the newspapers. I thought she would hiss that we had to leave Candy here, which is what I had been feeling, but Gina first pummeled me for five minutes with "I told you so," leaving me thoroughly chastised but obstinate, and then she hissed at me that we had to leave her here. I hissed back that I knew! I knew. We looked over. Ten feet away Candy stood in her little denim skirt, smiling ruefully at us.

"You have to tell her," Gina said.

"I know what I have to do," I snapped back.

After Gina vanished to the restroom, I walked to Candy.

"Look, I'm sorry," I said, "but I'm going to have to let you catch another ride. Terribly sorry. Too bad it didn't work out. Just one of those things. Wish you all the best. Good luck with it."

All she said was, "Come on."

"Come on?" I said. "Come on, what? Come on, don't be silly? Or come on, I won't do it again, or come on, I'm no trouble, or come on, I'll pay my way?"

Silence.

"Candy, I'm going to college next month. I've got to get all the way to California, possibly drop Gina in Bakersfield, find my mother in Mendocino, get all the way back, get ready, and leave— I can't be . . ." Can't be what? "You know."

She said nothing, just stood with her head bent.

"Gina and I agreed not to pick up any hitchhikers. We made a deal. I broke that deal. I feel guilty. It wasn't right." I was appealing to righteousness. I made a promise. I didn't keep it. That was wrong. Very good, Shelby.

I waited. "Aren't you going to say something?"

Her pink head was bent. She took a breath. "I am the least of human beings," she said quietly. "You owe me nothing. And you've been plenty kind already. I'm not upset. I wish you would continue to help me, but I know you're afraid. Maybe you can just let me stay with you till I-80? It's another six, seven hours from here. That way I'm on the road I need to be on, like you."

What could I do? She was appealing to righteousness, too, and I didn't have a good response, other than my own, "Come on." And that's all I had except a sigh, and hunger, and sandpaper eyes from not sleeping last night. Outside the day was beautiful and sunny. I wished I were swimming. By two, I'd drop her off; we'd be done. Maybe Gina and I could find a motel with a pool, dunk our bodies in the evening-blue water.

Brusquely, mustering coldness, hiding my anxiety, I agreed I would take her as far as I-80, but that was it, non-negotiable; did she understand? "Please don't make it harder than it needs to be," I said, and she promised she wouldn't make it harder than it needed to be.

Gina, however, saw it differently. When she heard of my plan, she crossed her arms and stood like a pillar by the mixed nuts, refusing coffee or food. She refused to speak even while we were on line at McDonald's. A group of truckers came in. They were morning loud, meaning, they weren't profane but slightly rowdy in their jokes and demeanor. One of them asked, "Hey, whose yellow 'Stang is parked outside?"

I was about to raise my hand, like I was in class, but Candy, standing in front of me, pulled my arm down. She pressed her back into my front, and shook her head. "Shh. Please," she whispered, her hips flush with mine. I could smell lemon cream on her skin, I could smell her moussed-up hair. Gina and I glanced at each other in confusion.

Moving away from me, Candy slunk out, blending in with a family of six carrying McMuffin meals.

"She's getting weirder," I said, getting our own hashbrowns, McMuffins, and coffee.

"You think?" Gina snapped her fingers in disgust. "I really don't want to talk about her anymore."

"Hey, maybe she left us and hitched a ride with that nice family." I tried to be conciliatory.

"Only if there's a God."

When we got to the car, there she was, waiting for us.

"What'd I tell you?" said Gina.

I myself couldn't talk to Gina about this, not about *this*, and not when she was pointedly glaring at me, or rather, pointedly *not* glaring at me. I didn't even check the map, unnerved by the new tensions. We had come down south on I-55 from I-80, so I went back up north on I-55 to I-80. It seemed so logical. The constant of my ridiculous morning—taking not *one* second to be self-aware, because self-awareness did not come without a price. The price was denial. As in, it's okay. It will be okay. It's 300 miles. What could possibly go wrong? I shook my head, shook Gina off and, with the music eardrum-bursting loud, pretended not to think.

Now that the dog cage was gone, Candy was down on the seat, far down. She didn't speak. Things weren't adding up, but I was never very good at math. I didn't even know how to formulate my idiotic arithmetic question. The logic of it escaped me. Was she like me and afraid of the truckers' advances? She didn't seem to be, so why was she hiding from the truckers? And why would she not want me to say it was my Mustang? Truckers had been whistling to me for a thousand miles because of my car. Suddenly I had to hide my pride.

We drove on in silence. Trouble is, when three human bodies are sitting in a forty-cubic-foot capsule, there's nowhere to go, nowhere to turn, nowhere to hide. I did my best to study the road. Gripping the wheel, I pretended to concentrate on the Interstate—flat and straight for the next 200 Illinois miles, with dried up fields and sparse trees all around. Such a ruse. But what could I do? It was pointless to talk about it. Thank God for the radio.

He wanted to kiss me all over and loved me like crazy and only wanted to be with me and asked me to be his baby when he needed me and was torn between two lovers the night Chicago died. Everybody had a hungry heart when they went down to the river. I didn't want to stop until we were on I-80. This wasn't the way I wanted to travel, with heavy hearts and mute mouths. I had nothing but the barely clad girl with doe eyes on which to focus my restless heart, and hearts, *oh hearts could be that way* . . .

We got all the way to Springfield, the capital of Illinois, before Gina checked the map and said that I-55 was veering off course, bringing us east and north to Chicago where we didn't want to be, instead of west and north to Des Moines, Iowa. Disbelieving and cursing, I looked for a rest area to stop. Candy said, no, no, don't stop, keep going. Bring me to I-80, then let me go. But don't stop. Please.

I turned around and stared at her on the backseat a second too long, the wheels scraped the ribbed teeth of the shoulder-warning track. We pulled into a rest stop past Springfield, and I snatched the atlas from Gina. Sure enough, this one time in her life, Gina was right about directions. We *were* headed back east. Another day, why, and we'd be back in New York! And now, to get to I-80 and head west, we had to get off the Interstate completely and travel on slow local highways. Throwing up my proverbial arms, I said I needed to use the restroom (*way* too much coffee, but how else was I going to stay even half-awake?). No, don't, said Candy. Please. Let's just get going. Gina said she was hungry, wanted Roy Rogers chicken. Candy said we should buy it quick and eat in the car. *Suddenly* she was in a hurry? No one was eating fried chicken in my car—it'd be all over the floor and the smell would linger till Mendocino. Candy said she would wait right here.

I stared at her. "You're not coming in?"

"I'll wait here. But hurry."

Gina and I bought chicken, biscuits and Cokes, and sat in a booth. After spending ten minutes mostly silently eating and only briefly wondering what was wrong with Candy *now*, Gina ran to the restroom to wash her hands and apply a fresh coat of lipstick ("Who are you trying to impress? It's only us in the car") while I finished eating. I was about to get up and throw out the trash when a man sat down—in *my* booth.

I thought at first he'd made a mistake, with such purpose did he slide into the seat across from me. I even smiled, ready to accept his abashed apology. Oh, sorry, thought you were my sister, something like that.

But he didn't apologize, and didn't leave. He was wearing black and brown clothes, a studded leather belt and gold chains. His shirt-buttons were opened one too many, his chest hair grizzly. He was in his thirties, I'd guess, and his long, matted blond hair, cultivated to look unkempt, drooped to his shoulders. His eyebrows and eyelashes were bleached-out red; his cheeks and chin fuzzed with week-old stubble. He had two fresh cuts on his forehead. His unblinking blue eyes stared at me intensely from across the table. "Do you know who I am?" His voice was low and slow, with some kind of twang. Not New York.

"No."

"She didn't tell you about me?"

"Who?"

"Don't pretend with me, darlin'," he said. "Do I look in the mood for games?"

"What?"

"Your little hitchhiker."

Because I've always had trouble putting two and two together, I said like a dunce, "What hitchhiker?"

"Let me tell you how it goes," he drawled, slower and more menacing, leaning across and banging the table with a stiff index finger. "She ran away, and I've been looking for her for two weeks. Her mother's frantic with fear."

"Who?" I stammered. What I meant was, "Who are you?" but was just too turgid to get the rest out. It did occur to me in a flicker that at any second Gina would come back, Gina, who was quicker on her feet and who felt nothing for Candy's predicament, and who would not hesitate to say, oh, Candy, she's in the 'Stang. The blood left my brain. What little remained in my empty skull, however, told me loud and clear that I did *not* want to point this man in the direction of the girl who had pressed herself into me at our last rest stop to hide, who spent her time traveling with her head as low as the Chihuahuas, and who was now in the backseat of our car, waiting. I didn't know if he was telling me the truth, and I didn't want to get into an argument with him about my deep skepticism. Stunned and confused I said nothing that would point a finger to the parking lot and my car. Desperately trying not to gasp, I said, "I don't know what you're—"

"Look, missy, don't play fucking dumb with me. I talked to the driver of the black truck, the one who kicked her out in Maryland. He's a friend of mine. He told me about you and your little yellow Shelby."

"The who? The what?"

"We've had trucks trailing you through four states."

"*Trailing* me?" Or did I mean, trailing *me*?

"*Tracking* you! You'd disappear, reappear." He wiped spit from

169

his mouth. "They've been on the lookout for my kid. First in Pennsylvania, then Ohio, then off the map, then in Illinois, then off the map again, and this morning, back on the road here. I been following you since Staunton myself. Now—where is she?"

"Mister," I said, "I promise you, I didn't pick up no one who got kicked out of a black truck in Maryland. We didn't stop for nobody. I can promise you that." Suddenly talking like a girl whose lifetime ambition was to become night manager at Dairy Barn.

"Is that so?" he said, biting off his filthy nails and spitting them on the floor.

Cringing, I nodded. Please, Gina, please, apply one extra coat of lipstick.

"My name is Erv Bruggeman," he said, through his tight cold mouth. "My daughter ran away. She ain't eighteen yet and she needs to come home. She's breaking her mother's heart."

"I'm sorry about that."

He looked over the cups on the table. There were two cups of Coke, two half-empty baskets of chicken. There was no third basket.

"Where's your yellow 'Stang?"

"Well, I do have a yellow Mustang," I said, ruing the day. "But there are only two of us in the car." My fingers were shaking.

"Why your hands all nervous?"

"My mother told me never to talk to strangers," I said quietly, not looking at him, breathing out the words in a whispered lie.

"That was good advice. Candy's mother told her the same thing. Did she listen? Not by a long shot. Now, let me make *myself* perfectly clear," he said. "I need to find her not today, not tomorrow, but yesterday. You got that? You're telling me you don't got her. I say you lyin'. You too nervous to be telling the truth."

"I never met you before and you're talking to me like that," I said. "Of course I'm nervous."

"Well, you've got every reason to be afraid. I'm a scary guy. And I ain't stoppin' till I find her. Until I do, you and your little friend don't have a safe place on an inch of asphalt in this country,

170

'cause I got friends all over who are looking out for me, *all over*, you get what I'm telling you?"

Oh God! "Listen, mister, you wanna find your kid, I understand," I said, trying not to cry. "But don't threaten me here in Roy Rogers, okay? Let's call the police, and they'll help you find your girl. I saw a police car right outside. Let's go to them. They'll help you. They do this sort of thing all the time, find runaways."

"You think you're being smart?" He leaned forward again, his hard face stonier, colder.

"No." I was all little. I needed Gina.

"Listen, you smart-ass. I don't need pigs and smokies in my business. She can't hide from me. And you can't hide her from me, neither."

I tried to get up. "Okay, then, well, best of luck to you." What an idiot.

He grabbed my wrist, I yelped, sat back down. "Don't touch me," I whispered.

"Listen very careful to what I'm telling you," Erv said. "She took something that belongs to me, something that's mine, and I don't like people taking my stuff. Tell me where she is, and then it's not your problem anymore. You get into your yellow bird and fly away; don't think about her, or me, or anything. Just do what you do—which is nothing. Get me? It's so simple, and you wipe your hands clean. Trust me when I tell you, you don't want me on your tail. Now—"

That's the moment Gina picked to come back, all lipsticked and shiny, focusing on the man and frowning.

"He says he's looking for his daughter who ran away," I gabbled, struggling to my feet, not giving him a chance to interrupt. "He thinks we picked her up in Maryland." I was shaking, staring straight at Gina, who looked at me, trash in her hands, looked him over, and said casually, "What girl?"

I wanted to kiss her.

"Oh, for fuck's sake!" Erv sprang out of the booth. We staggered away, clutching each other.

171

"Mister, I told you and told you," I said, "we don't know about no girl. Go talk to the police, if you want to."

"I'm gonna follow you to your car," he said, pointing his dirty, bitten-bloody finger at us. "I'm gonna follow you down the highway. I'm gonna stop at every station you stop, at every hotel. I know all the motel managers from here to Oakland. How do you think you gonna hide from me? Where do you think you gonna go?"

Gina pulled me by the arm. "A strange and threatening man following two girls to their car in the parking lot? You know what I'm going to do? Talk to the cops. There's a patrol car outside. Shel, let's go talk to the police officer."

Together we backed away from him, then turned around and started walking. I couldn't even allow myself a glance, a breath behind me to see if he was following us. The police officer was inside buying a cup of coffee. Gina asked if he wouldn't mind walking us to our car because there was a strange man bothering us near the fried chicken. "What man?" the cop asked.

"Right there. Near the French fries." We pointed, but Erv Bruggeman was gone, vanished just the way Candy had in front of those truckers, vanished as if he didn't want the officer even briefly to see his face.

The cop walked us across the filled-up parking lot. "Nice 'Stang," he said, smiling. "Yours?"

"Yes, thank you. A graduation present."

"Nice, very nice. Well, be careful, you two. Don't drive too fast. Easy to do in that one. And don't talk to strangers."

"Yes, thank you, we won't, have a nice day, officer." Carefully, sideways, I glanced in. The backseat was empty! Candy was gone. We jumped in and locked the doors.

"Start the car," Gina said. "Quick. Start the car and peel away. Go."

"Gina . . ."

"Go!"

"What about . . ."

"Go!"

172

I started the engine.

"Oh my God, Gina, what are we going to do?"

"About what?"

"About Candy."

"Nothing."

"But she's there, with him! How's she going to get out?"

"Why'd she leave the car? Not our business anymore, Sloane. She can go to the police, like we went to the police. Besides," she added, "if he really is her dad, who are we to get in the middle of a family squabble?"

"But what if he's not her dad?"

"Not our problem."

"No?" I whispered.

"No," Gina said adamantly. "Drive, Shelby."

"Gina, I can't just leave her. I told her I'd take her to I-80."

"Yes, and you told *me* you wouldn't pick up any hitchhikers. You're not exactly as good as your word."

But I was stuck, I couldn't put my foot on the gas.

"That sick fuck is going to come to your car and smash your windows in, and then bash our brains in," said Gina. "Did you see him? Can you just go?"

She appealed to fear, and it worked. Taking one last desperate look around the parking lot for sight of a spiked pink head, I reluctantly drove away. We left the rest area, got onto I-55, found our way to local Route 72, and then drove west in darkened silence.

"Shelby, do you know what the lesson of that story is?"

"No."

"Don't ask for someone else's trouble. Don't talk to strangers. Don't pick up hitchhikers. Mind your own damn business. Keep your head down. There are so many lessons, we're going to need half a country just to sort them all out." Gina had adopted a light tone. "It's a good thing we got that kind of time in front of us." She had come late into my and Erv's discussion, she hadn't looked into his soulless glare, hadn't felt fear like me. Perhaps she wouldn't have from the get-go.

"Gina, did we leave her in a place where a psychotic man is looking for her?"

"Have you seen the way she behaves? It's only right that she should belong to him."

"Oh, Gina."

She patted my arm. "It's gonna be fine. Cheer up. At least we're rid of her. Hey, did you know it's against the law to get a fish drunk in Ohio?"

I didn't smile. "Glad we're not in Ohio."

"We may be. Have you looked at a map lately?" Gina pretended to think. "I hope you're not thinking of hunting camels in Arizona. Because that's also a no-no."

"I'm not thinking about it right now." I took my grip off the wheel. We were doing thirty on a local road. We had been traveling eighty on the Interstate. Now we were stopping at every light like we were back in Baltimore. The word Baltimore set me off, made me recall things. I felt so bleak. I was relieved for me, but so upset for her. My hands gripped the wheel again. "What have we done?" I whispered.

"Saved our skins," asserted Gina. "Doesn't that have any value?"

"But he was so freaky."

"Exactly." Gina nodded fulsomely. "She's not so normal herself. Shel, are we going to be passing through Wyoming?"

"At this rate, not in my lifetime, no."

"Well, if we are," Gina calmly continued, "we better avoid having sex in a butcher's shop's meat freezer."

Before I had a chance to chuckle, we heard a sound from the back, a strange, scratching sound. We stopped talking, and there it was again, like something thumping against the backseat. My hands clamped around the wheel. With the next thump, the seat back fell forward, and from the recesses of the dark trunk, crawled Candy.

"Oh my God," said Gina, putting her face in her hands.

Candy climbed out, pushed the seat back to its upright position, stretched, and sat looking at us. "You're right not to trust

174

him," she said. "He's no good." She paused, while we remained without speech. "He is not my father."

"Oh my God," Gina repeated. "Is this ever going to end? Ever?"

We were stopped at a light; it turned green, I didn't notice until an angry honk from a Greyhound bus.

"I should've known," said Gina. "I suspected something was wrong with you. I should've known you were trouble, you with your skanky makeup and tattoos. What are we going to do with you now?"

"Who is he?" I breathed out.

"No, don't ask," Gina interrupted.

"What are you afraid of, Gina?"

"That she'll tell us!"

"You don't want to know?"

"No!" Gina turned to the back. "I'm sorry you didn't just get out and hide someplace else. I'm sorry you're still here, making our simple life so screwed up. I'm sorry we ever picked you up. I don't want you in our car. I wish you'd go away. I thought so from the very beginning."

"I know," said Candy. "You've never hidden it."

"Why didn't you just go back with him?"

"He's not my dad, I told you," said Candy. "He's the man my mother lives with."

"Your stepfather, then?" Gina said, attempting to be acerbically clever.

"Would be if my mother was actually married to him. She isn't."

She was talking, she was back there, and I don't know what Gina was thinking or feeling, but two feelings of equal weight were boxing it out inside me during these middle rounds. My whole soul wanted to sigh with despair that this day and this part of my life were not over, but at the same time I was being knocked out by relief that I didn't abandon her in the truck stop with a man who was not her father and not her stepfather, yet needed to find her not today, not tomorrow—but yesterday.

"Is your mother really worried?"

175

Candy shrugged in the rearview. "I'm not entirely convinced she knows I'm gone."

"Candy, he said you weren't eighteen," Gina said.

She didn't reply.

We sat. I drove. What are we going to do now? Who asked that question? Did anyone speak? Sheepishly, Candy picked up the atlas lying in the footwell and started examining it, like she knew where we were. "Oh, look," she said. "Shel, there's a whole town named after you. Shelbyville. We're going to pass it soon."

"What are you talking about?" I whispered.

She didn't answer.

"How old are you, Candy?"

"Don't ask, Sloane," said Gina.

"For once, she may be right, Sloane," said Candy. "Don't ask."

"For *once?*" Gina's voice was irksome and high.

"I'm kidding."

"If you're not eighteen," I said, "perhaps he's got a right to look for you."

"He has no rights at all," she said. "If he had any rights, you think he wouldn't have gone to the cops?"

"I don't know. What about your mom?"

"Don't you think if she had any rights, she'd have gone to the cops?"

"Are these rhetorical questions?" Gina snapped. "Your *mother* has no rights to you?"

"Let it go, Gina," said Candy.

I glanced in my rearview mirror at her pinched face. It was superimposed on Bruggeman's ice face, his blank gaze telling me he was capable of anything and everything. We passed through Shelbyville. We didn't stop. Candy said she knew of a place we could stop, and it wouldn't be very expensive; it was near Rock Island in the Quad Cities, Iowa. We were all thirsty. Music made us thirsty and shallow, reduced everything to a parched throat and a few miles of corn fields. Don't give up on us, baby. Boogie woogie woogie, get down, if only you believe in miracles, baby. Baby, come back.

"Candy, I'm telling you, I will not take you all the way to Paradise," I said. "So think quick of what else I can do to help you, as long as it doesn't include that. Okay?"

"Okay."

"Was Erv his real name?"

"Yes," she said.

"Would you like to tell me how Erv Bruggeman found me and my car?"

"Probably Citizens Band radios. All the trucks carry them."

"How would you know anything about CB radios?"

"Erv has had many dealings with truckers over the years," she replied.

"What kind of dealings?"

"The shady kind. Truckers live on C-band. They can find anyone. Erv was able to locate a friend of his in New Mexico using one of those things."

"If you're a runaway, why doesn't he call the police? The law's on his side, you know," Gina said.

Candy shook her head. "Law's not on his side, *believe* me."

"Well, we got us a situation," I said. "Because my car is the most conspicuous car on the freeway. Once we get on I-80, another truck will spot me in five seconds. I'm like the sun on the horizon. Seen from all directions. They'll give your Erv my location faster than we can stop for gas. Which, by the way, we're going to have to do soon. I was shocked into an idiotic response the first time. I won't be able to fake it the second." It dawned on me. "Is *that* why you've been hiding out in the back?"

"You just realized this?" said Candy.

"But why would they think you got into our car?"

"Probably because of fucking Trent in the black truck," she said. "He squealed like a pig."

Gina, too, was beginning to comprehend a few things. She was twirling her hair, and twitching her lip in assent. "Well, clearly you can't be traveling with us in the yellow car," she said triumphantly. I said nothing. She might be beginning to

177

understand a few things, but not all things, not even the most important things.

What Gina wasn't getting was this: if not in my yellow Shelby, bright as the sun, how *was* Candy going to travel? She couldn't get inside a truck, and who else would take her anywhere? She looked so desperately endangered. She was like a white tiger. Any man who picked her up could be looking only for trouble; girls wouldn't pick her up: she looked too threatening with her kohl eyes, ruby lips and blue mini-skirts.

Though *we* had picked her up.

I know Gina was hoping that it would soon stop being our problem, that somewhere between Shelbyville and Dixon, between the Illinois and Iowa fields, Candy would be gone. But even if she were, how could I convince Bruggeman, who'd catch up with me on the straight line that was the cross-country open road, that Candy wasn't with us? I could let him search our car. Perhaps he could travel to California with us, sitting where Candy now sat, just to make sure. I felt sick. I felt nauseated. I don't know how I continued to drive even thirty miles an hour. I kept blowing all lights.

Gina finally caught on to something. I'm not saying she caught on to much. But something became illuminated. "Sloane, why are you so glum? What are you so worried about? Look at you. You look like death."

"*She* may not be our problem. But Erv is definitely our problem."

In the back Candy didn't speak. Her lips were moving, her voice inaudible.

"What are you doing?" I asked.

"Praying."

"Why?"

"St. Paul told us to pray without ceasing."

Candy might as well have blinked and turned herself into a fruit fly. Her words seemed that incongruous, like pigs having wings. After what seemed like minutes of Gina looking at me with an expression of rank befuddlement, she finally said, "I think the time for prayer has long passed."

"Oh, not at all," said Candy. "It's just beginning."

"You know what?" Gina said. "No offense, but you don't seem like the kind of girl who prays, pardon me for saying."

"How little you understand. I'm exactly the kind of girl who prays. You know why? Because I desperately need help."

We were going too slow for clarity. Speed is better for thinking through difficult things, for navigating through the turns of a treacherous mind. "Okay," I said. "Erv is looking for you. Why? Does he want you to come home?"

"Not necessarily."

"Hear me out. He wants you to come home. But you don't want to come home. So? Eventually he'll relent. I mean, eventually even you will turn eighteen and won't be called a runaway, right?"

"I'm not called a runaway now. Who calls me that? The police? They don't know I've gone. You? What's wrong with your thinking is what I said before. He doesn't want me home. The rest doesn't apply—relenting or whatnot."

"Don't you want to go back home?"

"I don't know," Candy said. "I'm never going back. Is that the same thing?"

I didn't think it was the same thing.

"Why is he looking for you?" I yelled. Did I sound hysterical? I think so. I didn't care.

"But Erv told Sloane he wanted you to come home," said Gina, putting a steadying hand on my arm. "Was he lying?"

"He was lying."

"So what does he want with you then?"

"To kill me."

Here was the gasp. Gina clutched to my arm. "He *what?*"

"Better stay off the Interstate, Shel," said Candy.

"What are you talking about?" Gina blurted. "You don't mean that. Why would he want to do that?" I don't know how I continued driving.

"Because I know too much." She was simple and direct. Somber now, not funny or sheepish. Plain spoken and grim.

179

"*You* know too much?" Gina finally managed to say. "Is that even possible?"

"Yes." Candy wouldn't be baited. "I may not know about your little music. But I know about some things. I know too much about him."

"And for this he wants to kill you?"

"Yes."

"Come on, you're exaggerating! You're being melodramatic."

"I don't know what that is. Don't believe me, if you don't want."

"Oh, Shelby," said Gina. "Oh. Shelby."

Oh Shelby was right.

I drove so slowly that I finally had to pull off on the shoulder.

"Don't stop," Candy said. "Just keep going."

"I begged you!" Gina cried, glaring at me. "I said don't stop the car!"

"All right," I snapped. "You were right, okay? It's too late for I told yous. Now we have to figure out what to do."

"Don't ask her any more questions, that's one. You keep asking and asking. You're just finding out things you don't want to know. Stop asking. And you"—Gina turned to Candy, sticking her finger out—"don't tell us anymore! We don't want to know. Understand?"

"Whether or not we know," I said, "we still have to deal with it."

"No, we don't. We don't have to deal with anything."

"He's going to find you," Candy said to Gina. "Confront you again. He's following you as we speak. He followed you to Illinois, he is following you now. He's convinced you lied about hiding me. You didn't fool him; he's got a sense about these things. He was right, you *were* lying, and he knows it. By the time you get to Iowa-80, which is the busiest rest stop in the country, he'll have every truck alerted to your yellow canary. You won't be able to move one mile down that highway."

Gina lost it. For a few aggrieved minutes, she flailed her arms and cried unquietly. "I don't want to be here. I want to go home! I want my mother."

"Me too," I said, quieter, grimmer.

"Not me," said Candy.

"Maybe Eddie has a car," I said, almost musing.

"Eddie? What does Eddie have to do with this?" Gina shrieked.

I was taken aback. "Well, nothing," I said. I began to tremble. "But maybe he can drive out, meet you."

"We might need to get closer than Ohio, don't you think?" Gina said acidly.

"We *are* closer than Ohio. We're nearly in Iowa."

"Closer than that."

"How close do we have to be, Gina," asked Candy, "before your future husband drives out and helps you?"

"Shut the fuck up!" Gina stared at me pointedly, and Candy caught it.

"What are you giving *her* dirty looks for? She's the only one driving."

Thus we drove through the corn fields of Missouri, winding our way on local roads, dreading the Interstate, which I instinctively felt would be our undoing, even if I didn't quite have a plan of how to avoid it. Neither did I know what to do with the tattooed chick in our backseat, or about the fact that we needed gas and food, or that I hadn't slept, and in Candy's words, "was the only one driving." We needed a plan. I had to get to Mendocino. Gina had to get to Bakersfield. Candy had to get to Paradise. Gina was upset, I was upset, but Gina was upset and helpless, while I was upset and without a plan. That was different. I wasn't thinking about the past, what I could do to undo it. I didn't think I could have done anything differently, that was the sober truth. It was only the first time, when I drove by her in Maryland, that I could, and did, look away.

I was becoming so bitter at my lack of plan, not the most attractive quality for an eighteen-year-old who patted herself on the back for her level-headedness and spiral notebook abilities. Fear was breeding square unthinking resentment in my heart.

We had to stop. No, let's keep going. Yes, she's right. If we stop, we'll be like flies, suddenly we'll run out of life. We go, go, go . . .

"Yes, and then flies die."

Pause. By everyone.

"Bad analogy. Let's keep going."

"We should stop. We have to figure out where to let her off."
That was Gina.

"I'm not stopping," I said. "Remember what happened last time
we stopped?"

"We'll need gas."

"Not yet."

"Shelby."

"Gina."

At a light, we both turned to face the girl in the backseat.
"Candy," I said, "do *you* have a plan?"

She nodded.

"Does your plan include me making it to California to find my
mother?"

"Hope so."

"Oh, she hopes so!"

But yelling at Candy was like yelling at a child. She became
overwhelmed and saddened, slunk into the seat, shutting her eyes.
But there was no denying it—we had a situation on our hands, a
situation intensified by the hissing whisper to my right. Gina was
whispering, thinking Candy, whose eyes were closed, couldn't hear.

"What?" I said, full of irritated exhaustion. "I can't hear you."

"Shelby, you're acting like a building fell on your head. You're
not even blinking. Wake up. It's not our problem."

"Did you see his face?" I said. "Did you see his eyes?"

"*Not* our problem."

"He is going to kill her."

"So she says."

"Does she strike you as the melodramatic type?"

"She strikes me as a type who needs to get the fuck out of our
car."

"And then what?"

"Not our problem."

I steadied my gaze on the road, hands on the wheel.

We were hungry. We had to use the restroom. What did Candy know about Bruggeman that was so bad he was willing to kill her for it? He said she took something of his he wanted back. My Larchmont self, who'd barely been out of the driveway and led a safe downtown life, couldn't comprehend it. Did Bruggeman cheat on indifferent Mom? Did he have a child by his mistress? Was he abusive? Certainly—*certainly*, Candy looked like the kind of girl who'd seen one of everything, and two of some things. But what could she have seen that would make a terrible man like Erv Bruggeman chase her from Maryland to St. Louis, and farther perhaps?

What would make Bruggeman summon the support of a fleet of 6000 truck drivers? My daughter has run away. She's only seventeen. She's been troubled her whole life. Help me find her. Please. Who wouldn't help a concerned father find his little girl? And if that wasn't the truth, what was?

Before I was out of my nightmare, Candy woke up. She said she was thirsty. We all were. How could I let her stay in my car? I didn't know her. She could well be lying. She was a kid, and Bruggeman was a grown-up. A scary grown-up, but a grown-up. I wasn't sure I could trust him, but I knew I couldn't trust her. The only thing I knew of her was that she was the kind of girl who would go into a room late at night and give a blowjob to the husband of a woman who had fed her and given her shelter. Was that kind of girl capable of anything? I didn't know. I had never met that kind of girl.

After looking at the map, Gina said I-80 was coming up. Candy counted out the miles on her fingers. This was ridiculous. We had to stop. But stopping meant I'd have to make a decision on what to do with her. And I'd be out of gas before I willingly made one. Was Bruggeman going to help me?

Was Candy?

It was me, I was at fault. This whole thing was my fault. And now, to hide from myself, and to avoid confronting Gina, I was driving on local roads through Missouri.

Finally, after the gas light was on for longer than imaginable, I made a series of turns to get away even from the two-lane road we were on, and stopped at a tiny joint, almost on a dirt road, a Ma and Pa wooden shack travel stop, which served coffee, as well as gas. And after refueling, we got a burnt coffee and sat at a picnic table in the back where the local boys must go to smoke because the butts on the ground were like wood chips. We sat across from each other and at cross purposes.

"We have to figure it out," I said at last.

"There's nothing to figure out," said Gina.

"No?" said Candy. "What are you going to do when Bruggeman finds you in Iowa? When he won't take no for an answer?"

"I'm going to tell him the truth," said Gina. "She's not with me. See? It'll be so simple. You know why? Because you won't be with me."

"It won't matter," retorted Candy. "He knows you were lying to him in Springfield, and hid behind the police to get away."

"I'll take my chances," Gina said bravely. "The truth will set me free."

"Not with him."

It was six in the evening.

"Candy, what are we supposed to do?" I asked.

"Stay off the Interstate," said Candy. "That's first."

"For how long?"

"Permanently."

"Permanently?" Gina raised her voice. "Well, how are we going to get all the way to fucking California if we stay off the Interstate?"

"What did people do before the Interstate?" I piped in.

"What did they do before the Interstate?" exclaimed Gina. "What did they do before shampoo, or eye glasses, or cars? I suppose they took their horse and buggy across the fucking prairie and washed their hair with ashes. But what does that have to do with us, what people did before the Interstate?"

"Fewer trucks off the Interstate," said Candy. "Less likely to be spotted."

"Yes, and if we found a cave, and sat in it for the rest of our lives, we'd be less likely to get spotted, too. We need to get going. I don't know about you, Candy, but Sloane and I have some place to be."

"Gina's right," I said. "It's taken us all day to go sixty-nine miles, after running into Candy's father."

"He's not my father."

"This is a big country, Candy," I continued. "The 4000 miles aren't going to drive themselves. And I don't know about your division skills, but 69 into 4000 is a fuckload of days."

Gina oohed at my dry wit and my swearing. Candy didn't. We gulped our coffees. I got out my notebook. I wasn't sure what to do. I'm always unsure what to do, which is why I usually end up doing nothing. Opening the notebook always made me feel, perhaps falsely, that I was about to devise some kind of plan and do something. "All right, girls," I said. "What do you see as our options?"

"We leave her here, we go," said Gina.

Candy said nothing.

This is the difference between dogs and people. Dogs—mighty annoying to have in a confined space, smelling of wet fur and farts; dogs—stepping in poop, licking their own balls, then expecting you to allow them to tongue-kiss you—all that was child's play, a measly game of jacks compared to the trouble a non-odorous, non-ball-licking (at least not her own) stranger brought into my life.

"Candy," I said. "You know this isn't fair what you're doing."

She nodded. "I know."

"It isn't right." But she knew my weakness, even if Gina, my friend since early childhood didn't. Gina, my friend since sandbox days, pre-school days, neighbors down the block, played in diapers, went to kindergarten, to elementary school, to junior high, to high school, were thick as thieves, and our honor was as thick, too. And it showed. And this stranger, a girl I've known for five minutes, knew about me what Gina didn't know and refused to know. Candy knew I did not want to be like the Black Truck Driver. *I do me—you do you* was not going to become my motto. Perhaps it had

185

been my motto to this point. I never really did think of anyone but myself. I didn't think of Gina when I stopped wanting to be friends with her because she became friends with Agnes, the dog of girls. I didn't think of Emma when I yelled those nasty things to her every time I got mad, I didn't think of Marc, or Gina's mother, or my friend Melissa, who wanted to come with us and whom I told no, because I thought she was too needy. I never thought about anybody but me. And it showed. I had no regrets. I was young, that's what the young are supposed to do, not think about much, not think about consequences, and so I hadn't. But I didn't want *that* black truck motto as my bumper sticker, no matter how funny it was to the passers-by. Perhaps *because* it was funny to the passers-by. It certainly had been funny to us.

"I just want to get to Paradise," said Candy, looking into her Styrofoam cup.

"I know," I snapped impatiently. "Who doesn't know this? Does Erv know this? That you're headed there?"

"No, I don't think so," she replied.

"What about your mother? Where's her allegiance?" Gina demanded.

For a long time Candy didn't answer, and when she spoke, she couldn't look at either of us. "Not with me."

We were all quiet after that.

"Like I said, Sloane," said Gina. "It's no choice at all."

"Let's paint the car," said Candy. "Paint it black, or something."

"Paint it black," I said. "That's good. That's rich. Should we do it ourselves, in the parking lot of Earl Scheib?"

"Who?"

"Painting the car costs money. I don't know how much but it's not cheap."

"Let's find out," said Candy. "In Quad Cities, we can find a paint store, ask."

"Paint store? You mean body shop?"

"Whatever."

Gina groaned in disgust. "My father painted his station wagon last year. It was a Chevy wagon, but it cost him a thousand dollars, and he didn't care about matching the car or lowering its value. To paint a Mustang is going to require some hefty cash. And afterward, it'll be worth nothing. You'll see."

"Let's look into it when we get there," said Candy.

"No. We shouldn't paint the car," Gina said. "We should leave you and get going, is what we should do."

"Gina, come on," I said quietly. I looked into my spiral. I had an empty page in front of me. Picking up a pencil, I wrote: Number 1. Look into car painting. Number 2. Think straight.

I couldn't think straight. I didn't want to glance at Candy and her doe-brown eyes. "Let's get to this place Candy knows, and then we'll figure out what to do. Candy, can we let you off there?"

"I don't know," she said. "If you wish. If you want to, you can let me off anywhere."

"Here?" Gina said, enthusiastically, and then was mock-deflated when she saw my glaring face. We threw away our Styrofoam cups, and got back on the road.

We were all young. We rebelled against despair, went into self-defense mode. Candy started talking about music, asking Gina questions. "What's the best song you've heard all year? Really? Why? And what about last year? What's this disco thing? Is it any good? You say you can dance to it? No, I've never heard 'I Will Survive.' Should I have? So what's Larchmont like? Are you close to the sea? Are there mountains? What is this Westchester? Shel, did you like living in Larchmont? Did Emma?" She didn't spit out the word *Larchmont* the way she spat out the word *Ppppparadise*, as if maggots lived there. But then why was she going to a place that disgusted her?

Thus we whiled away what remained of the road between Missouri and Rock Island, Iowa, on the Mississippi River. We sputtered forty miles an hour in my souped-up eight-cylinder, 350 horsepower, tiny loose cannon of a yellow car, a car that was like the Bullseye on the Royal Airforce planes during the war, making it so easy for Germans to see them and shoot them down. We got to the Quad Cities near sunset, so near sunset that we didn't have time to find a better place to park. We stopped at a rocky embankment near an industrial district and warehouses off River Avenue. There was a gazebo, and children's swings, some ducks in the water. Other people had come out, too. Gina said it was ridiculous to stop here when we were all so hungry and tired, but Candy said, "Gina, look, it's sunset over the Mississippi."

"Yeah? So? It's a sun and it's setting. Happens every day. After the kind of day we've had, excuse me for not waxing misty-eyed." Gina walked away and, propped by a tree, stood with her arms crossed.

Candy pointed across the river at a moored riverboat called "Isle of Capri." That was our hotel, she said, and she and I walked away, leaving Gina to herself.

Sometimes words fail me. Often they do. Our stomachs were empty and scared, our hearts sore and disappointed. I know mine was. I know Gina's was. This wasn't what I wanted. It wasn't what Gina wanted. But going to Baltimore and to Three Oaks, and to De Soto wasn't what I wanted either. And living without a mother wasn't what I wanted. Or a father. Or siblings. Out of this whole shebang, Candy was the only thing I chose.

I know this was why Gina was upset with me, and angry. I knew what she wanted back is what we had five minutes before Picnic Marsh, before that traffic light in Fremont. The dogs, the idle conversation about Valparaiso, the mild boredom, the anticipation of something. I knew, because I wanted it back, too. Perhaps it was the boredom that got us here. We were looking for something. And sure enough, sometimes when you look for something, you find it.

I felt absurdly responsible for our predicament, and scared for Candy, which was novel for me, feeling anxious for another human being instead of for myself.

But the sunset over the mighty river *was* blazing. For five minutes, in my head, it had stopped raining nails.

SIX

ISLE OF CAPRI

1

Eighteen and Twenty-one

I don't know how Candy knew of this place. Isle of Capri Casino Boat and Hotel. It was so cheesy with its stained old red velvet carpet. I asked her about it as we waited in line at the reception desk.

"Been here once before," she said, sucking a cinnamon Life Saver, making her breath fresh.

"Been here once before?" I said. "In *Iowa?*"

She didn't elaborate despite our stares. She was funny like that. She said there was a buffet, but it closed at nine. There was, and it did. We just made it with ten minutes to spare, and the crabby waitress said, "We'll be closing in five minutes, girls, if you want to go and get more."

The pot roast was dry, the chicken wings not spicy, the cabbage cold. We didn't care, we were so hungry. I had valeted my car, hoping that the valet parking lot was in the bowels of the building somewhere, not outside. It was dark. When we got back to the room, I fell on the bed, exhausted. Candy did not share my energy level. She wanted to go gambling.

"Candy, you're seventeen years old. Do you even have a fake ID?"

She showed me her ID. Candy Cane, it said, born May 11, 1963. "Candy . . . but that makes you eighteen."

"Yeah? So?" she said calmly. "What kind of a fake ID would it be if it made me my actual age?"

"Not a very good fake ID," said Gina, sitting on the bed. "When's your actual birthday?"

"November 11, 1963. Off by a few days."

"A few days?"

"Sure." She smiled. "What's 180 days in the scheme of things?"

I stared despondently at the ceiling as if hoping to find counsel there. Score that one for Erv. So he was telling the truth about something. What else was he telling the truth about?

Candy put on more gloop, and another shirt; she changed from blue to black, kept on the same blue mini-skirt, making me believe she only had the one, and said, come on let's go. Gina got ready herself. She'd never been gambling and was curious. I was drained. I didn't want to be a spoil sport, though; the girls were going, so what was I going to do, stay home like an old cranky mother, say, you young 'uns go, I'll sit here and knit? So we all put on our jean skirts and our faces, red lips and cheap perfume, we shared Jovan Musk between us, hoping it would smell different on each one of us, and took off for the casino boat, but not before I showed some practical angst. "How much is this going to cost? I can't bring too much. I didn't budget for this. I don't want to lose all my money."

"Why would you lose all your money, Shel?" said Candy. "You're so funny. Bring only what you want to lose, no more."

"Can I bring nothing? Because that's all I want to lose."

"Bring a few bucks."

"I didn't budget for this . . . I'll bring five dollars . . . oh, cover charge. Well, I didn't plan for more than two covers, and this is my second, so I'll bring ten dollars, but that's it."

"Bring twenty."

I'd never been to a casino, and didn't know what to expect. The young man taking my money and checking IDs at the door, smiled flirtatiously at us. "You girls ready to have some fun?"

"Well, we're certainly going to try," said Candy, raising her eyebrows. "That's what we came here for, some fun."

"You came to the right place." The lad grinned, but it turned out he was having us on, being wise with us, because under the merciless fluorescents, it didn't look like anyone was having fun. Middle-aged people in polyester suits sat near poker machines, pressing down on the big metal handles. The place was filled with cigarette smoke and men in cowboy boots. Some older men shuffled from game to game, from seat to seat, with beer in their hands. They must have spent all their money, because they were watching, not gambling, but watching in a desperate way that told me they'd be pulling that lever, too, if only they hadn't lost their last quarter.

Candy walked around and we followed. She seemed to know her way around, so she led. She didn't plant down anywhere, just watched, looking at the people playing the tables. Everywhere, at the blackjack tables, standing bunched and hunched over the roulette, people looked like they'd just lost their dog and were hungry.

"Why is everyone so gloomy?" I asked.

"They're losing."

The overweight couple with their little buckets of quarters rattling under the glaring lights, the wife saying to the husband, give me more, and the husband saying, I only got a couple left, Doris, did you spend all yours? She wasn't answering, Candy told us, because she was praying to Five Flower, the Aztec god of dance and games. "What do you know about Five Flower?" I said to her as we approached the blackjack tables.

"Not much, Shelby," Candy said, "but I know one or two things."

We watched two hands. The first time the dealer got a twenty-one after six cards, while the four victims each had two face cards equaling twenty. There was no stirring of hands or expression, no gasp of disappointment. One badly-dressed older woman took a sip of her drink, while the three men pushed their ante forward. The next hand, everybody's cards were awful and the dealer bust, and still no one made a sound, except to scoop their winnings into separate, meager piles.

"Do you know how to play blackjack?" I asked Candy.

193

"I do," she replied. "But I'm not going to play. No fun here."

"That implies that there's fun elsewhere."

"More fun other places, yes."

We continued our amble. Many of the tables were empty, dealers standing shuffling cards, trying to tempt us to sit down. We sat down. Candy tried to teach me, but I was a poor student, dunce-like in my denseness. I did what? What did I have to do? I had to give the grumpy Asian woman dealer five dollars of my money, and for that she would give me two cards? And the two cards had to come very close to twenty-one or equal twenty-one. "But what do I do to help the cards be twenty-one?"

"Nothing," said Candy. "But if the two cards add up to a small number, like a five or a six, you can ask for another card."

"Do I have to *pay* for another card?" I was so pragmatic. I liked that in myself.

"No!" Exasperated.

So I tried. I gave Asian Grumpy five bucks and bought a Jack (which Candy said counted as ten), and a two. "Now what?"

"Ask for another card."

I did. It was another Jack. Candy shook her head. "Twenty-two. Not good, kid. You bust. Wanna play again?"

"Why would I?"

But I did. I gave the silent woman another five dollars and this time got a ten and a three. "Now what?"

"Ask for another card."

"But what if I get another ten?"

"That's the risk you take. You can hold at thirteen if you want."

"I'll hold." The dealer got twenty. Gina and Candy glared at me as if it were my fault. "That's it," I said, taking my three chips and jumping off the stool. "I don't want to play anymore."

But then two studs came over and sat down next to us; the waitress took our drink orders, and they played while I watched. Gina lost a little, won a little, but Candy steadily won while the dealer steadily lost, turning her twenty dollars into $150 before my drink was up. The boys, impressed with her skills, begged her to impress them further, and she duly obliged. In five minutes Candy made more than *twice* the money that Gina and I had made driving 800 miles across three state lines to deposit two dogs into a home of a woman who nearly came after us with a shotgun.

"I don't understand how you did that," said Gina. "How could you bet a *hundred* bucks?"

"Fearlessly. Bet if you feel like you're going to win. If you feel like a loser, walk away from the table. Keep the stakes low if you're cold. Ride it out. But if you're hot, bet your house, baby, because the cards are with you."

"But you could've lost!"

She shrugged. "So? It's not my rent money. This is just found money. I still would've had more than I started with, which, as you remember, was nuthin'."

The boys didn't want to leave Candy's side, were mesmerized by her long bare legs, smiling, enigmatic eyes, and painted lips. This vision, perched on a bar stool, was making their heads swim. Clearly, the Jovan Musk did smell best on her. Even the name Geeeena did nothing for these drunken gambling boys.

Finally Candy grabbed her money, stopped smiling, and despite their loud protests, said to Gina and me, "Let's go."

"You didn't like those boys?" asked Gina. "They were cute."

She shook her head. "There were two things wrong with them," she replied. "They were drunk, *and* they were broke. That's an especially unattractive combination in men."

The one drink was knocking me out. And unlike Candy, I wasn't fearless. Talk about an especially unattractive combination: terrified and drunk. I was afraid to lose my hard-earned money. For me, it was like electric shock therapy watching Candy at the blackjack table putting another fifty-dollar chip on her doubled down ten. Behind her, we strolled one more time around the stained carpet and the shuffling, penniless men with drinks in their hands. Finally deeming us done with the place, she sat down "for just five minutes" at one of the poker machines.

An hour later, Candy was still playing on the same twenty

bucks. She had won fifty, lost it, and was now trying to win it back. Gina and I played, too. I liked poker better than blackjack, it was safer and slower for a coward like me. I could bet a quarter, and if I lost it, it was no big deal. If I won, it was also not a big deal. Candy tried to explain to me that betting a quarter, getting a flush and winning only seventy-five cents was squandering the blessings of the gambling demons. That's what she called them, the "gambling demons." "What's the point?" she asked. "Are you having fun, winning and losing the same twenty-five cents? You have nothing at stake, you win nothing."

"Yes, but I lose nothing."

"Yes," she said, "but you *win* nothing."

"I'd rather not lose, than win."

"Wow." She turned back to her machine, bet the maximum, got a full house and won seventy-five bucks.

"You will learn, Shelby Sloane," said Candy Cane, our resident philosopher, "that sometimes you have to gamble everything to win everything."

Gina was trying to imitate Candy, and though she wasn't brave enough to bet quite as much, she was doing well betting a dollar here and there; she was four times braver than me. Gina got so into it that an hour passed, then another, and suddenly I asked what time it was. No one knew; there are no clocks in casinos, there is no time, no day, no night, only the moment and the machine. The same heavy-set couple was still there, the wife following the husband, saying, give me a quarter, just a quarter, and him saying, I'm almost out, Doris. I keep giving you quarters and you keep losing.

"What time is it?" I asked. They looked at me as if I were nuts. Doris eyed me suspiciously, clutching her empty bucket. He looked at his wrist.

"Three o'clock," he said.

"It's three o'clock!" I hissed into Gina's ear. "Let's go. Let's go right now!" How did it get to be three o'clock?

"How did it get to be three o'clock?" said Candy. "Maybe because we got here around ten, and it's five hours later?"

196

"We've been gambling for *five* hours?" I said, aghast.

"Well, no. Gina and I have been gambling. I don't know what you've been doing."

Gina laughed heartily. Gina! Laughing at me, taking Candy's side. Oh, yes. They were pals now, a little gambling, and they were best friends. "Can we go?" I said, tersely. "I won't be able to drive tomorrow." I was such a wet blanket.

"Sloane!" exclaimed Gina. "I've never had this much fun. Let's stay one more night."

"You're crazy." I walked away, left the boat and went upstairs. In all my clothes I lay on the bed, waiting for them to come back, and when they didn't, I sat so I could see the sunrise over the Mississippi and opened my spiral notebook to make a new plan, look at my budget, write down a summary of yesterday. Sunset, sunrise both over one river, strategies, and suddenly I was unconscious in all my clothes on top of the bed. When I woke up, it was light, past sunrise, and the industrial warehouses were gray with morning.

My two traveling companions were still nowhere in sight.

I couldn't believe it. They hadn't come back yet! This was Gina, Gina, who not long ago had been saying how we had to drop Candy off at the nearest road sign, throw her out of the car like an empty can and move on, on, on, and here she was, out with Candy till half-past morning.

2

Five Flower

They strolled in around eight, as refreshed and alive as if they'd had a full night's sleep. They were joking, talking about their winnings, bumping into each other; they jumped on the bed, sat cross-legged and counted out their money. Gina did respectably—she got seventy-five dollars for her full night of trouble. But Candy laid out three hundred dollars.

"I'll give you a hundred bucks toward painting your car," she offered.

"I simply don't understand how this is possible," I said.

Candy threw back her head and laughed. "I'm so hungry. Let's go have breakfast."

"Candycane, I'm famished too," said Gina, "but when are we going to sleep?"

"We'll eat, then crash. We'll stay another night. It's on me, girls."

"We're staying here *another* night?"

"Why not? Don't you have to check out Earl something or other? Look, you," Candy said when she saw my sour face. "Yesterday, you went sixty-nine miles in six hours, dragging your ass through Missouri dirt roads. When we go again, you're going to have to drive properly. Or you'll make us all insane."

Gina agreed, head nodding, arms flailing. She seemed to have forgotten that we were all set to leave Candy here in Bettendorf.

Downstairs at the breakfast buffet, the corn beef hash tasted suspiciously like yesterday's pot roast. "Aren't you tired?" I asked. They didn't even answer, they were too busy chatting about poker strategies, blackjack theories, patterns of winning. They were talking about the luck of the draw the way I talked about budgeting time and money for a two-week trip. Candy had even introduced Gina to the roulette table. "She's so reckless," Gina kept saying, but in the tone of someone who was saying, *she's a genius.* "She's trouble." *She is amazing.* "She makes me take ungodly risks." *She is my hero.*

"Not ungodly," said Candy.

"Does God approve of gambling?" I asked sourly. Jeez, I was turning into the mother I never had. Just great. Dandy. Emma was never like this.

"No," Candy said happily. "Certainly not. The Five Flower Aztec god approves. But you know what our Lord approves of, fully and completely? Joy! And Gina, we had us some joy last night, didn't we?"

"We sure did, applecakes," said Gina. "We sure did."

They ate, drank coffee, and then, with the caffeine still hot in their veins, crashed upstairs on the same bed, clothes off, just in their bras and panties, covers off, while I clucked around, walked gingerly like a chicken, ten o'clock, eleven, planned, wrote things down, fretted, then lay down and fell asleep myself.

When I woke up, it was three or four in the afternoon, and the girls were still asleep, their bodies barely having shifted. It was quiet in the room, only the occasional footsteps in the corridor told me we were not alone. I took off my makeup, had a shower, put my makeup back on. I made much noise, which did not bestir them, so finally left for the lobby to find a Yellow Pages and call Earl Scheib about the Mustang.

The news from Earl wasn't good. The shop couldn't do it; the unfriendly voice on the phone told me I had to contact a Ford-authorized Mustang paint shop, of which Scheib wasn't one. "Can you recommend somebody?" I asked.

"What am I, the Yellow Pages?" the guy growled. "Try Peter's Paint and Body in Moline."

Peter's in Moline also didn't do it, but Friendly Auto Painting (which was not Friendly) in Davenport, did. Shelbys were made in only seven colors in 1966. I wanted black with white stripes? They would have to order the two sets of paint from Ford in Detroit, it would take three to four weeks to arrive, they'd need the car for three days minimum, and it would cost $1500.

I nearly passed out.

Paint was expensive, Ford surcharges exorbitant, car needed a primer, two coats and a lacquer, the stripes were difficult, work labor-intensive. "You want it or not?" Friendly snapped.

"Not," I snapped back, but when I hung up, I was sad. Fifteen hundred dollars! Were they kidding me?

I called Earl Scheib again. "I won't do it," the guy said. "Not even for two thousand. I'll paint any car for two hundred bucks—except that one. My guys won't deface a Shelby Mustang with a generic paint job. It's pure vandalism. We can't guarantee it, I can't use my primer on it, the car will have to be stripped of its original color first. You want me to give you the labor charges on that? The car will be worth nothing after I'm done. Is that what you want? Why do you even bother having a Mustang if that's how you're going to treat it? Just get yourself a Maverick and be done with it." He hung up before I could think of a witty reply.

I trudged upstairs where the girls were stirring. When I told them of the paint charges and the wait times, they both snorted and sneered. "I told you," said Gina. They filed into the shower, and by the time they were dried and made up, it was dinner time again. I couldn't believe a whole day had gone by like this, a morning and an afternoon, of nothing, just sleeping in an unfamiliar room after pulling a metal lever the whole night and yelling into the phone at rude men.

"You don't find us despicable?" I asked them as they were putting on their shoes.

"I find us kind of cute." Gina smiled. "Come on, Sloane. Think about how depressed we were in that car. This is better, no?"

We *were* depressed in that car. So what's changed?

"Should we just stay here?" I asked. "Maybe I can call for my mother to come and meet me in a casino in Iowa."

"So you know where your mother is, then?" asked Candy. I said shut up, and Gina laughed.

"Sloane, it's very clear to me and Candy that we can't come with you," she said, twinkling. "You're too dangerous. Why don't you just head out by yourself. We'll take a train."

"You're joking, right?"

Gina tickled my ribs. "Scared you for a minute, didn't I? Come on, let's go. I'm starved."

We went to the buffet again. Candy, feeling generous, paid for us all, even bought us a beer, though Gina told her not to do that, since the drinks were free at the casino, and I said, "So what? We're not going back to the casino, are we?"

"Sloane," Gina said, "we've been sleeping all day. What the hell are we going to do? Lie in bed and stare at the ceiling? We're not leaving till tomorrow morning. We'll go play for a little while."

"Famous last words." I was sounding more and more like fifty-year-old Emma.

Famous last words indeed. We went, and my true colors showed again, but one thing was different tonight. Candy showed me how to bet on roulette. I played five times, and on the fifth, my silly number nineteen came in, and I won 210 dollars on my five bucks. I got so excited that even I forgot about time for a while under the fluorescents. The older couples were still there, and the shuffling old men, and the sullen bikers, but there were some college students, too, and we hooked up with them during the latter portion of the night; Candy disappeared somewhere, Gina was still on the slot machines, and I was being wooed by a cut young man with glazed eyes. "Are you drunk?" I asked him.

"You bet, baby," he said, and laughed. "But even if I wuzn't, you'd still look pretty to me."

"Aw, that's sweet," I said, pushing him off my shoulder, but gently, because he looked like he might topple over any minute, and also because he was so adorable, with his stubbly face, slick short hair and gleaming eyes. "But riddle me this," I asked, remembering what Candy had said the night before. "Are you broke?"

"I'm a sophomore at Iowa State. All college students are broke. Aren't you broke?"

I wasn't a student this summer and actually, I was a hundred bucks flush. I said nothing. Deciding I didn't mind his drunkenness and brokenness, I went outside with him and we made out under the poplars for a while. It was late, yet still warm and humid, the crickets were out, like we were out, and he was insistent and drunk, but we were in such a public place, on a bench just off from the valet parking, the cars still coming and going. He smelled good, he was sweet. I didn't know what to do with him. He asked if I had a room here. I said both my friends were there sleeping, and asked if he had a room. He said, no, he still lived at home, but he had his "carrrrr."

"You're going to drive in your condition?"

"Who said I'm going to drive, baby?" he drawled, grinning widely.

I had nothing better to do. So I went to his car. It was his parents' car, I could tell, because it was cavernous, like a Caddy or a Pontiac. The backseat was as big as my bed upstairs. We fumbled and sweated up all the windows, breathed hot and heavy, and got partially disrobed, me almost entirely disrobed, but unfortunately Shakespeare was right about my friend. Though the *will* was certainly there.

In the end, after fumbling and failing, he fell asleep on me. I sat with him for a while, too long a while, I think, and then shook him awake. He barely stirred, just enough to let me move away. I got dressed. "Bye, Todd," I said, and he mumbled, "I'm not Todd, I'm Jason."

"I know," I said. "Just checking if you're paying attention. Careful going home."

But he was unconscious, slumped over the backseat. I left him there, and locked him in, in case someone decided to steal him. In the three hours we'd been together, he did not ask for my name.

Upstairs, Candy and Gina were on the bed counting their money. "Good morning," said Gina.

"Shut up."

"That boy, I know he was drunk," said Candy, not looking up from her stash, "but tell me, was he broke, too?"

"Shut up."

Candy and Gina shook their heads and laughed. "It's okay," said Candy. "You'll learn."

"Learn what?" I took off my shoes, dropped the contents of my purse on the bed.

"That it's just as easy to fall in love with a rich boy as it is with a poor boy."

"Who said anything about love?" I said, pulling out my chips and cursing. In the midst of my little rendezvous I forgot to cash in.

"I'm just saying," said Candy. "There. Another 170 dollars. We're flush, girls."

"I can't believe the money you made," said Gina. "I don't know how you do it. I thought I did okay, and I made eighty."

"You did great. Eighty is great. What about you, Shel?"

"I have eighteen five-dollar chips," I said, letting them fall on the bed from my hands.

Candy nodded. "Ninety bucks. Not bad."

"Ah, so you can count some things, Candycane?"

She smiled at me. "Some things, yes. And don't worry. You must be lucky in love."

"Not very lucky," I said, thinking of my one failed love affair, the only one I ever had, the various Todds and Jasons and Tony Bergaminos notwithstanding. "But you must be *un*lucky."

"So unlucky," agreed Candy. "But lucky in other ways." She threw her money up into the air, and it floated down, landing on the bed with her.

"We're checking out tomorrow," I said. "No matter what time it is, we're going."

"Don't be so hasty," said Gina. "What's the rush?"

"Let me put it another way. *I'm* checking out tomorrow. That's what you want, isn't it?"

They groaned and teased but ignoring them, I got out my maps and planned my course from the Quad Cities, down I-80, across the entire state of Iowa, to Omaha, Nebraska, right on the border. I calculated the distance to be about 300 miles. Even with getting out late, and stopping six times to pee and get a drink, we could do 300 miles in one day, couldn't we? Then the next day we'd be in Wyoming, the next in Utah, the next in Nevada, and then California. Just a few days, and this would all be over.

My reverie was ended by Candy pulling the map from the bed and throwing it on the floor. Grabbing my spiral notebook from me, she dodged and weaved around the room, squealing, "Let me read, let me read, come on, I want to know how far you went with that drunk boy." She raised her voice to mimic me. "Dear Diary, I think I'm in loooove. His name is Sal, and he's sooo cute, dear Diary, I don't think I'll be able to sleep tonight, thinking of him as I do, oooooh."

"Candy, give it here!"

Raising her arm away from me, she opened my notebook. She was quiet a moment as her eyes scanned the page. "What *is* this?"

Gina was rolling on the bed, laughing. "This is her diary, Candy," she said, barely able to get the words out. "Dear Diary, today, I want to do some planning. Here are my charts, schedules, flows, summaries, and miles for the next forty years of my life. I think I finally figured out a way to plan, monitor, and control—everything. I hope you're pleased with me. Tomorrow we will be on our way. We will sleep exactly seven hours and forty-two minutes, and then after fifty-one minutes of getting ready and packing, we will go eat breakfast for thirty-seven minutes. After that we will take Road 10 five miles and Road 5 ten miles. Then we'll switch for exactly thirty minutes."

Candy was holding her stomach. "Stop, Gina, stop. I can't take any more."

Snatching my journal from her, I closed it up and put the pen away. "Are you two happy now? You're enjoying yourselves?"

"Shelby, why are you so funny?" asked Candy. "Aside from the subject matter of your so-called journal . . ."

"It's not a journal, it's a planner," I said, extremely defensively.

"Oh. Right. Well, aside from the subject matter of your so-called planner, one thing in it struck me as funny." She paused a moment for emphasis. "You know we can't go on I-80. So what the heck are you wasting your ink on?"

We weren't despicable. What these two days of sleep and revelry had allowed us was an escape from the important things, an escape, a denial of decisions, a refusal to make choices, to decide to take a different road, to plan Candy, to discuss. I clung on to my earlier positions like a vine out of quicksand. All pointless and pointed disquisition ended at the blackjack table. Time stopped. And even now, when we knew we needed to decide one thing, one day, one morning, one turn in the right direction, we were too tired to talk. Barely undressing, we climbed into bed; Candy lay next to Gina for a while, then got up and crawled into bed with me. "I figure it's only fair," she said, giving me a little nudge in the ribs. "You don't want Gina having me all to herself, do you?"

I said nothing. The curtains were open. Gina was already in twilight, sleep-muttering. Candy and I stretched out with our arms above our heads and stared at the ceiling.

"Forget the Interstate, Shel," Candy said. "No more Interstate for us."

For us. "Okay." I lay next to her thinking regretfully of the twenty minutes of hard planning I had just done. "Does luck sometimes run out?" I asked.

"I don't know. Other people's luck certainly does."

"Does yours?"

"Sometimes. But you know, I don't believe much in luck, except at the gambling tables, and I don't have much to lose. I'm not afraid," she said. "That's the only difference. You're afraid."

"Sometimes you can be plenty brave and lose anyway."

"Sure. But I don't care. That's the beauty of it."

We lay.

"You must care about some things," I said.

"Desperately," said Candy, turning on her side to me. "The things I'm afraid to lose."

"That man . . . Erv . . . Candy, you didn't really mean what you said about him, did you?" The night was too quiet to say the awful words out loud. That he wanted to kill her. *She took something of mine that I need back.* I lived in suburban Larchmont, not the Beirut war zone. I didn't know about these things.

"Tomorrow," Candy said, by way of answer, "we should drive up to Dubuque."

"Why? More casinos?" I said nothing about her coming with us, as if, of all the things to decide, that was no longer even on the table. What happened to *I'm going to let you off at the next Interstate junction?* Once Interstate was removed from the equation, easing her out of my car was also removed from the equation.

"Hah. No. But U.S. 20 runs through there."

"Is that north or south of here?"

"North."

"Candy, why would I be going north? I have to head west!"

"U.S. 20 runs through Dubuque."

"Um, is that somewhere we want to be?"

"Oh, yes. U.S. 20 isn't the Interstate, but runs near clear across the country. I think it will bring us to Reno."

"Reno?" I lowered my voice. "Reno, *Nevada?* Are you crazy? Candy, what does Reno have to do with California? And do you expect me to *take* you to Reno?"

"If you get me to Reno," she said, "I'll be fine from there. There's a chick there, a friend of mine, who owes me a solid. She'll help me."

"She owes you a *solid?* How would you know anybody in Reno?"

"I know people all over."

"No kidding. But come on, why can't we just stay on I-80?"

She sighed. "Shel, up near Dubuque, maybe sixty miles from here, lives my old man. I'd really like to go visit him."

I didn't say anything.

"Please help me out. I haven't seen him in years."

I still didn't say anything. I wanted to ask and didn't know how to: are we visiting or are we . . . dropping off? But what's worse, I didn't know which answer I wanted. I stared at her in the dark, her peculiar punky hair, her slowly blinking brown gaze, her bare shoulder sticking up from the sheet.

"There's something I need to leave with him," she said.

"Is it the something you took from Erv?" I whispered.

She sucked in her breath. "What do you know about that?"

"Nothing. Just what he told me." I waited. "Well?"

"Yes," she replied.

Oh no. Score two for Erv. Was this worrying, his record of accuracy? Yes. Yes, it was. What if everything he had told me was true? What if this girl *had* run away and left her mother broken? What if he would not stop until he found her? The pit in my stomach got darker.

"Does your dad have money?" I asked. "Maybe you can borrow some."

"Dad's broker than me," said Candy. "So no. Besides, we have a little money." She smiled in the night. "A few hundred bucks."

"Well, all right," I said. "We'll go. He *is* your father." I would've liked to visit my father. I would've come to Iowa to see him. I wondered if he had been like Emma, being her brother and all. Jed Sloane. Had he been stalwart? Had he been true? "What's your dad's name?"

"Estevan," Candy replied. "Estevan Rio."

"Huh. Not Cane?"

"No, not Cane."

We lay quiet.

"You think I'm going to find my mom, Candy?" I whispered. I

207

don't know why I was asking her these things, and worse, I didn't know why I expected her to have any answers. *Say hi to Shelby. Mendocino, California.*

"No, sweetie-girl," she whispered back. "I don't."

She took my hand in the dark, and her mouth moved silently, as if in prayer, and we lay there on our sides, our hands under our cheeks, until we fell asleep.

3

A Race Not to the Swift

The next morning Candy was up before us. Washed and dressed, she sat quietly in the chair, waiting for us to stir. She wasn't completely ready: her makeup wasn't on. When we were ready to check out, I looked at her still motionless in the chair. "You gonna put your face on?"

"Not today," she replied. Her piercings were out, even the tongue ring; she had on no jewelry, no hair gel. I'd never seen her eyes so bare, without heavy liner, thick mascara. She looked like a different person. Her hair was clean, streaks of pink sad and down; her cheeks pale, her skin opalescent, blemished only by wearing too much makeup and never washing it off.

When Gina found out we were going to visit Candy's father, she laughed. "Nice face, Cand, but what are you going to do about the tattoos?"

"Hide them."

And to me, in the hallway, Gina said, expectantly, "We're dropping her off at her old man's, I hope?"

"Dunno." I didn't want to say more, which was: don't think so. Or even: hope not.

Candy was unusually subdued during breakfast, not chirpy at all. I wanted to believe that the events between St. Louis and Isle of Capri would take the chirp out of white-throated sparrows, but she had just spent two days on the gambling boat feistier than a single gal on ladies night.

Yesterday she had asked to borrow a pair of my jeans and one of my T-shirts. She herself, I guess, had nothing to wear for a visit with her father. My jeans were too big on her, my T-shirt too long. She was a little shorter than me and thinner. I didn't realize how much thinner until I saw her in my clothes. I began to reconsider my bagel with cream cheese and my second helping of eggs and bacon. And I'm a runner—was a runner. It's not like, in the words of Woody Allen, I had fat dripping off my body like hot fudge off a sundae. Thinking about running made me feel bad, as if the different parts of my life that had been most important to me, had defined who I was for many years, were being washed away with the tide like seashells.

This morning I tried to interpret her quiet face. I liked Candy's eyes without makeup. They were real. She had something going on beyond the façade of her usually madly black-lined eyes. I'll admit it disconcerted me to see her in my running shirt. "NY STATE CHAMPION, 1981, 2-MILE." The waitress came to pour us a little more coffee and said to Candy, "You were the New York State Champion in the two-mile?"

"Huh?" said Candy, who had obviously put on the T-shirt without so much as glancing at it. "Not my shirt." She pointed to me. "Her shirt."

The waitress looked at me questioningly. I shrugged. "9:52."

"Is that fast? I don't know."

"Good enough for a record," said Candy, which I found amusing—her defending me when two seconds earlier she didn't even know I had ever run, or won.

Now it was the waitress's turn to shrug. "Are you really the state champ?" asked Candy after the server ambled away.

I nodded.

"How come you're so casual about it?"

"You have to put the thing in perspective," I said. "The running is the thing. That's everything. The winning is . . . I can't explain. Nice. But temporary. And ultimately, meaningless."

"Why do you say meaningless?" asked Gina. "You were the pride of our whole high school. I've never won anything in my life."

I wanted to say that Gina had won some things in her life, but didn't. "Well, you don't run," I said. "But if you played the piano, it'd be the piano playing that was the important thing. Look," I said when I saw Candy and Gina's uncomprehending faces. "It's like this. The year before, in 1980, the girl who won ran the two-mile in 9:42. In 1981 she had an appendectomy."

"And didn't run?"

"Oh, no, she ran. Just ran it in 9:58. And that's with fifteen stitches in her stomach. I got lucky, that's all."

"Come on, Sloane," said Gina. "You're going to a very good college because of that championship."

"Well, that's true," I agreed, looking sheepishly into my cup.

"That's not so meaningless," said Candy. "You go to college, get a degree, a good job, all because you ran that one race. That's not temporary. Nine minutes and fifty-two seconds equals all future roads."

"Well, that could be true," I admitted.

"Is it a good college?"

I demurred. "Pretty good."

"You could say, pretty good," said Gina, poking at her cold bacon. "She's going to Harvard." She said it without looking at me, but then looked up with a tight smile. "It's really great." She had been accepted to State University of New York in Geneseo for teaching.

"On a track scholarship," I said apologetically, in four words demeaning myself, Harvard, track, scholarships, and prepositions.

I don't think Gina deemed it fair I got a full scholarship just because I moved my feet quickly from point A to point B. Now, if I had counted some numbers at sonic speed, or combined gold and nickel and made a new alloy, or perhaps created a paramecium out of nitrogen gas, or wrote a poem, *that* might be fair. But moving fast didn't seem to fall into the same category of stellar achievement. I don't know for sure that Gina felt this way. But I know *I* felt this way. Therefore, slightly ashamed of my own good luck because of someone's ruptured appendix, I kept mostly quiet about my college choice. Though I will admit, I was going to find my mother so I could tell her these things about me, including what college I was going to, because I thought she might be proud. Thinking about my mother made me think about what Candy had said to me last night, and I started to feel bad, and pushed my coffee away.

Candy was blankly silent. "Is Harvard a good school?"

I laughed. "That's *exactly* what I'm talking about," I said to Gina, getting up. "Come on, let's get going."

Gina stood from the table. "Shelby got real lucky," she said. "But sometimes luck does run out, don't you think, Candy? I read in the paper that five upstate New York girls were all killed in a car wreck, less than a week after graduating from high school."

"That's not luck," said Candy. "That's destiny. You best pray it's not yours."

SEVEN

NEW MELLERAY

1

Hours of the Divine Office

We were on the open road away from the Quad Cities by 9:30. The road was a rolling highway between Iowa farms and corn fields, the day was gray. There were no trucks, no cars, sky to the earth was empty, and up and down we went, like on a rollercoaster, flying along, the view and the silos forever.

After we'd gone about sixty miles, Candy asked me to slow down and peered at the road signs. Making a left, we drove up and around a winding road where the Iowa vistas disappeared; what was left was tall pines and shady canopies. It didn't seem like Iowa at all, no fields till the horizon, but forested and woodsy, like Maine, where I'd been once with Emma. I wanted to ask if her father was a farmer, but didn't. Everything was very still and there were no other cars on the road. We passed a small cemetery on the left, and up ahead on the hill, partially covered by trees, stood a brilliant snowy stone building, like a historic school, or a museum from the Middle Ages. Solemn, it stood like a beacon and Gina said, "What *is* that?"

"That's the New Melleray Abbey. Make a right here. On Melleray Way."

"New Melleray?" I said. "Does that mean there's an even older Melleray?"

"Yes, Mount Melleray Abbey in Ireland," replied Candy as if she knew about these things.

We drove through the pristine green grounds and tall pines. There were benches under the trees near a statue of the Holy Mother. The large light building stood silent, as if deserted.

"We're going to the abbey?" I asked.

Candy nodded.

"Why?"

"Because my father lives here."

"Your father *lives* in the abbey?" Gina said, while I attempted not to crash into the statue of the Holy Mother.

"Careful," said Candy. "Don't drive like a maniac."

"Why does your father live in an abbey?" Gina asked.

"Because he's a Trappist monk."

"Your father is a *monk*?" I had stopped the car in the empty parking lot—more like screeched to a diagonal stop. When I spun around to look at Candy, I took my foot off the brake, and my Mustang pitched forward and went over the curb onto the grass.

"Shelby! Please."

Brake slammed on, car reversed, gingerly parked, ignition off, I turned to Candy. "Your father is a *monk*," I repeated.

"Why is that surprising?" she asked, frowning. "Do you *know* my father?"

"Uh—no," I said cleverly. But, I wanted to add, I know *you*. "You don't seem like a . . ." How to put it mildly? ". . . a monk's daughter."

"I did not choose who I was born to," she said. "When he was in college, he went looking for answers. First he had a thing with my mother, then he petitioned the Formation Council about joining the Cistercian order."

"Not because of your mother, I hope," I said.

"Your mother went to college?" Gina asked disbelievingly.

Candy squinted from the back. "Do you know my mother, Gina? Shel, open the windows, we're gonna die in here."

We rolled down the windows. No one was getting out of the car.

"So your mother went to college?"

"She cleaned the humanities building."

"Your father is a monk?" exclaimed Gina, as if just hearing it. "Oh my God."

"Shh." Candy crossed herself.

"Oh, for God's sake!"

"Shh!"

"Candy," Gina asked, "does your father know the kinds of things you've been up to?"

"Gina, *you* have no idea what I've been up to," said Candy.

We sat. "So what do we do now?" I asked. "Wait for you?"

"No. We leave the car, go inside. Ask for him." She paused. "But look, just so you know—they don't care what you do outside these walls. Really. So don't have that worried face on, because then for sure, the brothers will think you were up to no good, you look so guilty. And because you are guests, announced or unannounced, they will welcome you. That's their way. But please—respect their rituals. Do not talk inside the church or the cloister. Do not say, 'Oh God,' as often as you take a breath. Don't laugh."

Gina rolled her eyes.

We left the car and went inside, Gina and I *extremely* reluctantly. There was no one around to ask for Candy's father. We wandered through a small unattended bookstore ("Aren't they afraid someone is going to steal stuff?" asked Gina, and Candy replied, "In a *monastery?*") through a room full of urns and caskets (!), through a stone hall, opening and closing heavy solid wood doors, and finally found our way into what Candy whispered to me was the tabernacle.

"Is that a place of worship?" I whispered back.

"Yes!"

It was a long narrow hall, plain and rectangular, built in stone and wood, with ceilings tall like Ponderosa pines. The oak pews were in the back, where we sank down under stark shadows. The church was filled with light, streaming through the clear glass of the stone arched windows. A long way in front of us stood twenty white-robed monks in two straight lines on opposite sides of the church, in stalls, chanting a monophonic song. I thought at first it wasn't in English because there was not one word of it I understood. But then something plain filtered through, like the wiping away of snow on the windows and glimpsing beyond. *My soul waits,* they sang. *I wait. My soul waits for the Lord . . .*

Their somber voices filled the church. *I wait in hope for the Lord . . . in his word do I hope . . .*

We had come at the tail end; barely minutes later it was over. They crossed themselves, and filed out, leaving the place in echoing silence, almost as if the semitones of their last hymnic notes still lingered in the wooden beams, reflecting off the glass windows.

"Which one was he?" I whispered.

"Shh," Candy said. "Don't talk inside the church."

I was as quiet as can be. I told her so.

"What, you think God can't hear you?" she said.

Gina had been rendered mute by all this, not out of reverence but out of critical astonishment. I, on the other hand, especially after hearing that mystical singing, felt as if I had been walking in mud and then accidentally stepped into an alluvial deposit. It was still mud, and I couldn't for the life of me get my feet out of the morass, but underneath, in the wet slickness, I felt there was something gilded this girl was showing me with her extreme life that was out of my existence, beyond my understanding, and almost out of my reach.

"I'd never been inside a church, you know."

Candy looked at me with the kind of incredulous expression we must have been bestowing upon her these last days for not knowing the words to Blondie and Andy Gibb.

"What service was that?" I asked. "I didn't know they had services in the middle of the day."

"They have services all day long," Candy replied. "Seven separate services of the Divine Office, not including Mass at seven a.m. That one was sext. The noon service."

"What was the song they sang?"

Candy stared at me. "Um, Psalm 130," she replied slowly. Much the way we had said, *um, Baby, Come Back.*

"So you do know some songs?" Gina smiled.

"Yes," said Candy. "Psalms, the songs to God."

We loitered in the store. Eventually but suddenly a monk appeared, as if out of thin air. One moment there was no one near, the next, he, in his white tunic and black apron was walking past, his hands folded together. He looked at us and said nothing. "Hello, Brother Placid," said Candy. "Can you please tell my father I'm here?"

Brother Placid, a short squat man, observed her pink hair without reaction, cocked his head, nodded slightly, and poof was gone. His shoes, his robes made no sound, not even an echo off the walls. We walked outside into the square stone deck with benches and waited there. It was quiet outside; the air smelled of pines, and we didn't speak. Finally, the tall, narrow, solid oak door opened, and out came a tall narrow man who looked like solid oak himself, with gray hair and glasses. He was clean shaven, blue-eyed, grave. He wore a white robe and a sleeveless black tunic over it. He came out, stood still, and Candy got up off the bench, stood still also.

"Hello, Dad."

"Hello, Grace," said the man she had called Estevan Rio.

❧

Grace? I whispered sideways to her, as if in tranquiloquy.

"These are my friends," Candy said. "Shelby and Gina."

Estevan Rio nodded without expression. "Your friends are always welcome here."

They walked away from us then, down the steps and across the garden.

"She's using the term *friends* loosely," whispered Gina.

Was she? "Shh." I stepped away from her. *Grace?*

The grounds around the abbey were vast and Gina and I would every once in a while glimpse Candy and her father on the meandering paths, beyond the trees, behind the statues. Gina said she was hungry.

"Okeydoke. Thanks for letting me know," I said.

"How long is she going to stay?"

"I don't know."

"Five minutes? Five days?"

"I *don't* know!" I sounded churlish and silly.

"You think they'll feed us?"

"Candy did say they receive guests. They'll probably feed us."

"But when?"

"Man does not live by bread alone," said a male voice behind us, and as we turned around, a monk walked by, bowing his head slightly. He had a bemused, exasperated expression on his face, as if he had seen the likes of us many times and didn't know why the likes of us continued coming. He said he was Brother Benedict Babor; could he help us? We explained that we were waiting for our friend, the daughter of Brother Estevan; could we walk the grounds in the meantime?

He waved his hand, curlyQ in the air, meaning, go, do what you like, just don't shout, you spoiled children. "Of course," he said. "All are welcome here."

So we walked the grounds, our conversation stilted. We expressed surprise at the gust of wind that had blown us into an abbey. "Can you imagine, Sloane, *you* in an abbey?"

I was offended for my own agnosticism. "Well, perhaps I would've gone to one, but there weren't any abbeys in Larchmont," I said, huffing.

"How do you know? Have you looked?"

What an odd question. "Have *you?*"

"I've been to the Ashram many times," Gina said loftily. "Same difference."

"Is it the same difference? And what does that mean, same difference? Are they the same? Or different? Or it doesn't matter?"

Pointing to me, Gina said, "Now you got it." She wiped her perspiring face. "For God's sake, are they *ever* coming back?"

Out of nowhere, footsteps behind us made their own shuffling noise, and a male voice said, "Children, respect the premises. Don't blaspheme on our grounds. We don't pray in your nightclubs, do we?" It was Brother Benedict Babor again.

Chastened, intimidated by his robes and authority, I clammed up. Gina whispered, "Why is he following us?" We turned around. He was gone.

Unnerved by the magical realism of his effective transformations, we hastened our step and walked back inside the abbey. For some reason it seemed safer to me. Not talking also seemed safer. "Maybe she isn't coming back?" Gina ventured after half an hour had passed. "Let's go. What's she gonna do? She's in a monastery. She'll be fine."

"Gina . . ."

"What, you don't think she'll be fine *here*?"

Before I could say that I didn't think *I'd* be fine, Gina announced she was bored. And hungry. She wanted to go—now. "It'll take us a while to find a McDonald's."

"Let's go inside the church," I said. "Another service might be beginning." I wanted to hear the singing again.

"Are you out of your mind? I'll go crazy if I stay *outside* another minute, and you want to go *inside*?"

"Just to note," I said, "I don't remember you rushing me along out of the casino—for two days straight."

"Why would I?" she said as if she had no idea what on earth I was talking about. "The casino was fantastic and fun. This is slow death."

I looked at her as if I had no idea what on earth she was talking about. Throwing up her hands, she stormed outside to the car. "Don't stay in the car, Gina," I called after her. "You'll suffocate. It's so hot. At least crank open the windows."

She waved me off the way I used to wave Emma off. I sighed.

There was no one inside, and though I peeked in one of the corridors, I got nervous. What if I wasn't allowed to walk here, look here?

I went in to the casket room. The Melleray monks supported themselves by making pine and walnut caskets out of indigenous wood. The three they had on display looked well made.

I knew I was allowed inside the chapel, so that's where I went, tiptoeing, not wanting to make a sound, holding my breath, clutching my purse so the keys wouldn't jangle. I sat in the back again, resting my hands on the wooden pew in front of me.

I was the only one inside. I guess it wasn't time for songs.

I sat and waited.

What was I waiting for? I wasn't sure. What was I feeling? A little like a dry sponge onto which warm water was dripping. At the Isle of Capri, I had been bone dry for two days.

I stayed past the point of reason, waiting for something that refused to commence; just sat in that long narrow tabernacle, and waited. The wooden pew was warm under my fingers, the stone floor cool under my sandals.

The absolute silence unnerved me. There was no music playing, no clanging, no clinking. It was as if I had gone deaf. The solid oak doors and the hardwood floors muffled all comings and goings. Now contrast with the river casino last night: few human words, except for "Deck shuffle!" but a constant din, an endless clatter of levers, of cherries lining up, drinks falling, and the ching-ching-ching of the quarters dropping through. Here the world was on mute. Nothing but the noise inside my head.

What was surprising about the noise inside my head, however, was how low-key it was compared, say, to the car when the music was at the seventh decibel, blaring of the warm smell of eucalyptus, my head screaming about California, and injustice, Emma, guilt and fear. Here, even Lorna Moor receded. I was not thinking, not feeling, just breathing, my eyes open, a sponge, warm water dripping onto me. How many hours had passed since the tall man said *Hello, Grace?*

This child named Candy was known to him as Grace. What did he know of her? At the hotel last night she told me she hadn't seen him in years. But when would she have seen him at all? Yet he recognized her instantly. He wasn't surprised, he didn't look like someone who was seeing his child for the first time. *Hi, Dad. Hello, Grace.*

What would it have been like for me to see my father? *Hi, Dad. Hello, Shelby.* What would it be like for me to see my mother? *Hi, Mom. Hello, Shelby.* And then we would take a long walk in the tall pines. Would it be a little like that? Would she recognize me the way Estevan Rio had recognized his daughter? Lorna Moor, was she in her version of a monastery? Did she run off and join the Order of the Childless Mothers? Or was that a paradox I couldn't deal with, sitting in an empty tabernacle, waiting for the monastic choir? Did Estevan Rio, the Trappist monk, write his daughter, call her? She didn't seem nervous or afraid of him, like I imagined I would be facing my own parent, trembling with panic at the prospect of finding my mother.

I thought Candy had kept her makeup off and her clothes plain because she was wary of her father, but now I began to think that maybe she did it out of respect. Respect the rituals. *Man does not live by bread alone.* No? What else does he live by?

I sat so long that the shadows blackened and the light glowed vermilion before the monks noiselessly glided back in. I had been waiting only for them and now sat breathlessly as I absorbed the beginnings of their measured incantations in that monolithic chamber. Nothing was familiar, all was new and strange. But I had my answer. *Man does not live by bread alone,* the monk leading the service sing-songed, *but by every word that proceedeth out of the mouth of God.*

Is that what man lived by? What man? Not me. Not Gina.

Did Candy?

Finally, my keenly awaited Psalms. I tried to hear the words, tried to glean meaning, like in the car when Candy was telling me about Judas, but just like then couldn't grasp the threads of it. Ah, finally! Something I understood. *It is vain for you to rise up early . . . to sit up late . . . to eat the bread of sorrows . . . for so He gives His beloved sleep.*

That *was* me!

Behold, children are a gift from the Lord . . . the fruit of the womb is a reward . . .

Suddenly Candy, like a Trappist, appeared next to me in the pew. "What are you doing?" she whispered, pulling on me. "I've been looking for you everywhere!"

I closed my mouth, said, "Shh!"

"Come!" she whispered.

"Shh," I said. "Don't talk inside the church. What you think, God can't hear you?" And before I saw her reaction, I turned back to the choir. She sat next to me until the service was over.

"What in the world are you doing?" she asked when we came outside.

"I don't know. What are *you* doing? Where's Gina?"

"In the car suffocating herself in the heat. She fell asleep there and is now livid and starving."

What a combination. "What time is it?"

"Was that vespers?" said Candy. "Maybe six o'clock."

"Six o'clock! We've been here over six hours?"

Dragging me outside the abbey and lowering her voice, Candy said, "Gina did something to herself."

"Oh, God, what?"

"Shh! She—I can't explain. Shel, she doesn't have any eyebrows left!"

"Oh." I laughed quietly. "Don't worry. She does that sometimes when she's nervous."

"I don't know if you heard me," said Candy, "but *she doesn't have any eyebrows left.*"

I prodded her down the steps to the parking lot. "So? She'll draw them on with a pencil. They'll grow back."

"Why does she do that?"

"Nerves, I told you."

"But she's in an abbey!"

"What does that tell you?"

We crossed the parking lot to my car, where Gina, looking

bloated from hot sleeping, now sat on the black-striped hood perspiring.

"Where have you been?" said Gina. "Are we going? Because I'm absolutely at the *end* of my rope." And so she was. Her eyebrows were gone. Her eyelashes too. Gone. Her blue eyes looked raw and stark.

"Why'd you do that?"

She blanched, turning away from Candy. "I don't want to talk about it. Do you have any idea what time it is?"

I didn't know where the time had gone.

Candy said we weren't going yet. It was late; we had to eat; we would stay the night at least. I instantly agreed. Not so Gina. She wouldn't come inside until someone told her when, "in the name of hell," we were leaving. This is crazy, she kept saying. We have to go. Did you forget we're driving cross country? Did you forget I have to get to Eddie? Is there a phone here? I have to call him. Did you forget about your mother? Did you forget about Harvard? That we still have to drive back? Did you forget we're in flippin' Iowa, and not the middle of Iowa, but easternmost Iowa, we aren't even halfway done!

How was that possible, I thought. On the one hand, Maryland and Aunt Flo seemed like a day away. On the other . . .

"When's the next service?" I asked.

"Compline at seven-thirty," Candy replied. "But why don't you wait for the vigil at three-thirty in the morning? You might like that better." She smiled. "They sing beautifully. Psalm 77. *I call to remembrance my song in the night*. I think you'd like it. Come, you. While we wait for vigil, let's go have dinner."

"They go to service in the middle of the night?" I said as I followed her.

"It's not the middle of the night for them," she replied. "It's the beginning of their day. They rise early, go to bed early. Like farmers."

"You mean like the Kirkebys?" Gina shot.

Candy slow blinked at her. "Yes, just like them."

225

I pulled Candy's arm, detaching her from Gina's glare. "Why do they get up so early?"

"I thought you listened to Psalm 130. Because they wait and watch for the Lord," she replied. *"Yes, more than those who watch for morning."*

I must have stopped hearing anything after *My soul waits . . .*

"Did you finish your business with your dad?" I asked as we made our way inside. What was I asking? Did you give your father what you took from Erv? Or perhaps my emphasis was more on the *finish*, instead of *business*. Perhaps I was hoping she'd say yes. Sure, Shel, haven't seen Pop in years, but a few hours with him, my business is finished, and I'm good to go.

"Yes," she replied, like the enigma she was. "But I'm not done. And he wanted to meet you."

"Why does that terrify me?"

"No, no. Don't worry." She squeezed my arm and laughed. "He is so gentle. You should never be afraid of him. Besides," she added, warmly batting her long lashes and brown eyes at me, "it's good for us to hide here for a couple of days. Erv is looking for us on I-80, in Nebraska, maybe Colorado by now. He's like you, with his timelines and miles. He's calculating."

"I'm not calculating," I said. "I'm cautious."

She chuckled quietly. "I know. It's been three days since St. Louis. By the time we leave here, he'll be looking for us in California. That's good for us."

"Well, yes," I said. "But you know what would be even better?"

"If he wasn't looking for us at all?" She circled the crook of my arm. "Since that's not possible, Shelby Sloane, with generous endurance of small and large hardships, accept all things."

"I don't know why I have to," I grumbled as we walked behind Gina, who didn't know where she was going, but still kept trucking angrily down the corridors. "But tell me, do you consider yourself to be a small or large hardship?"

Candy took and kissed my hand. "A very large one," she said. "Gina! Go right, not left."

2

Estevan's Stories

"How long do you intend to stay here?" Gina said challengingly to no one in particular.

"Not long," Candy replied. "Monks aren't crazy about our noise. Maybe a couple of days. Gina, when you walk through the cloisters, you have to be absolutely silent."

"Why?"

"You just do, that's all. Those are the rules of the monastery. The cloisters is a sacred enclosure."

I wanted to shout, *I'll be quiet!*

We had come to a small room with tables and benches that was the guests' refectory. There was a pulpit under the Cross of Christ, and a plaque that read, "*O Beata Solitudo.*" Candy had known where to go. She had a sure foot leading us through the limestone labyrinths.

"Did you have a look around?" she asked. "Did you find the library?"

"There's a library?"

"A very large one. I looked for you there. I thought that's where you went."

I shook my head.

"How do you know where the library is?" asked Gina.

"Used to spend a lot of time there."

"Where? At the *library?*"

Candy laughed, soundlessly. "It's not your kind of library."

"Oh." Gina looked notably relieved. "Because I was gonna say . . ."

"Come, take a look," said Candy. "While we wait for my father to bring us something to eat."

"Is that going to be soon?" said Gina. "Because . . ."

"I know, I know—you're starved. Yes, it's going to be soon. Come."

Back through the cloisters we went, and this time, Gina was silent, though huffy. The library was old-fashioned, furnished with shabby wooden tables and chairs. It had some magazines, even newspapers. But when I walked down the rows of shelves, looking at the kinds of books the monks might read, although the words were in English I found the titles unfamiliar and strange. *The Rule of St. Benedict* in fifty different tomes and styles. St. Thomas Aquinas. St. Thomas More. St. Bonaventura, *The Mind's Road to God*. Francis of Assisi's *Little Flowers of Saint Francis*. "He didn't write it," Candy explained, walking alongside me, touching the spines of the hardbound tomes. "A monk wrote it a hundred years after St. Francis's death."

And to that I said, "Who is St. Francis?"

Candy looked at me with bemusement. "If you haven't read it," she said, "it's a must-read, especially in the translation of Raphael Brown. I'll see if my father can get you a copy."

There was the Vulgate, a hundred different Psalters, the Books of Common Prayer, all the works by C.S. Lewis ("Hey! I know him!"), two rows of Thomas Merton, a row devoted to someone called G.K. Chesterton, translations of St. Jerome, of Abelard, and Boethius' *Consolation of Philosophy*. I saw Dante and Milton, St. Augustine's *Confessions* and *The Orations* of St. Athanasius. Also: a complete collection of poems by e.e. cummings. "One of my dad's favorites," Candy said to me.

"Have you got any Sidney Sheldon?" Gina asked. "I'd like to read a few pages of him before I go to sleep."

"We don't have him," Candy said. "Do you want to try Anselm of Canterbury instead?"

"I want to try some dinner," said Gina. "Can we try that? Then we'll see about Anselm."

"This is what you read when you were young?" I asked, my hand on Candy's forearm, slowing her down so I could stay a little longer, see the books a little longer.

"Some of it. Much of it. And other things, too." She smiled. "Malachi Martin has quite a discourse on the Buddhists. Gina would appreciate it. And the Jesuits. And the devil."

Summarily we returned to the refectory. But Estevan wasn't yet there. We sat at the long dining table, and Gina put her head down and groaned. "When will they feed me?" she wailed. "When will I be fed?"

I turned to Candy. "Does your dad know the trouble you're in?"

"He knows some of it." Candy paused. "Not all of it. He can't know all of it. What he knows is bad enough. That I ran away. That one of my mother's friends is trying to find me."

To find me. What a euphemism. "*Grace?*" I said.

"Well, sure." Candy was sitting across from me. "Who in their right mind would call their child Candy?" She laughed lightly, as if it were a joke.

Gina lifted her head. "So what do we call you now?"

"How about Candy?"

"Does your dad know your name?"

"Clearly. He calls me by my name."

I waited. "Does your mom?"

"Ah. Yes. I guess. But she," said Candy, "calls me Candy."

We sat. I drummed on the wooden table, my eyes only on my new friend. "Does he want you to stay?" I asked carefully. One question, laden with layers. Does he want you to stay so we can go without you and be free, and my conscience be free also? Does he want you to stay, because what father wouldn't? Does he know what danger you're in? Can he help you? *Please*, can he help you?

"He wishes I could stay, yes."

And in her reply, years of conflict—in her profound eyes, in her grave face. He wishes I could stay because, for a moment or two when he sees me, he wants to be living a life in which his kid could visit, and he could say, spend as long as you want with me. He knows the pickle I'm in, and he wants to help, beyond the food and the prayers. He wishes he could help me more.

"You act like you've been here before, Candy," said Gina. "I find this odd, to say the least, because I can't imagine coming here willingly for one minute."

"You're funny," said Candy. "Been here? I lived here till I was almost twelve. My father raised me."

Gina and I frankly stared, waiting for her to say it was a joke.

"You were raised here?"

"Yes."

"In a monastery?"

"Yes."

"And you didn't listen to music?"

"Only to the Psalms."

"And you didn't read?"

"Voraciously. But only what's in that library."

"TV? Radio?"

"Nope."

Then I was speechless.

"When he was a young man," Candy told us, "my father, disillusioned with himself, and therefore with the whole world, had been contemplating joining the seminary for two or three years, trying to educate himself, trying to see if he could cut it."

"Three years to think?" I asked.

Candy nodded, talking slowly. "The fear was great." She smiled. "Though not as great as Gina's when she is in this place."

"I'm not afraid!" Gina exclaimed. "I'm bored, to tell the truth. There's a difference." Her hands went up to her eyebrows, but there was nothing left. "Crazy *bored*," she whispered to me testily, fingers running over her face. "Not afraid."

"Same difference," I said to Gina, and pointed at her before she could speak.

"Yes, well," said Candy. "The spiritual pressure to make the right decision, to be worthy of living in a place like this when you're in your twenties is enormous. Because what if they won't take you? I mean, that's like God not taking you. Like God saying to you, no, Estevan, I'm afraid you're not right for us. My father was thinking that if he wasn't right for God, who is supposed to be more charitable than men, he was doomed."

"Understandably he dragged his feet," I said.

"Maybe he just didn't want to join the seminary," said Gina. "Did you think of that? He was young. Perhaps he had other things he wanted to be doing."

"He did a bunch of those things. Which is the reason I'm here. Obviously he had a lot of doubt about what the right thing was. On the one hand was the blinding fear that they wouldn't take him. On the other was the blinding fear that they would. So like this, between a rock and a hard place, my father spent his sophomore and junior year at U. of Iowa in Dubuque. And then as always, these things work out in certain ways. Not how you planned. After much hand-wringing, my father resolved that the monastic life was for him. He had been living here for weeks at a time, meditating, praying, reading. Finally, they accepted him into their Order as a novice.

"It was then that my mother told him she was pregnant. She didn't have to tell him. She was almost seven months at this point. They hadn't been together for some time. She had gone to clean other buildings and he had gone searching for other things"—she smiled—"like the Swami. He didn't know what she wanted him to do. She said she was about to have a child out of wedlock, and had no insurance and no job since the university fired her when she became in no *condition* to work. She needed to take care of the baby; would he be interested in marrying her? So: in front of him was my mother with me in her belly, and also in front of him was a monk's life. Both paths offered a choice of living for something other than himself. For a moment it seemed like a way out of the Order. Not a good way, but a way. That's when my dad realized he didn't want a way out.

"He still felt responsible for my mother, though. He told me even when he was young he felt that every time a child was born it meant that God was not yet disappointed in man. So he went to talk to the abbot, who told him that the Lord was deliberately making his path not straight, so that by his faith he would come to stand straight. The abbot asked my father if his decision would be harder or easier if he loved my mother."

"Good question," said Gina. Even she had put away her hunger and was listening.

"Yes. My father replied that he did love my mother. It was she who had a fickle heart. Not to put too fine a point on it. My father could not live his life with such constant anguish. But now there was a baby." Candy sighed. "To make his long story short, my dad didn't take his vows. He continued to stay here in Melleray, leaving after compline at seven-thirty to go be with my mother, who was living at a local shelter in Dubuque. Two months went by like this, shuttling from life to life—my father uncommenced to the abbey and uncommenced to my mother. In these muddled circumstances, I was born." Candy smiled. "And then a funny thing happened, Dad said, and that was the strange effect that babies have on adults around them. They reorder everyone's priorities. Babies come in and sweep the dust into corners and bring out the good china. He named me Grace, because that's what he said God had given him. My mother hated that name, but he didn't care. He would bring her and me here to Melleray, and she would sit much like Gina sits now in the refectory, disaffected and grim, while my dad carried me around to show the monks. Eventually he had to make a decision."

"Well, we know what he chose," said Gina.

"Yes," said Candy. "To marry my mother. He said he heard God's calling. At that point my mother refused to marry him. Apparently she had met a young man from New York who wanted to take her to meet his family. My father dryly asked if she intended to take her baby with her to meet them. She asked him to look after me for a couple of weeks until she returned. She promised to come back and my father promised the abbot the baby would be a temporary thing."

"Did she," I asked haltingly, "come back?"

"No."

I couldn't speak. I lost my appetite. In my greatest silence, I stared at Candy, my soul crying out, watching her intently, wanting to know how she repaired herself, how she made it out in one piece. She didn't have Emma. What she had was someone who renamed her Candy.

Gina, who had a mother, and a father, and a sister, and a home in the suburbs with dogs, was the only one to speak. "The man she was with . . ."

"Was not Erv, no. Two or three guys before Erv. She did write, care of the Melleray Abbey, telling my father she was living in Hartford, Philly, Dover, Blacksburg, finally Huntington. She would come for the baby when she could. In the meantime, my father stayed a postulate for two years, then a novice for four, and by that time I was six. He didn't take his solemn vows until I left him the summer before I turned twelve."

The room was quiet and absorbed all sound.

Estevan Rio picked that fine moment to show up with bread and butter, hot tea, and a bean, corn and rice stew, which, he said, he had made himself. He perched down on the bench, next to Candy, while Gina and I ate across from him. I was too nervous to eat voraciously like Gina. I pecked at my food as if I were royalty. The stew was good. Plenty of salt in it.

"So you're Shelby," said Estevan, gazing at me. "Grace told me a lot about you."

With fear, I glanced at him, at her. She smiled.

"She told me you're going to Harvard. Congratulations."

"Thank you."

"On a track scholarship," Gina put in, her mouth full.

His manner was gentle, but he didn't smile at anyone. Only when he looked at Grace, did his face soften. Is that what a man who is a monk looks like as he gazes upon his own flesh and blood? I wondered, gaping at him greedily, picking at my food.

"Is there anything you want to ask me, Shelby?" he said. "Or, is there something you want me to ask *you?*"

"Is there something I *should* ask you?" I said, looking away in embarrassment, my throat tightening.

"I can see by your face that Grace has been telling you her stories about me," he said, almost smiling, almost amused.

"It's not a secret, Dad."

"No, of course not," said Estevan. "You're a good girl. It's meant to encourage."

"Encourage, really?" That was Gina.

"Why?" said Estevan. "Is frighten a better word?" When Gina didn't respond, he said, "Has Grace told you her favorite one? About Judas? She does this especially to mortify people. It's her version of Edgar Allan Poe's 'The Tell-Tale Heart.' Don't despair." Estevan put his hand on Candy's shoulder and patted her affectionately. "Child, don't you think Luke 10 and the Hymn of Cassiani might be a better story for these two?"

Candy shook her head. "Don't think so, Dad. Too soft."

"Hymn?" I said. I had liked the hymns today. "Will they be singing the Hymn of Cassiani tomorrow?"

Estevan shook his head. "No, that hymn is sung only one night a year, on Good Tuesday. But ask Grace to tell you about it."

"Too meek, Dad. But the food's good." She had some bread, some stew, sitting close to her father.

"Shelby," said Estevan, "I'm going to tell you a story. Because you look like you need to hear it."

I wanted to ask if I looked like I needed money, too. Aunt Betty had thought so.

"How come you're not telling *me* a story, Brother Estevan?" said Gina.

Estevan smiled. "You don't look like *you* want to hear it. But all right, I'll tell you something. You know why I joined the Cistercian Order? Because I was in revolt. I rebelled against my meaningless life. I was confused and needed refuge. Until I found my way in here, I simply could not remember who I was. Here, songs grew up around me like a jungle. And every day since, the Psalms have pierced my heart. We all yearn for meaning, don't you agree? For the revelation of the divine mystery. That's the single-minded quest of all our existence, especially when we are young."

"But *I* know who I am," said Gina.

"That's very good." He nodded. "I commend you. Most of us are not as lucky." He turned his solemn face to me. "Now, Shelby," he began, "the evening after Jesus died and was buried, the chief priests and the Pharisees came to Pontius Pilate and asked for help. They were afraid the apostles might steal Jesus' body from the tomb and proclaim that he had risen. They asked Pilate's permission to put armed guards at the stone, 'Lest the disciples come by night and steal him away.'" Estevan paused. "Shelby, do you know what Pilate said?"

He waited. I was mummified. "Well—uh—no," I stammered.

"Do you know what he didn't say? Oh, you fools. Or, don't worry. It'll be fine. That's what he *didn't* say. What he said was, 'You have your watch. Go. *Make it as secure as you can.*'"

I waited for him. He waited for me, for my face to understand, for my dumb mouth to close. Was it a riddle I was supposed to figure out? I wasn't going to Harvard for my brains! I wanted to shout to him. Gina told you—track scholarship. Estevan smiled. "Just remember this. That Friday evening, Pilate was telling them that their fears were *not* unfounded. They had reason to be afraid. And perhaps he wasn't talking about a mid-evening kidnapping. There was terror on the Pharisees' faces as they left him. This was not at all what they had hoped to hear."

Stammer again. "Brother Estevan, forgive me, is it, um, something, that, um, *I* want to hear?"

Estevan nearly laughed. Soundlessly, like his daughter. "I don't know. Only you know." Reaching across and patting me gently on the top of my confused head, he got up. "Listen to the Psalms. They're the songs of mankind. Well, goodnight. I hope you have everything you need."

"We don't," exclaimed Gina. "We don't have a room. Or meat. Or, most important, a telephone. Is it any wonder we're not in the mood for parables?"

"You have a room," Estevan said. "Everything else will wait. And that was not actually a parable. A parable is a simple story told by Jesus to illustrate a spiritual or moral lesson. And in my story, Jesus was no longer telling stories. He was dead." He blessed Candy's head before he left, he kissed her, and made a sign of the cross in the air in our direction, which I was grateful for, while Gina scraped the bottom of her stew bowl like a raven and didn't look up.

Candy pushed her own bowl toward Gina after her father left.

"You guys are lucky," said Candy. "He must like you. My father is usually a man of few words. He probably spoke more to you than he has spoken in five years. The Trappist monks live a life of contemplative prayer. They say they can't hear God when they speak."

"Why?"

"Why what? There are many things that God wants to give us," said Candy, "but can't, because our heads and souls are filled with too much noise, and our hands are full. The monks here are silent so they can hear. And as for the rest of us . . ." Candy smiled, raising her arched brows and opening her hands. "Every once in a while, God empties our hands."

My heart drummed in my chest. *Empties our hands.* Why did that sound so ominous? The room faced north, was silent and dusky. There was no light save the small decorative fixture shining down on the long table. Suddenly the room began to remind me of the room Judas had crawled into, crawled into thinking he was finally saved and was told that no, his real sorrows were just beginning. It made me hurt for him, and scared for myself, and unhappy at eighteen to be thinking of such things. What was the point of your father's story, Candy, I wanted to ask again, but didn't dare in this room. What if she told me something that might relate to me? I didn't want anything in that story to relate to me.

"Why'd you leave this place?" I mouthed.

"It was time for me to go," said Candy. "I was getting too old. And I knew—my father could never enter the order until I left him. Besides, I did have a mother, after all. I wanted to meet her."

"God, Candy, don't say that," I whispered, my arms stretched out on the wooden table, like on a tree.

We fell quiet. Gina loudly gulped her water. "What did he do with you when they went to pray? They pray every five seconds around here."

"Seven prayer services, not including Mass. Ten hours a day in prayer during Lent. Holy Week, twelve to fifteen."

"Now I know," said Gina. "You lost your mind back then."

Candy shrugged. "I dunno. When I was little, I stayed in the tabernacle. They'd sing the Psalms. I'd draw or sleep."

"It's true," said Gina, "those Psalms would put anyone to sleep."

Why did it seem like joy to be serenaded to sleep by those mystical lullabies? Maybe I had lost my mind, too.

"What did they teach you here?"

"How to make caskets. I have one actual skill," said Candy, grinning. "I can go to work anywhere, making caskets. And you say I don't know how to do anything. Bet you don't know how to make caskets."

"Bet you're right," Gina agreed. "I'm not sure I know how to do some of the other things you do either."

There was a pointed silence. "Come on, Gina," I said in a low voice. "I'm pretty sure you know how to do some of those things." I turned my face to Candy. It was getting dark, I could barely make her out in shadows. "Why didn't you and your dad both leave?" I asked. "Get a place in Dubuque, finish school? Have you ever been to an actual school?"

"Stop teasing. And about the other thing: my father didn't

know how to live on the outside anymore. His days here were hard but after compline, he fell into bed and was asleep before he could finish his prayers. That's how he knew he was all right. Because when he had been in college, he couldn't get to sleep until the monks got up for lauds. His whole life had been inverted."

"So what did he do, put you on a bus?"

"Yes!" Candy exclaimed, but not too loud. "He gave me money, put me on a bus in Dubuque." She sighed wistfully. "I went looking for my life, and by God, I found it. Another girl would've run and not got off in Huntington city 'cuz it looked so pretty, but I did, and found her on the banks of the Ohio."

"What was her name?"

"Dana," she replied. "Dana Cane."

"Was she . . . happy to see you?" I asked, my voice almost breaking, not looking at her.

"She was surprised," Candy replied dully. "She said she had always liked surprises."

We had long stopped eating in the dimly lit wood and stone room. The food was cold, as were the bare limestone walls. It was dark and preternaturally quiet, so quiet, you could hear the rumblings in my heart, and in Gina's stomach. Everything was heard. There was no cover. Candy was right. It *was* terrifying and I was not prepared for how it made me feel. *I* wanted to turn away. I did turn away. From Candy, from Gina, from these walls.

"So you lived with your mother," I said, "and were with her until this summer, when you left."

"Something like that." She sounded dubious. "We moved around a lot. From place to place, state to state, town to town. Like vagabonds. Finally settled back on the Ohio." She stood from the table and took her plate. "I'm exhausted," she said. "When I'm here, my body remembers thousands of days waking up at three in the morning for vigil, and lauds and Mass, and all the little hours. By compline I'm falling down myself. What time is it? It

238

must be past nine." She smiled. "When I'm not here, I'm not asleep before nine in the morning. Right, Gina?"

"Hallelujah," said Gina, finally animated about something. "Now that was some fun."

Candy nodded. "Everything was inverted," she said. "Come with me. Wash your plates and I'll show you your room." She said she was going to sleep in her old room, next to her father's. "He left it empty all this time. Even my old blanket is still on the bed. He said he washes it every two weeks because he never knows when I might drop by to visit."

3

Rock, Paper, Eddie

She left us then, this shadow Candy of the real Grace, a girl who colored in the tabernacle and read the Bible and Merton and Martin and e.e. cummings her whole life, a girl who walked by her father's side, her father the Trappist monk, who lived in silence for hours in a mute sanctuary. She left me thinking of her here, and also in De Soto, her head lowered between the legs of the husband of the woman who took her in and gave her food. It occurred to me then how much there was in this world I did not know, did not understand, and could not hope to understand. I must have muttered something to this effect, something to express my bewilderment at the things I was discovering here, but Gina, hostile and alert, getting ready for bed, said, "You don't understand *her*? Why look so far, Shelby? Let me ask you, do you understand how a girl could sleep with her best friend's boyfriend, knowing that he is the love of her life?"

Ah. I sank to my bed, my hands consigned to my knees. Here it was. Where do you go from here? Where do you turn? There is no Andy Gibb coming between us telling me that love is thicker than water, no Rod Stewart telling me that if loving you was wrong I didn't want to be right. The Bee Gees were not staying alive, Mary McCormack was not torn between two lovers, Gloria Gaynor did not survive, and Molly was not between us, no Molly, no Aunt

240

Flo, or Aunt Betty, no dogs, no Candy. There was just me and Gina on opposite sides of our own little tabernacle, in our gray wooden stalls, and between us Eddie, that fire-brand hobo, that scarred, jumpy, black magic artist, unworthy, undeserving, unjust, disloyal, so disloyal—oh, the fickleness of his Eddie heart!—and how do I tell Gina that, unbelievably even to me—mostly to me—Eddie is also the love of my life.

The stone floor beneath my feet was cold.

How do I say to her that he told me things that no other boy ever said to me, that he made me feel like no other boy made me feel. Granted, my experience has been more limited than Gina's. I don't have her sexy name and frame. I looked almost like a boy, but was a girl who ran track and field faster than most boys. They had to catch me first. I didn't strut my stuff in tight jeans. Still, Eddie saw something in me. Maybe just that I was so open. But I don't like to believe that; I want to believe he saw something more. I thought we had had something more.

Hard to call it love, I thought, as I bent my head in a guest room at the abbey. I was grateful it was so dim, and Gina couldn't see my face, but surely, she could see me in front of her with my head bowed, as if I were praying or asking for forgiveness, except I was doing neither. I bent my head so she wouldn't see the truth of things in my eyes, ashamed only of how I felt about him, and wishing fervently to this day and at this hour that I had not felt that way.

But I had.

I still did.

He was hot, and he knew it.

Gina had been going out with a high school superstar, the basketball player all the girls swooned over. John Neal. He was lanky and lovely to look at with his black hair and blue eyes. And what's more, he was crazy about Gina. She went with him, and then met Eddie at the beach, just like she always tells it. Eddie was eighteen, by his own account a genius, and in Larchmont because his mother, a gypsy like him, moved there with her new boyfriend. So Gina, admired like a queen for snagging the basketball hunk's intensely sought-after affections, took up with Eddie, who was the direct complement to John on the color scale. Where John was tall, Eddie was—how shall I say it kindly—not tall. Where John was lean, Eddie was squat, with blunt hands and a bull neck, bow legs and thick feet. Where John's face could've been that of an Irish king, Eddie was small-eyed and Brillo-haired, more like the Irish king's servant. And yet . . .

Gina continued with John, and with Eddie, keeping their hearts in her pocket—and then Agnes got grounded.

Gina asked me instead to come out to the Hobbit Hole with her and Eddie. "You'll love him. He's so funny!" When we were barely seventeen, we went to a local bar that looked the other way at all the young girls and boys coming in. Eddie parallel-parked the truck in a spot no girl could have gotten into, he swaggered, pulled out a chair for me; he ordered us drinks and clinked with me, he drank only Melon balls, and became giddy. I'd never had Melon balls. I drank three, and became giddy myself. I want to say it was the Melon balls. He talked Morrison's poetry and Spinosa's philosophy—how could I know he was full of shit, he sounded so worldly. So otherworldly. At the end of the night, he drove us home, dropped me off first, and like a gentleman said he would walk me to my front door. While Gina waited in his truck, Eddie in one second, in the dark, just inside the front door, had me pressed against the wall, flat against it, kissing me so feverishly, I thought we would wake Emma two flights up with our agonized breathing. It was five minutes of unconsummated rapture, and he kept whispering he had to go or "Gina would get suspicious," and so he went, closing the door behind him. I was open like a door ripped off its hinges by a tornado.

In school the next day I carried the glazed look of someone who'd been hypnotized. After I got home, the phone rang.

He was at my door in thirty minutes. I told Emma I was going out for a little while. He took me to his mother's house (his mother was not home), where we spent an ecstatic and perspiring hour. God, I long to feel again with another human being how

Eddie made me feel that afternoon. Afterward, while stroking my trembling body, he called Gina to say he'd be a little late picking her up and told her he loved her. "I have to say it," he said to me, "otherwise she'd get suspicious." I nodded as if I understood. On the way home, I sat next to him on the bench seat, his arm around me, while Irene Cara's "Fame" played on the radio. He said that's how he felt. Like he was going to live forever. He sang along to it, and I gazed up at him transfixed, thinking he had the most beautiful out-of-tune voice. It was summer and warm outside, and Dan Fogelberg's "Same Old Lang Syne" played while we drove down the hills of Route 1 from Mamaroneck back to my house. We too sang a toast to innocence—mine—there and gone.

Things I did not understand then. Eddie was a player. But you know what? That was okay, because I wasn't going cross country to marry him, Gina was, and she *still* didn't understand he was a player. Eddie hadn't wanted Gina to be going out with John. And when Gina suspected the worst, she broke it off with John, and Eddie backed away from me. We needed to cool it, he said, see what else was out there. Gina, too, backed *far* away from me. I was the casualty between Eddie and Gina. She took him on any terms, and *that* I understood because I would've taken him on any terms, too. Had he said to me he was going to continue to see Gina, and Meg on the side, and Casey in California, I would have said, do you want me to be ready for you at midnight?

I had confessed to nothing; Gina never asked me. We just quietly and without fanfare stopped being friends. I blamed it, as I blamed all things happening in the world, on vile Agnes. For the entire senior year we did not speak, until the afternoon she accosted me unclothed in the girls' locker room and asked to join forces in our fight against loneliness across the prairies.

Bottom line: it was here in New Melleray Abbey that Gina felt impelled to confront me with this for the first time, and it was in New Melleray Abbey that I, who had been thinking up tomes in response to that question, suddenly had nothing to say.

"I'm sorry," I said. "I don't know what you're talking about.

243

You're imagining things." Truth was, I didn't want to talk about it. There was nothing to talk about. She clearly did *not* feel that there was nothing to talk about, developing a keen sense of right and wrong, of personal ethics, of certain things one did and did not do. For me to pretend was fatuous.

"How could you do it?" she said. "That's what I want to know. How *could* you do it? I thought we were best friends. I thought you were the only one I could trust."

"I'm sorry. I wasn't thinking. I shouldn't have done it. Knowing what I know now, I would never do it again." Knowing it was all for a heartless pilgrim.

And there I stood, with my bestest friend, my sister, on the cold stone floor of the abbey, while the pierced hitchhiker we'd picked up near Valparaiso—who not long ago had given head to a married man in De Soto, two states away—was in compline praying for the benevolence and intercession of the Holy Mother for the forgiveness of her sins. Mealy-mouthed, I said casually, "I didn't know it would upset you." That's what I said. I didn't know it would upset you, me sleeping with your boyfriend. After all, you had two, and I had none. How was that fair? You're the one who keeps talking to me about freedom. "Gina, you're the one who's always saying, you gotta be free, gotta act free, gotta live without guilt because guilt weighs you down. You only have one life, live it, take it, make yourself happy, you've got only one chance at this, have fun. So I did."

"I didn't know you were going to take my advice so much to heart, Sloane," Gina said bitterly. "Didn't you know I was full of shit?"

I did know. I just didn't want to think about it. I wanted what I wanted. "You had John, Gina."

"But you knew I loved Eddie!" she cried.

"Yes, but you said you loved John, too!" I cried back.

"We were best friends," she said. "You don't do that to your best friend."

"We weren't best friends. You were best friends with Agnes.

244

You replaced me. I was a stand-in friend, a substitute. You knew I didn't like her, yet you dragged her into our friendship and didn't care how I felt about it."

"I thought we could all be friends!"

"I hated her guts! How could I be friends with someone I hate?" I got scared and lowered my voice. I didn't want Estevan Rio to come knocking on the door asking why we were shouting in the abbey and why Gina was so upset.

"So you betrayed me because you didn't think we were friends anymore?"

"That's right," I said in a tiny voice.

"But, Shelby," she said intensely, "you know that *I* still thought we were best friends."

My head so low, I said, "I'm sorry, Gina."

She turned away. "Too late for sorrys," she said, lying down on a bed that was hard as a tombstone.

And I didn't say what was a hot brick in my throat, in my heart. Gina! I didn't say, I know you're upset with me. But for a second, think about me, and how I feel, knowing that the boy I thought was the love of my life, chose *you*, not me, to be with, to love. He had a choice. Stay with me, or go with you. And he did not stay with me. I know you might say it's my just punishment, but think how this makes me feel—about you, about him, about myself.

I lay down on my own bed. We didn't speak after that. There was nothing to say. Elton John was wrong. Sorry wasn't the hardest word. I said it aplenty. I sang it from the rooftops. *Love* was the hardest word. What could I do, Gina? was what was hardest to say. Forgive me. I loved the bum. I don't want to tell you because I don't want you to ask me the follow-up: do you still love him? On top of all my other sins I don't want to lie to you in an abbey.

A restless night passed and a silent, restless morning. We had slept turned to the wall in all our clothes. Possibly I cried. Or dreamt about crying. A monk brought us our Spartan breakfast—a piece of bread and some black tea. I asked him when the next service was, and he looked at me like I was asking when his next breath was. "Terce at 9:15," he said brusquely and vanished. We ate, I took a shower, and while Gina was taking hers, I sneaked out and meandered my way out of the maze through the cloisters back to the front of the abbey, where I tiptoed into the tabernacle. The men in white and black were chanting. I sat and closed my eyes to the morning. *Open my eyes that I may see . . .* they chanted. *I am a stranger in the earth . . . My soul breaks with longing . . .*

Lauds, Mass, Terce, Sext, None, Vespers, Compline, Opus Dei . . .

Gina and Candy pulled me out. The monks were still chanting. "Terce is long," Candy said.

"Ironic, that."

"Did you want to get going?" she asked. "We've been here two days."

"Have we? Oh, what's the rush? You haven't seen your father in years. I don't want to cut short your visit. I know how hard it must be. I understand. Take all the time you need." I glared at Gina's glaring. "*All* the time you need. Never mind us. We'll be fine. Right, Gina?" I turned to go back inside, to listen to them finish.

"No," Gina hissed. "Not right. We won't be fine. We've got two thousand miles to go!"

"Oooh." I waved my dismissing hand at her. "Look at you, always rush, rush. A couple of days isn't going to kill us."

Candy took me by the arms. "Sloane, you are *too* funny. But here, I have to agree with Gina. We have to go." She shook me lightly. "Come on, snap out of it. You've sat through all the hours. Twice. Besides," she added, her voice teasing, "Gina will have no hair left soon."

"Oh, nuts," said Gina, not teasing. "So she *is* coming with us? I thought we might leave her." She waved her hand with irritation. "You know what? Get me to Bakersfield, then do what you like. I won't care then. I'll be with Eddie. But let's go."

Slowly I shuffled back to the guest room to get my things. "Still don't know what the rush is," I kept grumbling. "After the dogs and the aunts, and two days at the casinos, everybody's acting like their dog's on fire."

"I'll sing the Psalms for you in the car," Candy said. "Any one you want. You see they repeat them so that they sing all 150 every two weeks. Every two weeks, for eleven years. I know them all by heart."

Gina was skeptical but apathetic in the muggy morning, which, she pointed out, was hardly morning as it was nearly noon. "Sloane, how far do you plan to drive today?" she asked sourly. "More than sixty miles, I hope. Because that's about what we drove three centuries ago when we first got to this godforsaken place."

Estevan was at the car with Candy. I sat behind the wheel, while Gina stood impatiently, tapping her foot, waiting for them to say goodbye so that Candy could get in the back.

"You know, *you* could get in the back," I suggested pleasantly. "That way you don't have to wait."

"Oh, you'd like that, wouldn't you?" snapped Gina. "No way. She's not even supposed to be here. She gets in the back."

I strained to listen to Candy and her father, but they were saying things to each other I didn't understand.

"Remember the Publican first, child," said Estevan.

"I never forget," said Candy. "I don't raise as much as my eyes."

"Remember Cassia. Remember what she wrote, what she sang about Luke 10. No one is deprived of absolution, no one. He is forgiven much who loves much."

"And I love much," Candy whispered. "Which is good, since I have to be forgiven for much also."

"Out of my heart for you flow rivers of living water," said Estevan. "I never condemn thee. You know that, don't you?"

"Of course I do, Dad. Don't speak about me to anyone. Please. And keep safe what I gave you."

"All right."

"Unless something happens to me. And then . . ."

"Nothing is going to happen to you. All things that are impossible are made possible. Now go with God. Be a lamb among wolves."

"Can I be a wolf among lambs?" She smiled and took his hand.

"Be of good cheer, Gracie."

"Always, Dad. You, too."

He kissed her head and blessed it. I watched them in the side-view mirror. She stood in front of him for a little while longer, buried in his cowl and tunic, then got in the car. Estevan looked in. "May you be filled with joy," he said to Gina, blessing her. "It is a privilege of your age." She rolled her eyes. To me he said, "Go ahead, Shelby. Make it as secure as you can." In mass confusion I drove out of the parking lot, and before the curve in the road, Candy turned and waved to him through the rear window. I watched him. He waved back.

"How does it end?" I asked. "You dragged me away, and I couldn't understand all the words, but how does that unending Psalm 119 end?"

"Much the same way it began," said Candy. "*I have gone astray, like a lost sheep. I long for salvation. Let my soul live.*"

EIGHT

LOOKING FOR
THE MISSOURI

1

Gina's Boredom

For a while we drove in near silence, with Candy directing us out of the rambling roads of the monastery. We were trying to find U.S. 20.

Between Gina's boredom, Candy's compline and my barely felt apologies, it was implicit that Candy would come with us; we would drive her out of state and across the country. Nothing was spoken, it was just understood that was how it was going to be.

I'm pretty sure Gina wanted it to be another way, because the first thing she said was a combative, "You know your father's logical error in that story about the Pharisees and the tomb? I mean, he's your dad and all, Candy, and I respect that, but you know his error? It's that you have to make anything secure at all. I'll give you an example. Say I don't believe there's a Loch Ness monster in a Scottish lake. And the reason I don't believe there is one, is because there isn't one. Would I really need to make my boat secure against it?"

"I don't understand your comparison," said Candy with a puzzled stare into the rearview mirror at me. She scooted to sit toward the middle between us.

I said, "That's because you haven't taken the SATs, Candycane, and don't know about analogies." I glanced at Gina. "Don't make trouble. And in any case, your analogy sucks."

"I don't think so."

"It does," I said. "The Loch Ness monster is something horrible that eats people."

Gina was quiet with meaning. "I rest my case," she said. "How can you have faith in something like that?"

"Oh, come on."

"You come on." We hadn't been on the road five minutes. Maybe this was Gina's payback for Buddha. I sped up. Maybe if I drove eighty, she'd stop talking.

"I'll give you another comparison," Gina said. "Witches. Warlocks. Ghosts. Ghouls. The Cyclops. Zeus. If you don't believe in them, why would you need to secure that rock?"

Candy's expression was too serene for a fight. She wasn't in it. She was still trying to guide me onto U.S. 20, to scratch the soles of her feet. She casually said, "Honestly, I don't get your comparisons. Are you mocking God with metaphor? The Pharisees and high priests, who didn't believe he was God, like you, still asked for the stone to be guarded. Why would they need to do that?"

"I don't know. Maybe they suspected foul play."

"That's what they said, yes," said Candy.

"Maybe they suspected the disciples would steal him away and pretend he had risen."

"Are these the same disciples that abandoned him and hid away in fear of their own lives, fully believing that all they had been taught was gone and God was dead?"

Gina said testily, yes, those same disciples. "Clearly the Pharisees thought they might kidnap him."

"Imagine their surprise, then, when Pilate, instead of saying, don't be silly, you lumpfish, said to them dryly, 'Go ahead. Make it as secure as you can.' What do you think they made of that?"

Gina tutted impatiently.

"Why would he say that?" continued Candy. "Was he laughing at them? And why would they need to make it secure? To use your

Loch Ness analogy, would you need to make anything secure against something that had no probability of being true? If someone told you, you needed to close your windows because locusts the size of cats would fly through your curtains, you'd laugh, wouldn't you? You wouldn't go to the mayor and say, perhaps we need to cement our windows in case cats with wings come calling in the next day or two? Dear Mayor, we're afraid the Joneses down the road might fake people out by rigging some flying cats. What can we do?" Candy chuckled in good humor. "Clearly the Pharisees were afraid Jesus rising from the dead *might* come true, *could* come true, and Pilate, calmly, and without himself questioning anything, said the worst thing, from their point of view, he could say. He didn't say they were silly to worry. He wasn't skeptical. He didn't roll his eyes. He didn't even tell them to make a superfluous effort. He said: Go ahead. Keep watch. But by all means, do your best. Make it as secure as you can. That doesn't sound to me like Loch Ness, is my point."

"It's all nonsense, is *my* point," Gina said. "You can live out your whole life, and never think about any of this, never sing the Psalms and die unrepentant and completely happy."

"You're so right," said Candy with a hearty nod. "You can live out your whole life and never think about any of this."

Up and down the hills I drove, between fields and trees, corn husks littering the road, beneath a relentless gray sky filled with swift-flying swallows. The morning was overcast and thick and all I could hear was the echo of the monks singing.

"What does that mean?" Gina said after an hour had passed. "Why do I have a feeling you were trying to insult me and I missed it?"

"Candy, can you sing Psalm 150?" I asked.

"Don't change the subject, Sloane," said Gina.

"I didn't know there was a subject."

Turning up Supertramp on the radio, Gina turned to the window. "Well, I don't want to hear the Psalms," she said. "I'm all psalmed out."

253

"I think someone is afraid of the spiritual pressure of the monastery," said Candy lightly.

When I was young, it seemed that life was so wonderful . . .

When that song was over, Gina turned down the radio. "You want to know what your problem is?"

"No," replied the amiable Candy.

"You refuse to accept that you could be wrong, that other people might have a different opinion."

"What opinion?"

"About your little abbey, and your little Psalms and your little God."

"My little *God?*" Candy repeated.

"Yes. My aunt believed in God. Look where that got her. Dead."

"Do you think she got dead *because* she believed in God?"

"Clearly it didn't help!"

"Clearly."

"That's my point."

"Um—can I ask what god was this?"

"No. 'Cause it's a stupid question. A god that couldn't help my poor aunt, that's what god. In other words, a useless god."

"But that's what I'm asking. When Moses went to Mount Sinai to meet God, his people prayed to the golden calf. He was pretty mad when he came down that mountain. Smashed the stone tablets to pieces."

"My aunt didn't pray to the fucking golden calf, Candy," Gina said slowly, turning around. "What are you talking about?"

"You're right, nothing. Let's drop it."

"Yes, let's," I said. "Candy, sing me Psalm 100."

"No Psalms, I said!" said Gina, cranking the radio volume. Just as quickly, she twisted it down. "I have a goal," she said to Candy. "I'm going to get married to a young man I love. He's the only one I want to be with."

(What about Todd from South Bend? I wanted to say, but of course, *of course*, didn't.)

"We're going to make a family," she continued. "That's what I want to do. I'm going to go to school, then teach elementary school. Get a little house. Have kids. Does that sound so wrong to you? What do *you* want to do?"

"Gina, that's good," said Candy. "It's good to know what you want at a young age. I'm glad you have your ducks all in a row. My father said he thought you did."

"I don't think I do—I *do*!"

"That's what I meant."

Were *my* ducks all in a row? I had thought so, but I couldn't say. I didn't want to invite Gina's scorn.

"So, Cand," I said, "look at those well-planted trees, those silos. Is Iowa a rich state or what?"

"And I'd know this how?"

Gina didn't let me change the subject. "I like spiritual people. That's why I followed the Swami for a while."

"The Swami," Candy said slowly. "Is that who you not three seconds ago called a useless god?"

"No! He was very spiritual for the living, and taught wonderful and helpful life lessons. He was kind and forgiving. Nothing could have helped my aunt."

"Okay, Gina." I tried to diffuse her.

"Perhaps you're right," said Candy. "Then again, perhaps you're not."

"Candy, come on, let it go," I said quietly.

"You don't think I'm right!" Gina exclaimed.

"Gina, I'm allowing for the possibility you may not be right, yes," said Candy. "There is at least that possibility, no? That another God, one of comfort and love, might have helped your poor aunt?"

"I hate religious people," Gina declared. "They're so judgmental and dogmatic."

"What's the difference between spiritual and religious?"

"Spiritual people are *good*," said Gina. "Religious people are always telling you how to live. They're zealots. They have this holier-than-thou attitude I can't stand. Spiritual people just believe what they believe and don't bother anyone else. That's what I like. Not to be bothered."

"Well, sure," said Candy. "Who wouldn't? But am *I* telling you how to live?"

"Yes! You and your father. You think I'd be better off being like you."

"Not at all," said Candy. "Not in the slightest. I'd never wish that on anyone."

"Who are you to judge?" Gina went on. "Who are *they* to tell me I'm living wrong, just 'cause they wear a robe and have a cross around their necks?"

"*Is* there a right way to live?" Candy asked.

"I don't know. No one knows! They're guessing, just like me. We all have to figure it out for ourselves."

"Do we need a little help now and again?"

"Not from them."

"Who is this them? And if not from *them*, from who, then?"

"From other people. People you respect."

"Like who?"

"I don't know. Other people. Teachers. Politicians. Your friends. The voice inside your head. Listen to that, Cand."

"But what if the voice inside my head tells me to hope in God?"

Gina shrugged. "That's your trip, man."

"But priests know nothing?"

"Right. They're always on the news, saying, don't do this, don't do that. A lot of stuff we *can't* do. It's just not appealing, to be perfectly frank," said Gina. "All that parochialism, that arrogant attitude."

Candy said nothing.

"They're living in la-la land. They can't keep up with the times. All these people who don't know me, telling me what to do," Gina continued. "They don't know what's good for me. What's good for one person may not be good for another. I hate being dictated to by complete strangers. Really turns me off."

"You've been a church goer, then?"

"No, I never go. I *choose* not to go. The likes of you keep telling me I have free will."

"So who's dictating to you?"

"They would if they could," said Gina. "I won't let them."

"All these barricades you've set up for yourself," said Candy. "Is it to prevent yourself from thinking?"

"What barricades? I think plenty, just not about your stupid bullshit. Nobody owns me. Nobody owns my life. Sloane here agrees with me. She wants to have the free will to kick a puppy," said Gina. "Right, Sloane?"

"Leave me out of your little analogies."

Like I hadn't spoken. "What I'm asking is," said Candy, "are there absolute things that it's bad to do?"

Gina stared at me. "I guess," she said. "A few of them."

"Like what?"

"Look, can you two stop this?" I snapped, speeding up.

"We need to be more forgiving," said Gina. "We'd all be better off."

"Where did this whole concept of forgiveness come from?" asked Candy. "Forgiveness means, you did something wrong, and someone said, it's okay, don't worry. But the wrongdoing is essential. Otherwise there'd be nothing to forgive."

"Well, maybe forgive is a wrong word then," Gina amended. "I mean more, like, let it go, man. Just let it go."

"Like all things, let it go?"

"Sadly, yeah."

"It's all okay?"

"I guess." She shrugged. "Clearly, not all is okay. Kicking puppies, for example. And other things." She took a breath. "But some things are up for dispute. Why is the church always telling me I can't have premarital sex, or use contraception, or have an abortion, or whatnot? That's the kind of stuff I mean."

"Okay, sure, abortions are good," said Candy, "but what about

257

the other stuff? Like burning the houses of people you don't like, or putting water in someone's gas tank, or siccing your dog on a human being, or—"

"Jeez, Candy, you're so literal. Obviously," said Gina, "those things are wrong."

"Says who?"

"Says society."

"Where'd society get all that from? Why did they decide that you stealing money from an open cash register is wrong?"

"Because it hurts other people."

"Ah. So things that hurt other people are wrong?"

Gina tried very hard not to look at me. "Yes."

"What about things that hurt yourself?"

"See, no. If you hurt yourself, it's your choice."

"Isn't stealing also your choice?"

"But it affects other people!"

"What if you steal from someone who is very rich and barely notices? What if you take a diamond necklace from your friend, and she's got three of them. You don't have any, she's got three. Is that wrong?"

"Yes, stealing is wrong."

"What if you eat the dog's food and the dog starves?"

"That would also be wrong."

"But a dog is not a person."

"God, you're so literal! Other living things, okay?"

"Plants? Ants? Snails? Lilypads?"

Gina rubbed her face. "Shelby's right. This conversation *is* ridiculous."

But we were trapped in the car on the open road with nowhere to go, and the Top 40 was boring us to tears. Gina refused to allow the Psalms, and we couldn't talk about Erv because he was all too real, so we talked about this.

"What you do to yourself affects other people, too," said Candy. "Say you take drugs. And your kids run around neglected. That's hurting somebody, no?"

258

"Yeah, but if you take drugs and you don't have kids? Who does it hurt, then?"

"I don't know. Do you have parents who love you? Brothers? Sisters? An elderly aunt? Your best friend? What about the dog that'll die if you don't feed him? Or the cat that needs a drink while you're strung up on smack? You say you're free, but aren't you just as enslaved, to drugs or drink or whatnot? Aren't you enslaved to sin?"

"I totally disagree with this whole notion of sin," said Gina.

I furrowed my puzzled eyebrows. *Do* you, Gina, I inaudibly whispered. You didn't last night. How did she manage to argue this on both sides of the aisle?

"What about all the kids you could have and don't because you're tripping out?" Candy asked.

Gina breathed out in frustration. "This is just idiotic. So what?"

"I don't think you've thought deeply about this, is what," Candy said calmly.

"How do you know what I've thought deeply about? You have no idea."

"I do. By the things you say. I get the feeling that there are some things you feel are absolutely wrong, but if you say so, it'll weaken your argument. So you throw up your hands and say I don't want to talk about it, but what you really mean is, you don't want to *think* about it. Which is fine. But if you were a little more honest, you'd have to admit that if there *is* a Truth out there, then it demands certain things from you. It's like a path. You have to know what the path is, and where it is. It's nice and convenient to pick and choose the parts of the road you like, and reject the parts you don't want to apply to you. You're not really walking the road, then, are you, you're just flailing, hitting every tree in the forest. Because I guarantee you, Gina," Candy continued, not letting Gina interrupt, "that drug addicts are as vociferous defending their drug use and their consequent neglect of everything else in their lives as you are defending your positions on free sex. Bank robbers have a thousand good reasons for robbing banks and how society is to

259

blame. What I'm saying is, everybody defends their own sin, while managing to be smug about other people's. Mine is not so bad, but yours, now yours is *terrible*. But either there is such thing as sin, or there isn't. You say there isn't. Okay. But if there is, then it's governed by forces other than you. Either there is Truth, or there isn't. That's your choice: live your life like there is Truth, or live your life like there isn't. I have no problem with anything you say. It's your selective morality I question. I noticed how all the things you picked that were against some vague notion of right and wrong, you yourself do not do. I assume you don't do drugs or kick puppies. But all the things you rail at some phantom priests for judging you for, I assume you do or would like to do. You want a live and let live policy toward yourself, but we all want that. You want acceptance, we all want it, addicts and thieves, and killers."

"What the hell . . ."

"And by the way," said Candy, "just so we're clear, I am the first of all sinners. I tell you this like I'm in the confessional. I am less perfect than you can ever imagine. You are an angel of the Lord compared with me."

Gina scoffed. "No kidding."

"But I don't pretend I'm doing anything else but wrong, and then spend my time justifying it. I don't go around saying there is no wrong, and all the things I do are right. Just the opposite. I judge myself harshly, and give everyone else a break." Candy smiled. "Let them work out their own salvation."

"The only thing I agree with," said Gina, "in your whole mess of nonsense is that you're right—everybody does defend their own sin." She tried very hard not to look at me, and I tried very hard not to look at her.

"Truth comes in many faiths," Gina added after half an hour had passed. "I don't have to be a believer in any particular one. How can you be so certain about something you have no proof of? Me, I like to keep an open mind, that's all."

"Ah," said Candy. "Now you're getting somewhere. So you'd like God to supply you with proof so you can believe?"

"That would be nice. He wants me to believe? Then he needs to prove himself to me."

"So now God is your little performing monkey? Jumping through flaming hoops on your command?"

"No, and I don't want to talk about it anymore!"

"Sort of like the devil asked Jesus to be a little performing monkey for him. It wasn't enough for Jesus to turn stone into bread, he had to throw himself on the rocks and then miraculously come back to life."

"I said I didn't want to talk about it!"

"The people at Calvary said it, too. If you're God, come on, come down from that cross. Show us. Prove it. Nah-nah."

"How many times, how many different ways am I going to have to say it?" Gina yelled.

"Okay, fine. But, Gina," said Candy, "don't forget. Make it as secure as you can."

"Holy God!"

"Guys, can we *please* talk about something else?" I said.

"Like what?" Gina snapped. "Like what she's doing in our car? What danger we're in because she's in our car? How I told you not to pick her up and you didn't listen to me, and now look. Is that what you want to talk about?"

And from the back, Candy intoned, "O Jesus, hurl yourself from the cross, show us what you're made of!"

"Ahhh!" I think that was me.

Thus we reached U.S. 20 and drove for a long time without stopping, we crossed half the state, and it took us half a day. Iowa didn't look like Maryland—the trees in Iowa were all planted in purposeful clusters around the farms to protect them from tornadoes. The more trees, the more prosperous the farm.

Were farms prosperous? This is what I was reduced to, in a car where no one was speaking, and where REO Speedwagon kept on loving me except they didn't know what Joy Division knew, that love would tear us apart, I was thinking of living on a farm, hidden in the trees, the tornadoes coming every summer and tearing the whole place down while The Jam went underground. Candy started to sing. *Remember, O Lord, Your tender mercies . . . do not remember the sins of my youth, nor my transgressions; according to Your mercy remember me . . .*

"What did I say?" barked Gina.

Was Styx right? Was this the best of times? I wasn't sure. I hoped not. I was an American girl driving across America the beautiful, the sky above me, the golden valleys, one of my companions was hostile and not speaking, and her hostility was preventing me from hearing the loud Elton rock or from daydreaming about being torn apart by tornadoes.

There was plenty like me to be found, but not like Candy, a mongrel who didn't have a penny . . . I wished I could stop driving because the thing I wanted to do was look at her, not like Gina with irritated puzzlement, but with bewilderment. As in: who are you, you who waltzed into my car? Who are you that came first on a road I was never going to go on, and I passed you by, then you came to me again, on another road I was never going to go on, but this time, I stopped. Now, you're saying things in my Mustang that I've never heard, making me think things I've never thought, and do things I'd never dreamed of. You are not even eighteen. Who are you?

2

Hoadley Dean

We stopped for a late lunch and gas in Waterloo in the middle of the state. After that the road got bleaker, the sky got grayer. I was closing my eyes in a narcoleptic funk as I drove, but Gina and Candy got their second wind.

"Not atheist, agnostic!"

"What's the difference?" asked Candy.

"Oh, same difference," I chimed in, but Gina didn't think I was funny.

"You want proof? What about Design as Order?" continued Candy as if there had not been a three-hour break in the conversation. "What about Purpose, Simplicity, Complexity? Sense and Coherence, Information and Cosmic Constants, the laws of physics, of nature, and nature itself, the beauty of the world? One has to try very hard to be an atheist in this world, one has to have real blinders on."

"Not atheist, agnostic!" Right into it, that Gina, the salsa not dried at her lips. "Open-minded. I'm saying I don't know. I'm keeping an open mind. Leaving my options open. Because I *just* don't know."

"Okay. But in your world of open-mindedness, you have to somehow acknowledge Jesus, no? Even to reject him. Or to refute him, if you're able, to react to him in some way. In the world of

'I'm keeping my options open,' why isn't he even making the cut at the bottom of your waiting-list? How did you manage to discard him without so much as a mental argument with yourself?"

"I don't know what you're talking about. I think about other things."

"Yes, you talked about Baba, about Ashram, dualism, a little monism. What about equal time for Jesus?"

"You know why? Because I'm just not interested in your philosophy."

"Then how can you say you have an open mind? Open to what? Everything other than Jesus?"

"Yes. Because the whole Jesus thing is not important to me."

"But it speaks to the heart of man."

"No, it doesn't."

"The God question *is the* most fundamental question of human existence."

"No, it isn't."

"What was he? Tell me. In your opinion."

"I have no opinion on the subject."

"Why not? You have an opinion on everything else."

"No, I don't."

"Did he exist?"

"I don't know!"

"So he didn't exist?"

"I never said that."

"No, you didn't say much. Okay. So if he existed, what was he? One way or another you have to recognize his presence in the history of mankind."

"No, I don't."

"It's not *just* about the design or chaos of the universe. It's not about evolution or the Big Bang. It's not about something that impersonal and removed."

"Then what is it about?"

"It's about *the love that moves the sun and the other stars*," said Candy. "It's about Sin and Grace. The Holy Trinity, God speaking through Beauty, through sex, through marriage. It's about the Sacraments, prayer, the Gospels, Freedom, Virtue, Christ's two commandments, the historical value of the New Testament, oh, and let's not forget His Incarnation, Crucifixion and Resurrection. Doesn't an open mind imply that you *have* to deal with at least some of these questions?"

"No, it doesn't."

"This is what I think," said Candy. "I don't think you've thought about it and dismissed it. I think you're dismissing it because you don't want to think about it."

"I'm dismissing it," said Gina, "because I don't give a shit."

"Exactly." Candy was very hard to offend or goad.

"But you can't make me care by badgering me! You can't force me to care about your little beliefs. You know what my most fundamental question is? How long is it going to take me to get to Bakersfield. I like music, I like to hang out, I like my friends, I love my family, I *love* my fiancé. And, unlike the person sitting next to me driving this fool car, I love dogs. I try not to hurt other people, I keep to myself. I'm like your black-truck driver. I do me, and you do you. What's wrong with that?"

"Is that your philosophy of life? I do me and you do you?"

"Yes! Mind your own damn business and I'll mind mine."

"Then why were you lecturing me about the married guy up in the hills?"

"Because that affects me! I care about that. I don't care about your Jesus. I. Just. Don't. Care. And you can't make me. It's like when Shelby starts talking about geography. My eyes glaze over."

Like I was saying, said Candy.

Like I was saying, said Gina.

I, Shelby, who had contributed nothing to this entire exchange, coughed to clear my throat, and said, "But, Gina, if you're all about the live and let live, why did you, along with your mother, for three years try to convince me of the rightness of Baba and Hathayoga?"

"Because I cared!"

265

And now I said okay. Candy laughed and because she could never stop, even when she was a word ahead, said, "There are some people who hate Christianity and call their hatred an equal love for all religions."

"I don't hate Christianity!" exclaimed Gina. "That would imply a degree of involvement I don't have. I'm exactly like Shelby in this."

Candy prodded me, twirling the hair at the back of my head. "No, I don't believe you are."

I, Shelby the diplomat, said nothing, by the art of my own omission managing an affront to atheists, agnostics, my best friend, a well-meaning hitchhiker, *and* Jesus.

It started to rain. It was four, then five p.m., and we were straggling at thirty, forty miles an hour behind an oil truck. I couldn't pass an oil truck. I had visions of slipping on the ice, so to speak, ramming into its side, and burning to death. I slowed down. The cars behind me honked furiously through the rain. The oncoming traffic was too heavy for them to pass us, and I followed that truck through every town in western Iowa. I guessed it was headed to Nebraska, like us. Candy had been sleeping, but the first thing she said when she woke up was, stop, pull over, what are you doing? Let it get ahead.

I pulled over and we just sat for a while watching the rain. So she didn't think we were safe even here. Would the truck driver have spotted our small yellow car tucked behind him on a wet one-lane road? What if he did? "Get it through your head, Sloane," she said. "A truck is like a direct phone line to Erv. And I mean that literally. They call his handle on the CB, straight from their vehicle, and they talk to him about us." No music, no metaphysical argument could take the place of facing down the miles talking about this.

When at last Candy felt it was safe to get going again, it was excruciating to watch the time tick away, one minute at a time, and to know that in that one minute we'd gone maybe a third of a mile. Traffic lights were on every corner and were all red. Farms receded into gray fog. Now, as the sky shaded to dark blue, the rain slashed harder. The lights, red and yellow, glistened off the streaming black asphalt and pierced the night like bullets. I longed to ask Candy if she thought Erv knew where she was, but I didn't want Gina, who looked to be almost sleeping, to become reacquainted with our troubles. I wished Gina would sit in the back and sleep so I could talk to Candy.

"The Jews didn't need a Savior," Gina said suddenly. "Why do we?"

Wow, I thought. New Melleray really got under Gina's craw. She just couldn't let it go. Half asleep, Candy replied. "Was Jesus a simple man? A great man? A chosen man? A delusional man? A clever promoter of himself? An imaginary man? Or God Himself walking around Galilee?"

"Take your pick. Nobody's right, nobody's wrong. We're all right in a sense."

"It's like the United Nations." That was *my* one contribution. Gina turned away.

"Who'd want to live in such an arid desert?" asked Candy. "Who'd want to miss out on the most sublime gift ever offered man? Not me."

"I don't think you know *where* you want to live, Candy," said Gina.

Both road and sky had darkened. I had driven for so long I couldn't believe we were still in Iowa, that we hadn't yet reached Sioux City on the river across from Nebraska. How was it possible that nearly a week had passed and we were in the same state? I was so weary of being behind the wheel, and it was too dark to see the map. We had been rolling steadily uphill, and I made a lame joke about a city that was *right* on the river being so *high* up in the hills. Gina humorlessly said that was because we were still *miles*

away, and that just depressed me further. I thought a road trip was supposed to be fun. How much money did I have left? I was afraid to count. Every time we stopped we bought bagfuls of chips, pretzels, popcorn and Cokes. The car was filling up with greasy plastic bags like a water tank.

"Don't worry, Shel," said Candy. "Look, let's stop here. I see a place."

On our side of the highway stood a drab little unit called Pines Motel. It was set back from the road, which both Candy and I liked, and in front was a bar, with flashing red neon that blinked "Bar n' Grill." Candy said a bar was good. I said a grill was good for my empty stomach, but she was already out of the car and inside the tiny office to get us a room. Neither Gina nor I moved. We sat and watched her through the two sets of doors and windows. It was still raining something awful.

"God, what's wrong with you?" I said.

"What's wrong with *me*? I can't believe you have the nerve to ask me that."

"I'm asking. You've been picking on her the entire day."

"Gee, I wonder why."

"Look," I said, "I'm doing the best I can."

"Are you, Sloane? Are you really? Doing the best you can?" Gina emitted a black chuckle. "Nicely done."

I swirled away in my seat.

"Look at where we're staying," Gina said. "A few days ago we'd never be caught dead staying in a place like this. We'd pass it on the road and say, aren't we lucky we're not the type of girls who stay in a fleabag motel marked with omens and evil portents."

"It's not marked—"

"Shelby, don't be so fucking naïve. Stop pretending you're ten. Look around you! Open your eyes. We're hiding out in a trash dump because the chick *you* insisted on picking up is being followed by someone who wants to kill her. What do you think is going to happen to us when we become witnesses to her murder? You think a man who will kill her is just going to leave us alone? You didn't listen to me, you didn't listen to a word I was telling you. You wouldn't take my advice. You acted as if you were not my friend." She shrugged. "Well, why not. And you ask what's wrong with me!"

"Gina, I am your friend, come on," I whispered. "I'm sorry for this. But it'll be all right. We're just going to drop her off in Reno. It's on the way—"

"Have you asked yourself what business she has in Reno? And how do you know she's not going to need your help after she gets there? What gives you the idea that she won't be requiring your services past Reno?"

Grimly we watched her paying, talking to the office clerk, smiling. Gina was right. "I will tell her that after Paradise we'll— I promise. I will tell her—"

"Shelby, give it a rest. You're going to be carrying her water until you save her. I know it. You know it. She knows it. The only thing you don't know that I know—and that she also knows, by the way—is that you *won't* save her. You're spinning your wheels for nothing."

"What you're saying is not true," I said, ashen, but I couldn't look at Gina. "What you're saying isn't right. I'm not carrying her water. I'm just helping her out."

"Can't you see? She's using you!"

"Abandoning her is wrong."

"Yes, and we know how you're all about the right and wrong, Shel."

I tutted in wretched frustration, but thankfully Candy opened the door, like Pyrrhus. "We can park over there, by the last cabin under the trees. Won't be able to see the car from the road at all. The manager said they serve food at the bar till two in the morning, so we're all set. Come on."

I did as she told me. I drove to the room, parked behind the bushes. We unloaded. The room smelled unsavory, of unsavory people and their unsavory lives. Gingerly we put our things on the chairs, and walked back across the gravel to the bar in the rain. Before we left, Candy had transformed herself once more. She had reapplied her black liner and red gloss so dark it looked black too. She moussed her hair, put on her own clothes, a mini-skirt and short white T-shirt with no bra. Her nose-ring went back in, so did the belly-button ring. I'd never known anyone who had had her belly button pierced and wondered if it had hurt her.

At the bar, we drank enthusiastically, and ate listlessly. We were the only girls in the bar, and while this made me distinctly uncom-fortable, Candy seemed to revel in it. Gone was the girl from the abbey, walking quietly with her father through the pine paths and falling mute in the cloisters. She was flirty on the barstool, smiling tantalizingly at the truckers. Gina admonished her to be more careful but Candy shushed her to be quiet. At that, Gina tutted and said she was going back to the room. I got to my feet and said me, too. Shrugging, Candy barely looked up from her drink, her coquettish eyes lowered to the bar counter while a very inebri-ated, heavy, older man spoke close to her ear. I was almost out the door when I turned around and saw her, a young girl in a bar, verbally jousting and coming on to truckers. Torn for a moment between acting in my self-interest (mollifying Gina so she wouldn't leave me) and Candy's, I sighed and turned back. Gina swore, but I was already sitting down at the bar, pretending I hadn't heard. What a funny animal man is—when faced with a choice between his own preservation and the protection of the assuredly lost, he opts to crawl back to the barstool. Peculiar and distressing as it was, I crept back to the inexplicable.

There were a few tables, a few patrons; everyone smoking; on the jukebox Fleetwood Mac was *so afraid*, probably of the *devil woman* and then Billy was a hero. And when Billy was being a hero, I started paying attention to Candy's new squeeze. He was young and countrified, had a nice little drawl; Candy and I enjoyed listening to him. He said yes, m'am, and hello there, miss; he was polite and young. I was wearing a baseball cap because my hair was wet and gross from the rain and had on no makeup. I felt more wretched than usual, which is saying a lot, while Candy sparkled and smiled, her eyes made up, her tattoos hidden, looking petite and so pretty. The young Kentucky stud, whose name was Hoadley Dean, went on and on about driving on I-80 for the last four hours and hating the rain. We nodded in vigorous agreement. He asked where we were headed. Demurely Candy said Rapid City. Bat eyelashes. Ah yes. Hoadley had been there. "Yes," Candy said. "Me, too. My aunt and niece live there. My aunt was married but her husband just died. I'm going to visit them." She introduced me. "This is Virginia. My cousin." She stuck out her hand to Hoadley. "I'm Ronnie. Short for Veronica."

"Well, good to meet you, Virginia and Veronica," said the milky-haired, spotty young man shaking our hands and smiling from behind his beer. "Don't meet too many nice girls on the road."

"I bet you don't," said Candy. "And who says we're nice girls?" She threw back her head and twittered, he twittered back and leaned his body closer to her on the barstool. They talked about Rapid City. I had thought much of what came out of Candy's mouth was a lie, but she talked about Rapid City as if it were not. There was a place on the map called Rapid City, South Dakota, and Candy spoke of the Fire Brewing Co. on Main Street and Wall Drug, where she said she had worked for two summers while staying with her folks. The aunt used to have this cute little car, she said, a hand-me-down rusted red Camaro, which she let Candy borrow.

"Hey," Hoadley said, "as you were driving, you didn't happen to see a cute little yellow Mustang on the road, did you?"

"No, why?" Candy smiled. I froze. "Should we have?"

"There's a reward for finding a runaway in it," he replied with a shrug. "It's all over the CB."

"Oh, yeah?" Candy said, perking up. "How much of a reward?"

Hoadley eyed her, his casual gaze becoming less casual. "A few bucks," he said carefully. "Nothing major. What's it to you, sweetheart?"

Candy circled the air with her finger, as light as if she were at a ballgame. "Just makin' conversation, cowboy. Haven't seen the

271

yellow 'Stang. But let me ask you—if we see it, how do we let you know?"

He admitted that would be difficult. "I wasn't askin' you to look out for it in the future. I was askin' if you'd seen it in the past."

"In that case, no," she said. "We only came up from Waterloo, though. Took us forever in that rain."

"Tell me about it. It took me longer to go the few miles north from Omaha to Sioux City than it took to drive all day 'cross Iowa." He drank. "They wouldn't be local, anyway. They're on I-80. Heading west. But still, thought I'd ask, just in case. No harm in asking."

"No harm at all," Candy agreed.

Hoadley lowered his voice. "Reward's five thousand bucks."

Candy whistled. "Wow. Nice chunk of change."

"No kidding. I'm gettin' married next month. Could really use it."

"I bet. Someone must really need to find that girl."

"Three girls." He eyed her. "About your age."

"I'm twenty," said Candy. "But three? That's a lot of runaways."

"The other two are transporting her. I bet they have no idea it's a felony to knowingly transport a minor across state lines."

"Well, we'll be on the lookout," Candy said quickly, while I sat with a paralyzed grimace on my face. "So are the police involved, then? The FBI, if it's an interstate thing?"

"Nah. Man who's looking for her says it's family business. He prefers to keep it that way."

"I see. Though like you said, I doubt they're this far north. But you think it's the only yellow 'Stang on the road?"

"Probably." He downed his beer and inched closer to Candy. "I've never seen one." He settled around his barstool and hung his arm near her. "So what do you say, sweetheart?"

I tried to excuse myself, like a child who walked in on her parents and just as awkwardly. Candy said quietly, "Where's your room?"

"Right out front," he said, all perked up, as if he didn't think it would be that easy.

Lowering her voice, she said, "Tell me your room number and I'll meet you there in fifteen. I just have to tuck my cousin in."

He grinned wide. "Bring her, too," he said, with a double lift of his brows.

Candy smiled. "Tempting. But I don't think she'll go for it. A bit of a prude, you know?"

"Ask her."

But the prude was already off her barstool, moving fast toward the door. Candy caught up with me. "We gotta go, *now*," she said.

"Really? Oh, well, only if you think that's a good idea."

"Stop," she said. "Go quick. Pack up the room."

"What about Gina?"

"Bring her, too. No use leaving her behind. She'll get cranky."

"When we drive out the only exit, and his room is right at the front, you don't think he'll notice?"

"I don't think he will. He's pretty wasted. Just go back to the room, get our stuff, load up, and let me worry about him. Be ready with the car running in twenty-five minutes."

"Twenty-five minutes, you're joking!"

"He won't last longer than that."

"For goodness' sake! I don't mean that," I said, impatiently. "I mean twenty-five minutes is not enough time to pack and get out."

"Shel, just quit yakking and get packing, will ya? We have to go!"

"After you've finished with him," I persisted, "you know he'll go straight to the office and ask what kind of car the devil girls were driving."

"Boy, you sure do worry about a lot of stuff," Candy said, urgently prodding me along the gravel. "When he goes to ask, the office manager will tell him we were driving a brown Comet, 1973. License plate fake. Let him try to track it down."

"Candy, you're too much."

"Thank you. Now do you remember what you have to do?"

"Hmm. Gina'll go through the roof."

"What else is new. Go. Get everything out of the room, including my stuff, and wait for me outside with the car running."

"I know, I know."

So back she went inside the bar to Hoadley, and I ran to the room. As predicted—though it didn't take a Nostradamus—when Gina, who was undressed and watching TV in bed, found out that we had to leave, she went berserk. She said she wasn't going. Absolutely *not* going. She turned up the TV, then started yelling over it. I argued back and forth with her for a few minutes, then threw up my hands and started collecting our things. I told her I was getting in that car in seven minutes, and if she wanted to get to Bakersfield she'd better move her ass.

We were both hyperventilating by the time we slammed shut the motel door and jumped inside the Shelby. "This is sick," she hissed. "This is demented. We've been driving all day, it's pouring out, we haven't slept, we're disgusting and unshowered, and when she says jump, you ask how high without even a blink. What the hell's wrong with you?"

"What's wrong with *you*?" I retorted—there was a rap of knuckles on the window. Gina slowly, theatrically, furiously, opened her door, got out, stood glaring threateningly at Candy, who pulled forward the seat and hopped in.

"Let's go," she said. Gina took her time. I didn't even wait for her door to close all the way before I stepped on the gas ("What the fuck is your problem!" she yelled), and the sound of spinning tires on wet gravel was like a million nails on a million blackboards.

It resounded in my ears as I made a right and kept going. I didn't stop. No one was out in the courtyard in the rain, where the wet Christmas lights twinkled all year round.

"Where's Hoadley?" I breathed.

"Asleep in his room. He had a lot to drink. He was tired."

"Did he know you left?"

"Nope." Candy stuck her hand clutching a wad of twenties in between the seats. "But did give us a little money for our trouble." She chuckled.

"It's all so funny to you," Gina hissed, with unsuppressed hatred. "My whole life since we met you has been one unending nightmare."

"Melleray was a nightmare?" I asked.

"Shut up! Yes, everything's been a nightmare! You and your pretend indifference to what you're doing to us. Sloane, why is she still in our car? Just pull over on the side of the road and open the door. What are you worried about? Clearly she's going to be fine, better than you and me, who are being dragged out of an infested bed at midnight. How long is she going to be with us? Let her out right now!"

I didn't answer. It was raining. It was night. My mind, my heart was closed to it. I couldn't even entertain it as a hypothetical option. I knew Gina wasn't serious, I knew she knew I'd never do it. "Come on, Gina, stop. Be reasonable." But this made Gina only more heated up. "No, of course not. Why would you?" I was having a hard time concentrating on driving.

"Don't you understand?" she said to Candy. "You are not my friend. I'm sorry, but I don't care what happens to you. I just want to get to California, to my boyfriend, and never think about you again. That's what I want. So don't try to appeal to my better nature, don't try to tell me to help out my fellow man. I can't help myself! I have less than zero interest in helping you."

Candy said nothing.

"Look what's happening, and all because you're in our car! God, I'm so sick and tired of this!"

I gripped the wheel harder. I couldn't see the slick road for the rain. I was driving real slow, thinking that whether or not Candy was in our car, it was obvious that cowboys like Hoadley were everywhere, even on U.S. 20, looking to score five thousand bucks, off me, off Gina, off my Shelby.

"Let me tell you something," Gina continued. "You are not normal. This isn't normal. In a normal world, this doesn't happen. Mothers stay with their children. Mothers don't throw their children out."

"What's that got to do with anything? And who says my mother threw me out?"

"Girls, please." I was trying so hard to see the road, to not hear them.

"She didn't stay with you, though."

"So that's *my* fault?"

"I don't know. It's somebody's fault, isn't it, Candy?"

"Gina," I said. "My mother didn't stay with me, either."

"You're both screwed up!" Gina cried. "You know perfectly well, Sloane, that there are screwed up things in you, and I'm not blaming your mother, I'm just saying it's weird, and maybe this is why you do the things you do, but all I know is that in *my* world, mothers stay with their kids."

"And the kids become normal like you," said Candy.

Gina shrugged angrily. "No comment. Just saying. Just pointing things out."

"Stop, okay," I said. "I can't concentrate."

Nothing would stop Gina. "This is what I get for picking up a Jesus freak. It's punishment. Oh yes! I used to attend a Jehovah's youth group. Before the activities began, we usually sang hymns or some shit. We'd sing, and then pray for hours. That's when I lost my faith. And look at you—proof positive—all your praying did *you* no good, as I suspected all along. Oh, they used to pray for all those who hadn't seen the light yet, who weren't Christian. They wept! They felt sorry for three billion people who hadn't opened their hearts to Jesus. Like you do for me. You feel sorry for me. And yet do you see me jumping into strangers' cars and turning their life upside down? No. I know my fucking place. Do you? You look down on me and Shelby because we're not like you."

"I don't look down on Shelby," interjected Candy.

"Fuck you!" Gina was incensed. "The Nazis felt the same way about the Jews. Except with killing and stuff. You are one of the most condescending unpleasant people I've ever met. Everybody else but you are headed to the rings of hell, the Chinese, the

Muslims, the Buddhists, everybody else is wrong and you're right, and yet, you're the one fucking up my life, and I've never done anybody any harm. You think you're so pure."

"Is that what I think?" said Candy. "You obviously haven't listened to a word I said."

"No! Because I don't give a shit! Ah, but you know what, that's right. You tell me what a good Christian you are . . ."

"Never once said that. I love Christ, but I'm a terrible sinner."

"That's right! You do reprehensible things, and still manage to come on all high and mighty. I don't do anything bad, but don't act like that. See how it works? I don't swoon at the mention of Christ *or* hurt other people. I'm not a hypocrite, pretending all the things I want to do are dirty and inhuman. Give me a break. Fuck you for trying to convert me."

"Is that what I've been doing?"

"Gina, enough already."

"Fuck you for feeling sorry for me. Fuck you for praying for me. Fuck you and your deluded salvation. You make me sick."

"Jeez, Gina," Candy said, calm and unflappable. "You're right, you sure don't hate Christianity. You have an equal love for all religions."

"I want her out of this car!" yelled Gina.

"Stop screaming! I can't see the road!"

After midnight in the rain, in these spirits, we drove downhill to the Missouri, to Sioux City, trying to find another motel, more hidden, more unnoticed and unnoticeable than the hole in the ground we had just crawled out of.

There was nothing on U.S. 20.

"Tell me," Gina began again acidly, "is there going to be a Hoadley Dean at every motel?"

"Yes," said Candy, ending it.

I thought Candy was precocious with her answer. I wasn't sure if Gina was inquiring after her safety or making a backdoor swipe. It was dark in the car, and nobody but me cared either about the question or the answer.

We had been lucky this time that Gina had stormed off and there had been only the two of us at the bar. Next time we might not be as lucky. Though it was hard to define our present condition as fortunate, wet and drained as we were, in the car twelve hours, unrested and unreconciled to each other. Don't think it hadn't occurred to me on that road to nowhere in the black abyss, that if only I'd pulled over and swung open my Shelby door, and kicked Candy out, things might have gotten easier for me and Gina. But that was like saying, if only I hadn't run so fast, I wouldn't be going on a scholarship to the best college in the country. Yes, that might be so, but so what. I did, and here I am.

"We'll be fine," I said, to no one in particular. "We're so far north. He expects us to be on I-80. We're okay. We just have to get some sleep."

"Yeah, that's likely," Gina muttered, turning her gaze to the dark hills leading to the Missouri. I wished it were day and not raining. I wished this day were over. I wished we weren't in Iowa anymore. I wished for many things.

If wishes were horses.

It's impossible to explain how interminable seems the road when it's late at night and you're exhausted. There is no mile that doesn't go by in slo-mo, no traffic light that doesn't stay red for hours. We were stopped behind a line of cars at such a light. A few streetlights, cars, fast food joints. That's how we knew we were coming back to civilization—a McDonald's followed by Kentucky Fried Chicken. Was Candy scared? I couldn't tell; in the rearview mirror, I could see she was looking out the window.

In Sioux City, there was no Holiday Inn or Budget Inn, and the Best Western and the Clarion, too rich for our blood in any case, were sold out. We didn't dare pull into a gas station to ask about lodgings because it suddenly dawned on me that perhaps every gas-station attendant had a CB, and no sooner than I'd put a drop of fuel in my car, he'd be calling in my latitude and longitude to a man named Erv.

Where was Erv? Was he traveling on I-80 in his own car, staying in touch by radio? Or was he centrally headquartered like a general, perhaps in Nebraska, ordering other people to find Candy and bring her to him? I glanced at her in the back. She had given up even looking outward. Her eyes were closed.

Near a muddy canal that couldn't *possibly* have been the Missouri River, we found a shining, neon-blinking casino, the Argosy, more colorful and trashy, if such a thing were possible, than even the Isle of Capri. The only room they had for us was a penthouse suite for six hundred dollars a night. Politely we declined, and cursed like sailors out in the parking lot.

Gina said we might as well go inside and play a bit. Exhaustion and anger were gone from her face. I looked at her as if she had two heads. "You were in bed two hours ago telling me you were too tired to be a *passenger* in a car. Now you want to go play a bit?" I was incredulous.

Shrugging, she said, "I got my second wind. Is that a yes or no?"

"Uh, that'd be a no from me, Gina," I said.

Even Candy, who was up so high at the Bar n' Grill, shook her head. "Count me out, no pun intended."

"What? Is tomorrow going to be any better?"

"There is always that hope, yes," said Candy, "plus tomorrow I will have slept."

Will have slept. Sometimes she spoke as if she read Henry James. I wanted to cry. All that driving, and no bed, no pillow for my head, no sheets on which to stretch my sore and aching limbs. I was all day behind the wheel, and now had to sleep behind it, too.

"God, sing me a Psalm, Candy," I muttered. "I need something to fall asleep to."

Gina, upset with us before, was upset again for denying her the only fun since the last bit of fun she had. With her huffy arms crossed, she sat and complained, while we sat with our eyes closed. I opened the window. "Go ahead, Candy," said Gina. "Sing for your ride." And before the girl could begin, Gina said, "I don't believe the both of you. All day and night in the car, and now we're cooped up again. Instead of stretching our legs, walking around a little, sitting down, having a free drink, enjoying one minute, one *second* of relief after this wretched day, after *all* these wretched days, this is what I get. You're forgetting yourself, Sloane. You're supposed to be *my* friend, remember? Fifteen years friends, how quickly we forget, one evening at a bar, and the whole friendship right out the window . . ."

I remembered coming over to Gina's house when we were twelve or so. She'd just gotten a new puppy, and we sat in the summer grass with him between us and played. Our feet were stretched out, the heels, the soles and the toes pressed against each other. I remember this because her feet had been warm, but not sticky, and I worried mine might be and that any minute she'd pull her own nice dry feet away. But she didn't. We sat there, and let the puppy bite and chew us, and roll around between us. Oh, Gina.

"Go ahead, Candy," I repeated miserably. "Sing for me."

"The Lord is my light and my salvation," Candy sang. *"The Lord is the strength of my life; of whom shall I be afraid? When the wicked came upon me to eat up my flesh, they stumbled and fell . . . the Lord in time of trouble shall hide me in his pavilion, shall set me up upon a rock . . . When my father and mother forsake me, then he will take me up, lead me in a plain path away from my enemies. I would have fainted, unless I believed to see the goodness of God in the land of the living . . ."*

There, in the parking lot of a seedy canal-side casino that was too pricey for us, regretting leaving a room in a dank dump I should have never pulled into, Candy placed her hands on my shoulders. The rain came through the open window onto my slumped and despondent head, the night air cool and fresh. It smelled like the river was near, smelling of distant cities, of ships, and seas, of other seafaring people's safe adventures. There once was a time I dreamed of running away with Eddie, just the two of us, getting into his beat-up GMC truck and just driving, not stopping. We'd head somewhere into the great unknown. But now, drifting off on the watery border of Iowa and Nebraska, in the land of *such* unknown, both geographically and emotionally, I couldn't picture Eddie in my dreams anymore. The only thing in my head was the plain, solemn face and unadorned eyes of a girl slowly approaching a tall man in white robes, bowing her head to him. "*Hello, Grace.*"

"What's in Paradise, Grace?" I whispered. "Can't you give Erv what he wants and be done with him?"

But no one answered.

3

Argosy Pavilion

At the International House of Pancakes the next morning we ordered breakfast and Candy paid. "It's on Hoadley," she smirked. She sat across from me, Gina next to her, not angry anymore, just bleary, and in the gray of the morning, my mind addled, my heart as sore as my body, I said, "What are *you* so chipper about? Give me the map. I need to plan our route." My hands were scraped, my knees damp.

Candy took the map from Gina. "Don't worry about today," she said. "We got some bucks, and I know the way to Rapid City."

"To where?"

"Rapid City."

"Give me the map."

"It's in South Dakota."

"South *Dakota?* Give me the map, Candy!" I ripped it away from her and Gina smiled smugly. My olive tank top felt rank; I needed a shower, I needed to change. "Rapid City is completely and totally out of our way," I said, tapping emphatically on the map. "Completely. And totally."

Candy tried to wrest the map back. I wouldn't let her. "Shel," she said gently. "Have some French toast. Have some bacon. Relax. Eat a little. You look terrible."

"Gee, I wonder why."

"You should've come with us," said Gina. "Serves you right. We had fun; what did you have?"

Candy squeezed my grumpy hand, circled it with the tips of her fingers. "Shel, listen to me. There is no such thing as out of our way. Out of our way means out of Erv's way, and that's good. Don't worry so much. In Rapid City lives my very good friend Floyd, who has a wad of cash that belongs to me. I need to get it before I get to Paradise." She cheerfully raised her eyebrows. "He's got *plenty*. I'll pay for your gas all the way to California. Okay?"

"Candy . . ."

"We'll take the backroads to Valentine, Nebraska, through the Sand Hills, and then go north and west through South Dakota to Wall Drug. That's where Floyd works. We'll stay overnight at the nicest hotel in Rapid City, my treat, and the next morning drive down through the Black Hills. Sounds like a plan?" She grinned at me like a circus clown. "I know how much you like plans." An endearing circus clown. But still. "We can't take the straight and narrow anymore," she went on. "We can't get on I-80 in your little yellow canary and smoke 300 miles in three hours. Can't do it. We either do the backroads where the trucks don't come or we travel at night, off the main drag. We need to be extra careful. Okay?" She pushed the map back to me. "Now go ahead. Study the map. Plan. You see how Rapid City is right on the border with Wyoming? After Rapid City, I figure we'll have it pretty easy till Utah. Then we'll see."

Throughout this exchange Gina had barely been paying attention. She was giggling, trying to peer over Candy's shoulder at the map while picking at a soggy hash brown. I used my thumb knuckle to measure out the distance between International House of Pancakes in Sioux City and Rapid City, *South Dakota*. "I hate to point out the obvious, Cand," I said, "But it's 460 miles. You plan to do 460 on the backroads?"

"Finish your food. We need to hammer down. I have to be in Rapid City tonight."

"Why?"

"Why? Because my friend's expecting me tonight, that's why. And because," Candy added, "we still have a long way to go, and I really do have to be in Paradise, *very* soon. But first I have to get my money from Floyd. I don't have time to dilly-dally."

"Good plan, Cand," said Gina. "Spiffing." She gulped down the last of her coffee. There had been a polar transformation in Gina's disposition toward Candy, a nice tropical thaw. After all the things Gina had shouted at Candy last night, I was surprised Candy would ever talk to Gina again. This could only be explained by a trip to the casino, a calculated move on Candy's part to avoid a repeat of last night's virulent tantrum. Candy needed Gina in her camp if she was going to get where she was headed in one piece.

"I thought I was only taking you as far as Reno?" I was the moody, dour one this morning.

"Reno!" exclaimed Gina, *so* brightly. "How long till then?"

"Candy," I said doggedly. "You told me Reno."

"Look, let's take it one day at a time, 'kay? 'Kay." She patted my hand.

I persisted. "Who's in Paradise?" Though I didn't take my hand away.

"A friend." She paused. "Mike."

"Sure got a lot of friends, girlfriend."

"You're going to Paradise for Mike?" Gina asked incredulously.

"No, I'm not going to Paradise for Mike," Candy said, mimicking Gina's tone, turning her steady, amused gaze at the girl. "Though your surprise is ironic, coming from someone who's—going to Bakersfield for Eddie."

Gina got defensive. "Bakersfield for Eddie is better than Paradise for Mike."

"Really? Well, if you say so. Personally I think going to Bakersfield for Eddie is just the beginning of your sorrows. But as for me, I'm not going to Paradise for Mike." She lowered her head a moment. "Not anymore."

"But it's Paradise for something, isn't it?" I asked.

"What does that mean?" Gina snapped. Candy had a knack for saying just one sentence too many.

"Nothing," Candy said to Gina. "A dumb joke." And to me she added, "Yes. It's Paradise for something." She got up. "Let's go. Shel, do you know where you're going?"

"Do I know where I'm going?" I got up, too. "You mean like Mendocino, California? Or do you mean like a hotel, with a bed and shower and sleep?"

"Don't worry. You'll get that. In 460 miles. But you really gotta make tracks, girl. Floyd's getting off work at six."

It was ten in the morning. I was so fidgety and unsettled. Last night after Candy had relented and gone with Gina to the Argosy, I fell into restless sleep. Cramped and miserable, in a sitting position, trying to get comfortable, I half-opened my eyes at one point—and screamed. A man's face was peering at me through my open window. I staggered sideways from him, dragging my legs over the clutch to get to Gina's seat. I started to whimper and cry. He stuck his head in and looked around the car. "You got somebody else here with you?" he barked.

I pretended I didn't hear.

"Hey! You alone?" he yelled.

How did I answer that? To say I was alone was unthinkable. To say I was with two other girls, one of them pink-haired, was also unthinkable. I didn't answer. I was crying because he looked like any minute he would open the door and fling himself on me. Thrashing from side to side, suffocating in my panic, I pushed open the passenger side, fell out of the car onto wet pavement, struggled up, scraping the palms of my hands, and sprinted toward the Argosy doors, leaving my car, my bags, my money, everything. I didn't think he would outrun me; after all I had once run the 440-meters in fifty-seven seconds.

A group of people walked out; I rammed headlong into them. They walked me to my car, looked around, assured me there was no one there; giggling, teasing, they advised me to lay off the hard stuff next time. A little calmer, I locked up and, taking my keys this time, limped to the lobby, where I dropped onto a stiff couch, waiting for the girls to return. That's where they found me, asleep. I said I'd had a bad dream and left it at that.

And this morning, I didn't want to tell Candy about last night, turning my face away from her questions and soft gazes, looking down at my raw palms. I didn't see the point. The terror had been so real.

NINE
BADLANDS

1

The Bartered Bride

The road is like a drug. It's like hypnosis. I'm staring into the long distance, tires whooshing, the soporific rhythm of the wipers battling to clear the pearly road spray. We crossed the Missouri in the rain, found a dinky two-lane road. Up down, up down, where we are, no one knows. Candy said, a long way away, that's where we are. No effing kidding was Gina's comment. We bickered. We didn't listen to music. Oh, we tried. But how many times are you going to hear tide is high, *so I'm moving on*, before you scream? Gina's morning gloss was gone—gambling gets you only so far, and there were no more casinos to relieve her stress. I had the wheel to relieve mine, which I gripped with both hands like a new driver. Candy sat in the quiet back, eyes closed. She always managed to achieve that—stillness. Was she listening perhaps for God's voice, for help, for direction. I didn't know. I was beginning to suspect Candy had more resources to cope with anxiety than either me or Gina, and I envied her that. I wished she could teach me how to keep body and mind so calm, when ahead and behind was so much imponderable noise, when all three of us waded through a loud mire of delusional shallows.

Partial list of my delusional shallows: everything is going to be okay. What else could possibly go wrong? We'll fix it. We'll work it out. I need to find my mother. I wish the girl weren't with us.

"So Nebraska is landlocked, right?" That was Gina. She had her mischievous face on. She was always good for a laugh at times like these. Except when she wasn't.

"Yeah, so?"

"Well, how do you explain that a quarter of it is covered by sand?"

"What?"

"Exactly. And not just sand, but dunes of sand. A quarter of the state, an area nearly as large as New York state, 37,000 square miles, covered by hills of sand that blew in, formed into dunes and remained. How do you explain it?"

"Since I didn't know about it, I don't explain it," I said. "How do *they* explain it?"

Gina waved her hand at me. "*They* say it's glacial outwash from the Rockies."

"Well, if that's what they say, that's what it is."

"What the hell is glacial outwash?" Gina exclaimed. "Nobody can explain *that*. And while we're on the subject of things no one can explain, the Rockies are 500 miles away from here. Dunes usually protect a coastline fifty to a hundred *feet* away. We're talking about 500 miles. Must be some pretty strong wind glacially outwashing sand from *mountains*."

"What are you getting at?"

"It's a geological impossibility."

You know what was a geological impossibility? Meeting a human being named Candy, materialized—for the second time—out of thin air at a traffic light at a picnic marsh. Every other imponderable paled by comparison.

Leaning her head through the seats and smiling impishly, Candy said, "Maybe it's an act of God."

"There you go again." Gina pushed her slightly back. "It's science!"

Candy wobbled back in, like a weeble. "Well, then explain it."

"I can't. But scientists are working on it."

"Any time, then?"

"Shut up."

"Can scientists explain why we give alms to the homeless?" asked Candy.

"Shut *up*! We're talking about the Sand Hills of Nebraska."

I piped up. "Where is this famed sand?"

"It'll be hard to miss. Sand 2000 miles away from an ocean. And Candy," Gina added, "why would God need to put sand dunes in the middle of landlocked Nebraska?"

"How should I know? That's why it's called a miracle. Because we don't understand it."

"I never called it a miracle. I said a geological impossibility."

"Same difference."

That's when I laughed. "How does it feel to be hoisted by your own petard, Gina Reed?" I said to her, finding her ribs to tickle.

That took three miles and five minutes.

Without music or the petty banter of three bored girls, the atmosphere within the car grew ever more bleak, somewhat like the surrounding landscape. We passed through wet, fog-shrouded hills, no lights showing anywhere, no other cars for miles down the road, and every once in a while a small farm, dripping farm equipment, a factory. Nebraska, at least in these parts, did not resemble Iowa. Now I knew the difference between a rich state and a poor state. Iowa farms were big wealthy plantations, painted and landscaped. Here, rust powdered overgrown front fences, and the houses were ramshackle and neglected. There was some farming industry, but we saw no stores. Not one. There wasn't a single sign that pointed to a gas station, a deli, a happy ice-cream parlor, or a shoe shop. There. Was. Just. Nothing. Except the endless rain, fog and grassy hills. Like this we traveled on U.S. 20 for a hundred miles. Laurel, Randolph, Osmond. Once in a while a car would pass us. The bright lights jumped in the fog, got larger, then whoosh, disappeared. It was quiet. Plainview, Royal . . .

I longed to hear about a girl named Grace, but instead, Candy leaned between the seats, close to my ear and Gina's ear and quietly began to tell us about a man named Erv.

"He was a coin collector, and in construction," she said. "Then he got involved in photography, in video production. All cash business," was how Candy put it, slowing down her speech a bit just as she was exhorting me to speed up. "Some of his cash business was procuring girls for his many friends. Not his businessmen friends, more low-rent than that. Workmen, truckers." She paused. "And . . . I was one of those girls."

Ah. So I *was* hearing about a girl named Candy. "You were?" I didn't believe her. "What do you mean?" I said. "You're only seventeen."

"Yes, nearly too old for him. I started four years ago."

"When you were *thirteen?*"

"Yes."

"You've given yourself to men for money since you were thirteen?"

"I have."

"Oh my God, Candy." I suddenly felt sick.

"What?"

"Why would you do that? Why would you agree to that?"

"It was very good money."

Her hand patting me, Gina turned her body to Candy. "Candycane," she said mildly, "what about your mother? How could she allow something like that?"

I'd been hoping Candy would say, *my mama didn't know*, because that was the only thing that would make sense to me.

"My mother liked Erv and wanted to keep him," said Candy. "Her previous boyfriends had been such losers." She fell silent a while before continuing. "I stopped going to school a few years earlier, and that was why we had to keep moving, so the school attendance board would get off our back. I slept during the day and worked at night. I brought home a paycheck. It wasn't too bad."

We didn't stop listening, but she stopped talking, as if suddenly she'd run out of things to say. When we reached O'Neill ("The Irish Capital of Nebraska!") we gassed up and got some coffee.

Gina asked, "If you needed a job, why didn't you just get a job at Burger King?"

"I was too young. Who'd hire a minor under fifteen?"

"Dear God, Candy," I said. "You could've babysat."

Candy waved her hand. "Babysitting paid a buck an hour. And I was making ten to twenty, plus good tips that I sometimes didn't share with Erv. Ten bucks for ten hours or 200 for ten hours. Big difference, no?"

"How much money did they have to give you to do something you didn't want to do?" asked Gina.

"I'd guess about ten to twenty an hour," replied Candy.

We got back in the car and I just drove, swallowing away my nausea, aching and sad for her. Miles passed. It stopped raining, the sun peeked through clouds and, finally, the road dried.

"Did it mean anything to give it away?" I asked, almost in a whisper.

"Who gave it away? Not me. Maybe you. I gave something they wanted in return for something I wanted. That's not giving it away. That's being smart. I placed no value on the thing you talk about. It was just a means to an end. But money—now *that* had value. Money would buy my ticket out of that life."

"Where's that money?" asked Gina.

"Well, I used to keep it with me. But Erv was a big spender. He bought a boat, two trucks, a summer house on the Chesapeake. When he was short, he'd take from me. He'd ransack my room till he found it. He'd say without him I'd have nothing. Which was true, but when he took it, I also had nothing. So I had to start hiding it. I kept some with me, like a decoy for hunters, but the rest I sent away. Some to my dad, some to Mike in Paradise, and to my friend Jess in Reno, but most to Floyd, the one we're meeting tonight."

"I can't believe you sent *any* to your dad," Gina said. How respectable she had become between South Bend and O'Neill! "Candy, don't you think Erv knows who you wired the money to? One Western Union receipt and he knows. What if he got to Floyd first, and is waiting for you in Rapid City?"

"I'm not stupid, I kept all the receipts." Her lips tightened. "Receipts, the Bible my dad gave me when I was a kid." She paused. "And the thing Erv wants to kill me for."

We waited, me barely breathing so I wouldn't miss a thing.

"I took a reel of 16mm film," she said reluctantly, eyes downcast. "One of the more recent films Erv had made. From this master reel he dubbed cheaply made things called video tapes and sold them at an enormous profit. The reels were guarded like gold at Fort Knox. It was a miracle I was able to take even the one."

"Why in the world would you take something like that from a man like him?" I gasped. "Don't you know him? Don't you know better?"

"I know him," she said. "I took it because I needed protection. Without it, we'd all be dead."

"You took a reel of film from him for which he wants to kill you," said Gina, "and you call that *protection?*"

"You don't understand anything," said Candy. "Yes, protection."

"What's the film, Candy?" I asked.

"Oh, under-age girls doing over-age things," Candy replied tiredly. "In one raw, unedited footage, Erv tied me to a tree and . . . well, sort of tortured me in front of the camera. Hurt me, like he was killing me. Did all kinds of things to me, then pretended like it was a snuff film. He's been making these for a couple of years now, selling them on the black market, since they're illegal and all."

"Illegal? You don't say," said Gina. "Under-age girls and a faux snuff movie?"

"Is there a market for something like that?" I asked skeptically and incredulously, my naïveté morphing into revulsion.

"He made a fortune. You wouldn't believe what a cash cow it was," said Candy. "He was making so much money that he could've stopped pimping me out, that became just pocket change to him. In films, instead of selling one me to one or two men, he was selling one me to 4000 men."

"I think," I said, "*you* were the cash cow, Candy."

"You could be right. Which is why he was so reluctant to part with me. These films are the reason why the truckers are so eager to help him. He supplies them too. It's the most profitable thing he's ever done."

"Candy," Gina said officiously, "don't you know it's against the law to transport across state lines any obscene, lascivious or filthy matter of indecent character, particularly of a graphic visual representation of children?"

"You *are* a font of information. I'm not transporting it anymore. I gave it to my father."

Gina and I took a breath. Mine was more like a gasp. I stared at Candy through the rearview. "Candy, the blue film Erv made that broke all U.S. and international laws you gave to your *father?*"

"Yeah, so?"

She must have taken our shocked silence as judgment because she said, "You think you're better than me because you give it away for free to complete strangers? That doesn't make you better, it makes you stupid."

I don't know about Gina, but I hadn't been judging her. I was imagining the Trappist monk Estevan Rio, in the monastery for fifteen years, spooling Candy's film onto Melleray's only projector in the small rec room off the library, flicking it on, sitting back. Perhaps other monks were in the screening room with him. Did they get popcorn and candy, a little Coke, as they watched Estevan's fourteen-, fifteen-, sixteen-year-old daughter being tied naked to a tree and sexually tormented?

While driving through Nebraska, though, I did silently judge Estevan Rio for not doing more to help his child. My opinion of Bruggeman had not changed. He was beyond disapproval. It was like judging a rock. No matter how much you judge that rock, it will never make a very good goldfish. For one, it's too heavy.

The man from last night came back to my eyes. Had that man been looking for Candy to give her back to Erv so he could make more movies?

Gina could not believe the film had been bequeathed to Brother

Estevan, but what I felt was a melt of relief that it was not with us, a short-lived melt, to be sure, since to convince Bruggeman it wasn't with us, I knew was beyond my capabilities.

"Candy, I know you think it might be Christian of *him* to take it . . ." Gina continued, and couldn't finish. Even the fearless Gina couldn't finish!

"I had no choice," said Candy. "I didn't take the stupid reel to blackmail Erv, or to bribe him. I took it so he would let me go. It needed to be safe."

I began to understand why Erv wouldn't want to let Candy go.

"The demand for these movies is greater than anything you can imagine," Candy told us. "And the supply is real low. In the last two years, since he got into it, he must have made, and I'm not exaggerating, maybe three, four million dollars."

"How much did *you* make?" I asked.

"A few bucks." She sounded evasive. "Enough to change my life. Now we have to collect my money."

"*We*? We're going to be pretty busy," said Gina. "Bribing pornographers, driving points home, shaking people down for money in Rapid City." She snickered. "That's rich, Cand. What's Sloane's role going to be?"

"The most important one. Driving the getaway car."

I groaned.

"What's *my* role going to be?" asked Gina. "Breaking their kneecaps when they don't pay up?"

"Why wouldn't they pay up? Floyd's my best friend. I wire him my money, he gets to keep half, the rest he saves for me." Her voice was low, almost like she were speaking in the woods at night. "With him keeping half, my share is still about twenty grand. Just think about that." She laughed softly. "Not bad for a seventeen-year-old, huh?"

"Yes, not bad," I said. "Why did you stop? You didn't want to do it anymore?"

"Something like that," she said vaguely. "I said I was leaving, but Erv saw it differently. He refused to let me go."

"Ah. Well, why would he?"

"At first I thought it was because of the money, losing his income. But his partners had other girls they could've used. No, for Erv it was about something else." She furrowed her brow. "When I saw he wasn't going to let me go easy, I tried to force his hand. I got myself tattooed so filming me would be impossible." She smiled bleakly. "I thought that no one would like a tattooed chick." Shaking her head, she went on. "But he just beat me and started hiring me out again by the hour, saying there were plenty of men who'd take a girl with tattoos. I know he wanted me to stay, even though he was pretty mad about the tattoos, and normally I would've stayed, but I *had* to go. None of my pleading, or tattooing myself, or telling him I didn't want to do it anymore was driving home the point. I knew I had to find a way to convince him. I had to leave, and he needed to leave me alone. So I took the reel."

"Ah. How'd that work out for you?"

"Admittedly not great."

Gina stared intensely at me. I narrowed my eyes on the road and didn't return her glare. What had we gotten ourselves into? Gina and I were momentarily speechless—for about thirty miles.

"He's pursuing you," Gina said, "because he's afraid if that film gets out, he's going away for life. And he's right. You're a threat to his entire existence. He knows if he gets the film back, he'll be safe."

"Yes. Which is why I can't let him get his hands on it." Candy tutted. "I told him and told him to leave me alone. I begged him to let me go. Is it my fault he's stubborn and refused to listen to reason?"

"No, *that's* not your fault," I drew out. We were so screwed. My hands were shaking. Erv, the pornographer, knew his work was not for public consumption. His ouvre, for example, was unlikely to be released at the local movie theater. And he was in the reel of film with Candy.

"What kind of a fucked-up mother did you have?" exclaimed Gina. "Where the hell was this woman while this was happening, while you and her boyfriend were doing this? Did you have a work studio right in the house?"

"No. We went someplace else."

"Oh, well, that's all right, then!"

"Look, my mom's had a real hard life," said Candy. "She ran away from home herself when she was thirteen, lived on the streets with her boyfriends, had one child before me who died, had some serious health problems, calcification of the kidneys, cirrhosis of the liver, her boyfriends beat her, and her sister was strangled by her newly-wed husband two months after the wedding, and," said Candy, widening her eyes, "on top of all that she got *impetigo*."

"What the hell is impetigo?"

"It's some kind of a horrible skin infection," said Gina. "Yuk."

"She'd been living pretty dire before she met up with my dad. He was probably the nicest to her, but she was too flighty to settle down. She didn't see that life for herself. My mother is not a very spiritual person. She's not exactly looking for answers to things. When I came east, she was scared at first of having me with her, but then she lightened a little. Saw the potential. My money allowed her not to work, to have things she liked."

"Like what?"

"Like Southern Comfort and cigarettes. It allowed her a new Maytag top-loading washing machine and a Frigidaire fridge and freezer. She bought the house she lived in and wasn't a renter anymore. She bought herself a truck. I was her only child, and I made my mother's life a bit better."

"I don't know how that can be," said Gina. "She's still with Erv."

Candy stared at the back of Gina's head for longer than I thought necessary, as if trying to force a quest for reflection on her own choices, but Gina was thinking only of Candy and didn't feel the pointed stare.

"Your mother bartered you for a Frigidaire?" I finally said.

"For a life full of Frigidaires. Everybody made out."

"Did they?" I said. "If everything was so hunky-dory, then why are you running away?"

"I'll tell you," said Candy. "It has absolutely *nothing* to do with the business, nothing to do with my mother, and nothing to do with Erv." She moved to the back. "I got my own personal reasons. I really don't want to talk about it right now." She stared out the window. "I just wanted out. I needed out. But when I told Erv I had to go, he went crazy. I was his bread and butter. I had no choice. I had to take the film and run."

"Did you leave him and your mom a goodbye note?" I was big on goodbye notes. I wish my own mother had left one for me. I wish my father had left one for me. I got a note post-maternally. "*Say hi to Shelby*" was what I got from Lorna Moor.

"Yes," Candy replied. "In the empty reel case. I wrote, *Erv, it's like this. The world is big enough for you, and for me. Let me live my life. I will never speak about you to anyone. No one will ever know your name. I promise you. Just let me go, and go on doing what you've been doing. Big world. You in one corner, me in the other. I swear, unless something happens to me, that reel will never see the light of day. You have my word. Otherwise, it's going straight to the police and the* New York Times. *Just let me go.*"

"Good letter."

"Yeah," said Gina, "but something tells me Erv didn't take her advice."

"Maybe he's still thinking it over?" offered Candy. "I seriously figured it would take him and his camera guy a week or two to find it missing. I was wrong about that, judging by how quick they tracked me down. It took them no time at all."

Gina emitted a short disbelieving laugh. "My God, Candy," she said. "How in the world does Jesus factor into the life you've been living?"

"What do you mean?" said Candy, frowning. "Who do you think Jesus is for? Saints?"

"I dunno. But he seems pretty far away from the life you had with Erv."

Candy didn't reply, slumping into the backseat. I wish I could be a fly in the corner of her soul.

"Candy," I asked, "that thing you used to do . . . with men . . . for money . . . that was because of Erv, right? You don't do that anymore, do you?"

"Not if I can help it," she replied.

What to do with the minutes that the thoughts are filled by? Rather, what to do with the thoughts that the minutes are filled by? Candy's mother? I couldn't bring myself to think of her in any terms other than from Candy's point of view. *Candy had a mother*, was the only thing I could muster. Pathetic, I know. Abortions, health problems and truancy, and perhaps some bad decisions. Even impetigo, whatever the hell that was. Still. She was Candy's *mother*.

I opened the window, breathed the Nebraska air, barreling through the countryside, past Inman, pop. 22. It was flat, hot, windy. All oxygen had been sucked from the car by Candy's words.

After a few miles of road had passed, I told her about my rock metaphor for Erv. She was quiet for a few moments. "I guess," she said, then added, "Except for one thing. Jesus. He's the one who makes goldfish out of stones. With Him all things that were impossible are made possible. People don't change much, that's true, but they can. And you don't stop helping them, making an effort on their behalf. That can be *your* true nature. And it will be good enough. Just because it's the scorpion's nature to sting, that does not change the turtle's nature to save. That's the Jesus answer."

This is a consequence of being in the car for hundreds of miles. Things are revealed and reconciled without so much as a change of seating. You are shocked. Wait thirty miles. You'll be thirsty. You'll have time for a drink, for melancholy, for fear, for more trivia about Nebraskans, for a pervasive feeling of queasiness about the things you just heard, and then a gasp of astonishment at the geological impossibilities seen through your front windshield—ocean dunes rising out of the sagebrush grass, flat plains sloping up onto rippling sand dunes. You felt bad, you gasped for air, you picked up speed, scratched your head, moved on. What choice did you have really? Scorpions, turtles, Sand Hills, Ervs, Danas, Candies, and the voices of twenty men, singing, *He brings wine to gladden the heart of man, and bread to strengthen man's heart.*

In the afternoon, when we were *finally* in the northwestern part of Nebraska, amid the eternity of the stretched-out Sand Hills, Gina told us a story of two sisters who lived in Jonestown, Nebraska, in the 1800s. One Sunday they asked their mother if they could go visit their older sister who was working in town. The mother agreed. The girls left after Sunday church. The mother had warned them to stay on the road, but the older girl saw some beautiful wildflowers and went to pick them, to make a bouquet for the sister she was going to visit. The younger sister helped her. The girls got off the road.

They made a beautiful bouquet, but when it came time to get back, they couldn't find their way. It was yellow sand and blue sky everywhere they looked. They went this way, that. They wandered around. Night fell. The next morning, they walked, calling, calling. Another day passed. Meanwhile, a posse had been arranged by the frantic parents, with all the townspeople looking for the girls. On the third day, the older sister told the younger one, who was getting weak without food and water, to stay put, to sit tight, that she would go find help. So she left, the other one stayed put. Night fell, morning came. Eventually, the small girl got up and started walking.

She was found by the posse who had been looking for them for five days. The mother, sick with grief, couldn't even go out searching for her girls. The child was brought to her mother, and then the posse went back out. The sister was found under one of the creosote bushes, her cardigan under her head, lying on her

301

side, as if she knew she was lying down to die and wanted to make herself comfortable.

"How old were the girls?" I asked.

"The older one was eight, the youngest five."

"God, Gina!"

"Yes, they were young. What did I tell you? Sand Hills."

Bassett, pop. 743. Jonestown, pop. 57. Straight out of the 1800s. Until Valentine, the "heart" of the hills, I thought about the girls off road and lost and their mother home grieving. I spent most of my life dreaming about getting lost, so my mother would hear of me, and be moved to grieve, to feel, to do something. To return for the funeral perhaps. How good I was at daydreaming this, of getting lost in the untouched remnants of the vast prairies that once covered all the Plains states of America and finding my mother.

The hotels of Valentine came upon us—in resentful, isolated silence. The town was closed for lunch. It was scorching, the merciless sun beating down. Only a couple of bars were open, but I wasn't going into a bar during the day. Out of one of these, staggered an inebriated American Indian, a corduroy satchel on his back. He followed us down the street trying to speak to us in slurred English while we ignored him the best we could.

"We have to get something to eat," said Candy. "There's nowhere to stop between here and Wall Drug."

"How the hell do *you* know this?" I flung open my map of South Dakota.

"You'll see," said Candy. "It's just a sea out there. A sea of wheat waves. Beat it, cowboy," she said to the Indian, smiling a little, her pink tank top riding up, her thin straps falling. He loitered near, not taking his unfocused eyes off her. The pink of her hair complemented nicely the pink of her top, and between them her brown eyes sparkled, far, far older than seventeen; my own soul was heavy with those eyes, with her life.

We found a run-down Mexican place; we ordered burritos and

ate them quietly, opening our mouths just long enough to argue whether a burrito was a sandwich or whether it wasn't. Candy maintained it was a sandwich. Gina disagreed. "Well, if it's not a sandwich, then what is it?"

"A burrito!"

"And what's a burrito?"

"Meat wrapped in a tortilla."

"Kind of like meat wrapped inside bread?"

"Kind of."

"So it's a sandwich."

"No. A sandwich is a sandwich. And this is a burrito."

"Which fits the description of a sandwich."

"So does an Oreo cookie."

"No, it doesn't."

"Why not?"

"Because it's sweet."

"So? The beans inside the burrito have sugar in them. They're sweet. Maybe my burrito is an Oreo cookie."

"Now you're just being silly."

"*I'm* being silly? I'm not the one calling a burrito a sandwich!"

On and on. I wondered if I should send Emma a postcard. For some reason I wanted to. Emma had never been to Nebraska. Had never been anywhere, except that one trip to Maine we took. She had been saving her money to go visit my father in prison, but then he died and we didn't go.

Candy studied me, burrito in hand. "Have you sent her a postcard from anywhere else?"

"We weren't near a geological miracle."

"The Missouri? The Mississippi? Lake Michigan? Those aren't miraculous?"

"I'm going to dazzle her with water? Larchmont is on Long Island Sound." Emma told me she had always liked water. She said she didn't want to live inland. I didn't even know if she was born in Larchmont. I couldn't believe I never asked her that. Ah, one more thing to feel queasy over.

"She's going to think something is terribly wrong," said Candy.

There was a pause between the three of us. Was there something terribly wrong? "Candy's right, Sloane," said Gina. "Better send nothing."

We sat on a little patio on Main Street in the western, nearly-abandoned town. Gina and I bent our heads over the atlas, going from page 57 and Nebraska, to page 140 and South Dakota, because the atlas was foolishly and illogically arranged alphabetically, not geographically. We didn't think Candy was right about U.S. 83. Clearly there were markings on the map that signified life. One town, another, and they were named; she should like that, she liked things named.

Candy was paying no attention to our musings. She was scanning the street, her gaze traveling across the houses, peering at the few people window-shopping. She watched this Valentine scene intently, without blinking. "Girls, what you think? Would a town like this be an okay town for me to hang my hat?"

We didn't even bother looking at the street. "It's like that old joke," I said. "You and I are both looking at the people getting off the train. You think, how marvelous they are, look at their adorable little lives. And I think, 'People get *off* here?'"

She frowned blankly. "Where's the joke in that?"

I slapped the atlas closed. "Let's go. Candy, what are you getting all wistful about Valentine for? Aren't you headed to Paradise?"

She rolled her eyes. "Not permanently, duh."

She amused even Gina. Gina!

"But it's named *Paradise*," Gina teased. "You're the one going on and on about names giving value to things. How bad could it be?"

"This is where it shows that you don't know everything," said Candy. "Back when the gold rush ran like madness through California, particularly that area, some men used the town as an outpost for all kinds of unsavory activities. One of the saloons in the area was named *Pair O'Dice*. Get it?"

After a few times of mouthing it to ourselves, we got it. "Exactly.

304

So don't wax all rhapsodic. Mike said the town is the most boring place he'd ever been to."

"What, all the saloons closed?" said Gina, smiling.

"Each and every one."

At our car, the Indian was parked out. "You girls feel like giving an old man a ride?" he slurred, leering at Candy. He was old, probably in his late twenties.

"Uh—no."

"Come on, just up to Mendosa. I'll get out then, I *promise*."

"Where did we hear that before," I muttered to Gina, and louder said, "No, no. *We* promised our mothers we wouldn't pick up hitchhikers. Sorry."

Our mothers.

He grinned lewdly. "You don't look like the kind of girls who always listen to their mothers."

It was three in the afternoon! Gina didn't even look his way as she got in the car, modestly pulling down her short shorts. It was Candy who appraised him. "Got any scratch, cowboy?" she asked—and before I could yank her by the hand, he said, "I like your little yellow vehicle. I like it *very* much."

Candy didn't need any more prodding to slide in behind me on the driver's side.

"Are you crazy?" I said. "You want to get us into *more* trouble? Besides, it's three in the afternoon!"

"What, time not good?"

"Candy," I said, "keep your eye on the prize. You've got bigger fish to fry. Wall Drug by six."

"You're so right," she said. "Paul and Silas said that. Keep your eye on the prize. But I wasn't going to sin. Just have some fun. Having fun is an admirable quality."

"So is prudence," I said. *I!*

I peeled away from the curb so the Indian couldn't take down my license plate number. I didn't get a chance to send Emma that postcard from the Valentine Sand Hills.

After driving for a while, Gina broke the silence. "Let me ask you, Candy Cane, when you lived your nocturnal life on the Ohio River, did you ever make it to a place of worship?"

"Every Sunday," Candy replied. "And do not think of yourself more admirably than you ought, Gina Reed. Appraise yourself, not me, with sober judgment, recalling the measure of faith God has given you."

"How about if I just appraise *you* with sober judgment," said Gina. "Because my faith is small. Step on it, Sloane."

We had cheered up after we ate and the rain stopped. From my nightmare at the Argosy to now was barely the breadth of half a day, and yet we, our backs hurting, my sandpaper eyes burning, and watching always for the shape of a truck, were now managing to be less caustic with each other. It was better.

Too bad it didn't last.

I had to agree with Candy, though, and her compelling argument. The burrito was a sandwich.

2

Lakota Chapel, All Welcome

Something happens to you on the road. Something happened to me. You're driving, humming, looking around, or you're tense and fretting, chewing your nails on the hand that's not clutching the wheel, you're arguing and dreaming. Meantime, the fields, the trees, the farms are passing by. Jersey and Maryland, you're barely paying attention. Pennsylvania is familiar, Ohio full of trucks. The Interstate, I realized now, is the death of all cross-country travel. You can go 2000 miles and all things on the Interstate look, smell and feel exactly the same, the rest stops, the steel rails, the cat's eyes and the trucks. There is no life on the Interstate. Ohio showed me that.

Iowa, Iowa, Iowa. It rained there, and the rain washed away some of the familiar things I'd seen, the fields, the trees, the silos; the rain washed away the colors of my old life, and it rained through half of Nebraska. I was deceived by the plainness of it, the ostensible blankness of it. But somewhere in Nebraska, on that empty road, while listening to Candy talk about her torn-up life, going seventy an hour, I blinked and suddenly realized I had been transported to a different life.

She did this to me. Nebraska did this to me.

By the time we got to South Dakota, by the time we took U.S. 83 north, I was an unmoored ship at sea. There were no Iowan farms, or Nebraskan fields, no people, no trees, just nothing, but waves and waves of grass against the endless sky. It was like nothing I'd ever seen, ever imagined, or even begun to imagine.

Simply, I left one life behind and entered another, one state of being, one way of understanding and entered another. Where precisely this happened I didn't know, but I knew it was irrevocably so when my eyes saw the waves of the sea in the flowing, yellow-ochre grass of South Dakota. When I looked at Candy, she no longer looked the same to me. I couldn't say what was different about her, the eyeliner was still black, the bra still missing, the legs still slender and smooth. She was composed and calm-eyed, her pink hair familiar, but she simply didn't look the same after all the things she had told me.

When I tried to explain to the girls about South Dakota, which was the only thing I *could* talk about, I don't think I did a very good job. Gina obviously thought I was crazy, while Candy looked at me like every place she'd ever seen was how I was seeing South Dakota now. "There is beauty everywhere," she said. "*He sends springs into the valleys and they flow among the hills.*"

"Beauty?" Gina said. "This burned grass is beauty? The sand in Nebraska was beauty?"

"Oh my God, yes! Beauty," I said. At ninety an hour on a deserted road in the middle of an ocean, the windows open wide and wind roaring in the joytruck, we blew by a town comprised of two businesses: a garage and a church. Lakota Chapel, it read. "All Welcome."

"This is how people describe their conversion to God," Candy said. "They use the same language you're using now, Sloane. They repeat Oh my God about a thousand times. They say, there I was just living my regular life, minding my own business, going about things in the same old way, muddling through, but always, imperceptibly, moving on the path to God, and suddenly exclaiming, 'Of course! I see it now. Every old thing is not like before. All things are made new.'"

Is that what I was feeling? Is that what I was trying to say? My whole chest was sick with it. "But you do see it, Candy?" I asked, my voice high, almost pleading. "You do know what I'm talking about, don't you?"

"I see it," she said. "I see it everywhere. In the canals of Isle of Capri, the rush hour of Chicago."

"On the Iowa-80 truck stop?" Gina inquired dryly.

"Especially there. Sun sets there, too."

"Sloane, close your window. I can't hear a thing."

The air stopped gushing through, and now it was as if we were watching a movie again. We were behind glass, and the land was beyond the glass, separated from us, like moving pictures. It wasn't as dramatic. It wasn't like living it. But now I could hear Candy.

She told us that Floyd had come out to West Virginia for a family funeral. His folks had been cattle-ranching in South Dakota for generations, and they soon returned home, but Floyd came back to stay with rels. He and Candy had met at Our Lady of Martyrs church, where they both sang in the choir and had become tight.

"Tight? Or thick as thieves?" Gina commented. "Floyd. What a name. Does he look like a Floyd?"

"Sure does."

"You'd think Floyd wouldn't want God to know him by his name," mused Gina.

"I guess. I wish God wouldn't know me by Candy. Grace is so much better." Candy sighed with conflicted resignation. "But." She shrugged. "Candy made me more money."

"It does reveal the essence of the thing, don't it," I said, glancing at her in the rearview mirror. Candy. Like a strawberry lollipop. Without the makeup, plain and waving on the side of the road. Grace.

Like this we rode the sea of sage and brush and rolling grasslands, not seeing a soul until deep in South Dakota when we got onto I-90. Candy slunk down on the seat again, the hundreds of trucks unsettling us, so we took the next exit and drove the parallel service road instead. It was almost six.

It looked like it was about to rain; by the time we got to Wall Drug, black covered nearly the whole sky. It was dinnertime, yet the place was empty. Wall Drug maybe began as a drugstore years ago, but when it decided to become a tourist attraction, it branched out into a restaurant and a trinket shop. Perhaps they had some Band-Aids and an aspirin hidden somewhere, but on display were stuffed jackalopes.

Candy came up to a man behind the counter. "I'm looking for Floyd," she said. "He around?"

"Floyd?" said the man gruffly. "Floyd Lashly? He don't work here no more."

"But I just spoke to him and he told me to meet him here."

"I don't know what he told *you*, all I know is, I fired his ass three weeks ago and haven't seen him since."

Candy shook her head, not comprehending. "No, no. He's worked here two years."

"I know! I hired him, I fired him."

"He told me to meet me here," Candy said, nearly crying, but the burly plaid-shirted guy had already turned away.

She called the number she had for him, but no one answered. "I don't understand," she whispered to me and Gina after dialing twenty times. "I just spoke to him yesterday."

"Maybe he's not home?" Gina said helpfully.

"I came all the way from West Virginia to see Floyd," Candy said to the woman serving coffee and toffee donuts, her voice breaking. "He just moved out from his folks a little while ago. Do you know where he lives now?" Standing behind her, I didn't see her face, but I saw in her strained calf muscles intense anxiety. "Please," she whispered. "Please. He's my good friend."

The coffee was cold and weak, the donut pretty good. The lady shook her head. "He left on bad terms. I don't got that information." She was not particularly friendly or sympathetic, but she was a woman, and she saw something in Candy's glazed despair

310

that obviously made an impression on her. The manager yelled at the waitress to get back to work, "before he fired her ass, too." She picked up a coffee pot, poured some into a cup for Candy, fussed with another donut, and as she took two dollars from her, said, "Go through the Badlands, at the junction of 44 and 240 there be a town called Interior, you'll see a yellow trailer with a red roof. That's Floyd's."

Candy smiled. "Okay," she said. "Thank you." She gave the woman a ten-dollar tip and left, without taking either the coffee or the donut.

"Take the donut, Cand," I said. "It's delicious."

"Suddenly, I lost my appetite. I'll get hungry again when we find Floyd."

"Candy," said Gina, "what does he do? Keep the money you send him under his pillow?"

"I don't know where he keeps it."

I didn't say anything. I was not the kind of girl who'd say, oh, you're going flat across the entire country to find your mother, but what if she doesn't want anything to do with you? And so, in this instance, neither was I the kind of girl who said, even teasing, so you called this Floyd yesterday to tell him you'd meet him today at six, and he said okay, sure thang, sweetheart, and when you got there, you found out he'd been fired three weeks ago Tuesday. This doesn't crash alarm bells through your head? But it wasn't my style, particularly if I suspected that the teasing struck too close to the truth, so I kept my mouth nice and shut as we crossed the divided highway and drove south into Badlands under the black sky. The summer tourists must have heard a storm was coming: there was no one on the road except Bambi, his mother, and us.

"Badlands," I said to Gina, as a matter of statement. "Didn't Bruce Springsteen write a song about them?"

"Who?" Candy said from the back.

Gina and I both groaned theatrically.

And from the back, we heard her voice, lowered two octaves, suddenly sing, *I believe in the faith that could save me . . .*

311

When she saw our comically struck faces, she threw her head back and laughed her sing-song, contagious child-like laugh. "Badlands I know," she said.

It was an endless winding way through the Badlands to Interior. The turns were hairpin and we could go no more than twenty miles an hour. The black clouds were building ominously ahead. A few times it felt like I could easily slip off the road. Once I got so scared we had to stop at a scenic view to collect my bearings, which I had lost around the last hairpin. Candy wanted to keep going. There was a twitchy nervousness about her. "Come on," she kept saying. "Come on. Let's go." But I had to stop long enough for my hands to stop shaking. It was tough Gina who got us through it. It was Gina who looked out her open window and said, "Oh my God, will ya just look at this?"

We looked, but we were too preoccupied with our fears to fully appreciate what we were seeing. "Girls, do you even see what I see? You two are unbelievable. Three days you gawked at a field in Iowa, you were breathless about sand, and don't even get me started on grass in South Dakota. 'Loooook, grass! It's God, oooh.' And here's something you've actually never seen before, and you couldn't care less."

Candy and I pretended to care. For five minutes we stood at the top of a crest overlooking what seemed to be the entire north of all the Dakotas, north and upward to the dangerous sky.

"The Sioux Indians," said Candy dully. "They stood right here, motionless, watching buffalo at sunset. They would take out their suncatchers, little bits of stone and wood with holes in them, to reflect the sun into the buffalo's eyes. The buffalo would become dazzled, one would buck, then another, there'd be a confusion, then a stampede. That's when the Indians would run down the hill and slaughter the animals that had fallen in the frantic run. They would have food and skins for the winter."

Gina and I stared at her like she was a buffalo.

She pointed to the National Park sign at the edge of the view. "INDIAN SLAUGHTER GROUNDS."

"All right, let's go," said Gina, reaching for a word of comfort and failing to find it. All I could see was Erv sitting across from me, his ice eyes trying to penetrate my secrets, and now that I knew what kind of a man he was, it made it harder for me to look straight at Candy. Too much vivid imagining. If we hid, our hiding gave us away. If we remained in plain sight, our gawking gave us away. Everything gave us away while we were exposed on the plains like this.

"Why would Floyd lie to me?" Candy asked. "Maybe he forgot. Do you think so?" She sounded so scared.

"I think so, Candycane," I said, squeezing her arm, not lifting my eyes. "He just didn't want you to worry. He'll be home. You'll see. Come on."

The Badlands are a steep rock gully, an intricate, meandering ravine of eroding sedimentary rock that goes on for a hundred miles. I wished we could look at it with eyes not dimmed by Candy's worry and my lies. As I was making razor turns down steep inclines between mountains of prehistoric rock, it started to rain again. Pretty soon it was so heavy I could see nothing but the streaming hood of my yellow Mustang. I had to stop, but there was nowhere to pull off. We were stuck on a two-lane road going blind down a mountain pass, so we idled in the car, but that inching forward was even more frightening. At any moment, someone could come plowing into me from behind, send me flying into the ancient clay and mud. We were just sitting, waiting for something bad to happen. "Hence, the name," said Candy. "Badlands." She was no longer serene. "Come on, Shel. Please try to hurry. It's just a few more miles, right? We're almost there."

3

Broken Hill

It took us *two hours and five minutes* to make the 33-mile journey
to Interior. The rain had stopped, and the sun was setting behind
the wet rocky Badlands, which were now behind us, too. The town
of Interior was a gas station, closed, a produce stand, closed, a bar,
open, and a mini-mart, closed. The few dilapidated trailers were
peppered right on the sagebrush. We saw Floyd's yellow trailer with
the red roof right away. It was hard to miss. Candy made us wait
in the car while she walked up the rickety steps and knocked on
the door. With her gamine legs, slender white arms, and spiky hair,
she looked small, so vulnerable standing by the metal door, knocking
with one hand, holding on to the rusted railing with the other.

No one answered. She came back to the car and leaned in
through my window. Her eyes were wandering. He wasn't home,
Candy said, like a truism. What did we do now?

Nothing to do, Gina announced. "Let's go to Rapid City, rest
a bit, and come back tomorrow."

Candy shook her head. "You don't understand."

"We do," I said, touching her hand, clutching my driver door.

"No." She shook her head vehemently. "You don't. This money
is my life. Without it all the plans I've made are ruined. I can't
leave until I get my money. Everything I've worked for and planned
for is with Floyd. I'm not going anywhere till I see him."

314

"What about Jessica in Reno?" I said, beseechingly, cajolingly.

"She's got a few bucks," she cried, "but Floyd's got twenty grand! You see the difference?"

"I do, I do. He could've gone on vacation." I didn't add, *with your money.*

"There's nothing to do around here," said Gina. "If he's not home, where is he? We know he's not at work."

"Maybe he found another job," I said.

"Yes. Or," said Gina, "he could be in Rapid City himself. It's Friday evening, after all."

"Saturday," I corrected.

"Even better. He's out clubbing. He's a young guy? Clubbing it up."

"Saturday night, clubbing it up before church on Sunday?" Candy was dubious.

"What's the difference?"

Candy waved her off.

"Gina's right about one thing, Cand," I said. "We could wait all night."

"Then that's what we'll do. Wait all night."

"No!" Gina exclaimed. "I'm not sleeping another night in the car."

"You hardly slept last night, girlfriend," said Candy. "You were in the Argosy with me."

"I'm not staying all night in the middle of nowhere!"

I hated to admit it, but Gina was right. This *was* in the middle of nowhere. If I had black visions in a full parking lot in Sioux City, think what might happen here, on the edge of the Badlands, with only grassland in the other three directions, and not a light in sight, nothing but the gas station and trailers with their rusted railings. And because I'm not that kind of girl, I didn't want to point out the obvious: that a person who would live in this kind of trailer would hardly be the type who had made twenty thousand dollars for himself, and was keeping another twenty thousand dollars safe for a friend.

"I'm not going anywhere," said Candy, "until I speak to Floyd." She turned away from the car. "Go if you want. Go."

I exchanged a look with Gina, who shrugged. "Great. Let's go."

"Something tells me the girl don't mean it," I said, turning off my engine and heaving a childish sigh of pained distress.

One thing about sitting on the hood of your car while waiting for a stranger to return to his trailer to give you back the money he owes you is this: it's scary in Interior. I thought I'd feel safer with no trucks speeding by, but the town was so isolated and the Badlands so ominous, just shadows now that the sun had gone. As the last purple light faded from the sky, an eerie quiet settled on the land, and I just knew that at the moment when the sky finally shaded from violet to black, there would be neither sight nor sound and I would long for the din of a thousand trucks hurtling along the Interstate. I *really* wanted Floyd to come home before night fell.

I asked Candy to put on a pair of jeans. With the Horseshoe Bar right next door, I didn't feel safe with her pale bare legs stretching out on the hood, next to me. The bar was on mute, too, as if there were furtive goings-on inside. The road, U.S. 44, stretched straight through the grassland to Rapid City. Rapid City, where there would be lights, people laughing and joking, eating. I jumped off the hood and leaned against the car. It had been a long time since Valentine, where we'd eaten real food, the sticky toffee donut at Wall Drug not counting. Funny how you could go without food for so long, and then suddenly be famished, ravenous, thinking about burgers and fries, onion rings, and pickles dripping vinegar into coleslaw. I wished I were back home, on my little couch, getting ready for a quiet evening of TV, a little "Jeopardy", and "Dallas", and Emma in the kitchen asking if I wanted lemon with my tea. That's what I hankered for.

Gina didn't seem to feel the same way I did about Interior. She was sitting on the hood of the car, next to Candy, humming to the radio. It was playing quietly; loud seemed obnoxious here.

I got back into the car and drummed the wheel, watching Gina and Candy's backs and butts against my window. They were chatting. How long had we waited? Only an hour, it turned out. Insufferable.

Gina and Candy suddenly announced they were going to the Horseshoe to get some food. I shook my head vehemently, bounding out of the car.

"But there'll be food."

"Let's wait."

"But we're hungry *now*," whined Gina.

"I'm not going into that bar." I propped on the hood, faking casualness.

"Why not?"

"You figure it out," I replied. What a stupid conversation. "Three girls in the middle of nowhere, going inside a bar full of drinking men who live in a place like Interior? Are you out of your mind? How do you think you'll protect yourself there?"

"Why would we need to?" said Candy.

"Candy, you *are* out of your mind," I said. "They'll assault you, then kill you and throw your body in the brush over there, mine too. We won't be found for a thousand years, not even a thought of us will remain in anyone's head."

"Fine, Drama Queen, stay," said Gina, complacently unconcerned. "We'll go. We'll be right back. We'll bring you something."

I started to say, okay, do whatever you want. But I stopped. I hopped off the hood, very roughly, I almost fell. I slammed shut the open car door; the sound echoed in the prairie. "No, Gina." I was adamant. "We either go to Rapid City, or we stay here. We're not going inside that place."

"You don't have to."

"And *you* won't. I don't know how to spell it out any clearer, how I can be more plain. You can't go in there, because if you do and something happens, there's only me out here. When they've

317

finished with you they'll come for me, and I won't be able to do a single thing to help either you, or myself. Now do you get it?"

That stopped Gina in her tracks. "Okay, okay. Take it easy." She motioned to Candy. "Come on, let's go."

"Gina, Candy, if you two go," I said, left with no choice, "I will get into my car and leave you. I will not stay here another minute. Now, decide what you want to do."

Gina turned. "Don't threaten us, Shelby."

"I'm not threatening you. You're not my child. I can't tell you what to do. But this is my car, and my life, and I am going to get into my car and drive the fuck away if you set one foot in there."

Candy diffused the situation; stepped away from Gina, toward me. "She's right, Gina," she said. "Let's not be foolish." She sprung back on the hood and lifted her hands up to the sky. "*From the deep water, I cry to you,*" she intoned. "*Hear my prayer.*"

To escape the mugginess of my own resentment, I moved a few feet away from them, leaned against a wooden post, listening for cars on the road, milling, kicking up dust. Why couldn't Gina see the truth of things without my having to point it out so forcefully?

Seems I couldn't see the truth of things myself too well, either.

I cried out to God with my voice, sang Candy. *And he gave ear to me.* She lifted her hands again. *My hand was stretched out in the night without ceasing. I complained and my spirit was overwhelmed. I remembered God and was troubled. I am so troubled I can't speak . . .*

She turned to me. "I know you're hungry and you want to go, Shelby. Honest, you can go. I won't be upset. But *I* can't go. There's no other time for me. There is Floyd and my money, or my life is over."

Reaching into her hobo bag, she pulled out a postcard. It was getting hard to see, but it was a picture of a band of green light over a night sky. "A postcard!" said Gina. "Excellent."

"It's a postcard from Paradise," said Candy. "A few years ago, Paradise, which is *not* near the North Pole, got Northern lights streaking across the sky. Apparently a unique phenomenon in that part of the world. Hence the postcard."

"So you're going to Paradise," I said slowly, "to catch some Northern lights?"

"Foolish," said Candy. "Turn the postcard over."

On the back of the card, beside the address, were two words in sloppy teenage print.

Mike died.

That's what it said, and that's all it said. Gina and I twisted our mouths, glanced at each other, squinted our eyes. "Is this *your* Mike?" I finally asked.

She nodded. "Let me tell you a story of three boys," said Candy. Floyd was nowhere in sight. Not a single car had passed through Interior in an hour. "Three boys went out partying and drinking on a Saturday night."

"Much like tonight."

"No, not at all like tonight. On this particular Saturday night, the three boys were joyriding, and there is no joy tonight. One of them was a security officer at a local bank, one of them had a gun, one of them was fifteen years old. They were playing around, but they'd been drinking, and driving; the gun was playfully pointed, they hit a bump, the gun went off. No one meant for it to go off, but it did just the same, and hit one of the boys in the neck. They stopped the car, the bleeding boy fell out onto the sidewalk." Candy was spinning the postcard in her hands. "You know neck wounds."

"We don't know neck wounds," I said quietly. We were all leaning against the hot Mustang.

"There's a *lot* of blood. It looked pretty hopeless. And the boy who shot him was so distressed, so horrified at what he'd done, that he turned the gun on himself."

Gasping, we said nothing.

"The wounded boy on the sidewalk," said Candy, "lived. Got a scar in his neck. Will talk funny for the rest of his life, but lived. The fifteen-year-old wasn't harmed."

"Oh my God," I said. "The boy who turned the gun on himself was your Mike?"

"The boy who turned the gun on himself was my Mike."

"And his friend?"

"They weren't friends. They were brothers. All three of them."

We were quiet for a long while. The last purple streaks on the western horizon darkened finally to black while we struggled to find something to say.

"Are you going to the funeral?" asked Gina. "Because you're taking your time, if you are."

"I'm not going to the funeral," replied Candy. "Mike's parents would have me arrested if I ever came near them."

"They hate you?"

"Like the plague. They thought he was too good for the likes of me."

You were trouble, I wanted to say. You are trouble.

"Well, if he's dead, and they don't want to see you, why are you risking your life going to Paradise?"

"Because Mike was the father of my baby girl."

"You have a *baby*?" gasped Gina. "But you're only seventeen!"

"What, not old enough?" Candy said ruefully, pulling a small envelope from her Mary Poppins bag and handing it to us.

Plenty old, I thought, old like a wizened woman. But still a child, too. I turned on the dashboard light, to see the small card, written in the neat scrawl of a child.

"Hapy Valentin, Mama, wen u com, I giv u chokolats and roses. From Tara."

"I had her five years ago when I was almost thirteen," Candy said, taking the card from my hands. "That was the whole problem. I got to my mom's, met Erv, met Mike, and got pregnant straight out of the gate, so to speak. Wham. Before anything else. So, what could I do? I had the baby, and she lived with him. I visited her all the time, but then they moved." Candy spat on the ground. "She was two. They took her, took her deliberately away from me, pretending it was for work or some shit, and moved to that

320

god-forsaken hole in the ground, Paradise. Mike didn't want to go, but what could he do? He was just a kid himself. He hated them for it, hated that place like I can't tell you. Whenever I talked to him, he'd tell me he was counting the days until he was out of school and could get a job, move away. He said it was like prison, like hell on earth." Candy made a stricken noise. "Mike was the only decent one in that whole family. We were both saving money so we could take our baby and be together. But now that he's dead, I'll be damned before I leave her another day with those blood-sucking sons of bitches."

"You're going to Paradise to take the girl?"

"Yes."

In the dark I swallowed air, like a fish, as if I wanted to breathe and couldn't. "Are . . . they going to be okay with it?"

"Well, I'm hardly going to ask them, am I?"

"Is the girl going to be okay with it?"

Candy paused before she slowly replied. "Shelby, a small girl needs to be with her mother, that's all there is to it." When I said nothing, she said, "What, you don't agree?"

God help me, I *still* said nothing. I was panting. In my universe, these were undreamed of dilemmas. I had once thought, once believed the answer to that question was so simple. "Yes," I finally said. "Yes, I agree."

"But what are you going to do?" asked Gina, her voice transformed, considerably softened. And why not? Nothing she had hitherto known about Candy made more of an impression on Gina than this small, but monumental fact. She was a *mother*. She had a child. She didn't have a hairbrush, yet she had a child. She didn't have a suitcase, or a wallet to put her earnings into. She didn't have a pen, or a plaque. She looked like she'd never *seen* a doll, much less played with one. She was younger than me. This person had a *child*. At seventeen, I was sucking lollipops in the hall, pining after Tony Bergamino and running 440-meter sprints.

Gina said, wishful hope lifting her voice past the peaks of the

Badlands, "So you started doing what you were doing to make money for the baby?"

"Uh, no," replied Candy, who, for all her vices, found it difficult to lie. "I don't think it was that thought out. I just sort of, walked into it. Knowing that I had experience—having given birth and all—Erv asked if I'd be interested in making good money for a few hours' work. I said why not. I bought Tara a few things, treated her well for Christmas. After they left, I worked, sent Mike some money. But one day, his bitch of a mother opened his mail, saw the cash from me and flipped out. After that, it was hard to send money. You have to be eighteen to receive a Western Union wire or your parent has to sign for you. But then I started sending some to a woman named Nancy, who owned a bookstore in Paradise. I'd wire it to her, and she'd give it to him."

"There are no easy answers," Gina said.

Candy frowned. "No easy answers to what? You don't wrestle with the question of the meaning of life, but this gives you pause? I need my kid. I need my money. She and I disappear, start a new life, away from everything. What answers are you talking about? You think I got dealt the wrong hand? Or that I should be unhappy with the hand I was dealt?" She shook her head. "I never complain."

"Oh, I know that. That's not what I meant."

"Then what did you mean?" But before Gina could think of a response, Candy added, "And you know what? I knew a girl during the five minutes I went to school, who was four foot ten and picked her face so bad it bled all the time. None of her clothes fit and the boys laughed at her. All she wanted, and I mean, *all* she wanted, was to be able to wear a mini-skirt. So she did. Her rolls of fat spilled under her halter top, her legs were trunky and hairy. Her face bled as she applied her mascara and blush, but still, she put on her mini-skirt, and every night asked God for only one thing—to fit into it, to just once be looked at by the boys the way I was looked at by the boys. Everything I had she wanted or so she thought. But you know what? Not for anything would I

322

give what I got dealt to be her. So she prayed to God and asked him for what I had, and I prayed to God and asked him to help me make sense of what I had been given."

"Some of it not so good, Candycane!" said Gina, scooting a little closer. "Personally, I'd ask, what the fuck?" I scooted closer on the other side. Candy stared at us from one face to the other.

"What's wrong with you? Are you worried? Don't worry," she said. "Floyd will be here soon."

Touching her bare arm, I said nothing. She took my hand and, for a few moments, held it.

How long could we sit and wait in the dark at the foot of the Badlands for Floyd to arrive with Candy's money? It was unbearable for me. What was it like for her?

"Do you see why one way or another I have to get my money? Because without it, I can't have a life with my baby. Without it, I can't change anything."

I think I nodded. I may have wished I did. "But, Candy," I whispered, "where is there to fly where Erv can't find you?"

Candy moved away from my patronizing, compassionate handwringing. "I'm not writing poetry here," she said. "I'm going to get us a plane ticket and she and I are going to Australia. Just me and her."

From the hood of my car, I could see the dark outlines of those monolithic, ragged rocks rising out of flat ground. The neon of the bar was broken and intermittently flashing. Not "Horseshoe," but "Horse hoe." There wasn't a car in sight, nor the sound of one coming. "You're planning to go to *Australia*?"

"Yes."

"Do you even know where Australia is?" said Gina.

"Har-de-har," replied Candy.

"That's your plan? Take her and fly to Australia?"

"Yes."

"*Australia?*"

"Yes! No one knows us there. Erv won't find me, and I can

323

begin afresh. Tara will be starting school next month. I have to think about making a stable home for her. I can't just be traveling from bar to bar."

"No, no, of course not." I rubbed my chin, not wanting Gina to catch my incredulous stare.

"Australia *is* exotic, Sloane," said Gina, trying to find something positive to say.

"Yeah, but no one speaks English," I said.

"What language *do* they speak?" said Candy. "Australian?"

I was skeptical.

"They speak the Queen's English," Gina said slowly. "Sloane is just fooling with you."

"I read about a place there," Candy said, unbaited, "a little mining town in the middle of vast semi-arid desert lands called Broken Hill. It's nicknamed Silver City and that's where I want to go live with my Tara. In the outback of Australia. Silver City. It's just right for me, but to get there I need my money. Do you see how badly I need it?"

"I do, I do." Hopping off the car, Gina started to dance, inexplicably swirling and skipping, accompanying herself merrily with song.

> "Up jumped the swagman, sprang into the billabong
> You'll never catch me alive, said he
> And his ghost may be heard as you pass by
> That billabong
> You'll come a waltzing Matilda with me . . ."

We watched and when she stopped the odd revelry, I said, "What about passports? You'll need those, too."

"Oh, Sloane," said Gina with a disapproving frown. "Leave the girl alone. Let her have her dream for five minutes."

"Passports? To Australia?" Candy seemed surprised by that.

"Yes. It's a *foreign* country. You need a passport to travel out of the United States."

Candy thought about it, then shrugged. "Well, I'll get these passports if that's what I need. How hard can that be?"

"You need a permanent address," I said.

"Sloane!"

"You need a birth certificate," I continued. "For you *and* the baby. You need pictures of her and you, certain kinds of pictures, certain size, certain profile. You need identification, and you need to wait for a few weeks, until you get them."

"Shelby!" exclaimed Gina. "Her parade is so short-lived. Why do you want to rain on it?"

"Because I want her to succeed. And she can't go without the passports."

"I don't have birth certificates!" Candy said. "My father might have mine, but I don't have Tara's. I wouldn't even know where it might be. I've never seen it."

"Mike's parents should know where it is," said Gina. "You'll have to ask them."

"I don't have weeks to wait," said Candy. "You know I don't have days. I was going to take her, go to 'Frisco that very day, fly out the next. I didn't know I needed passports. And you know I can't ask Mike's parents for anything. They hate me, I told you. They're not going to help me with shit. I'll be lucky if they don't call the cops on me for taking my own kid." She started to cry. "They won't give me her birth certificate," she whispered.

"You are her mother," I said. "They will."

"You *are* her mother," agreed Gina. "Sloane's right. They should."

"I am her mother," concurred Candy. "I need to get her somewhere safe. I can't fail her. I have to help her. She can't grow up without a mother."

Mutely, I pressed my sad hands around Candy's shoulder.

She lowered her head. "I've seen some bad things in my life." Restlessly she looked down the road, one way, the other. "I want to keep Tara from them."

The night became hot and humid. We were stuck to the car, and the accidental touch of another's bare clammy skin was unpleasant. Candy jumped down from the hood and started pacing. I started twitching. Gina was curious. I wanted to talk about the baby; Gina wanted to talk about Mike. Did Candy love him?

"We were twelve, thirteen."

"I know. But did you love him."

"I guess. I thought I did."

"Did you want to get married?"

"We were *thirteen*."

"Did you talk to her on the phone?" I asked, and held my breath for her answer.

"Yes," she said. "Mike would take her out for a walk in the stroller, and I'd call them at the library, or the bookstore."

It was so dark, so quiet, so frightening. Where was Floyd?

"How far do you think you can run from your life, Candy?" asked Gina.

"Ten thousand miles to Broken Hill," she replied.

"A man like Erv, you don't think he'd miss you? You don't think he'd notice you were gone? All the things you know about him and what he's done to hurt young girls, the film you stole from him, you think he'd just let you wander the earth? You could have him put away for life."

Candy was pacing, not answering. "Yes," she said at last. "I told him in my letter. As long as he leaves me alone, I'm forever silent. He knows that. I once believed he'd let me go. He as much as said so. 'Any time you want out, darlin', you just tell me, and you're out,' he told me. No fuss, no muss." She paced more furiously.

"Not really a man of his word, is he, Cand," I said.

"I got mixed up with him, he was no good, and my mother couldn't help me. But you'll see. I'm going to be a better mother to my Tara. I'll put braids in her hair. She'll play with her dolls, and wear pretty dresses, and I'll *never* let her wear makeup till she's sixteen. I'll be so strict with her. Strict but fair. I'll home-school her, so she stays away from the bad boys. She is so beautiful. She needs to stay far away. Tara is going to have a long childhood, I'm

326

going to make sure of that." Suddenly she swore. "Where *is* that fucking Floyd?!"

I couldn't stare down the dark road anymore, waiting for his lights. I hopped off the car. "Do you know how to braid hair, Candycane?"

"No," she admitted. "I don't know any lullabies either. But I'll learn."

I walked to the trailer. "We've been waiting for over three hours," I said.

"Going on three," corrected Gina.

"Thank you. How long are we going to sit here? Will we stay the night?"

"I don't want to," said Candy. "But what choice do I have? He has my money."

"Where do you think he keeps it?" I asked. "In a bank?"

"I don't know," she said. I was quiet. She stared at me. "What are you getting at?"

"What I'm getting at," I said, "is perhaps he keeps it in his trailer. He's not here. It's your money. You see what I'm getting at?"

We ransacked the place. We were like drunk ATF agents on a gun raid without a warrant. The trailer was locked, but Candy crawled through the bathroom window, and let us in. We were quick and careless. We didn't worry that he'd know we'd been looking for her money: the place was a biological and human dump, he'd never notice. It was a trash heap of someone's life, and all of it was on the floor, on every available flat surface. "This doesn't seem like Floyd," said Candy, looking around. "I've seen his room. He was always so clean. I used to call him tidy Floyd."

"Maybe you were being ironic?" said Gina.

"Perhaps he has a messy roommate," I countered.

After twenty minutes of looking, in dusty corners, under a

ravaged mattress covered with grime and gunk, we finally found a metal box with a lock on it. It took an energized Candy, a hammer, pliers and five minutes to break the lock. Inside was cash.

My relief was short-lived.

"This can't be right," she said after she finished counting. "There's only a thousand here."

"Maybe he divided his talents among little metal boxes," said Gina. "Maybe he doesn't want to keep his treasure all in one place."

"Yes, yes," I said in vigorous agreement. Gina and I stood close together, watching Candy on the floor with the metal box.

We searched some more, but it felt futile. There were no other metal boxes. "This has to be some kind of a mistake." She shook her head. "Floyd is a good guy. This must not be my money." She went to put it back.

Gina and I, gesticulating wildly at each other, took her by her arms and persuaded her not to. It was insurance money, we said. If it's a mistake, you give it back. When he gives you your money, you return this and apologize.

She kept it. "Floyd wouldn't do this," Candy insisted. "He went to church with me. He sang in the choir with me. We sang hymns and Psalms together, every Sunday." She wouldn't move from the now empty metal box, holding on to the fifties. "What if this is all that's left?" she whispered. "It can't be. It just can't!"

"It's not," I reassured her, patting her shoulder, trying not to touch anything else, trying even not to touch her. Imagine patting someone without touching them, it's not easy. I wished I could float and not stand on the filthy floor. And all the while, my heart thumped dully, thickly in my chest, all the while, I kept listening for the sound of Floyd's car, dreading the confrontation.

"What are me and my baby going to do?" Candy whispered. "It's not enough to get to Australia."

I took a breath. "Candy, we'll have to make you a plan B. Just in case you can't get the passports and all."

"I don't have a plan B," she said, clutching forlornly at what she suspected was all that was left of her money. "I have only one plan. To take my money from Floyd and go to Australia."

"You'll make it," I said. "You'll see."

"I have to start a new life," she repeated stubbornly. "I can't start it on a thousand dollars."

"It's not the money, it's the life," I said.

"No, philosopher queen," said Candy, "in this instance it *is* actually the money."

Dejectedly, we looked once more for other boxes, other hiding spots then, filled with disappointment, we lowered the busted blinds, turned off the lights, and left.

Candy refused to leave Interior. We could go if we liked, that was fine, but she wasn't going anywhere until Floyd returned and gave her her money. While Gina banged her head against the car door, I tried to convince Candy to come back in the morning.

"Let's go," Gina said finally to me. "She told us to go. Let's go."

"No."

"If you want, we'll come back for her in the morning. I can't stay here another minute, can you?"

"We'll stay one more minute."

"Can we at least go to the Horseshoe and get some food? It's after eleven!"

Suddenly, Candy said she'd be right back and disappeared, running down the road to the bar. I called after her, but it was too late. She was gone fifteen minutes, during which Gina exhorted me for each one of those 900 seconds to get in the car and *go*. Then Candy was running toward us, her hands full of warm bacon and cheese potato skins. "Get in," she breathed. "Eat. I found out where he is."

The guys at the Horseshoe knew Floyd. They said he hung out at the Fireside Brewing Co. in Rapid City. Apparently, he had a really cute girlfriend.

"Why didn't we think of asking at the Horseshoe earlier?" I wondered, starting up the Shelby in relief and inhaling the skins.

"Because you, genius, said you wouldn't go in there," Gina pointed out. "We'd be sleeping by now if it weren't for you."

After nearly two hours and a hundred miles on a threadbare Route 44, no lights, no other cars, we got to Rapid City's old center square nearing one in the morning. Rapid City surprised me because it wasn't the western town I had been expecting, a hole in the wall with tumbleweeds. It was laid out on a wide grid, the buildings square, six-storied, and orderly. It looked like an old small town. Candy knew the manager at the "historic" Alex Johnson hotel; unfortunately he was off duty at one in the morning, so we had to pay for our room up front, eighty bucks. I paid. I felt bad for Candy. We parked in an alley behind the hotel, off the street where the car would have been in full view, dropped our things in the small room on the top floor and ran to Fireside Brewing Co. before it closed at two.

Inside the loudly crowded bar/restaurant, it took Candy less than a minute to scan the place, say, "I don't fucking believe it!" and walk from the bar to a small group of rowdy studs. Gina and I followed.

"Well, well," said Candy, loud, her hands on her hips, eyes blazing. "If it isn't fucking Floyd." Her denim skirt was short, her pink halter top faded in the smoky light.

A boy with nappy hair looked up. He was flushed and smooth like a baby, but unlike a baby, inebriated and sheepish. "Hey, Candykins," he said. "What are *you* doing here?"

"What am I doing here? Don't screw with me, Floyd. I talked to you four weeks ago, told you I was coming. I talked to you yesterday and you told me to meet you at Wall Drug! Or did you forget?"

His eyes were darting from drink to drink. "Oh, yeah," he drew out. "Was we supposed to meet tonight?" He chuckled. "I didn't think you meant *tonight*. Sorry, hon. Did you wait long?"

"Yeah, about four fucking hours at your hole in Interior." She looked over the guys sitting with him. "You want to talk in front of them? 'Cause I don't mind." Candy's hands were still at her hips. Floyd's friends were tipsy and equally useless at wading through the bullshit. Should they stay or should they go? the song kept insistently asking. They decided to go, tripping over each other in their intoxicated effort to make tracks.

"So, how are you?" He looked broke, and was just making conversation.

"I'll dispense with the niceties," said Candy. "Where's my money, Floyd?"

"Money?"

"Don't play stupid with me, like you never heard the word money. Where's the forty grand I sent you over the last two years?"

"Forty?" He shook his head, tried to focus, tried to solemnize. "I don't think it was that much, sugah."

"Oh, you can be sure it was," said Candy, yanking a white envelope out of her Mary Poppins bag. "It's all here, the dates I sent the wires, the amounts."

He was red in the face, and she was impressive the way she stuck up for herself, how she didn't back down. He hemmed and hawed. He said the money was in the bank, and it was Saturday night, the bank wouldn't be open till Monday. "But if you wanted to come back . . ." he drawled in his false tenor.

"I'm not leaving without my money," said Candy. "So cough up, buddy. Don't give me any of that sugah shit. You made 20,000 bucks for doing nothing but keeping it under your pillow, as per my instructions. Remember?"

"I do, I do. But I don't have it right now. It's in the bank, I tell you. I'll get it for you Monday. Are you girls hungry?"

"Yes—" That was Gina.

"No!" Candy slammed the table. Floyd recoiled. "Let's go, and you can show me the bank statement, Floyd. Your most recent bank statement with the balance in black print."

"Oh, I don't keep that stuff. You know me." He giggled like a girl, his contrite head bobbing on a thin gooseneck, his face round

331

and flushed pink. "Don't be upset, hon. I'm always happy to see you."

"Fine, you didn't know we were coming, but now we're here, and we'll be out of your hair in a jiffy, just as soon as you get me my money."

He coughed. He said tomorrow banks were closed. No one opened up banks on Sundays, not around these parts.

"Floyd, you told me to meet you in Wall Drug!"

"Oh, yeah . . ." he drew out slowly. "They sacked me just last week."

"We spoke on the phone yesterday," Candy said, just as slowly. "Your exact words were, I'm getting off work at six, I'll see you then."

"I might've misspoke, hon," said Floyd, his eyes darting to the black bag on the floor near his booth.

"Point is," said Candy, "while sitting around waiting for you, and we had plenty of time, you know, we had a drink out of the sink, and then I thought I'd write a card to my mother, telling her I arrived at your Interior abode safely. And I couldn't find a pen that worked, though believe me, I looked. I couldn't find any stamps, or envelopes. I couldn't find," Candy said caustically, "my Western Union receipts, the receipts telling me how much money you were stashing for me. Zilch. You know what else I couldn't find? A checkbook. Imagine that. Keeping thousands of dollars in your account and not having a checkbook."

The visibly shaking Floyd, I was realizing with increasing concern, looked strung out, not drunk. I've seen drunk plenty, but I've seen a guy on junk only once, and he was almost walking until the police picked him up. I thought that was worse. Gin was cheap. Drugs were not. Floyd was shifting his weight, nervously ticking away the seconds under Candy's glare by obsessively rubbing his fingers, like he was washing his hands. His mouth kept moving in a silent defense, but he wasn't looking at her. The music was loud. The waitress came over to ask if we needed something.

"Yes, twenty grand," said Candy. "Got some of that?" The waitress slunk away.

332

"Where's my fucking money?"

"See, that's what I'm trying to tell you, Cand, and you're not listening."

"Oh, I'm listening, all right. Where's my money?"

Floyd lowered his voice. His body swung from side to side.

"I can't hear you," said Candy. "What?"

"JD has it."

"Who the fuck is JD?"

"Well, I thought he was a friend of mine," Floyd replied theatrically, drawing out the word *thought* so that it sounded like *thawwwwwght*.

"I hope you're not wrong about that," Candy said, "especially if he has my money. And why has this JD got it anyway?"

"He has to give it back to me. I'll get it for you, sweetheart, I will. I just need a little time."

"I don't have time," said Candy. "I don't have five minutes. I need my money, and I need it tonight."

"Oh, darling, I don't know where JD is," he wailed plaintively, as if he were about to cry. "I need to find him myself. I'm looking for him."

"Floyd, Floyd." Candy took deep breaths. Floyd was shifting, avoiding her gaze. Things were looking bleak for Candy's money, judging by Floyd's ungainly jitters.

A girl stepped up. "Floydie," she squealed, "where you been, baby? I thought you were going to meet me at Justin's. I've been waiting, like, five minutes."

"I'm here, hon," he said, turning her by the shoulders to face Candy. "Hon, this is my friend from back east. Remember I told you about her? Candy Cane? Candy, this is Lori. She's my girl."

Lori was a bird of a girl, dressed in black, and wobbly herself. Beside Floyd, she didn't seem too bad, but standing close to Candy who was motionless, you could tell that Lori was a parable, a cautionary tale of what happened when you weighed eighty pounds wet and did too much junk. Her black tank top revealed bare, skeletal arms, the insides of which were scarred from bicep

333

to wrist with the livid track marks of needles. Candy did not shake her trembling, proffered hand, she barely looked Lori's addled way.

"I appreciate your fine manners, Floyd," said Candy, "but I don't have all night to stand here and make nice with your bag brides. Now where is my money?"

Floyd pushed Lori away. "Go and get us two beers, hon, please? You girls want anything? Go, Lori. I gotta finish up here."

"What money she talkin' 'bout? You owe her money? And what did she just call me?"

"He doesn't owe me money," snapped Candy. "He *has* my money, which he needs to fork over, my 20,000 dollars."

The girl threw back her head and laughed, a good, merry laugh. Floyd pushed her a little more forcefully. "Just go, I said. Go get me a beer, will you."

"Floyd, is she crazy? You ain't got that kinda money."

"Lori!" He lowered his voice. "Seen JD?"

"No. That punkhead's vanished."

When she left, Floyd turned to Candy, whose angry arms were crossed on her chest. "Look," he said, "sit. Sit for a sec. I need to tell you things. I'll get you your money, but I gotta talk to you first."

Candy did not sit down and motioned for Gina not to. "Floyd, you know my situation. I don't have to tell you what kind of trouble I'm in."

"You and me both, girlfriend," Floyd said tiredly.

"You're wasted, strung out, blasted and lit-up," said Candy. "It's none of my business. Float all you want. I just want my money."

"That's what I'm trying to tell you. I don't have it at the moment. JD has it. But we're going to get it back from him. You'll see. Come with me. We'll find him together, you'll explain the situation. He's an okay guy. Except for that last thing . . ." Floyd shook his head. "Don't want to talk about it. But other than that, he's been pretty good to me."

"I'll ask you just one more time," said Candy. "Why does JD have my money?"

"To help me out," said Floyd. "I needed a little help. So I gave it to him to hold."

"Why?"

"I was afraid I was going to spend it. And I didn't want to do that. So I gave it to him to hold for me. But every once in a while I'd come to him because I needed something, and he'd give it to me. Then he'd say, this is on the house account, this little bit. I didn't know what he meant, so I'd say, yeah, fine, whatever, but this last time he gave me stuff, it was no good. It was just gunk, horrible. I had to get more stuff from somewhere else, because his was ridiculous, just blanks, blanks and blanks—"

"Floyd, you're a beamer?" A beamer is a serious addict.

"No, no, I'm just an ice-cream user. A baby. Just once in a while. It's so good, Cand, you gotta try some, you just have to, you won't go back. I'm not a beamer, oh, every once in a while, if I can't get the good shit, I'll have some light brown sugar, but I hate it, really."

"So let me understand," said Candy. "You gave your candy man, your balloon JD, from whom you get regular antifreeze, my money to hold so it would be safe from you?"

"You got it, baby."

"And then you keep going to him asking for dirt and he gives it to you, saying it's on the house account?"

"I thought he was saying it was *on* the house."

"See, different meaning there."

"Last time, he gave me gaffel, he gave me fake stuff."

"You don't look like you're on flea powder now."

"I had to go get me some from somewhere else, didn't I? His dust was no good!"

Candy and I exchanged looks. I hope I didn't look as helpless as I felt. Candy, I thought, still wasn't getting it. I stood shoulder to shoulder with her. Gina flanked me.

"What money did you use to get dust, Floyd?"

"Don't you worry about that. Not yours."

"So what's with the 1000 bucks I found under your bed? Whose money is that?"

"Candy!" He became so agitated. "I can't *believe* you looked under my bed."

"You keep a messy house. You need to take better care of your things," Candy scolded.

"You have no right to look through my things."

"Ha. Yes, and you have no right to take my money. Twenty thousand dollars. That's robbery, larceny, embezzlement, all in the first degree, you name it. Right, Gina?"

"Right."

"You either get me my money or I'm calling the police."

"That 1000 bucks is mine. I saved that from working."

"Really? That's convenient. And how come Lori doesn't know about it? Would it upset your little girlfriend if she found out that you've been keeping that hunk of change under your bed?"

"You left it there, right? Because it's *my* money."

"I tell you what," Candy said pleasantly, "you get me my twenty grand, I'll give you back your 1000. Deal? Where's JD?"

Floyd ordered Lori to stay put, and we left the Fireside Brewing Co. and walked down Main Street. Floyd went into every joint, as if on a mission, looking for his zoomer. The absurdity of what we were doing seemed lost on Candy, but not on me—searching for a drug dealer to ask for the return of money he was holding on behalf of a heroin user who was hitting him up daily for dope.

We found JD, an unsmiling Indian with hair down to his elbows, in the back room of a seedy small-time bar, counting out some change. Floyd introduced him as JD Soderquist, but the first thing JD said to Floyd was, "Get the fuck away from me, man. I'm sick to death of seeing your face. I don't got nothing for you, understand? And who the hell is this with you?"

Floyd used his soothing tone, he patted JD on the arm, made cooing noises. He introduced us as his close friends, tried to explain the situation. Floyd talked to JD like a son who wants to appease the father before hitting him up for the keys to the Alfa Romeo. It took Floyd ten stilted struggling minutes and JD another incongruous five to understand what it was that Floyd needed from him.

"What money, Floyd? What the hell are you talking about? The money you gave me two weeks ago?"

"No, no, not two weeks, a long time ago. Months maybe."

"Two weeks ago. And you didn't give me twenty grand, you gave me five. And let me just say that since that day, you've come to me twice a day, asking for scag. You say, a little hit, a little stash, but Floyd—twice a day! Who do you think pays for that?"

"I only wanted a little tiny bit," Floyd said beseechingly.

"Twice every fucking day! What do you think I meant when I said this is on account?"

"Yes, yes, yes, yes, yes," said Floyd, hurrying him along. "But that last batch, it was blank, baby. Blank, blank."

"It was not blank," said JD, twirling his mustache, completely in control and straight. "It was blue velvet. It was cut. And it was cut for two reasons. One, you're out of fucking money. You ain't got a house account no more, because the five grand you gave me, you blew on blow, you chased yourself out of Rapid City with your little balloon habit. And two, I was doing you a favor. I thought you were getting so far strung-out, soon we wouldn't be able to bring you back. I was watching your back, Floydie-boy, and this is how you repay me? You bring me your pussy posse, more bag brides to pay for your fix? Where's your regular skeezer, where's Lori?"

"Bag brides?" mouthed Gina.

"Pussy posse?" mouthed I.

"You spent 5000 dollars of my money in the last two weeks?" said an aghast Candy.

JD looked us over. "I'll give you a hundred and a dime bag for the three of them for an hour. But that's it."

Floyd said, "Now, JD, if we could be reasonable about this . . ."

But Candy had had enough. "I want my fucking money. My twenty grand, and I want it now."

337

Next thing you know, we were all out on the street, shoved none too gently by two of his bouncers. The door to the bar slammed. There was no re-entry. We didn't move from the sidewalk.

"I don't think he's right," explained Floyd. "I think he's hanging on to my money. Our money. Your money. Honest, I didn't . . . I just got a bit a day, to tide me over, I didn't . . . honest, Candy, you have to believe me."

"Did you give him all of my money?" Candy said in a low voice, struggling to control herself.

"Really, I think I gave him much more than five. I'm almost sure. I thought I gave him everything. For safekeeping."

"You gave my money to your dealer for safekeeping," she said flatly. "Where's your share of my money?"

"Long gone, baby," croaked Floyd. "Long, long gone."

We walked beside him down the dark street. There was no one out, but the lights were on in the two or three bars still open. He swayed while walking. I wondered about Lori; JD called her a bag bride, so did Candy. What did that mean? I tried not to glean meaning from its use in the sentence JD used, but to do that, I had to not think of the sentence, and that sentence kept parading in my head like Macy's giant balloons on Thanksgiving. *A hundred bucks for the three of them for an hour.* I held on to Gina's arm. She held on to mine. Candy walked unsupported, as if she had to stand a little stiffer now that her meager dreams had turned to ashes. Music piped from the bars, and the jukebox, even in this remotest of remote corners, as if having only one universal song, was playing "I Will Survive," *I will survive*.

"Floyd, I thought you were my friend," was what Candy managed to say when we reached the Fireside Brewing Co. where Lori was waiting.

"I was. I am." He stumbled, he stammered. "I'm sorry, Cand, I wouldn't have gotten so hooked without your money, but the money was there, and the dope was there, and I really thought JD was gonna keep it safe for me. He gave me bad stuff that last time. He shouldn't have taken anything for it."

"I think by the time he gave you gunk instead of junk, you had nothing left to pay with, Floyd," said Candy, without looking at his pale, slightly remorseful face.

"I'm sorry."

"This sorry of yours, is it going to buy me two tickets to Australia?"

"You don't want to go to Australia, baby," said Floyd. "Alligators there."

"It's crocodiles, you moron. I thought you were like me, Floyd. I thought you and I understood the same things." She was crying.

"We did." He bowed his head. "Harry Jones was stronger. It's my Judas."

She slapped him hard across his pink face. He was crying, too. Then she walked away. We hurried past, not looking at him. "Was nice to meet you, girls!" he called after us. He called after her, holding his face, "Candykins, honey, sugah, you left my money alone, right, baby? You left it for me in the box?"

"Yes, right next to my two tickets to fucking Broken Hill," she called back without turning around.

We were alone in the street after he shuffled inside. I was afraid Candy was going to break down completely, and I didn't know how to deal with her despair. I'm not very good with extreme emotion. I don't know what to do when I see it, when I feel it. It frightens me. Tomorrow was Sunday. What were we going to do? What was she going to do?

The Alex Johnson historic hotel was around the corner from Fireside, and we trudged our way up six flights of stairs, because the elevator was being serviced at two in the morning.

"Cand, Floyd's girlfriend, what does she do?" Gina asked.

"What do you mean? She's obviously an addict herself," she replied.

"*Does* she sell her body for dope?"

Candy shrugged. "We all have to feed the monster," she said. "So I guess that's what she does."

Gina realized she was talking to the wrong person if she wanted to elicit shocked condemnation in response to a young man pimping his girlfriend in return for some poison. She turned to me, but I was beyond shock at this point. Candy looked so forlorn, sitting on the bed, shuffling through her bag for comfort, an explanation, a solution. She was counting the money she had won at the Isle of Capri casino, the money she got from under Floyd's bed. I went to sit next to her. Putting my arm around her, I said, "Don't worry, Cand, it'll work out. Honest, it will. How much is the chick in Reno holding for you?"

"Floyd was my best friend," she said. "He and I were soul buds. If he didn't keep himself, how could Jessica? She's like me. She went out to Reno to make a little more money. I gave her a thousand to take with her." She continued to count. "I got twelve hundred bucks," she said, putting the greenbacks on the bedspread. "Enough for nothing."

"It's better than nothing," I said. "It's probably more than I got."

"Yes, but you didn't bring enough for a two-week trip! This money is for my whole life."

There was nothing I could say, my own petty thoughts notwithstanding. *Not enough for a two-week trip? But I counted so carefully!* Gina sat on the other bed, looking at us, fretting. She kept giving me looks. I didn't know what she wanted, so I ignored her.

"I trusted Floyd," said Candy. "You don't know. That guy you met, that's not Floyd. Floyd was the nicest, sweetest boy. He prayed, he promised he would help me. His mother told me he was an angel. He cleaned up, made dinner, washed her floors. One Christmas, he asked for a hand-held vac. That was Floyd. He was a good friend. I never doubted him. I thought my money was safer with him than at a bank." She started to cry again. I didn't know what to do with my insufficient arm.

Gina came over and sat on the other side of Candy, patting her, comforting her. "It's okay," Gina said. "Really. You have 1200 dollars. That's a lot." She smiled. "And maybe when we get to Reno, we can gamble a little, win some more. One good win, and you'll be back in business."

"We're talking 20,000 bucks, Gina," Candy said, swiping the tissue I was handing her. "We're not talking about quarters in your poker machines. Do you know how many frogs I had to kiss to get that money? How many dances, how many laps, how many movies I had to make to earn that money? You'll never understand." No amount of tissues were going to be enough.

"I can't imagine."

I couldn't imagine.

After a while she calmed down. "Oh, well," she said, blowing her nose, getting up, fetching a drink. "Oh, well. Easy come"—she smiled—"easy go. The things you come by without grace, you lose without grace." She said it, but you could tell, she couldn't make peace with it.

Later that night lying in bed, not sleeping despite body-bending exhaustion, she said, her voice breaking, "I saved it for her, my baby. I saved that money, denied myself everything, didn't put myself through typing school, didn't stop working so the baby could have it. I gave it to Floyd, and now look. Had I kept it, Erv would've taken it. Or my mother would've spent it. Mike's mother confiscated it. I couldn't give it to my father. Made me feel too guilty. What was I supposed to do?"

There was nothing to do. We closed our eyes. "What do you say at the end of a day like today?" I whispered to Candy on the clean linens. "A day that's long like a life."

She turned her body to me, crawled close, put her head in the crook of my arm. I held her lightly, her legs next to my legs, her stomach next to my ribs.

"You say, *O Lord Jesus Christ, please show me the path of my life. I am poured out like water, my heart is like wax. It is melted into the heat of my bowels. Be not far from me, hasten to help me, deliver my soul from the sword, and bless Tara and save Tara and give her eternal life.*"

I spooned her, drew her near.

"*I am guilty of an abundance of sins,*" Candy continued to whisper, "*but I would wash Your feet with the abundance of my tears and wipe*

341

them with my hair. I don't want to be deprived of absolution for the many wrongs of my life. I reflect on the magnitude of my shame, but, though in terror, I foolishly remain in my sins. I live in the night of carnal desires, shrouded in the dark moonless love of night. Do not despise Your servant in Your boundless mercy. My sin is ever before me. The harlot from the depth of her soul cries out, do not cast me away or destroy me, O my God, but receive me in my repentance, and save me." Candy sighed painfully. "That, Shelby Sloane," she said, "is the Hymn of Cassiani."

TEN
MAKING THINGS WRIGHT

1

Surio

Sunday morning came too soon. Candy, early to rise, was up and dressed before I stirred. She said she was going to church; would we like to come? We were in bed! We said no, though I may have said yes, had it not been so early. "This is what I'm going to do," Candy said to Gina and me. "I'm going to walk the three blocks to the Priestly Fraternity of St. Peter, and attend the ten o'clock service."

"Why?"

"I like church," Candy replied in a chipper voice. "And apparently they celebrate the liturgical Latin Mass. So. That's what I'm going to do. Things change, and I have to make other plans. I have to figure things out. Doesn't seem ideal, I know, but I've got to play it as it lays. You two pack your things, and go downstairs, get some brunch. It ends at noon, so I suggest you hurry. I'll take the one bag I've got with me. When you're having your hash browns, talk it over and decide what you want to do. About me. I won't be back until 12:15. If you want to go, walk to the alley, get in your car, and drive away. Shelby, don't forget to study that map, because Wyoming is a big state and has mountains everywhere. You want to be careful to avoid them, but going around them is going to triple your distance. Talk about it, decide, and then don't think twice about me. Absolutely go. But if at 12:15

345

I come back, and you're still here, I'll know that you have chosen to stay with me. There won't be anymore of this, woe is me, if only we'd not picked her up, kept on driving, blah, blah that you're both so prone to, especially you, Gina, but then you make Shelby feel guilty, too. So decide. Walk across the street, get in your car, drive, or wait for me to come back from church and we'll go together. It's as simple as that. You have over two hours to mull while you're having stale coffee."

With that, she walked out, and the door swung shut behind her.

She was wearing my floral skirt and Gina's collared white blouse, which I guess she wasn't giving back if we were leaving without her.

We tried to cook up a plan, for her, for us, to help her, to help us. Suddenly she was our problem, our thing to solve, like Professor Plum in the study with a candlestick. We sprung to dialogue slowly, almost reluctantly.

"She can't go to Australia." That was me.

"Duh. That much is obvious. But she's got to go somewhere." That was Gina.

"It's unbelievable about Floyd. What a loser."

"Yes. But she's got to move on. He spent her money, and that's that. He doesn't have it to give her. She's lucky she managed to get a few bucks of it back."

"I can't believe she was so trusting," I said, a little more animated. "I would have never given my money to anyone."

"But that's you. You also wouldn't do a number of the things she does."

That was true. "But now what's she going to do?"

We beat around that question, tried to figure it out. What would *we* do, if we were in her shoes?

"I'd never have had the baby," said Gina. "I'd never give my body away for money, I'd never star in a porn film, I'd never hitch-hike, or steal the film hoping to bribe the man who made it."

"She's not bribing him. She's insuring herself. Stay away from me, she says, because if you touch me, you'll go down."

"I'd never get mixed up with a man like Erv," said Gina. "I wouldn't go to Australia. Australia! What is she thinking? So the answer to your question of what I would do—*that*. I'd never be in this position in the first place."

I said nothing. Easy for Gina to say. Nice loony mother, nice busy father, a sister, a grandma, dogs, cats, suburban house, pleasant Christmas. Aunts. One less than before, but still. Family things. What would *I* do? I must admit, I couldn't see myself to this point either—because along the way I would've made different choices that would not have brought me here. I wouldn't have given myself to men for money either, but if I had, I would not have sent my money to Floyd, no matter how dependable Floyd seemed to be. But then, if I didn't work at a job like Candy's, I never would have made 20,000 dollars at seventeen. I would have made 600 bucks working at McDonald's, and it would have gone on sandals, shorts and maybe gas for the car. Australia would be out of the question, but then so would many things. Hitchhiking. Having a baby at twelve. Mike dying would not be an issue; he would die, and I would feel sad 3000 miles away and go work my afternoon shift serving burgers to a lunch crowd, making thirteen dollars after taxes. So, like Gina, I also couldn't figure out what I would do based on what I would do, and thus we sat on the bed, counting out the minutes. We were on the sixth floor and outside the small window we saw the tops of other buildings, down below a movie theater and an empty street, with our little yellow roller skate parked in an alley somewhere yonder back, out of sight. I was hungry, thirsty.

We jumped up, got ready, flew out. It was eleven. We rushed downstairs with all our luggage, because the alley where I parked was two blocks away. We got a table, nesting our suitcases with us. The restaurant was dark, down three steps, almost in the basement, while outside was light and sunny. I wanted to be outside, to go for a walk. To go swimming.

The food was sub-par, but on the plus side it was almost warm. The minestrone soup was too salty, the coffee weak, the corned

347

beef hash greasy. The sweet potatoes were pretty good, had marsh-mallows. I ate three helpings. It was 11:35.

"She gave us an out. It's our ticket out," Gina implored me. "We can't help her, Sloane. I know you want to. I do, too. She's really grown on me. But we can't. I'm telling you, we can't. We did all we could. Look how far we got her. From Maryland all the way to South Dakota."

"We can't really lay claim to Maryland."

"She told us it would be all right. We should run while we still can. No guilt, no worries. That's why she goes to church, so she can forgive people like us."

"That's not why she goes to church," I said. "And forgive us for what? I thought we did all we could."

"You obviously don't think so."

"I don't think so because we haven't. You want to go after what happened to her yesterday? After all you now know about her? After what she's been through?"

"How are you going to help her, Sloane? How are you going to get that monkey off her back? What are you going to do? You have money? You don't have enough to take this trip without me. You can't lend her a few bucks until she gets back on her feet in Sydney and wires you some kangaroos instead of repayment."

Gina was right.

What if Mike's parents wouldn't give her the baby? What was her plan then?

God, what if they did? What was her plan *then*?

We sat heavy-hearted at the table and outside across the street, Audrey's Wedding Fashions was opening up for a few hours on a Sunday, and a young girl with her mother stood expectantly outside its doors. The girl was holding her mother's hand.

It was 11:55.

"Come on. Please," said Gina. "Please." She squeezed my hand. "I came with you," she continued, "because I wanted us to be friends again. I didn't know how we were going to do it. But we were once so close. I wanted that again."

"Is that why you brought Molly?" I smiled lightly. "And wanted to move in with Aunt Flo? And didn't want to go on the road alone with me?"

She shrugged sheepishly. "I admit I was a tiny bit conflicted. But you fixed that whole alone thing, didn't you?" Her eyes were not accusing, her familiar face, minus eyebrows, minus most eyelashes, was staring at me beseechingly. A few years ago we had gone down to the Jersey shore with our friend John Turner and his parents. We spent all day, all week jumping the waves together. Then she and John would bury me in the sand. It was one of the greatest weeks of my life, the week coming with full acknowledgment of feeling happy to be alive, to be carefree. And then Gina went and ruined it with awful Agnes. Still. I achingly longed for that feeling again, of riding the waves in the sun without a care in the world.

And then I thought of Candy. What if she never in her life had had a day like that, frolicking with friends? She probably never had. My warm flush of flashback cooled as if vaporized.

Reluctantly—looking away from the wedding shop, where I was trying to catch another glimpse of mother and daughter through two sets of reflecting windows—I opened the atlas. "I know you're right," I said. "But I just can't go."

"Sure you can," she said hurriedly. "We'll figure it out."

"Gina," I said calmly. "Figure what out? We'll get in the car, I'll put it into first—and then what? Left or right? Or straight? Which way?"

"We'll figure it out!"

"Which way out of the alley, Gina—left or right?"

"I don't know!"

"Precisely," I said calmly. "Which is why we have to look at the atlas."

Noon.

12:05.

I couldn't find adequate roads to lead us from South Dakota to Utah through Wyoming. I saw only I-90 up north, which we couldn't take, and I-80 down south, which we also couldn't take.

From the looks of the atlas, it seemed as if Wyoming had no other roads.

We paid and walked outside, dragging our suitcases behind us. Sixth Street was empty and sunny. Gina's shoulders were slumped. Mine too.

12:09.

We walked to the intersection, slowness guaranteed by our suitcases and the duffel bag on my shoulder. And by other things. At the corner of a deserted Main and Sixth at high noon on a Sunday, Gina said to me, "You're stalling."

"I'm not."

"You are! You are stalling. You don't want to leave without her."

"I'm not stalling," I repeated. "But, no, I don't want to leave without her." I took a breath. "Gina, you should know me better by now. I'm not going to leave without her."

Gina took a step away. "It goes against all reason. It's illogical, it makes no sense." Her gaze clouded. The light turned red, green, red. 12:12.

I stared at the pavement, my head hanging, my eyes cast low. I didn't want to spend a minute more either in this town or talking to Gina about Candy. "We can't leave her, Gina," I said. "We just can't and that's all there is to it."

Candy was right. Things had changed. You never noticed as they were changing. Like the transformation of America, from east to west. The transformation was always in the past. Somewhere in Nebraska. By the time you got to South Dakota, you looked and things were different. Gina and I, childhood friends—with nearly forgiven though unforgotten Eddie between us like a fishbone in the delicate lining of the throat—looked for the girl we picked up on the side of the road, like a bag of trash we were going to discard later when we could find a receptacle, the girl who sat on the hood of my car in Interior, a deserted western town, and told us how she was going to find a place to raise a child she gave birth to, like I hoped my mother had gone to

350

Mendocino to find a place to raise me. And maybe my own mother, too, sat on the hood of someone's car and told them how she was going to come and get me, and she and I would find a place to live together.

No, not like that, I thought, closing my eyes, squeezing them tight so Gina wouldn't see. More like my Emma found a place and raised me. She didn't want to; who'd *want* to be saddled with a baby, with someone else's baby? And she was once young, she told me she used to sing, and wanted to go to dance school. But then instead she found work cleaning other people's houses. And after my father left, there was no more talk of dance or singing. Instead, she bought me a bed, and a little lamp with horses on it, because she knew I liked horses, and every night made me dinner, and washed my pillowcase with pink flowers on it. When I needed sneakers, she bought me sneakers. When I needed to go, she bought me a car.

I didn't know: did my mother leave and hope to come back, like Candy, and just couldn't; or did she leave and know she was never coming back? Did her postcard words mean, *I will see you soon, Shelby,* or *Say hi to Shelby because I'm not going to see her anytime soon.*

I couldn't take it. I told Gina to go back to the hotel lobby and wait for me, that I would be right back. Rushing across the street to the corner, I stopped at a phone booth and dialed Emma's number collect. It was Sunday afternoon, but the street was empty. There was no one strolling, window shopping, pushing babies along the way. Only my soul was outside. Gina had gone back to the hotel, dragging her suitcase. With my own suitcase at my feet, I pressed my head against the dirty glass.

"Emma," I said, when she accepted the charges, "it's me."

"I know who it is, Shelby. What's wrong?" She sounded concerned. "Where are you?"

"I'm out on the street," I said. "How are you?"

"How am *I*? I'm fine. How else should I be? What street? How are *you*?"

351

"Oh, fine, fine. We're in Rapid City."

"South Dakota," Emma said. "You're so far. You sound far away. Are you having fun?"

Forehead pressed hard against the filth of the phone booth, keeping my voice like glass too, I said, "Oh, sure. I'm having a *great* time. Thank you for my car."

"What's wrong?" she said. "Are you in trouble or something?"

"No, no."

"You need money?"

I hesitated. "No, no."

"How much do you need?"

Twenty thousand dollars? "I'm okay. Really." I couldn't say anything, and she didn't say anything. "How do you know where Rapid City is?" I asked instead.

She laughed lightly into the phone. "You think you're the only one who was ever young, child?" she said. "Once upon a time, I too traveled across the country."

"You did?" Why was that so shocking? "By *yourself*?"

She laughed. "No. I went with my boyfriend. We were three months on the road."

"Three months! And then?"

"Then, I don't know. We must have broken up. I came back home, got a job."

"I can't believe it. Where did you go?" I wanted to keep her on the phone.

"Where didn't we go," she said. "Alaska. Hawaii."

"So funny," I said. "And there I was thinking you've ever only been to Maine. With me."

"Well, that's right," said Emma. "You think the universe began with your birth." She changed the subject. "Tell me you're all right. Or I'm going to worry."

"I'm fine. Honest." I swallowed so my voice wouldn't break. I couldn't explain to her on the phone what was happening to me, not when it was costing her $3 a minute to talk. "Is everything okay at home?"

352

"It's swell," she said. "The Lambiels have moved out. They're getting a divorce. We got new tenants now. You'd like them, they have two sons your age."

"Two?" I almost laughed. "Yes, but are they French?"

"*Mais naturellement, mademoiselle!*"

"Oh, Emma . . ."

"All right, all right, this is costing me a fortune," she said. "Promise me you'll be careful."

"I promise. You know me. You know I will."

"You haven't picked up any hitchhikers, have you?"

"I really gotta go, Emma, don't worry about anything, bye!"

After I hung up, I don't know if she felt any better for my having called, but I was pretty sure I didn't. I wished again I'd sent her a postcard from Valentine. *Someone's thinking of you here, in the heart of the Sand Hills.*

I turned to go—and gasped startled. A homeless Indian man was standing nearly flush with me. "Hello, darling," he said. He was a few years older than me, with long slick hair tied in a pony tail; his ripped layers of odd clothes smelled; he was very dark, round-faced, smiling. "My name is Surio. Hope you having a nice day. Do you have thirteen cents I can borrow?"

"What?" I wiggled my way past him and onto the street.

"Yeah, that's all I need. My friend over there, do you see him? He's sitting by the wall, he's not feeling too good. Just thirteen cents will be enough for us. Have you got that?"

He was wheedly, and polite. Why did he scare me almost worse than Erv? Because his menace was so contained.

"I don't have thirteen cents."

"Oh, come on," he said, his manner less polite. "You're walking around here in your expensive sandals and your expensive jewels. You don't have thirteen cents for me and my sick buddy over there? Just come with me for a minute, come talk to my friend."

"I'm not going anywhere with you," I said, my voice starting to shake. My gaze darted around the street. "My sandals are Dr. Scholl's, and my beads are from Genovese Drugs." There was no one on the street! It was a Sunday afternoon, Main Street, and there was no one except me and him. I turned out my pockets. "Look," I said, "I'm out here just taking a walk. I brought nothing with me."

"Except your suitcase."

"Uh—"

"Your suitcase and everything in it. Including possibly thirteen cents?"

"Nothing but clothes," I said, cursing my suitcase. "No money, no change, no cash. I wanted to stop by the bank, but it's Sunday. I guess I'll have to wait till tomorrow. Now can you leave me alone?"

A car passed. He backed away one step.

"Hey!" someone called from behind me. I turned my head. It was Candy, running across the street. Quickly she came up and put her hand on my shoulder. "What are you doing?" she asked. "Who is this?"

Surio looked Candy up and down with great interest. "He wants thirteen cents," I explained.

"Hang on a sec," said Surio, his attention firmly fixed on Candy. "There are ten trucks a day who come by looking for a girl like you, a young girl with pink streaks in her hair, riding shotgun in a yellow bird, the kind that's parked in the alley my pal and I live in. Strange to park a car like that in an alley, not on the street, almost as if hidin' it, but whatever. Ten truckers a day blowin' by here for weeks, askin' 'bout a yellow rollerskate and three pretty seat covers. Go figure." He smiled. "Until today, my answer's always been I've seen nothin'."

"Give him the thirteen cents," Candy said to me, "and let's go."

"I don't have any change!"

"Tsk. Tsk. Might need more than thirteen cents, now, sweetheart," Surio said pleasantly.

Candy and I exchanged a look. She shook her head. "How much do you think you might need now, cowboy?"

"Dunno. Reward for finding the car *or* the girl is a hundred dollars."

Candy whistled. "A hundred dollars, huh."

"Somebody must want you pretty bad if they're willing to pay a hundred." He stared lewdly at her even though she was wearing church clothes.

"Let's go," Candy said, pulling on me, and after waving to Surio, she called out, "Tell them we're headed to Denver, pal. Don't forget now!"

"A little scratch for me and I'll keep my trap shut."

"Why would *we* pay you? We're not looking for the car or the girl."

And in the Mustang, Candy said, "Thirteen cents, a hundred bucks, five thousand, it won't matter. The next trucker through here will know all about us for a bag of weed."

And I thought that if we didn't know all about us, how could they?

2

Hell's Half-Acre

Gina wanted to go to Deadwood. While she was waiting for me, she talked to the doorman at Alex Johnson who told her there was gambling there. "Gina," said Candy. "There's gambling in Reno, too."

Except that Deadwood was forty miles away, Gina unhappily pointed out, and Reno was 1200. "Half an hour's drive," Gina said. "Come on, girls, how often do I ask?"

"Every time you think there's gambling somewhere," retorted Candy. "Sorry, Gina, the Lord said, no gambling on His day."

"How long is it going to take us to get to flippin' Reno?"

"The way we've been driving, a month," I said. No one laughed, and though I think I was kidding, I couldn't be sure.

Needless to say, we didn't go to Deadwood. We headed south, winding and loopy, for the Black Hills.

"The car is trouble, Shel," said Candy. "Real trouble."

"The car," said Gina pointedly, "is not the real trouble, Candy Cane."

Candy ignored her. "As long as we have it," she continued, "we're going to have problems."

"You talking about the car?" Gina said. "Uh, okay."

"Well, then, we're going to have problems for a long time," I told Candy, "because Emma gave me this car. Why don't you cut your hair, girlfriend, or paint it black, get rid of the pink, wear a hat, start with that, then worry about my car?"

"Okay," she agreed. "Let's find a drugstore. We'll buy some Clairol peroxide."

But there were no drugstores in the woods. The one strip mall we passed was closed on Sunday. "You see?" Candy said to Gina. "Sunday is a day off for everybody."

"Can it be a day off from you?" snapped Gina, back in her funk. "I didn't think so. Funny how that works. No respite there."

On the weaving roads in the pines we drove, the evergreen foliage so thick and dark green that it looked black. Hence the name—Black Hills. During gray days or winters, it must be frightening to drive up and down these roads through the tall and brooding pines.

It felt like August, and someone, maybe Gina, said it's the dog days, because it was very hot and felt like that. We opened the windows for some air and the breeze whipped through the car, and on the radio, for the rest of your life played Ricky, don't lose that number. Candy tried to sing along to the chorus, but got it all broken and wrong. Why did Candy's not knowing any regular songs suddenly make me pity her so exquisitely? What are you going to teach your baby if you don't know any songs? I wanted to ask. Where are you going to run, so you can fit in, where people aren't going to look at you and say, what do you mean you don't know "Hush Little Baby?"

But she knew the Psalms. One through one hundred and fifty.

"Candy, any Psalms appropriate for little babies?" I asked.

"Oh, sure," she said. "Psalm 123 isn't bad. *Onto thee I lift up mine eyes, as the eyes of the servants onto the eyes of their masters . . . have mercy upon us, O Lord, have mercy upon us.*"

"Yes, lovely," said Gina. "So much better than 'This Old Man.'"

Through the Black Hills, past Mount Rushmore, across fake Western towns full of tourists, we rode. Down to the river.

Should we stop at Mount Rushmore? we asked each other, and feeling pressed for time, crushed down by all manner of things, decided not to; not even decided, just kept driving. Next time, we said, full of optimistic youth, one hundred percent certain there'd be a next time.

Maybe 99.9 percent certain.

"You know, if I lived here," said Candy, "you could come and visit me."

"Yeah, you'd be like Laura Ingalls," said Gina. "She lived here."

"Who?"

"God! Never mind."

"Live where? Mount Rushmore?" I asked. But Candy surprised me.

"Well, no," she replied uncertainly. "Not Mount Rushmore. But around here. One of these western towns, in the woods, hidden away. Tara and I could settle here, and I'd find me a job, a little apartment. She'd go to school. I'd work. And when you were off from college, you could come visit us."

I said nothing. Gina said nothing. Then I said, "What kind of job?"

Candy said nothing.

Then she said, "Making caskets?"

Kris Kristofferson's "Sunday Mornin' Comin' Down" played on the radio, and there was no way he could hold his head without it hurting. "Stormy Monday," when Etta James got down on her knees and prayed. "Gloomy Sunday," when Marianne Faithfull was slumberless.

"Boy, the DJ must have had a fight with his wife this morning," said Gina.

Soon we were out of South Dakota heading down a steep decline recently blackened by a severe and expansive wildfire, the ground singed for a swathe thirty miles long and wide all the way to the horizon, down to the flats of Wyoming.

"Wyoming has spectacular mountains," Gina said.

I forced myself to say an ironic "Oh yeah?"

"Yes. Some of the most dramatic, most beautiful mountain ranges in the U.S. are in Wyoming. The Tetons. The Wind River

Mountains. The Bighorn. The Laramie Range. It's the Rockies, you know, and they reach up grand into this state."

"Should we avoid the mountains?" asked Candy. "I worry we'll get lost."

"Nah. Shelby over there is like Henry Stanley."

"Who?" Candy turned her head to the window.

"I think the Great Divide is in Wyoming," I said. "I wouldn't mind seeing that."

We were just trying to make conversation, attempting to avoid our most pressing concerns.

Candy asked what the Great Divide was. I told her it was a split in the Continental shelf that made the rivers flow east to west instead of west to east. The Great Divide, I explained, changes the orientation of the things around you.

Candy was thoughtful. "And you can see this?"

"Absolutely. We're going to drive right through it. Map clearly says so."

"The Great Divide, huh? Wonder if there are any songs written about it."

We couldn't think of any. This occupied us. "Maybe Willie Nelson?"

Gina, though, couldn't avoid all topics for long. "Candy, is Floyd an example of your story?" she asked. "The Judas story?" We couldn't get our minds off his breathtaking disloyalty.

Candy sighed, looked thoughtful. I tried to sneak a peek at her in the rearview. "I don't want him to be," she finally said. "I'd hate to think this was just the beginning of my sorrows. I've already had so many. I was kind of hoping it was the end."

I think it's going to rain today. I think it's gonna rain today. Neil Diamond thought so.

She was quiet through Custer, a spooky place with wooden log cabins and log cabin bars nestled in the pines.

"Maybe here?" she asked.

"Here what?"

"Maybe I could live here with my baby."

"What would you do?"

"Dunno. Make caskets?"

"You know, Sloane," Gina said, "Candy may have a point. There's a call for certain professions everywhere. Don't you agree? I mean, for instance, every town needs a casket maker."

"Exactly!" said Candy, brightening.

I pushed Gina, silently exhorting her to stop.

What would Candy do anywhere? Wasn't that the eternal question. If we could have *that* figured out, I felt we could have many things figured out. Perhaps we were trying to figure out too much. We had only the day in front of us, and we were trying to imagine what we would do with our whole lives, what Candy would do. I felt as if any minute someone would yell at us: "Take human bites!"

"Could *you* live here?" Candy asked me.

I didn't think so.

"Could *you*?" she asked Gina.

"If I was with Eddie, yes."

Candy groaned. "Honestly, Gina, maybe we need to look past Eddie. To the rest of your life."

"But Eddie *is* the rest of my life."

"Okay." Candy sounded tired.

"What's the matter with you?" Some of the neutral feeling had gone from the car. "Haven't you ever been in love?"

Between the seats, Candy turned to look at Gina. "I got plenty of time to fall in love," she said. "I gotta fix my life first in the here and now. Gotta get myself together, get my baby sorted out. There'll be time enough for love."

There were no towns or mountains around us, just Wyoming, the silvery sagebrush sea, and flat grazing land.

"Didn't you love Mike?" asked Gina.

Candy tightened her mouth. She didn't reply for a little while. I say a little while, but we moved two longitude points on the map. Where were we going? No one knew. If there were only two roads, neither of which we could take, how were we going to get from point A to point B? We had said we would stop at the next

360

town. And here we were, looking for the next town, and that's when Candy said, "I once thought I loved him. He was my first proper boyfriend. I've never really had another."

"He's the father of your child."

"Yes." But she said it in the tone of someone who was saying, "No." Or "The time is 2:17," which it was. Where in heaven's name were we? And where were these fabled mountains? Nebraska was the Himalayas compared to these parts. The country, almost parodying life, or perhaps, life parodying the country, was constantly surprising me. I stared off at the muggy, blurred-by-the-sun line of the horizon.

The trees had been left far behind, in South Dakota. The hills, too. There was nothing here in Wyoming, except us, the road and the sagebrush. The only signs of civilization were the fences that ran along the miles of highway to keep the grazing animals from wandering out and getting killed. I wondered if it was to protect us or the animals. We didn't see any grazing. Neither did we see men, women, children, buffalo. There was no gas station, nowhere to get a Coke, no motels. There was no wildlife, no deer, rabbits, or birds.

"You want to live here?" I asked Candy.

"I dunno," she replied dully. "I have to live somewhere. Now that I've lost my money, I have to find a place where Erv can't find me."

"This ain't it," said Gina. "Here you might as well put an orange hat on your head, and signal him. Yo, Erv, I'm the only resident of Wyoming."

"What about Custer? We passed that a few miles back."

"It made even you depressed," said Gina. "I saw your face."

"It's not Custer that made me depressed," said Candy.

Suppressing a sigh, a sound of anguish, I said to Gina, "Show me a grazing animal."

"Perhaps they're all dead," Gina said wisely. "Maybe their ecosystem is already ruined. That's why compassionate people are fighting to save it."

Candy chuckled. "Look left, girls." As we passed a small beat-down farm, near the barbed wire fence lay two llamas, lazing not grazing.

"Llamas, Gina," I said, slowing down to take a better look. "Llamas in Wyoming. Interesting. Are they, hmm, indigenous to the sagebrush?"

Gina rolled her eyes. "Make fun. Go ahead. But when you can't get a decent burger in your cute little Cambridge, Massachusetts, you'll know why."

The grassland was like the Sand Hills in Nebraska. Infinite. After Custer and Newcastle there had been no towns. We'd gone a hundred miles.

"Where are we going?"

"I don't know."

"Where are we stopping?"

"I don't know. I'd like to find a place to live, if it's all the same to you."

"Here?" I threw out my arm to indicate the landscape, empty except for the interminable grassland, separated from the road by miles of chicken-wire fence. Candy laughed a little, then retreated once more to her window.

❧

Forty miles further on, just as I was worrying about running out of gas, out of nowhere, small suburban tract houses rose from the ground, clustered together in a housing development. We stopped, rolled down our windows. Some kids were skateboarding while their dad washed the car. "Excuse me," Gina said, "can you kids tell me what this place is called?"

One of the kids pointed at the sidewalk. "This is Wright," he said. "Who you looking for?"

"Gas," Gina said, glancing back at Candy. Slowly we drove through the development that was the town of Wright. The fascinating thing was that a quarter mile earlier there had been nothing, and now there were houses, but not a single business, no stores, supermarkets, or restaurants, no shops of any kind. Just private, close-together

362

homes with small yards. A minute later, we were out of the housing development, and the sign on the road said, "Thank you for visiting Wright, Wyoming, a good place to live and work."

"Can I live here?" asked Candy, looking around.

"Why not?" I said. "Llamas do."

Up ahead on the main road, we saw a gas station and a Subway deli in a separate building nearby. I pumped gas while the girls got out to stretch their legs, then we drove the five yards uphill to get a sandwich. The place looked closed, but only because there was almost no one in it. The only food game in town; yet there was just one customer inside, a burly tall man who looked like a truck driver. We saw him through the window, and even here in the middle of staggering nowhere, got a pang in our gut, and rolled around back, staying in the car until he left. The three of us said nothing as we waited for him to empty out.

The girl behind the counter was slicing cheese, the boy wiping the shredded lettuce onto the floor. We ordered, and while the girl was making our tuna and salami and roast beef, Candy asked, "Excuse me, but what do all the men do in this town?"

The server looked at her strangely, looked her up and down.

"I just want to know what people here do for work, that's all." Candy smiled.

"Well," the check-out girl drew out grudgingly, "the men pretty much all work at the mine."

"Mine?"

"Yeah. Thunder Mountain Mine. You'll pass it if you're headed to Casper."

Were we headed to Casper?

Thunder *Mountain* Mine? I wanted to ask her if that name was decided ironically but was afraid she might not know the meaning of the word.

"What about the women?" Candy asked. Such an innocent question, yet how could she keep her life out of her voice? She couldn't.

"The women stay home mainly," the girl replied, frowning,

rushing through the order. "But many of them work in the mine, too. Why?"

"No reason. Is the mine the only employer in town?"

"Well, this *is* a mining town," said the girl, trying to keep her life out of her voice, too.

"Or you could work here at Subway," Gina said to Candy.

"We're not hiring," the girl said quickly, wrapping the sandwiches in paper and pushing them toward us on the counter. "Will there be anything else?"

Now it was Candy's turn to look the girl up and down. "So where do you go shopping?"

"Casper."

I perked up in surprise. "On the map it looks a hundred miles away."

"It is," the girl said, in a voice that said, so what? "But there's nobody on the road. You can make that in an hour."

"Hour, really. Hmm. You must have a pretty fast car." Candy smiled politely, taking her sandwich.

A man came in wearing plaid overalls. He gave Candy the eye. Even in church clothes, she was a male eye magnet. She smiled at him. The girl behind the counter glowered. "Will that be all?"

"Actually, one more thing," said Candy. "Is there a drugstore around here?" She pointed to her head. "Need an aspirin."

"Casper," the girl said, turning away. "Everything's in Casper."

When we hit the road again, Candy talked animatedly about the town, and I said, "Candy, that girl has lived in Wright her whole life. I'm sure her parents were miners. And she's going to marry a miner. There is not even a bar in this town."

"Oh, you can be sure," said Candy, with a short giggle, "if it's a town of miners, there will be a bar in this town."

"And what are you going to do? Serve drinks to men?"

"Sure, why not? I can be a bartender."

"The women will stone you for sure." Gina laughed.

"Aren't you the parable-teller," said Candy.

364

"I'm not being parabolic. I mean that literally. They'll stone you. For sure."

After we left the deli at Wright, there was once again nothing around us. A few miles down we passed several orange signs that said, "BLASTING AREA UP AHEAD. STAY AWAY FROM FLYING DEBRIS." Next sign we saw we realized it said *falling* debris, not flying. Flying was better. Funnier. Thunder Mountain is the largest open-pit mine in the United States, and after we drove past it, there were no more llamas, no other grazing animals either. There was nothing at all, soon not even sagebrush.

Candy said that perhaps Wyoming wasn't for her since, except for Wright, there didn't seem to be anywhere to live. "Aren't there any people?"

"It's the least populated state in America," said Gina.

"No shit."

"Less than half a million people and half of those live in Cheyenne, the capital."

"Hmm." We debated whether it was better to hide in a small town in the middle of desolation or a large exposed town, heavily populated. That discussion took us fifty miles to I-25, but when Candy saw it, she said we couldn't go on it.

"Not even here?"

"Not even here."

"But there's no one on the road! And they're not looking for you here."

"I know. But all a trucker has to do is hear the call once on his CB, and think about that call. A 5000-dollar reward for locating a yellow 'Stang and three girls. That's something you don't soon forget. You might forget a red Camaro, because you see a million of them, but not this. He'll be calling me in as soon as he sets eyes on your yellow prize. This time it'll be on the open road near Casper."

"All right, so he calls you in," said Gina. "What's Erv going to do? Helicopter his way into the grassland?"

"You want him to know where we are?" asked Candy. "He

can do math, you know. All he's got to do is figure out how long it'll take us to get to the next Wyoming town, and goodness knows there aren't that many of them, and he'll be calling in for truckers passing through to be on the lookout. You want him that close?"

"Oh, you're just paranoid now," said Gina, but we all agreed we didn't want him that close. Reluctantly I stayed off the highway. We found U.S. 87, a dilapidated highway badly in need of repair that ran almost parallel to I-25, which allowed us to get nice and lost right as it started to downpour and the mountains we saw in the distance behind Casper disappeared in the mist. At least I think they were mountains. They could've been black clouds. We had to stop and assess our location by the side of the road called Lone Bear Road, near the barbed wire that kept in the llamas. No way around it—map said we were headed south to I-80. It was the only road leading to Salt Lake City, and the only road leading from Salt Lake to Reno. On the map it looked so deceptively close and the thought of being done, of getting Candy to her destination was so tempting, I just wanted to get on the road and drive a hundred without stopping. Three days, and it would be over. I hadn't yet figured out how I was going to let Candy go, but I'd deal with that later. I didn't want to think about Gina's words. *What do you think will happen when you get to Paradise? You think you'll be able to leave her there? Any more than you were able to leave her at a rest stop in Iowa?*

And other words, too. *How long are you going to be carrying her water?*

Candy said no to I-80. She didn't care what the map said about highways and mountain ranges. I thought the mapmaker had a sense of humor, a dry sense of wit. Whoever drew the map clearly had never been to Wyoming and discovered what I discovered— it was flat like a grill pan. All I knew was this: we were nowhere, it was still pouring, it was nearing evening, and we couldn't go on the Interstate. That was my now. Cramped by the side of Lone Bear Road in the flat, treeless, grass sageland.

So where could we go?

Which way did we run?

I handed Candy the map, more like threw it at her. The 'Stang was getting all fogged up on the inside, but if we opened the windows, water poured in from the sky onto my black vinyl seats. It was Biblical rain, Candy said, it was Noah's flood.

"That's just great," said Gina. "And how long was that guy out? Forty years? Wonderful."

Dejectedly we sat by the side of the road with my emergency lights on. "How long are we going to sit here?" Gina wanted to know.

"Until the rain stops."

"But you heard Candy! It's going to be forty years."

"I can't see. I can't drive if I can't see. You want to drive? Be my guest."

"Girls, girls," said Candy. "Come now."

"Yes, thank you, Miss Peacemaker," snapped Gina.

Candy thought the rain was cleansing—"That's the literal and figurative meaning of rain: it washes things away"—but I said, "Yes. Good things too," thinking it was a bad omen for the many off roads still to come. Gina said, "*That's* a bad omen?" and glared at Candy, who begged us not to talk anymore.

I watched Candy in the rearview. She wasn't sleeping. Her face pressed against the windowpane, she stared at the fields, perhaps searching for the place of her imaginings—as vivid as Australia, as remote as Australia, as safe as Australia. Except beyond her window all was black, the rain loudly drumming.

We must have sat in that car an hour. Finally I couldn't take it anymore and got going.

"How much money would you need?" I blurted on impulse. It was pitch dark all around me, the rain hardening to hail now, which mercilessly pounded the car. To say we were traveling slow would be to say that turtles traveled slow, or clams.

"How much would who need of what?" Gina asked, startled out of her reverie.

I tried to think quickly and managed no thought at all. "To get settled in a place."

"Well, I don't know, do I?" Candy didn't move her head from the window. "There are trucks on the road."

"Yes, but since visibility is zero," I said, "it's not an issue."

"I see them," she said doggedly. "They must see us."

"What, you want to go a different way? Gina, how long to Riverton?"

"About an inch," replied Gina. The traffic on U.S. 26 moved at the speed of water erosion on rocks.

Rubbing the damp moisture from the window, Candy said, "Look at this place. Maybe here?"

"Nirvana," the sign read. "Pop. 62."

"Candy, they'd all know you by name after a week. Not very good getting lost."

Coming soon, the green sign said, "Hell's Half-Acre."

"Wanna live in Hell's Half-Acre, Cand?"

I know she kept hoping for something else. I kept hoping for mountains, like in "Jeremiah Johnson." I loved that movie when I was a kid. Watched it with Emma every time it was on. It was so romantic in the mountains with broody Robert Redford. Emma liked it, too. And now that I thought about it, I realized I'd missed a great opportunity to tease her, as I hadn't connected the dots until now. It wasn't just "Jeremiah Johnson" Emma had liked. It was also "The Great Waldo Pepper" and "Butch Cassidy and the Sundance Kid," "The Sting," "Barefoot in the Park," "The Candidate," and Emma's favorite movie of all time, "This Property is Condemned." Oh, how she would wax rhapsodic about Tennessee Williams and Natalie Wood! They were just decoys. It had been Robert Redford all along! That Emma.

I should have heeded the last line in "The Candidate," should've listened to Robert Redford. After he wins the brutal, no-holds-barred, all-stops-pulled-out campaign, he sits in his election chambers, puts his hands over his head and says, "Now what?"

That's what we should've been asking ourselves. That's what Candy should have been asking herself every day of her life. I took Erv's film, now what? Floyd mainlined my 20,000 dollars, now what? I got into a car with two bystanders, involving them in my squalid life, now what? I, all seventeen years of me, take my baby girl and go somewhere, now what?

Eventually we're going to get to Riverton, now what?

The rain stopped, slowly, and the trucks became more visible; rather, we became more visible to the trucks. On a slick two-lane road, stuck between two eighteen-wheelers, no one in the car could relax. We sat like upright spring coils. There were still no mountains, but beyond the yellow wheatfields in the dark turquoise sky shone a double rainbow.

"Aw, shucks, look," said Gina. "A rainbow. But there's irony in there, no? I mean, wasn't the rainbow originally meant to remind man of God's promise that he would never again send a flood to cleanse mankind of wickedness?"

"Oh, look at her with her Genesis tales." Candy was almost smiling. "So where's the irony?"

"So what the hell was that just now," said Gina, "if not another one of God's broken promises?"

"So every time it rains and there's a rainbow, it's a reminder of God's *broken* promise to man?" Candy shook her head. "Man, Gina, that glass is almost all empty with you, ain't it?"

"Ain't it just."

"Candy, come on, tell me a story," I said. "Take your head away from the window. You're not going to live here, not anywhere near a town called Hell's Half-Acre, so stop looking. God, what a name. Gina, tell me, how much longer?"

"I'm not thinking about living anywhere right now," said Candy. "Just living. I wonder if they're calling us in on the CB radio. I wonder how long before Erv's in Riverton."

"About an inch," said Gina.

"Gina, shut up! They're not calling us in, Cand. They're trying not to crash, like us. They're not paying attention."

"You don't think?"

I groaned. I wish someone else would drive. I wish I could sit with *my* head pressed to the window. I wanted a nap, a drink, a blanket. I wanted out. I wanted Emma.

"When we get to Riverton, I'm going to call Eddie," said Gina. "Tell him I'm close."

Now Candy and I both groaned. "Yes, do that," Candy said, bouncing up and down on the backseat. "Ask him if Riverton is close enough for him to come see his future wife."

I got a black hole around my heart. What if it was? What if Eddie got in his truck and drove out to Riverton to meet us?

"Sloane," asked Gina, "when do you think I should tell him we'll be there?"

"About six inches," I replied, pleased by her har-de-har-har in a car full of long faces. "Tell me a story, Candy," I repeated.

"A parable?" she asked. "The parable of the twelve talents?"

"Okay."

"Or the story of Christ's fourteen stations with a miracle at the end?"

"Yeah, okay."

Candy was thoughtful. "Nah," she said. "I'm going to tell you the story of rugby players in the Andes."

"I don't think it's as good as a miracle." I was tired. I'd been driving all day, and it was nine at night. A little miracle might be just the ticket around here. Did we really leave Rapid City just this morning? It seemed a month ago. Wyoming was passing around us in slo-mo.

A plane crashed in Chile one Friday the 13th, Candy told us, in the Andes, with the Old Christians rugby team and their families on board. Many of the forty-five people were injured, half died. The survivors thought they'd be rescued any minute, but they were covered by snow, and the rescue teams couldn't spot them. So, with a broken fuselage, a little canned food, no heat, and no way to call for help they waited. No help came. More people died. The days passed. It continued to snow; they were utterly stranded in the blizzards. The cans of food had gone, and as time went on, the survivors eventually resorted to eating the freshly dead.

That got a gasp from me, a "holy shit" from Gina.

There was one avalanche, Candy continued, then another, which buried the wrecked fuselage *and* the survivors. They had to dig their way out. Finally two men said, we have to go to look for help. We know we're in the impassable Andes, and we have no compass. We don't know which way to go, we don't know if we have enough strength and we don't know if we're going to find anything. We may take a step and it will be in the wrong direction. We'll never know had we walked a different way if we might be saved. But one thing we do know for sure, for absolute certain. If we stay here, we're dead. We won't make it. We've been here too long, and no one has come. They've assumed we're dead, and why not? Most of us are.

Thus they set off. Wounded, depleted, freezing, they walked, in December, over some of the steepest mountains in the world and, after many days, finally found a peasant farmer, who ignored them, thinking they were joking. When eventually they were rescued, they had been stranded for sixty-two days.

"Oh my God," I said. "*How* long?"

"Sixty-two," repeated Candy. "Oh, that's not including the ten days they walked through the Andes. Seventy-two days altogether."

"So what's the point?" asked Gina.

"It's a story. Does it have to have a point?"

"To be any good, yes. To have lasting effect. To mean something."

"My story fits all those."

I drove slower. "That's an *unbelievable* story. It's not true, is it?"

"All true," said Candy. "My father told me. It happened a few years ago, in the early seventies, when I was still living with him."

"By Jove," I said. "You should've told me the story of Christ's

371

radio stations. This was the worst story I ever heard. It's worse than Judas."

"Worse than Judas, no! Why?"

"Because this one is real."

Candy raised her eyebrows at me and laughed. "Right-o. But you're looking at this all wrong. It's not the worst story. It's the best story. They did what they had to do, and made it against impossible odds. Sixteen of the forty-five people were rescued, two days before Christmas. The story of these rugby players is called the Christmas miracle. *O give thanks unto the God of heaven.*" She shook her head. "The worst story? You're nuts."

"Sloane's right," said Gina. "What about a little Christmas miracle for the other twenty-nine unlucky bastards who were eaten, huh? It all depends which way you're looking at that half-filled glass, Candy Cane."

"Yes, and the glass is overflowing. Just open your eyes, Gina, and you will see, and you will be answered."

"I'm not asking."

After thinking about that plane crash and 72 days in the snow, I don't know if we were answered in Riverton, which turned out to be a place for founded fears. It was a small frontier town, and what if East coast justice and Christian mercy had not come here yet? The town was isolated and mostly deserted. The Riverton Inn didn't look like a safe place for girls. Older men were camped out on folding chairs, smoking their cigarettes, looking for us to drive up to the reception area. Well, Gina and I weren't going to be the twenty-nine wounded on that plane. We drove away from Riverton Inn and found a Holiday Inn instead. It was too rich for us, too expensive, but at this point, I would have paid double. Of course after ten in the evening, there was no decent food establishment open. Only bars were serving food. Riverton was an outlier, and there was no way I was walking into a bar in a no-limit town with a no-boundary sense of justice.

"What are you going to do, starve because you don't want to walk into a *bar?*" said Candy. We were in the darkened parking lot of the Holiday Inn. That was bad enough.

"We're not bar food, Candy," I said.

"Candy's right," said Gina. "As always, you're being ridiculous."

I stared at her. She glared right back. "In Interior," said Gina, "I bought your little threats. I thought you were serious. But since now I know for a *fact* that though you might leave *me*, you will not leave her"—she pointed at Candy—"I'm going with her with no worries. Because I'm hungry."

"Park all the way in the back," Candy called to me as they strolled away. "Between two other cars."

"Why can't there be a Burger King," I whined, throwing up my frightened hands. "Why in this whole state can't there be a McDonald's, or a Kentucky Fried?"

They went. I couldn't. God, I was so afraid.

I stayed in the room tracing the map of Wyoming with my fingers, and my two food hunters didn't return till nearly midnight. The burger they were carrying was room temperature. My windows faced the unlit parking lot at the back where there were no cars except ours.

"Where's our stuff?" asked Gina, dropping my food on the bed.

"Still in the car," I replied guiltily. I couldn't manage my terror alone in the lot at night. I parked the car, but couldn't spend a second fussing with our bags, and left them all, every one, even the toothbrushes, and the underwear, everything, I just ran madly to the door. In front of my eyes was the man leaning into my car at the Argosy in Sioux City, and the strange staring men at the Riverton Inn sitting on their little chairs in the waning light, smoking, looking us over from the side of the road. God, all I wished for was a little courage, but it wasn't for sale in Riverton parking lots.

"Sloane, what the hell is wrong with you?" moaned Gina. "We went to a bar, but you can't get a bag out of a trunk?"

"Shelby," Candy said affectionately, "eat your food before it gets cold and gross."

I ate my food. It was already cold and gross.

We took off our clothes, washed our faces and crept under the sheets, unclad and fully burdened. Another long day tomorrow, said Gina.

"It's a long life," said Candy. "And even after the worst happens, and you don't think you can endure, can continue without perishing, you somehow do, beyond all scope of what you thought you could bear."

It was still such a long way to Paradise.

"You think I could live in Salt Lake City?" Candy asked me. She was in the other bed with Gina. We alternated Candy between us. It was understood that the one in need of the most protection was not going to sleep alone. I missed her. Last night in Rapid City (I couldn't believe it was only last night!) she was so warm and sad against me. I wanted the feel of her again. So tonight, missing her, I listened to her trembling question.

"How would I know?" I said. "I've never been to Salt Lake City."

"Why not?" said Gina. "You'd like it there, Cand. They're Christian."

"They're not Christian. They're Mormon." She lifted her arms straight up in the air, and caressed the insides of her forearms. "Question is, can I fit?"

As I lay in the bed by the window at the Holiday Inn under the pitch black Wyoming night, trying to catch the shadows of her on the wall, this is what I was thinking. I had initially believed that Candy was a small distressing part of my life. That I had been living my life, la-di-da, and she walked into it, like a dress on legs, flew in like the fly to the waiting spider. But here in Riverton, land-locked for good, it suddenly dawned on me at midnight: what if she is not playing a major part in my life, but I'm playing a minor part in hers? What if *she* is not the fly?

I had long put away my spiral notebook. I couldn't remember the last time I made a schedule, checked my to do list, wrote down the mileage. I felt more and more that not only was I *not* in control, not only was I not in charge of even the smallest detail of my own life, but that I wasn't even living my life. I was trespassing through Candy's—who was also not in control! Her life was the house, and I was crawling from the front door to the backyard.

As if to affirm the central role in *her* own life, Gina asked Candy a question she actually needed an answer to. "Candy," she asked, "why is it when you talk about Eddie, you sound so skeptical of him, though you've never met him?"

"I'm not skeptical. I'm cautious," Candy replied, winking at me in the dark.

"But why?" and when Candy didn't answer, Gina said, "Sometimes I think you want to say that the worst that can happen to me is if I find him unmarried in Bakersfield and hitch my star to his."

"I'd never say that."

"But sometimes I think you want to." And when Candy again said nothing, Gina said, "See?" and sighed deeply. Candy had fallen asleep. Curled up into a fetal ball, facing me, blankets over her hips, in her underwear, makeup still on her face.

"Sloane," Gina whispered, propping herself on her elbow. "You awake?"

"Yes," I said, but didn't want to be.

"What's she going to do?"

"Find her baby. Go live somewhere."

"Where? Here?"

"Maybe."

"Where can she live where Erv won't find her?"

"I don't know."

"But doesn't Erv know that she's got a kid? That's the kind of thing that's not easy to hide. A kid is like your yellow Shelby. If he can't find her on the road, here in Riverton, back in Wright, won't he then go to Paradise and lie in wait for her to come to the only thing that means anything to her?"

I sucked in my breath and held it, because it hurt to breathe out.

"Maybe he doesn't know where the girl is," I said.

Still curled up in a ball, Candy opened her eyes. She lay there blinking, her doe eyes dark and full of sorrow. For a moment she appeared to me like a fawn that had been shot and was lying on her side, only her eyes moving because nothing else could. I realized, somewhat belatedly, that the past radius of my life being confined to only a few miles was not just geographical. That the vast, mystical entities out there that were completely outside my understanding were not just about the spectrum of a country four thousand miles from stem to stern. I couldn't bear to look at her anymore. I turned away, and prayed, actually prayed. This is what I prayed for: *Please dear God, let it be morning. Let it be morning of someone else's life.* I wish I hadn't turned away, but I just couldn't face myself with her bleeding-out eyes staring at me.

3

The. Great. Divide

Riverton at morning was still an outpost of civilization. A few cars on Federal Boulevard, the main road, the mountains distant, the sky, too, the air thin, the people watching suspiciously. They answered questions but you could not call them friendly. More like reserved, with shotguns on their backs. At the agonizingly slow breakfast in the hotel restaurant, we were quiet, desperately trying to think of some trivia to pass the time. Oh for the Goethals and Outerbridge arguments! Oh for the talk about Baba, the spiritual swami! There was no one else in the place, and yet we had to wait ten minutes for someone so much as to take our order, and even that not until I stood up and said loudly, "We're the only ones here. I understand sometimes it's busy and you can't get to your customers. But what's your excuse this morning?"

Only then did a waitress drift over, obese and cranky, to silently take our order for eggs.

"Gina, aren't you going to call Eddie?" Candy asked.

"Yeah," I said. "Now's a good time. Before we get started again."

Gina, suddenly impatient to save time, said she'd call Eddie at the next stop, and reiterated that she thought we'd be okay on the open road, okay on the Interstate. Candy wouldn't even respond, drinking her coffee. I was torn.

"What do you think, Sloane?" said Gina. "You look so pale and exhausted. Look at your eyes, they're almost crystal clear, they're sapped of all color. Come on, a few hours on I-80, zip-zip, and we're in Salt Lake City."

Candy stared at me, her own leached-out eyes caked with yesterday's makeup, and the day's before. With all of Gina's eyebrows and eyelashes gone, I noticed a few bare spots at the crown of her head. If this trip went on any longer, she wouldn't have any hair left.

"I thought we were going to bleach you?" I said to Candy.

"Yeah. But." She sighed. "We checked out of the room already. And I want to get out of this town. It's not for me. Plus the few motels are all on this road. What if Erv is going from motel to motel, looking for our car?"

"Okay, back to reality," Gina said impatiently. "What do you say, Sloane?" she implored. "The Interstate?"

I looked from one wan face to the other. Imagine anybody in this world looking to *me* for answers to anything. Me! I nodded somberly. "I don't think we're safe on the Interstate. I'd rather take my chances on the smaller roads."

"Oh, God! You want to go through the mountains? Did you not hear the story of the mountain cannibals yesterday?"

"Yes," I said, "but I, for one, don't believe Wyoming has mountains, so there. We'll go north and be in Idaho tomorrow."

"Yeah, good luck with that."

"Fewer trucks in the mountains," said Candy.

"There *are* no mountains!"

"You two are ridiculous," said Gina. "Ri-di-cu-lous. Half a day from here to Salt Lake, or three days in the Snake River Canyon. Is that what you want?"

"I'd like to not run into Erv," said Candy. "If it's all the same to you."

Outside the remarkable morning, the parking lot didn't look as scary in the crisp, dazzling sunlight. There were no strange people sitting on benches, there was no noise. There was just one tall heavily-built biker guy smoking near his beat-up pick-up. We scurried like three blind mice. He walked over to my car as I was fumbling for my keys in my too-tight shorts pocket. Served me right. "How you doin', ladies? *Love* the car. Yours?"

"Thank you," I said. "Yes, mine." Still so proud!

"How much d'you pay for that?"

"Don't know," I replied. "It was a gift." Candy pushed me, wiggled her fingers into my shorts pocket herself, got out the keys.

"I had one once," the man continued, in a nostalgic drawl. "A 1966 light-blue 'Stang. Like yours, oh, it was a *beaut*. Paid fifteen for it. Would've paid twice that."

Candy unlocked the doors. Gina opened her side, pulling forward the seat. "Get in," Gina said to Candy. She didn't. She came to stand next to me on the driver's side. Gina started to say, "Cand—" but Candy interrupted her with a sharp loud grunt, like an ace serve in tennis, all without taking her eyes off the man. "Let's go," she said to me, almost in a hiss. "We're going to be late."

"You girls headed somewhere nice?" the man said amiably. "Skiing maybe?"

"Get inside," Candy repeated to me out of the corner of her mouth.

I didn't get inside. I was looking up at the man in stark confusion. Did he say $15,000? For a 1966 Mustang? "What happened to your car?"

Candy pulled on me, opening the driver door.

"Oh, you know," he said, taking a step to us and scanning the parking lot. "Sold it to pay the rent." He smiled. "Now I drive this." He pointed to his roomy GMC truck. "Not as good, but I can afford my pad. But your Shelby is even rarer. It's a collector's item. Might be worth twenty, twenty-five. And what a great yellow. I didn't think they made Shelbys in that color."

"Clearly they did."

Without referring to me by name, Candy bodily moved me toward the open door. The man took another step toward us and shook his head. "Seven colors for the '66 Shelby, none of them that one." He whistled. "I know that model like the back of my hand."

"Oh, yeah?" I said to the man, who looked down the road at two white pick-up trucks driving fast behind the Holiday Inn, about to pull into the lot. Without saying another word, he reached out and grabbed Candy by her forearm. I yelped, but she yanked herself violently away and kneed him very hard in the groin, instantly shoving me down into my seat, and while he was still doubled over in pain, kneed him again in the face, jumped over, *ran* over the hood of my car to Gina's side, threw herself in, clambered in the back, yelling, "Drive, Shelby! Drive!" the passenger door still open.

Gina must have slammed it shut, I don't know, but I didn't have to be asked twice to drive. I couldn't hear what the man was yelling to his buddies who had pulled up to him and were trying to block us, but he was shouting, incoherently, and gesturing to them like he was having a seizure. Going over a low curb, I screeched out of that parking lot. The white trucks weren't fast enough to flank me, though they tried. Right behind, they raced me to Federal Boulevard. My light was red, but Candy yelled, "Go, Shelby, go!" and I went through, which is harder than you'd expect, so hardwired is that stop on red. They followed us across the main road, one after the other. I made a sharp left, a sharp right into a residential development, right, left, right, left, right, left, I didn't know where we were anymore, but there was no stop sign I respected.

"Are they still behind us?" I panted.

"No," said Candy. "But they will be. Keep going."

"They won't catch us."

"They'll follow us. Keep going, Shelby."

"What in fuck's name just happened back there?" exclaimed Gina in a disbelieving, stunned voice.

"What happened," said Candy, "was our Shelby forgot who she was dealing with. Drive, Shelby!"

Gina started to wail. Her hands went up to her hair, twirling it around her fingers. By the time we got to Eddie, Gina would be bald. I know he liked her long hair, she'd told me enough times, but did he like her bald? Candy was panting in the back. I was crying, uncomposed, behind the wheel. My heart was thundering. "Are they behind us?" I asked. I was afraid to look in my rearview mirror.

"Yes," said Candy. "Go straight and make a right on the highway. Then drive, Shelby. Drive as fast as this car can go."

But they were no slouches in their Ford F-150 trucks. Those trucks must have had some power to them, too, because I came out onto the highway, revved up my engine from three to six in two seconds, and was hurtling at a hundred miles an hour, but when I peeked in the rearview, they were not receding as fast as I would've liked.

"Faster, Shelby," ordered Candy.

The road was not deserted. There were other cars, pulling into strip malls and gas stations, stopping at lights. I had to dodge and zigzag, I had to slam on my brakes once and swerve, Gina screamed, but I kept going, through three or four red lights. Finally we hit a flat stretch without traffic lights, red, green, or yellow, and I revved it up to 110, then 120, like all was one great big green light ahead of me. We were going too fast to see the road signs, Candy grim and silent, Gina praying. "Oh God! Oh God. Please! Oh God, we're gonna die! We're gonna crash! Slow down, Shelby, please, slow down. Oh God!"

"Don't you dare, Shelby," commanded Candy. "Go faster, if you can. Fly, girl, fly!"

So that's what I did. I flew. The Shelby Mustang the burly man was so envious of did what it was supposed to: rocket down the empty highway at 136.7 miles an hour without so much as a wheel tremble. Soon the F-150s were left in our dust, far away in our rear window, white dots now, small, smaller, then gone.

"Are we going in the right direction?" I breathed.

"Who the fuck cares?" exclaimed Gina. "Any direction away from them is the right direction. Oh, man. Oh, man."

I felt Candy staring hard at me from the backseat. "What?"

"*What?*" she said. "I don't understand you. What the hell were you doing back there, talking to him? Why in the world would you talk to a stranger in a parking lot, knowing what we're up against?"

"It wasn't Erv," I defended myself lamely.

"It's Erv's proxy! He just says, hold them for me, just keep them in place, and 5000 dollars is yours. Who knows, it may be up to ten now. Twenty! I told you. He can throw as much money at the CB handles as he needs to. This isn't Surio, bought for thirteen cents. The fact that there were three of them coming so willingly, risking themselves on the highway, says to me the ante's been raised quite a bit, raised to make it worthwhile for three men in fairly new Ford pick-ups to put themselves in such jeopardy. Why did you do that, Shelby? Why did you continue to talk to him?"

I didn't want to tell her why, feeling terror and guilt for getting us into such peril. I continued to talk to that man, because he said something I could not let go of, could not believe, and still did not believe. His regular, run of the mill '66 Mustang went for *15,000 dollars?* Fifteen thousand dollars for a 'Stang that wasn't a Shelby? If I sold mine, how much could I get? Was he right, ten, twenty? And if I sold it, could I give that money to Candy so she could take her daughter and fly away? Without wheels, to be sure, but still.

Sell my Mustang. It was like saying, *change your name.* How could I explain it to Emma? Did Emma spend that crazy money on me, a child not even her own? Was this my moral choice, and was it a fair one, to sell my only beloved possession given to me by my Emma (oh, see me calling her *my* Emma!) to give the money to a child gypsy who had a baby and now wanted to hide?

Yes, hide from men who wanted her dead. To save her, could I sell the car?

I tried to imagine it. I couldn't. Emma had given me that car. Where would she get that money from? And why? I would've been just as happy with a Ford Maverick, not a Mustang. Yet she had given me a Shelby, the labor of her love and the gift of the great burden of my freedom.

Selling it was impossible. Yet this is what I was thinking when the biker was talking to me. I forgot to be vigilant, and look what happened.

"I'm sorry, guys," I said.

Neither Gina, who was busy ripping out hair from her head, nor Candy, who sat with her hands on her lap and eyes closed, said anything. I slowed down a little, to ninety. I asked Gina to look at the map.

Angrily she did so. "Yes," she said. "We're going north to the Tetons. Is *that* what you want?"

That wasn't what I wanted.

The Wind River Range passed me on my left, laid out in the valley at the foot of the mountains, the top hits of 1981, "Hungry Heart," "Hearts" and "Stop Draggin' my Heart Around" passed me, too. Gas stations, Wind rivers, ragged rock peaks of mountains passed me by as I gripped the wheel and gradually returned to being myself. And what if I gave it to her and still didn't save her? Would it be worth it then? If I had a crystal ball and could see how this all turned out, would I give it to her?

"The trucks saw us going north on this road," said Candy grimly.

"So what? We smoked 'em," I said.

"What about the trucks up ahead at the next stop, at the next town, waiting for us?"

Almost in a whisper, I said, "You said there aren't any trucks in the mountains."

"Oh, my God, what a fucking disaster," said Gina.

So Wyoming did turn out to have mountains, after all. But my mind and heart were so full of other things, I barely noticed.

Gina spoke at last. "The Wind River Range was formed when a compression in the earth thrust a block of granite hundreds of miles long upward," she said, slowly twirling and pulling out strands of her long hair. "Nice, right?" She, too, slowly returned to the little she had in her arsenal to block out what she couldn't think about.

Candy wasn't speaking. Mutely she sat in the back, staring at the mountains, her face like a mask of a child, her vulnerable mouth slightly open, her deer-like eyes agape. Her lips were moving; in prayers?

"A penny for your thoughts, Cand," I said.

"A penny for yours."

I couldn't tell her. And she said to me, "I just want to get my baby, Shel. That's all, I just want to get her, and then find a little place for us where everything will be all right."

"I know, Cand," I said, wanting to stop the car, to hug her. I tightened my hands around the wood of the wheel.

"Candy," said Gina, in her practical voice, "I don't understand. Erv's chasing you because he wants to get this stupid film, which you don't have. Why can't you just tell him you don't have it? Ask the driver of the next truck we see to use his radio, call Erv's handle, say, Papa Bear, this is Goldie Locks, leave me the fuck alone, I don't got what you want."

"Okay," said Candy, "and Papa Bear says, Goldie Locks, if you don't have it, who does? What do I tell him then? Should I point him to New Melleray? Is Erv the kind of man who will back away when he hears the word Abbey?"

"No," said Gina. "just tell him you destroyed it."

After a pause, Candy said, "Oh, Gina. Why don't I just tell him a little fairy came and whisked it away, never to be seen by anyone in the land of sprinkle dust?"

"Fine," said Gina. "I'm just making suggestions here, and you're just shouting me down. That's what I get for trying to help."

"I'm not shouting," Candy said in a whisper.

We had driven through more than half the country now. Soon, I knew, it would be over. But I was thinking how not ready I was to face the last act of our journey. I couldn't fathom it. I didn't know how to get Gina to Bakersfield or Candy to Paradise. I didn't know how to get Gina to Eddie, Candy to Tara, me to Lorna Moor. I didn't know how to begin to look for my mother in Mendocino. As I realized this, my foot lifted off the gas pedal. I was flying through mountain passes, and the summer was here. The sun was shining, the valley was green with verdant bloom, and the river rushed by. Marty Balin was crying on the radio. *I really can't believe I'm here* . . . We were heading deeply north even though Salt Lake was south and west. We headed north even though Reno was south and west, though California and our mothers-daughters-lovers were south and west.

Lost in ourselves this way, we passed a small green metal sign. It was embedded at the foot of a mountain, tilted to one side, partly covered with leaves and twigs. The sign read: "CONTINENTAL DIVIDE ELEV 9658." I pulled over onto the narrow shoulder and stopped the car.

"What are you doing?" said Candy.

"So *this* is the continental divide?" I said, lumbering out. "This sign?" We looked around. Green fields full of yellow dandelions ran up to the feet of the mountains, the snow-capped ranges sloped high and wide.

And here, by the side of the road was my Great Divide.

The girls looked at me in frustrated puzzlement. "Um, when do you think we can get going again?" Gina asked.

"No, no, you take your time," said Candy. "It's not like we have anywhere to be. Or like anyone's following us."

We were completely alone on the road. "But Candy, this is it!" I said. "This is the Great Divide."

"Okay, Shelby, I can see I'm going to have to explain a few things to you," Gina said. "The Great Divide is not just one place."

"Oh yeah? Then how come this is the only sign we've seen?"

"Ahem, sign doesn't actually say Great. It says Continental."

"Same difference, smart aleck."

"Have we been looking for the divide?" asked Candy, prodding me to the car, pushing between my shoulder blades.

"*I* have." I wouldn't budge. "What I want to know is," I said, extricating myself from her, "is the change in me that apparent? Is it unmistakable, like that sign?"

"What change? What are you talking about?"

"See, I always thought the Great Divide would separate the country into a before and an after."

"Yes, Sloane," said Gina, "all your waters now run to the west."

They were making fun of me, even I could tell. But I really had expected the Great Divide to be a monumental thing, like a chasm in the earth that ran for miles that we had to zigzag around, something visible, something tangible. It wasn't called the itty-bitty partition. It was called The. Great. Divide. I got sulky. "Well, what about this sign makes the rivers flow west or east?" I said with indignation. "I just don't see how a little sign can do that."

"Kind of like the cross?" said Candy.

Gina and I both looked at her glumly. "No, *nothing* like the cross," said Gina. "The divide is an actual thing, not a symbolic thing."

Candy stared. "The sign that says CONTINENTAL DIVIDE is an actual thing?"

"Nooo," Gina drew out. "The ridge that runs underneath the sign that breaks the continent into an east and a west is an actual thing."

Candy nodded. "Like I was saying." She crossed herself.

Gina harrumphed back into the car. I stood forlorn by the pine. Candy draped her arm around me. "Honestly, Shel, do think of it in terms of the cross. This isn't *the* thing, but it doesn't make the thing you've been searching for any less tangible. Any less real."

But I didn't understand.

"Someday you might," said Candy. "You want me to tell you the miracle of the fourteenth station?"

"No," I said. "I want to understand now. And I don't." Unhappily I, too, got back in the car.

"All that time waiting for it," I said, so disappointed, "and that's all there is?"

386

"In the wintertime," said Gina, "the sign must be covered by snow." That's all she said, like it had some mythic meaning.

"Like that plane in the Andes," Candy offered as an example.

"Nothing like that plane!" Gina exclaimed. "In the winter the rivers can't see the sign, yet they know which way to flow. How do you think they know that, Shelby?"

"Oh, clever." I fell into silence. "Is there just one place for it?"

"Mostly Wyoming."

"What about Nevada? Montana? Utah?"

"Utah and Nevada are west. They're part of the Great Basin. Montana yes. The divide runs through there, too."

"Is it the whole of Wyoming?"

"No, Sloane." Gina was using her teacher to child voice.

"Is it a straight line, then?"

"Not at all. It's a meandering, freedom fault that trails for hundreds of miles. Like a river. Or a mountain range."

Back into silence I fell as I got on the road. I couldn't gawk at the mountains; I was driving and the road swirled downward along the decline of the hill. We would crash if I didn't pay attention.

"Your Great Divide," said Gina, "is part of the sagebrush sea, that vast expanse of sage-dominated canyon and range country that we drove through on the way to Riverton."

"Great," I muttered. "When it was raining and invisible?"

"But the rivers now all flow west!" Gina exclaimed. "That's not invisible. That's the most tangible thing there is. What did you think the divide was?"

"I told you," I said. "I thought it was going to be a canyon in the earth."

"So let's drive to Yellowstone," said Gina. "We surely want to get as lost as possible and it's only a few hundred miles from here. I'll show you what I mean. There's a place called Two Oceans Pass, where you can clearly see the thing you're looking for. One stream splits into two brooks. One brook becomes the Snake River 1300 miles to the Pacific. The other, 3500 miles away, is the Mississippi."

"How in the world do you know this?" Candy asked in amazement.

"I'm going to be a teacher," replied Gina authoritatively.

"Well, Professor Reed, we're not going to Yellowstone," said Candy. "That's where hell bubbles up from the earth every 90 to 120 minutes. Sloane is just going to have to take your word for it."

Like I would.

Gina had been right. The mountains did become spectacular, in deeper contrast to the sky and the flat fields; they turned into snow-capped towers, their outlines etched, their colors vivid. The river was greener, the sky bluer. There was a range up ahead particularly striking, and at the first scenic opportunity, we stopped. A river below us ran into the mountains in the far distance. Gina and I studied the map. She couldn't wait to get to a little skiing town called Jackson, right at the foot of the Grand Tetons. "Jackson has the world's largest ball of barbed wire," she said.

"Oooh, let's not miss that," said Candy. "What *are* we waiting for?"

No sooner had we pulled out of the rest area than we were stopped by a state trooper. I had just passed someone in my little bird, and his lights flashed on. I sat quietly, got out my license.

"Hello, girls," he said, leaning in, his eyes scanning the three of us. He was full faced, freshly and closely shaven.

I explained I was passing a slow-moving vehicle.

"Oh, I don't have a problem with that," he said. "What I have a problem with is you continuing to maintain the speed of seventy even after you passed him. The speed limit here is fifty-five, or were you going too fast to notice?"

My face must have registered rank shock because he said, "Do you know why it's fifty-five? Because of the wildlife. The bison keep crossing the road."

"Oh," I said regretfully. "It's to protect the wildlife."

"No," he replied. "It's to protect *you*. Do you know what happens to you when the bison hits your car at seventy miles an hour? You don't want to know. I've seen it many times, and believe me, it's not pretty."

"Although, technically," whispered Candy, after he took my license and went back to his squad car to call it in, "the bison is not actually hitting *you*."

"Well, why don't you tell that to the police officer," snapped Gina. "When he returns."

Candy just smiled from the backseat when he returned. And he smiled back. He didn't give me a ticket, just told me to be careful. "Okay, officer," I said. "Thank you, officer, have a good day, officer," and cut away from the curb at what I hoped was less than seventy an hour. Afterward I wasn't even noticing the countryside, I was so happy not to get a ticket.

My joy was short-lived. We were on a two-lane highway, a road so flat and straight in the valley between the far-away mountains, it went eleven miles to the horizon and still made no turns. His lights came on behind me again. With angst I pulled over.

"Officer?" My smile was so fake. "I wasn't speeding, was I?" I said through my teeth, staring at him pastily through my window.

He looked inside, eyed me, eyed Gina, stopped on Candy, stared at her a nice long time. Then he said, "Through the entire state of Wyoming we keep hearing CB alerts of a wild search for a yellow Mustang with three young women inside it. This wouldn't happen to be that yellow Mustang?"

My heart was on the floor. "No, officer."

"And you wouldn't happen to be the three young women, would you?"

"No, officer."

"CB keeps saying, one of them is a runaway minor."

"We're all over eighteen," I said. "Would you like to see our IDs?"

"I don't want to see your IDs," he said. He was a smart guy. "Where are you girls from?"

"New York," I said. "Larchmont."

"All of you?"

"Yes." Now I was outright lying, but he had said he didn't want to see our IDs. "We're high-school friends. Just traveling to California."

"Where to?"

"Mendocino."

"All of you?"

"Yes."

"What's your business there?"

I spoke slow and measured. "My mother lives there. Thought I'd visit her. Didn't want to go alone. They're along for the ride. They're my friends." My plates did say New York. The car was a Mustang. And yellow. There were three of us, and we were young, and I'm sure if anyone cared to give a description of us, he'd describe us pretty well. All he had to do is mention one girl's pink-streaked hair.

"Just so I understand," the trooper said. "Someone's looking for a yellow Mustang with New York plates and three women in it, and you're saying it's not you?"

"That's right."

He eyeballed me with a skeptical twist.

"Not us," I repeated. "It's a big country. Mine is not the only yellow Mustang on the road, is it?"

"No, no." He was pensive. "Well, yes, actually. But. What's odd to me is if there really *is* a runaway, a missing persons type of situation with a minor, the police are always involved. Why wouldn't they be? We get bulletins on runaways all the time from other states. Why would the truckers be involved instead? Why wouldn't the girl's parents get in touch with the police?"

"Good questions. All very good," I said, solemnly nodding my head. "This definitely bears further investigating." Candy kicked my seat from the back. I cleared my throat, lady-like. "Officer, if there's nothing else, we've got to be in Utah by nightfall. My uncle is meeting us in Salt Lake, and we've got a long way to go."

390

"You sure do. Because you're heading in the wrong direction. Salt Lake is at least 400 miles away, and you've got to go around the lee side of the Wind River Range. If you're in such a hurry to see your uncle, why are you taking the slow local roads away from Utah and north to Jackson? Why didn't you take I-80? You'd be in Salt Lake already."

"But then we wouldn't see the Grand Tetons. Or Jackson." I smiled sweetly. My hands were sweating.

"So do you have to be in Salt Lake by nightfall or are you taking in the mountainside? Can't have it both ways, girls."

"Oh, I think we can, officer," I said. "I think we can."

He let us go. Candy said she almost wished he hadn't. "He was so cute and protective."

"Stop it," said Gina. "He's not your type."

"No?" Candy smiled. "You did real well back there, Shel," she said, her voice low. "You're a good liar."

"You really are," said Gina. "*Scary* good."

I didn't look at her, she didn't look at me. Enough already, I wanted to say. I wished Candy were sitting in front and Gina in the back. We drove on, the snowy sharp peaks of the Grand Teton to our perpetual peripheral right, peripheral in every way, for central to us now was the hole in our life: what in the world do we do?

Jackson was a log cabin town, all western motif and dark wood, all the awnings, store fronts, benches, and brown signs. We sat across the booth at a mobbed for lunch log cabin Mountain High Pizza Pie and stared listlessly at each other across the wooden table, our feet on the wooden floor.

"If you had gone to the police," Gina speculated, "and gave *them* the reel of film, instead of your father the monk, you'd be protected and he'd be arrested."

"Yes," said Candy. "And my mother, too. That's what you recommend? Me turning in my own mother? Plus, I'd be remanded until

I turned eighteen, maybe even face some legal trouble of my own, who knows, some JD convictions for soliciting, for conspiracy to commit a felony, and I'd never get my little girl."

"Yes, Gina, don't be stupid," I said.

"And Erv in a day or two would be out on a $100,000 bail, anyway," continued Candy, "I'd be in even worse danger."

"Frankly, I don't see how that's possible," I said. The pizza wasn't coming. They were crazy busy.

"Candy is right, I guess," said Gina. "The penalties for multiple counts of a federal felony are grave. Twenty to life. Unlikely chance of parole, because the defendant would be considered too much of a hazard to the community, preying on children and all. He'd never get out."

"Right," said Candy, "so a man with nothing to lose, you think he's going to be more desperate or less desperate?"

"He seems pretty desperate now, Candycane," I said.

"Tell me something I don't know."

The iced tea came, the pizza eventually.

Afterward, without a plan, we walked a few blocks to a school playground and sat on the swings. Jackson was a skiing town. It was summer now, and dead (except for the rhyming pizza place), but you could tell by the fearsome quantity of ski shops what the town would be like in the wintertime.

"The car is *such* a menace," Candy said.

"Tell me about it." Gina came to sit on the swing next to her, as if they were commiserating with each other over the peril *I* had put them in with my bright yellow Shelby!

"The car is not the menace," I said, feeling tendentious. "Erv is the menace. The car is lovely." Exasperated, I sat on the seesaw nearby where I could still hear their bitching and moaning.

"What do we do?" Gina was saying. "We can't continue traveling in that thing. It's a danger magnet."

"I don't see we have much choice," said Candy, swinging back and forth, kicking her legs underneath herself like a little girl. Except this little girl was wearing a skirt so short a man standing in front of her would be able to see straight into her throat. And just like a little girl she wore no bra under her thin satin halter.

"We could take a train," suggested Gina.

"A train to where?"

"You to Paradise. Me to Bakersfield. Oh, that reminds me. I have to call Eddie."

"*That* reminds you? You need to be *reminded* of that?"

"What about a bus? Yeah, maybe a bus," said Gina. They swung as I watched them, my mouth falling open.

"You go to Bakersfield, I go to Paradise?" said Candy. "By bus?"

"We have to do something. At least I'm thinking. Coming up with ideas."

Candy glanced at me, not ten feet away, at my open mouth, my wide eyes. She winked at me, and then made a serious face for Gina. "Your plan is bold," she conceded. "Daring. But Gina, what about Shelby over there on the seesaw by herself?"

"Yeah, Gina," I said, getting up and walking over to them. "What about Shelby over here?"

Gina shrugged. "She can do what she likes. Right, Sloane? You like to do as you please."

"Knock it off. What are you proposing?"

"We have to do something, Shelby!"

"Why don't we get going to do something? I keep saying and saying that."

"Go where?"

That stumped me. "Well, to Salt Lake, like we planned."

Candy shook her head. "No. Not yet. I need to think."

"Think about what?"

"Shelby's right," said Gina.

"Yes, I am," I said, "but I don't mean, get going *without* me."

"No, no, I know." She wouldn't look at me.

"Gina," said Candy. "We can't really leave Shelby alone in Jackson, can we? You run off, I run off, and we leave her? That doesn't seem right, does it?"

Gina didn't reply!

"*I* could stay here, Shel," Candy suggested. "Get out of your way."

"And do what? Don't tell me make caskets."

"Why not? People don't die in skiing resorts?" She kicked up dirt under the swing. "I kind of like this town. I could even get a job as a waitress. I bet the tips are fantastic in winter."

"Well, you'd know about tips better than me," said Gina, quickly adding, "I've never worked as a waitress. But why would you want to live here? People coming in, out, transients all the time. No community."

"It *is* beautiful, though," I said. Did I want to leave Candy here?

"Is that enough?" Gina said. "Beautiful?"

"What else is there?" asked Candy.

"And how would you get from Paradise to here?" I wanted to know.

"How would I get from Paradise to anywhere? I'd have to somehow, wouldn't I?"

Disgusted with myself, with them, and helpless, I hopped off the swings.

Is that what they were both thinking? Gina take the bus, Candy stay in Jackson, and leave me by myself in my yellow pony while they roller-skated away, leaving me to the talons of Erv's fear and anger?

Is that what they were both thinking? That I wouldn't just carry Candy's bathwater, I'd drink it, too?

"Candy, how far are we from Bakersfield?" Gina asked when we had left the playground and started ambling back to Broadway Avenue.

"Geographically?" Candy wanted to know. "Philosophically? Metaphorically? Symbolically?"

"Timewisecally."

"That's a metaphysical question," replied Candy. "I don't know."

"God! Sloane, how long?"

"Gina, how would I know? I don't know when we'll get out of Wyoming! Ask Candy."

"Oh, for God's sake. Does anyone have any quarters? I have to call Eddie."

We had no quarters. "Why don't you call him collect?" asked Candy. "He *is* your future husband. What, you don't think he'd accept the charges?"

"Oh, the two of you!" We got some quarters from a hot-dog vendor.

We huddled around Gina while she called Eddie. She was nervous, twirling her hair like spaghetti around her fingers. What if he's not happy to hear from me? she asked. What if, when he finds out how soon I'm coming, he'll tell me not to come?

"What *if*?" said Candy.

"You know what?" Gina pushed Candy slightly away. "You don't know him, so don't stand so close. You don't know anything about us."

"I'm sorry," said Candy, putting her hand on Gina, pinching the back of her arm. "I'm just teasing. You're right. Call him. It'll be fine."

"But what if it isn't fine?"

"Then you come with me to Mendocino," I said, glaring at her. "Help me look for my mom."

"Come with you?" Gina repeated dully.

"Or you can come with me," said Candy. "To Paradise. Help me get my little girl."

Groaning, Gina dropped quarters into the phone and dialed Eddie's number. She had tried to call him several times since Isle of Capri, but each time she called his mother said he was out. Was he out—and if so, why so frequently, and with whom? And if he wasn't out . . . well, Gina wasn't prepared to face that level of lies. Being out with Casey at the bat was bad enough. Pretending to be out so he wouldn't have to talk to Gina was worse. So even this time, at the dusty Jackson phone booth near a sign for the

National Elk Refuge, it took her several minutes to get up her nerve to dial the tenth digit.

I didn't want to stand too close. I didn't want to hear his voice. I hoped he'd be out. I was upset with her for entertaining even for a second the thought of ditching me, but even if I weren't mad, how could I be a proper friend to Gina when my self-interest was involved to this degree? I couldn't counsel her, because I couldn't trust myself with my own advice. Not liking myself one little bit, I moved away, then forced my legs to step closer, and liked myself even less for that—forcing myself, like a sociopath, to do the right thing.

He must have been home this time. "Hey, baby," Gina said into the phone, smiling. "Whatchya doin'?" She turned her back to us, and lowered her head.

Now of course I struggled to hear his voice! I had always liked his voice, and wanted to hear it now—it had been so long since I had. My internal commotion must have been plain on my face, because I caught Candy staring at me with sympathy and compassion. Pulling me away from the phone booth, she whispered, "I cannot be*lieeeve* that after all you know about him, you can have that face on. You should be saying to yourself *there but for the grace of God go I*, not wishing you were in her Dr. Scholl's clogs. You should be *praying* for him not to be home."

"You don't know anything." I pulled my arm away. But I feared she did.

"What a silly sad creature you are," Candy said, gazing at me with strange softness. "Even when you know you're barely saved from a life of misery, you still stand here and wish you weren't."

"And your point?"

Gina ran out of quarters in seven minutes. She asked Eddie to call her back. I don't know what he said, but I know what Gina said. "No, no, I understand. Of course. Don't worry. I'll call you again in a couple of days, okay?"

They said goodbye; she turned to us reluctantly.

"So is he coming or not?" I asked.

"What? Oh, I didn't even mention it," she replied breezily, her thin lips stretched into a smile. She got out her red gloss, smoothed it on. "He's very excited we're close. He can't wait to see me."

Candy elbowed me, and I pinched her.

"He was happy to hear from me," said Gina defiantly. "He said he really missed me; wanted to know how soon I was coming."

"Is that what he said?" asked Candy. "Gina, babe, how soon you gettin' here?"

"Yes, about."

"Ah."

Gina stared at us. We stared back.

"So do you want me to take you to the bus station?" I said, trying to keep the challenge out of my voice. "You can take the bus from here to Bakersfield. We'll have to get your things out of my car."

Rolling her eyes, she said nothing at first. "I wasn't serious before," she said at last. "I was joking." She stared at me coldly. "After you leave Candy, you and I still have to make our way back home."

"Yes, we do, don't we?" I returned her stare, just as coldly.

Gina said nothing. That's where our alienation became visible, like the sign for the divide. She started rushing us, then. Let's go. We have to go. Now. I promised her Bakersfield, and she was going to hold me to it. But she had promised me that she would stick with me to the end, and I was going to hold her to *that*.

Though Gina was hurrying us it was such a long way from Jackson to Salt Lake, and Candy was daunted by the prospect of driving on the windy roads through glens, abuts, ravines and waterfalls and Citizens' Band radios announcing her every turn, that she wanted to stay in the canyon. We got a room at the Painted Buffalo Inn. "Candy, don't you want to go? Don't you want to?" I kept whispering. "How are you going to get to Paradise if you're going to let every state trooper and every white truck chasing us distract you?"

"I'm not distracted," said Candy, walking aimlessly around the room. "I'm despairing."

"You want to get your girl, don't you? How many miles to Paradise from here?"

"Eternity away," she said, sounding an eternity away herself, though she was only at the open window.

"It's not far. One mile at a time, Candy. We'd be halfway to Salt Lake already if we didn't stop here."

But she was looking for different things than us, than me. Gina's future goal was rooted in the past—to reach her wayward Eddie. Mine too was rooted in the past—to find my wayward mother. But Candy was searching for her future. She was going to change herself from something she was and try to become something she wasn't, and she intended to do this with another small human being for whom she would become solely responsible. She was searching for a place she'd never been to, and didn't know for sure existed, where she and her girl could build a small life brick by heavy brick. I let her alone to stare out the window. If she needed to stay in Jackson an extra day, who was I to argue? Our car was in the municipal lot, under cover, safe for now, out of sight, like us.

Gina wanted to know what Candy planned to do with her hair. "Are you *ever* going to bleach it?" she said, combatively. "We're just sitting around doing nothing. Now's as good a time as any."

"Oh, yes," said Candy. "Our problems would certainly be over. Three young women traveling in a yellow Mustang, but now instead of three brunettes, you've got two brunettes and one blonde—that couldn't possibly be them!"

Gina swiped a magazine off the table onto the floor. "What does your Jesus say about sarcasm?" she asked, plonking herself into a chair. "Anything in the New Testament about that?"

"Not a word. And the day I'm perfect like Jesus, I'll let you know."

She went out for a walk. We stayed in—for five minutes, and then, because I couldn't be in a room alone with Gina feeling as bad as I did about her, we went out, too, trudging along after her.

"You got us into an unbelievable mess and now you're upset because you think I'm looking out too much for myself?" Gina said to me. "But why would that upset you? You always looked out only for yourself."

I lowered my head. I had no defense against my anger, my feeling of distance from her. It was true. This was payback. "I said I'd put you on the bus, Gina," I said. "You want to go? Let's go now."

She fell quiet then.

Candy found a drugstore, and bought a bottle of Clairol peroxide. I thought about it for two seconds and bought one for myself. I bought scissors. Then we went back to the room, cut each other's hair, then bleached it. It didn't come out great, our hair was too dark, and the double process of leaching the black out and then coloring the hair with peroxide went awry somewhere. A professional was sorely needed, but this was cheap, only ten bucks each, and we did it in the room. After three hours of fuss and muss and mess, we were both spiky short-haired and the fakest blonde you ever saw, blonde tinged with orange, and inexplicably, Candy's pink strands had now acquired a disturbing shade of lime green. We stared at our faces in the bathroom mirror, hair still wet and moussed, appraising ourselves critically. "Well," Candy said at last. "That was a success."

We walked out of the bathroom. "Gina, what do you think?"

Gina looked up. She had lain on the bed reading *People* magazine she bought at the drugstore and then the Jackson Hole skiing brochures.

"That's great," she said. "Can we go eat? I'm starved." She had miserable bare spots near the crown of her forehead.

We found El Abuelito Mexican restaurant but that was closed. Candy thought perhaps she could get a job there. Walking down the street, we found a Laundromat. "To work or do laundry?" I wanted to know.

Candy didn't reply. We meandered our way back to the elementary school, and briefly sat in the swings. It would be cold here in the winter, she said. Would it be too cold?

"Too cold for what?" I asked.

"Can we go?" repeated Gina. "I'm *starved*."

"It would be dead in the summer," I added, as if Gina hadn't spoken. "Like now. Dead, but hot."

We dolefully agreed Jackson had everything Candy needed. A nightlife, restaurants, shops, a Laundromat, an elementary school.

That it was better than Wright, Wyoming.

"That isn't fair," said Gina. "Hell is better than Wright, Wyoming."

"Maybe we should go now," Candy ventured. "Drive at night when no one can see us. Truck drivers don't stop much by here. It's quiet. Let's go. Let's get me to Reno. My friend Jessica has a car. And my thousand bucks."

"I'm not driving through the woodlands of Idaho at night, Candy," I said. "I just can't."

"Besides we already paid for the room," added Gina. Candy glared at her as if that were not even a consideration.

I had to agree with Gina. It was a small consideration. I had already tapped into the money I needed to get back home, rationalizing it away by saying the return trip couldn't possibly take as long. I was deceiving myself, of course. I wasn't anywhere close to Mendocino, which was my halfway point.

On Candy's dime we went to the Million Dollar Cowboy bar and grill, because Candy liked the name. She said it sounded promising. Indeed it was popular and there we ran into our friend the police officer, who was now off duty and didn't recognize us with the blonde tresses. Once she reacquainted herself with him, his solemn face lit up like a Christmas tree. They struck up a brief flirtatious dance, and disappeared into the darkness. Gina and I sat, nursing our pathetic beers, paid for by Candy.

"Do you remember when you and I climbed out of my aunt's window and went to the Library Bar in Indiana?" Gina said.

"No," I said, turning away from her, feeling un-young and miserly. Here I was, sitting in a smoky, loud bar where "I Love Rock 'n' Roll" was blaring and young people were hooking up, while judging Candy and counting in my head what was left over of my money. To throw stones at her seemed petulant in light of Gina's remark. Still, though.

"Why does she always need to flirt with guys?" I asked. "Why can't she just sit with us, have a drink, go back to the hotel room, get a good night's sleep?"

"Tell me about it," said Gina. We huddled together like allies. "You know yesterday in Riverton, she went off with some guy, too. I was alone for forty-five minutes, in a bar in that town! I didn't want to tell you, didn't want you to say I told you so. But how ridiculous is that?"

I nodded vehemently. "It's ridiculous. Yeah." We clucked and tutted. Then I frowned. "But what about us in South Bend?" Was Candy right? Her flirtations were wrong, but ours, now ours were delightful!

"I guess," said Gina and smiled. "But that was so devastatingly fun, baby."

"The next day when we ran into them and they didn't even acknowledge us," I said, "was *that* fun?"

"Who cares?"

"That's right," I said. "You shrugged it off then, too, but I couldn't. Still can't. I didn't feel liberated. I felt diminished. Like I gave that guy something he wanted, but after I gave it to him, he held me in contempt. Why would he? I don't hold him in contempt for taking it. Why does he hold me in contempt for giving it?"

"Ask Candy. She's got a silver spoon in her mouth, according to you. Ask her why she doesn't care. Actually, it's the one thing I really like about her."

Candy didn't return in time for us to ask her. Why did it upset me so much, her going with him? He seemed nice, seemed to like her, why did it prick my heart? Tired of waiting and not wanting to pay for another beer, we left and walked back to the motel, a few blocks away. Jackson is laid out below one of the tallest mountains in the United States and the effect of the Grand Teton at night on a tiny town lying at its feet is staggering. A massive black monolith hulked threateningly over every street and alley, the thin crescent moon and the distant stars lighting up just enough of the gargantuan ebony outline to drive more foreboding into my heart. "I don't want her to live here," I said to Gina, hurrying along, looking at the pavement. "This place isn't for her."

"How do you know? Maybe the copper fell in love with her."

Candy came back after midnight. We were already in bed. Gina was asleep. I had nothing to read, so I was reading Gideon's Bible. When she returned I was leafing through "*What to read when you're feeling sorrow*" and "*What to read when you're feeling lost.*"

"Where've you been?" I closed the book.

"You know where I've been," she said. "With Ralph."

I waited for her to say more.

Candy shook her head. "He's a nice man. I told him I was looking for a place to live. He said if I stayed in Jackson, he'd make sure I was safe."

"Did you tell him you have a baby in California?"

"Not yet," she said, smiling tiredly, taking off her little skirt.

I examined her resigned face. "Did you tell him about Erv?" I swallowed.

"No. Did you want me to?"

I waited until she came back from the bathroom, her face and hands damp.

"So are you staying?" I asked haltingly.

"No," said Candy. "We're leaving tomorrow."

She took off her makeup and got into bed. Rather, she got into bed and then took off her makeup, her crumpled balls of baby-oiled tissue falling soundlessly to the floor.

I chewed my lip. I was happy she was back, to have her next to me. "Gina and I were talking," I began.

"About me?"

"Well . . . about the whole thing."

"The *whole* thing? Really? Because that's a lot."

"Well, just the boy thing."

"Ralph is not a boy. He's thirty-three."

402

I took a breath, and told her about the two Todds in South Bend. Finally, I said, "The way he looked at me made me feel so bad. That was the only time I had done something like that." That wasn't, strictly speaking, true. It was the only time I had done something like that outside of Larchmont. But there everyone knew everyone else, the boys saw the girls again, and after all, it was the melodrama, the false tears and the even more false promises that kept us all busy in our junior and senior years. If it weren't for the relentless and meaningless hook-ups in high school, what would any of us have to talk about?

"Okay," Candy said. "But what does it have to do with me?"

"Doesn't it make you uncomfortable that boys might feel the same way about you?"

"Nope," she said. "What surprises me when I think about it, and I don't much think about it, is how often they want something so bad they're willing to do anything to get it. To pay money for something I don't often want for free. I make it easy, and they like it easy. But that has nothing to do with me. It's got everything to do with them."

Turning slightly away, I stared at the ceiling. I'd seen a lot of ceilings on this journey with her. "Don't you want some love, Candy?" I whispered.

"I have love," she said. "You don't know yet. But someday you'll know."

I thought I might already know, but I didn't tell her that.

The next day we got up extra early at seven. We didn't want to hang around, Candy said, because Ralph was going to come looking for her.

"Why would he come looking for you?" an exhausted Gina asked, moody like Miami weather.

"He was pretty smitten," said Candy. And sure enough, his patrol car was parked in the front and he was sleeping in it! Making sure he didn't miss her. We tip-toed past him.

"Candy, if he was that smitten," Gina whispered, "why didn't you stay?"

"Gotta get my girl."

"So get your girl and come back."

"He was too nice for a girl like me," she said. "This place's too nice for a girl like me."

Not protesting I was relieved. Did you see the ominous Tetons, I wanted to ask. They were like a black premonition. It increased my speed.

We missed the Snake River Canyon, drove right above the river, didn't even notice it. We swept through the little towns, Alpine Junction and Freedom, Afton and Smoot, around the lee side of the Wind River Range, and then headed into Idaho, around the ragged cliffs of enormous Bear Lake that looked artificial and artificially green.

Then we made a wrong turn by a tumbling river and got lost in the woods. There was construction up ahead, we took a detour and by the time we realized we were heading north, not west, we'd gone fifty miles through woodlands in the wrong direction on a winding road. Candy stared out the window the whole time.

We were so scared, we stayed in Pocatello, Idaho, though it was nowhere we needed to be. Pocatello would have looked like Wyoming if not for the millions of birch trees lining the rocky grasslands.

Through it all, Candy stared open-eyed at the little towns on the banks of the Idaho rivers, and I stared, too, trying to see what she might see, to imagine what she might imagine. Could I live here? I wondered when we had driven through Smoot, a tiny western town on the northern edge of the Wind River Range. Car lots and industry, smokestacks and run-ons, a banner advertising a pig race and a county fair. No department stores, shoe stores, Baskin-Robbins or pizza parlors, no McDonald's even. Just bars and windows.

I couldn't live here.

But could I, if I *had* to?

Other people did. Other people maybe not like me, but like Candy? And who was like her?

"Candy," I asked in blisteringly sunny Logan, Utah, when Salt Lake City was within a hundred miles. "Could you take the baby and live with your dad?" He is sanctuary, I thought, in the full sense of that word.

"You know I can't. Tara's five. What happens in six years when she turns eleven? They gonna boot her out, too?"

"So don't live in New Melleray. Live in Dubuque nearby."

"In Iowa?"

"As opposed to Idaho?"

She didn't answer. "I can't live that close to him," she said at last. "You know that I'm no good. And I don't want him to know it, to think of me like he thought of my mother."

"Your God knows it," said Gina, piping into the conversation.

"God has inexplicable and undeserved grace," Candy replied. "And infinite patience. I don't want to put such an undue burden on my poor old dad. Besides," she added, "I think the earthly things weigh him down, bring him to a place he wants to get away from. He didn't join the Trappists, that divine refuge, to be dragged down into ice-cream parties, pig tails and time-outs."

"How do you know that's what your kid is up to?"

"Because Mike told me. He said she was a handful. He said I should feel lucky I wasn't dealing with her every day," Candy said, and, turning away from the bright, green and beautiful Logan so I wouldn't hear her, groaned in despair.

ELEVEN
BEYOND THE GREAT DIVIDE

1

Good Samaritans

Salt Lake was at least a city. It had gas stations and McDonald's, it had department stores, restaurants and coffee houses. There were mountains in the distance for beauty and the blood-orange sun melting into the mountains for awe. It was pristine, swept clean, in-ground-sprinkled, impeccable, tailored, and green. We found the address of the hotel manager Candy knew, on Seventh, at the Omni. He remembered her from his business trip to Huntington; he was mortified but happy to see her. He gave us a fantastic, ridiculously expensive room for free with a view of the Mormon Temple, and two queen beds with down quilts and pillows. He let us have room service "on the house"—which ended up costing twice the room by the time we were done ordering champagne and filet mignon. "Well, it's not on the *house*," said Candy. "But I know what you mean, Sloane." That night Gina and I went for a walk through town to look for life in Salt Lake while Candy stayed behind at the hotel. I didn't ask, didn't want to, didn't even want to think about what it was costing someone to get us down quilts, champagne and steak for one night.

There was no life in Salt Lake. But the thousands of flower beds in Temple Square were illuminated and impressive. "Let me tell you what I like about Salt Lake for Candy," said Gina. "It's in the middle of nowhere. No one would think to look for her here. It's counterintuitive. It's a big city—easy to hide. It's got stuff for her to do. It'll have schools for her baby, friends for them both. I think this may be just the ticket."

"You're not thinking it through, Gina," I said, and while strolling thus we argued about the merits and demerits of Candy's possible move to Salt Lake.

When we were done discussing her future life, we went back to the hotel and found her in the room getting ready to go for a drink with the off-duty bell boy. "He's my little Mormon friend," she said, grinning.

"I thought Mormons don't drink?" said Gina.

"They don't. I do." She was getting dolled-up. She had only two skirts, one bright blue, one denim, but every time she put one on, it looked like a different outfit. She had cheap jewelry that she alternated for effect with her pink and yellow halter tops, she varied her lipgloss and eye shadow, and managed to seem like a different girl, especially now with her cheap blonde hair. We watched as the mascara went on layer after layer.

When Gina told her about our plan for her future, Candy listened, looking at us both like she knew something we didn't. "You girls are cute," she said, her eyelashes black and fake-looking, her blonde hair short and fake-looking. "You're adorable. But I can't move here. The eagle at the gates to the city stands atop an upside down star. That may be all right for some, but not for me." Then she left.

"What did that mean?" I asked blankly.

"Damned if I know," replied Gina, turning on the TV. I tried to read, but the volume was too loud, "Mary Tyler Moore" reruns followed by the "Odd Couple." I fell asleep with Felix Unger still on. Gina and I could've talked about things, but we didn't. I didn't want to, and I suspect she didn't either. She just wanted all this to be over, I think, like me. I don't know what time Candy came in, but near dawn I woke briefly to find her lying next to me under the covers.

410

The next morning, Candy wouldn't wake up, no matter how much noise we made. "Check-out's at noon," I said into her ear. She turned her head away and pulled the blanket over her head. "In Reno by sundown," I tried with an upward inflection, thinking the reminder of Reno would be enough to get her going. Not so. Gina and I went downstairs to get a bagel and a coffee. It was a blue-sky morning, so hot and sunny that coffee and bagel in hand, we decided to walk to Temple Square. I didn't like my new hair-do. I attracted entirely the wrong kind of attention to myself.

The marble-like towers of the Church of Jesus Christ of Latter-Day Saints soared against the perfect sky like statues. But there was no cross anywhere—not on the doors, not on the cupola. The Temple also had no windows. No windows and no cross. Hmm. "Should we go in?" I asked, standing amid the glorious impatiens.

"Why would we want to?"

"I dunno. Just to see. We went in at New Melleray."

"Yes." Gina threw out her coffee. "Okay. But then I really want to get going. We're so close to Bakersfield."

If by close she meant eight or nine hundred miles through Reno, then yes. We walked up to the doors. But the church was closed, the door was locked. A man said into our back, "They won't let you in if you're not a member."

Swinging around we faced him. He was a businessman in a suit, on his way to lunch perhaps, standing at the foot of the stairs.

"How do you know we're not members?" I asked.

"Members don't try to break down the doors of the Temple when they know the Temple is closed."

"When does it open?"

"Sunday. Still can't go in. They'll card you."

He walked off. There was a wedding in the square; we watched for a while, the bride in white standing next to her black-suited groom smiling for the photographer. She was dazzling, as were the blue and yellow roses behind them. I wondered if Candy had woken up. We walked out of the square and down the street past the John Smith House and Museum. "Should we stop in at the museum?" Gina asked. "Learn a little about John Smith?"

"You want to?"

"No," she said. "I'm kidding. We have to get going." At the corner of Temple and State, we stood a polite distance away from Eagle Gate, a metal arc with an eagle perched on it. This must be what Candy was talking about. "I think it's hard to tell about the star, though," Gina said. "Don't you think?"

I squinted. "Star has five points?"

"Yes."

"It stands on two legs, with two arms outstretched?"

"Yes."

"And the fifth and remaining tip points up?"

"I guess."

We squinted some more. The star, heck, the whole gate started swimming in our eyes. We couldn't tell anything. Except this. The eagle's two clawed feet clearly stood on two upwardly pointing tips of the star. "Why is this significant?" I asked. "What does it mean to have the star upside down? Is that symbology or something?"

"Why don't you ask our resident theologian? She must be awake by now."

Not only was she awake, she wasn't in the room. Her stuff was gone. The room key still worked, and the maid had not been in, though it was nearly *two*. Where was she? And whom to ask? I wondered if she left a note. Gina said, "Maybe she's split."

My legs turned liquid. Just at the suggestion of it. "Stop it. She probably went looking for us. We didn't tell her where *we* were going, why should she?"

Where to look for her?

We went downstairs; the bellman and the valet were standing outside in the sun near the double doors, chatting. While the valet retrieved my car, I asked the bellman if he'd seen our friend.

"Who's your friend?" He was not friendly.

I looked Justin up and down. Was he pretending to be dense? Yesterday he sure noticed her. "You know, the one in the blue mini-skirt, the one you had a drink with?"

He turned red. "She went out earlier."

"When?"

"I don't know. Before noon."

Gina and I studied each other dumbly.

My car was brought, and before I got in, I asked Justin if there was another way to get to Reno.

"Another way than what?"

"Than the Interstate."

"Uh—no. Why would you? It's a straight line in. And it's not an easy trip anyway. Five hundred and seventy miles of nothing. Don't fall asleep."

"There must be another road, no?"

"In—Nevada?" He said Nevada the way someone might say the seventh circle of hell.

"Maybe a scenic route?"

He stared at me like he had never heard the words Nevada and scenic in the same sentence. "South Utah," he finally said. "That's one of the most beautiful places in all the world. I'm from there. From St. George. But Nevada, I know nothing about it. I go through Nevada only when I have to go to Reno."

"Oh yeah?" I sized him up. I took a chance. "I didn't know Mormons gambled."

Boy could he turn red. "I just go there with my buddies," he said quietly, backing away from me into the revolving doors. "Have a good day."

We got into our car. "We can't go anywhere," I said. "We can't do anything."

Gina's face soon changed, got harsh suddenly. She pointed down the street. "While we're busy not doing anything, look what your little Candy's doing."

And sure enough, there was Candy walking down the street. Next to her was a young blonde woman and a little boy. As they

413

got closer, I saw that the woman wasn't that young, and the boy not little, but almost the size of the woman, who seemed smaller because she was pulling a suitcase. "Candy, where've you been?" Gina asked sharply, rolling down her window.

"Sloane, can you pop the trunk?" Candy cut in.

"Who's this?" That was me, leaning out, my casual elbow resting on the door. "We got no room in the trunk." I popped the trunk anyway. Gina cast me the dirtiest of looks while Candy and her companions struggled outside.

I didn't see and didn't want to see. I didn't want to ask why this woman, or this woman's suitcase or this child was getting into my car.

"Are you *kidding* me?" Gina hissed.

At first I said nothing. Then I spoke. "Gina, let them get in."

The trunk managed to slam shut, and the three of them piled in, boy first, packing into the miniature backseat that had been barely big enough for two Pomeranians and now, no less incongruously, was cramming in three people, to a varying degree all strangers.

"This is Lena," Candy said, behind my seat, a big smile on her face. "And her son Yuri."

Lena, sitting in the middle, stuck out her hand. I shook it. Gina didn't. She wasn't even looking in the back. Her arms were crossed.

Candy announced she and Lena were hungry. "I'm not hungry," said Lena. "I'm thirsty." She had a heavy Slavic accent; Russian maybe? While I drove around unfamiliar Salt Lake streets, they decided they were more in the mood for a sandwich than a bagel. "Gina," Candy said, with an ill-received poke, "is a bagel a sandwich if you put ham on it?" She chuckled. Gina did not grace Grace with a reply.

Candy wanted eggs and hot oatmeal. And milk. This in addition to a good cup of coffee. Lena, who knew her way, badly, around Salt Lake, directed us to a sandwich place on North Temple that apparently had a bit of everything. Gina and I stayed in the car while the three of them bounded out and inside.

414

Whirling to me, Gina said, "Are you ever going to ask her what the hell she's doing?"

"Whoa. What's with the tone?"

"Shelby!"

"Gina!"

She swung her arms crossed on her chest nearly hitting herself in the nose. "You clearly have stopped caring a damn for what I think," she said. "I'm not going to waste my breath."

"Thank you. What will it matter if I ask? They're in the car. A mother and a child. What do you want me to do?"

"I wish I weren't here. From Ohio onward, I regret every second I didn't take a bus to Bakersfield. I should have put my foot down. Then. Now."

"Candy will tell us soon enough," I said, disengaging. There was no point. What was I going to do, threaten her again with the bus station at Salt Lake City? It was getting so old.

"Could we go anymore out of our way?" she barked.

"I don't think so."

"We put ourselves at risk every second. And now we've got Russians in the car! Tell me, will we be safer with them?"

"I think so." I smiled. "Russians are badasses."

Gina growled in anger.

"Would it make you happy if I asked who they were and what they were doing in my car?"

"Happy? No!"

"So why should I ask, then?"

They came back, carrying their hot coffees and milks, bagels and egg sandwiches, foiled squares, and potato chips. For people who weren't hungry, they sure were carrying a lot of food. Half of it spilled out as they were getting in.

After they were finally settled, I turned around in my seat to face them. The woman was a better bleached blonde than me or Candy, in her late forties, with heavy eye makeup and red lipstick. Her beige business clothes were tight, and her skirt too short for a grown woman. Her slight son was gray and wiggly. He had sallow

415

teenage skin as if he didn't go outside, and unwashed pin-thin black hair. Lena smiled at me. I gave her a perfunctory smile back. My eyes were on Candy, who had obviously been shopping because she was wearing a new pink halter, so thin it was see-through, and a white mini-skirt. Every time she moved, I could see her skimpy white underwear. She was holding five things in her hands, trying to figure out where to put the coffee while she ate her egg sandwich. I waited. I raised my eyebrows.

"Candy?" I said inquisitively.

"Yes, Shel? Yuri, can you please hold this for me?" Yuri reluctantly helped her.

"Candy." With my eyes, I gestured to Lena and Yuri.

"Oh, them," she said. "Remember last night I told you about the bartender I met? Well, that's Lena."

"Okay. And where is Lena going?"

"To Reno. I figure we were going anyway. I said we could give her a ride. I told her you wouldn't mind."

"Mind? Nooo."

"I can drive," said Lena in a heavy accent. "I learned in Moscow. I have my international license."

"No, that's okay. But thank you." I envisioned trying to stuff Gina back there with the mess of them.

"What's the suitcase for?" I asked.

"We're not coming back."

"No?" I said it so casual.

Lena shook her head. "I don't make too many mistakes in my life. But Salt Lake City is biggest mistake I ever made. Until I met this nice person, I didn't think anything else was possible. And your friend just said, let's go. Pack your stuff, tell them you're quitting, and let's go." She sat up straighter in the seat. "I work only one night per week at bar. My full-time job is at Nordstrom. I sell shoes. Do you think they have Nordstrom in Reno?"

"I really don't know," I replied evenly. "I've never been to Reno."

Lena told me my car was nice. Gina snorted. I said thank you. Candy said, "Nice—but noticeable."

"You want them to notice you, no? Three pretty girls in car like this. You must get so much attention."

"A little less attention would do us all some good," said Candy.

Yuri said nothing. He was squished, eating his bagel, turned sharply to the little window.

"Candy told me she was thinking of moving to Salt Lake," Lena said. "That's how we got to talking. I said not if you want to survive. Not if you want to live. If you want your soul to live, you can't come here."

"And I said," said Candy, "that I wanted my soul to live."

"Do you like it here?" I asked Yuri. Gina wasn't speaking.

He shrugged. "The Mormons are weird."

His mother put her arm around him.

"Weird how?"

"I dunno. Like there's nothing inside."

"That's because there *is* nothing inside," said his mother.

"Ma, I know how you feel about it, okay?" The boy tried to move out from under her arm.

Lena told us she came from Seattle to Salt Lake two years ago. "Seattle we lived for eight years. Seattle was beautiful. But the weather was terrible. Like Russia."

"In every place there's something," Candy said. "Never going to be perfect." Huffing, Gina turned to her window.

"I take rain every day rest of my life," said Lena, "than sunshine in Salt Lake."

"I told you, Sloane," said Candy, her mouth full. "You were so gung-ho on this town, but I told you."

"Candy, you tell me something's wrong with every place we've been to."

"Jackson took me a while to figure out."

"And what was wrong with Riverton?" suddenly snapped Gina. "What was wrong with Hell's Half-Acre? Wright? Rapid City?"

"You forgot Interior," Candy said.

417

"I know what was wrong with Interior," said Gina, the memory of its desolate loneliness and Floyd's heroin-soaked guilt stamped in my own eyes, too.

"There is nothing wrong with Broken Hill," said Candy in her rolling, lilting voice. "That's the one place that's perfect."

2

Open Range

The car was covered with bug juice, the windshield, the wipers, the doors, the grill, the hubcaps. The car was filthy dirty, inside and out. I wished for a carwash. As if by magic, it appeared near our entrance to the Interstate. By the time we, in a spotless and shiny yellow car, got onto I-80, it was after three.

"It's ridiculous, is what it is," I said.

"I'm surprised you don't like it here, Lena," Gina said. "It's so pretty. Wasn't Temple Square nice, Shelby?"

"The flowers were." I didn't mention that we weren't allowed inside a church. I glanced in the rearview mirror.

"So how come we can't go inside their church?" Gina asked.

The Russian bartender and shoe saleslady said, "They don't tell you why. They tell you to convert, become a Mormon and then they let you in."

"How come there are no crosses anywhere?" I asked. We were driving through miles of salt flats that looked like snow all the way to the distant foothills.

"I don't think they believe in Jesus," said Lena. "Right, son?"

"I don't know, Mom." Yuri was trying to stay out of it.

"Really?"

"Really," Lena confirmed. "The Mormons don't believe in or

celebrate Christmas, Easter, or the Feast days. They don't believe in the saints, or in baptism. They don't believe Christ was divine. They place Jesus on the same plane as John Smith and worship the latter slightly more."

"And their star is inverted," said Candy.

"That too."

"I bet the Mormons see nothing wrong with that. And," said Gina, as always finding provocation with Candy, "I think the Mormons would be pretty upset, Candy, to hear you call them not Christian."

"What I call or not call them doesn't change things, like that Great Divide sign. Whether the sign is there or not doesn't change the essential truth of—Shelby, off the Interstate!" Candy said suddenly.

"Off and go where?"

"I don't know. Just get off."

"No, no, don't get off," said Gina. "We're in the Great Basin. It's quite remarkable here in the playas and the salt lakes. Don't get off."

"Sloane, go!" demanded Candy, as if Gina had not spoken—certainly as if she had not spoken to Candy's best interest. Great Basin? Playas? But I had other concerns about leaving the Interstate.

"There's only one road to Reno from Salt Lake," I said. "Your Mormon friend Justin told me."

"That can't be true. Off."

"It's true. Just north is Idaho. You don't want to go to Idaho again, do you?"

"We'll go south."

"South? To the Grand Canyon?"

"Sloane, just—get off. We're almost where we need to be. Don't blow it now."

"We're almost broke is what we are," I said, getting off on U.S. 93 and heading south. It was only a seeming non-sequitur. A straight road meant I needed less gas, there would be less meandering, less meandering on the leeward sides of mountain passes,

420

less wildlife, less risk, and Reno was just one long drive away. Gina was angrily studying the map, telling me we were in the middle of an empty and vast Steptoe Valley.

"I got money," Lena said suddenly. "I don't have much, but I saved some, hoping I'd get out of that place one day. And you guys are helping me out big time. I'll be glad to contribute. I'll pay for your hotel, your food. Whatever you need."

Ashamed of complaining in front of a single mother, now unemployed, with a kid, I shook my head, but before I could speak, Gina said, "Thanks, that *will* be a big help."

After rummaging in her purse, Lena handed Gina a hundred-dollar bill. "I'll give you more if you need it." Gina felt better.

We rode alone through the Steptoe Valley, a Great Basin land with the Nevada Egan foothills in every direction. I thought Wyoming was desolate. Here, not even man-made cattle fences flanked the road to proclaim man's presence and to keep the wildlife from wandering out. Just two signs in a hundred miles with the following words: "OPEN RANGE."

No rich Iowan farms, no Nebraskan broken barns, no Lakota Chapels where all were welcome, no Interior with trailers and a neon bar, no llamas lazing by sheds, or fences keeping the buffalo in and out. No ski towns. No scenic turnouts. No electricity. Nothing. Two signs forty miles apart. OPEN RANGE.

That, and the road itself. A clean, smooth road with yellow double lines and an emergency shoulder to tell me civilization came here through the valley and paved me a gliding path so I could fly on my yellow bird and sing, there is no civilization, there is no civilization.

At the junction of 93 and 50 lies a town called Ely. Signs for that town started coming up thirty to forty miles ahead. Billboards announced that the Ely McDonald's had a great parking lot, and the Burger King had one of the best play areas in the state. And every mile or so, a big colorful billboard declared that you hadn't been to Ely unless you visited the "biker friendly!" Hotel Nevada for some "Western Hospitality!" And for the businessmen passing

421

through this part of the country, they could relieve their troubles and their stresses by visiting the VIP Spa, "with Truck Parking!" This was sung to me by a repeating silhouette of a voluptuous naked woman, like an X-rated chorus.

"Maybe Ely is the town for you, Candy," commented Gina dryly.

"Could be."

"No, no," said Lena. "Ely? I thought you were headed to California?"

"I am," Candy replied. "But not permanently. I'm looking for a permanent place."

"Stay in California," urged Lena, with a big red-lipped smile. She must have reapplied after the bacon sandwich. "Why would you want to leave? It's warm. It's beautiful. It's got a little of everything, not too much of anything. California is endowed with gifts."

We three didn't speak.

After a while Candy said, "Town I'm going to is terrible. The pits."

"Trust me," said Lena, "California is paradise."

In the narrow mirror, I saw Candy cringe.

"Let me tell you what's wrong with the people in Salt Lake," said Lena. "Last year I had some health problems. Just female things. And I was friendly with my boss at Nordstrom. She was—is—nice lady. I asked her if there was anything Nordstrom could do to help me out. Perhaps small loan, maybe raise, better insurance policy? You know, whenever money is involved, you can gauge many things about people. Their true hearts come out. So hers did. She refused to help me, said Nordstrom couldn't help me either, no loans, no raises, and when she saw my face, she patted me and said, 'Why don't you convert to Mormonism? They are very generous with members of their church. And they have plenty of money.'"

Candy shook her head. I withheld judgment. Gina said, "Sound advice. Why didn't you?"

"Why didn't I? Are you joking?"

"No, I'm serious. To help yourself, to pay for your medical bills? It's a no-brainer."

422

"I said to my boss," Lena continued, as if not addressing Gina, yet addressing only Gina, "why would I prostitute everything I believe in and turn my back on my faith for few pieces of silver? I'm Russian Orthodox. I'm going to become Mormon so they can give me money? There is a word for someone like that."

We didn't say anything. Gina spoke first. "But what if your faith isn't that important to you? What if you have no faith?"

"Then you're not giving anything up. It's like my Catholic friend who converted to Judaism because her boyfriend wouldn't marry her as Catholic. I said to myself, how serious a Catholic could she have been?"

"Maybe she was a bad Catholic. A bad Christian."

"We're all bad Christians," said Lena. "We should be better. But better Christians."

"But the Mormons call themselves Christian," said Gina.

Candy stayed out of it, smiling at me through the rearview. Lena was the only one in the ring with Gina.

"Yes," Lena agreed. "But they don't believe any of the dozen things you need to believe in order to *be* Christian."

"Well, they don't have to believe in every single thing—"

"They don't believe in a hundred things!"

"Just because they don't agree with *you*—"

"Oh, no. This isn't about me. This is about them. And all things they don't believe in."

"They're just different from you," said Gina. "Everybody's got their own opinion."

"Opinion is not religion, girl. Opinion is not Christianity. And you know what, Mormonism is not opinion. Judaism is not opinion. Religion is not opinion. Religion is religion. Opinion is opinion. Religion is not gambling either. Or Lake Tahoe. Or State of Nevada."

"I don't know what you're yelling about," said Gina. "Shelby, Candy, do you know what your new companion is yelling about?"

"Mom, honest, calm down," said Yuri.

"I'm not yelling," said Lena in a calm clear voice, as Candy

423

stared at her amused. We passed another sign for the Ely VIP Spa. DON'T DRIVE BY WITHOUT STOPPING BY! "If it's all the same, Mormons and Christians, then why didn't they just give me money without converting? They're Christian, you say? Well, I'm also Christian. We're all Christian. Why not give me money?"

"No one does that. The Catholics don't do that."

"Exactly. Because there must be some difference."

"Small difference."

"Is it small, Candy?" Lena asked.

"Um, no," said Candy. "*As man is, God once was. As God is, man may become.*" She shook her head. "That's not us."

"Exactly!" Lena smiled at Candy approvingly. "The Mormons don't believe the Trinity is three separate gods. Forget Christ, heck, they don't even believe in the divinity of God! They think God was once flesh and blood, had sexual relations with his goddess, and on another planet, they had children, one of whom was Jesus, and one of whom was Adam. And one of whom was Lucifer. So, Jesus and Lucifer were brothers! Adam was a god, and God was a god, and Jesus was a god, and all the good Mormons will eventually become gods, too. They pretend not to believe in polygamy, but they hold sacred, *sacred*, a man who had twenty-seven wives, and were founded in Utah by a man who had fifty wives, and fifty-seven children! Oh, and the cross is non-existent in their worship. There is no resurrection in Mormonism."

"Yes, but it's *their* Christianity," Gina insisted, stubbornly. "Just because *you* don't agree . . ."

"All right," interrupted Lena. "But then why can't *I* be a Mormon? They call themselves Christian, yet they don't believe basic tenets of our faith. I don't believe basis tenets of Mormon faith. Why can't I be Mormon?"

"I don't know why. Maybe you can."

Ely was ten miles away. Gina stopped speaking. I asked, "But what about salvation? Without resurrection, how are you saved?" HOTEL NEVADA: BIG MISTAKE IF YOU DON'T STAY WITH US!

"Salvation?" asked Lena. "In our faith, it's gift from God. Like this. Here. I love you. There you go. Now be good. But Brigham Young said that salvation comes to man only by professed belief in Joseph Smith. The false belief that salvation comes from Christ rising from dead was a lie spread by Satan to damn the world." Lena laughed. "Those are not *my* words. They're Brigham Young's."

Ely was calling. LIVE GAMING! PENNY SLOTS!

"But in the New Testament," said Candy, "Jesus said that the belief he was *not* divine was spread by Satan to damn the world."

"Oh, Jesus!" exclaimed Gina. "Same effing difference!"

HOTEL NEVADA: HOT PIZZA AVAILABLE 24 HRS!

Yuri cringed. "Mom, please! Look what you started *again*." He tried to stifle her apologetically. "You'll have to excuse my mother," he said. "There is *nothing* she likes to talk about more."

"Coming here has ruined our life, son," Lena said. "And you know it."

"All right, Mom, stop it already. What do these girls care? They're going to throw us out of their car."

Candy said no. I said no. Gina pointedly said *nothing*. "Same damn stupid idiotic difference," she muttered, hitting the hot window with her fist.

Ely sparkled in the sun. There was a park and a school, and indeed the parking lot in McDonald's did look quite parkable, and the playground in Burger King was, as promised, large. Hotel Nevada was out of the nineteenth century, and in front of it on a bench sat a toothless man, who looked as old as the hotel. He sat in his dirty denim overalls and no other clothes, with his legs stretched out, a cigar in his mouth, looking up and down the street. Behind him was a sign that cheerfully invited you in: "WESTERN UNION— INSIDE!" Figuring you were going to need it. Next to the old guy was a slot machine on which a young man in a sharp suit was pulling the lever. The old man waved to us, gumming a smile, the suit didn't turn around, sticking his hand into his pants pocket for more quarters.

"That looks like a nice place to work," said Candy. "I could be a waitress. I could deliver drinks."

"I'll teach you," said Lena excitedly. "We both get jobs."

"Mom, we're not living in Ely," said Yuri.

"Why, son? It looks like nice town."

"Have you looked at a map, Mom? Two hundred miles north, south, east and west, there is nothing."

"We don't need anything."

"How is Dad ever to come and visit?"

The mother scoffed. "The same way he came and visited in Salt Lake. Never."

"At least he *could*. He could if he wanted to. What's in Ely?"

"It has a nice spa," offered Candy. "For the tired businessmen."

We all giggled. I looked for a gas station. Gina wanted something to drink. "How many miles to Reno?"

"I dunno," I said. "Check the map. Three hundred?"

"Get out! It can't be. It's impossible."

We pulled into a parking lot, not McDonald's, but still comfortable, and sprung open the map. Lena took her son to the bathroom. As soon as they were gone, Gina, forgetting about the map, spun to Candy. "I don't like her," she said. "I don't like her, I don't like her tone, or her ways. I don't want her in our car. You are *so* inconsiderate. You didn't even ask how we would feel taking a stranger with us. You got no respect for us. It's Shelby's car, and you didn't even ask before you invited them in."

"I knew Sloane wouldn't mind."

"She does mind! She minds greatly. She is sick and tired, too!"

"Gina." That was me.

"You're taking advantage of her," Gina continued breathlessly, sticking her finger in Candy's face. "You're using her, knowing she can't say no, doesn't know how to, and you, knowing that, are abusing her every chance you get!"

"I can, too, say no," I meekly protested. Gina and Candy weren't listening.

"Sloane doesn't mind," Candy repeated.

"I can't wait to get to Reno," Gina said through gritted teeth. "You hear me? I. Can. Not. Wait. We're dropping you off and taking off. I'm not even staying overnight. Whatever time we get there, we're barely even slowing down, you're out, your new little friend is out, and we're gone."

"Okay, let's be reasonable. We're going to get there late . . ." That was me.

"I don't know what you're talking about," said Candy. "I'm stopping at Reno. I'm not *staying* in Reno. Jess there owes me a bit of change. And Jess has a car. But that's it."

"What you do after you leave *this* car is your fucking problem."

"Gina . . ." That was me again. When did I become so mealymouthed, so milquetoast? I'd prefer if they just didn't talk to each other. Where did my allegiance lie? Who did I side with? I didn't want trouble. That was me, I'd prefer things a little quieter, with less money dripping through my fingers, less angst, less Erv (God! Much less), less dog and hitchhiking mothers, and bars in tumbleweed towns. That's how I preferred my life, was that so wrong? Yet in front of me stood my lifelong friend, and the green-streaked, bleached-blonde waif with no bra.

Lena and Yuri returned from the bathroom. "Why are you all standing outside?" the woman asked. "It's a hundred and twenty degrees. Let's get in."

The air-conditioning system in the car was not strong enough to cool the small space with the outside temperature that high and the heat of five hostile people inside.

"No one wants a bite to eat?" I asked. "Burger King has a large play area."

"No," snarled Gina. "Let's get going. How many miles really to Reno?"

Turned out I was wrong; It wasn't 300. It was 369. Gina got even more sore. It was after six in the evening, though you couldn't tell from the sun, which burned so hot in the sky over Ely, you'd have thought it was equatorial noon.

427

3

The Loneliest Road in America

No one spoke for a hundred miles. We took a sharp right on U.S. 50—and kept going. It was just us—five of us, alone in the car. No one else on the road, except for the two birds that crashed into the windshield, one inadvertent, but one clearly suicidal, since it was high up and flew down to fling itself unto death. The mountains were spooky large, so too the distances between them and the sky.

The road in the flats between the mountains stretched out like a pencil line, was a hallucination. Occasionally it wound like string through the sunlit hills. I couldn't help it, despite everything that had happened, I was still thinking, God, how beautiful. How amazing. I can't believe I'm seeing this. I can't believe I'm living this. Nevada. Who would've thunk it was like this? Not Justin, the skeptical Mormon by the revolving doors. God. It's unbelievable.

Candy said, "Gina, did you know that Jean-Paul Sartre had to struggle with being an atheist all his life?"

"And this segued from what?" Gina asked. "From Nebraska? Never a good time to let it go, huh?"

"Well, not here," said Candy. "Anyway, often he would catch himself thanking God for a beautiful day, or for stunning views like these. He said it was a lifelong struggle to remain an atheist, because the whole world seemed to be made 'as if' there were a God."

"Not much struggle for me. Why can't you all just look at a mountain, or a leaf without attributing some larger meaning to it? Why can't it be just a mountain? Why does it have to mean something?"

I watched Lena put her arm around her son, and he didn't move away from her. She fixed the black greasy hair that fell into his eyes, and he let her, while mumbling, stop it, okay. She kissed his cheek, and he let her, then I caught Candy staring at me with a "*you see?*" expression.

"That's what you did for me, Sloane," Candy said quietly.

What did I do for you? I thought, saying nothing, catching Gina's closed face. I could've let her catch a bus. I could've done *that* for her. Gina, too.

"Guys, come on, what about Ely?" asked Candy. "I see *nothing* wrong with Ely."

"Girl, why would you want to live in Ely?" said Lena. "You're too young. You have to finish high school first."

So Lena didn't know. Candy didn't tell her.

"You have your whole life in front of you," Lena continued, the lines in her face deepening. Where was Yuri's father? Why was she still alone? She was fairly attractive. Perhaps it was the Mormons. Perhaps she couldn't find a match among them, and it made her bitter. Maybe it would make me bitter, too, if I were old like thirty-five or something, with a child, living in Salt Lake. "You know what I was thinking of doing?" she said. "If Reno doesn't have Nordstrom, I was thinking of taking class, learning how to be casino dealer. That'd be something, don't you think?"

"It would be," said Candy. "They tip you good. You'll have nice customers. And you'll meet new people. You dress up nice, put on your face, earrings. Men with money will come to your table. You'll be able to get a nice apartment, support your child." She smiled at Lena, while winking at me in the rearview. "It's a really good idea, right, Sloane?" That's how she and I communicated. By deciphering the meanings behind our glances in a two-inch by seven-inch reflective strip.

The loneliest road in America must have been misspelled. It wasn't the loneliest. It was the longest. There were only two towns from Ely to Reno, Eureka, pop. 640, and Austin, pop. 320, a Pony Express town, and as we blew through it, a handwritten poster stuck into the side of the road warned, "CAREFUL! SPEEDTRAP AHEAD." So I slowed down, from ninety to fifty, and sure enough the copper was sitting by the side of the deserted road. Not a thing was open in town, not a store, not a gas station, not a drinks place. There were no other cars, yet the trooper was sitting, trying to catch speeders like me.

"How long to Reno?"

It was interminable. We'd gone less than a hundred miles. Still over two hundred and fifty to go. Gina groaned and moaned, crumpling the map, curling into a corner and whining. Candy sat composed and cramped in the back. Yuri had fallen asleep. Lena was too tense to feel bored; she had her whole life to plan. Candy, too. But Lena was chewing her lips and cuticles.

The sun set in the mountains out of Austin, right in front of us, melting the cement on our distant road. It set so directly in front of my eyes, unfiltered by a tree or a bush, water or a moun-tain, that I had to stop driving, because I was blinded and couldn't see.

"Why are you stopping?" said Gina.

"Because I can't see." We rolled down the windows, we oohed and aahed.

Only Gina remained in her stone-like masquerade. "It's the sun," she said. "You're acting like you've never seen the sun before. Oh no! It's setting, look! That's incredible—a sunset. You mean the sun also sets in Nevada? Who'd have thought it? Wow. Is it ever gonna do that again? Because I sure want to be here for it if it happens."

"Nice, Gina."

430

Eventually night fell down around us on the road. There were no towns, no fences, no neighbors, no cars, and no lights. There was nothing.

"Don't break down, Sloane," said Candy. "God Himself couldn't find us here."

"Why not?" Gina grunted. "There's nothing but us for miles around. How could he miss us? We're the only things breathing. A blind man could find us here."

We entered Fallon around ten in the evening, then rode an hour or more through the black hills, down the dark mountainside to Reno, nested in the valley.

Lights! Electricity! Civilization! The first sign we saw coming in off the road was a billboard for RenoforJesus. "Lost?" the billboard asked. I blew by too fast to read the rest.

TWELVE

RENOFORJESUS

1

Lost

There is absolutely nothing in life that Reno can't make cheaper.

We arrived so late; perhaps we should have come during the day, but at night, the lights were sparkling and after 500 miles of driving through land no soul has been through except to pave the road, I became distracted, lulled into benevolence. Everything was looking good to me, even the shiny casinos. We passed a place called "Adventure Inn." It advertised "Exotic theme rooms." I wanted to see them. I thought it'd be fun. Stinger Good Times Bar and Grill had pink neon lights flashing and I said, "Look, Gina, wouldn't that be fun, so fun, right?" But then in front of Circus, Circus, two down and out guys were sitting waiting for the (very) late bus, both gray and stringy, caps on backward. They looked so broke, like the last quarter they had went on the poker machine on the street right behind them, and waiting for the bus was a futile pastime. Past them was the Wild Orchid Club, "with new girls every night."

"Where'd they get new girls from, and every night, too?" I mused out loud. No one was playing.

Jess, a friend of Candy's, ran a local motel, and had told her she'd let Candy stay there, so that's where we headed. "What's the name of the place we're looking for?" I asked.

"Motel."

"No, I know. What's the name of it?"

"Motel."

I couldn't see her in the rearview mirror. "Are you being difficult?"

"Motel! That's the name of it. That's what it's called. Motel."

We drove up and down the strip twice, looking. We couldn't find it. It was all Pines Motel, and Reno Motel, and Gordon's Motel, and Sunshine Motel. A dozen places, all with motel in the moniker. How would you go about finding the one with just *motel*?

I was so hungry, all I kept seeing was restaurants. "Look," I said. "Heidi's Family Restaurant. Pancakes, steaks, omelettes. Maybe we should get a bite before we continue?"

Lena thought that was a good idea. "The boy is hungry."

For the boy we stopped. I had to go to the bathroom; we all did. We pulled into Heidi's, parked the car, and ran inside. The boy went to the boys' room. All the girls piled in to the girls'. While we were washing our hands, Lena said, "Shelby, I need to run to the car for a sec. I forgot my purse."

"Car's locked," I said. "I'll come with you." I went out with her. She dropped her cigarettes and all her change in the dark, in the parking lot. I should have helped her, I felt bad, but I really wanted to go inside and order.

"Look," I said, "you don't mind, do you, I'm just going to run in, okay? When you're done, press down the lock and meet us inside?"

"Okay," she said, without looking up; she was bent over the passenger side footwell. "Could you order me a hot tea with lemon, please? And something for Yuri. Whatever he wants. Milk. I'll be right there. I just need to—Oh God! Sorry . . ."

But I was already inside. We all piled into a long booth, the three of us squeezed on one side, in a row like soldiers, leaving the seat across from us for Lena and Yuri. The waitress came, a bloated chick named Daisy. We ordered coffee, Cokes, tea for Lena. "What do you think Yuri wants?" I asked.

"I don't know," said Candy. "Chocolate milk? Apple juice? He's been in the bathroom a long time."

436

"He was saving it up. Like a camel." We chuckled, so relieved to be sitting down, nearly eating, and in Reno.

The waitress brought the drinks. "You gals ready to order?"

Tilting my head to see around her, I couldn't quite see the front door. "Well, we're waiting for . . ."

"Let's just order," said Gina. "They'll order when they come." The waitress agreed; we ordered soup, steaks and pancakes and French fries, a burger deluxe and a BLT. Daisy took our menus ("Wait, leave two!") and left. She brought bread and soup, which we devoured.

Fifteen, twenty minutes had passed.

"What the hell?" said Gina, glancing behind us. "Seriously, maybe something's wrong with the boy?"

"Well, how would we know? You want to go to the men's room?"

"You go."

"*I'll* go," said Candy.

"Really?" Gina and I giggled. "Be our guest."

When Candy came back, she stood at the head of the table. "Sloane, where did you say Lena—"

I must have spilled my drink, gasping, "Move!" shoving Gina so hard that she nearly fell out and onto the floor, as I jumped from my claustrophobic seat and ran through the restaurant into the night. The car was there. But Lena was not. I ran back inside and opened the door to the men's room. "Yuri?" I called. There was no answer. "Yuri?" I peered in the three stalls. They were empty. Candy was outside in the parking lot. She was standing near my car.

"I don't understand," I said, panting. "What happened to them?"

"Looks like they took off," Candy said, emptiness in her voice the size of Montana. "Unlock the door."

"Took off? Why? Where?" Her face was hollow, as she got out her Mary Poppins bag. "Took off in what? They have no car. Where could they have gone?"

"I don't know." She dropped her hobo bag back on the seat. "Caught a bus? Slipped into one of the casinos? Went to the train depot? I don't know." She wouldn't lift her head.

"Why would they leave like that?" I stuttered. "I don't get it. Did they take their suitcase?"

"I reckon they did. Open the trunk." Still not looking at me. She slammed the car door.

Then it dawned on me. "Candy," I whispered. "Oh, no, Candy."

I popped the trunk. Lena's suitcase was gone. I was afraid to look in my suitcase, afraid to look in Gina's. Candy looked for me.

"It's gone, Sloane." She groaned.

"What's gone?" I said inaudibly. I couldn't comprehend it.

"Our money. Yours. Mine. Gina's. She took it and vanished."

"What? How much?"

"All of it."

"What do you mean, *all* of it?"

"I mean, all of it. All my money, and yours. I'm assuming Gina's too. She kept it in the side pocket of her duffel? It's gone."

"Maybe she has another stash somewhere. I have a secret hundred bucks in my makeup bag."

"They took it, Sloane," said Candy.

"They took my *makeup* money?" I started to shake. I didn't believe her. I checked for myself.

Then I believed.

Gina found us in the parking lot, Candy standing over me, sitting on the curb, crying.

It was 11:15 at night, and all the Reno lights were on, like it was daylight in the desert. It had taken us 577 miles to get here from Salt Lake. I clocked it on my odometer. In the distance I could see the arc, like Triomphe, proclaiming, "Reno—the Biggest Little Town in the World." The traffic on Virginia Street was nearly at a standstill. It was dry hot, about eighty. The dirty hubcap of my driver tire was near my flip-flop. Maybe if I cried enough I could wash it off. For a moment I saw myself outside my own body, looking in, seeing me, helpless on the curb, Candy standing sheepish and guilty, and Gina, taking some time, like me, to understand what

438

was happening, what had happened. That woman and her son took every last cent of our money. We gave her a ride, and she robbed us. It took a while to sink in; that kind of thing wasn't easy.

At last, the cold reality of the night dawned on Gina. Conversely, as she became enraged, I stopped crying. I wiped my face. She was shouting at Candy, menacing her in the parking lot with wild gestures. "What have you done! You have brought nothing, *nothing* but trouble into my life! God, wake me up from this nightmare! Maybe it's all a mistake. Maybe we put it in a different place. Maybe we forgot where we put it. Oh my God, what have you done to us!"

She searched the car, front to back, top to bottom, back again, and once more. On the fifth time, I helped her.

Candy stood nearby and all I could hear from her was, *O Lord my God, I cry out in the night before thee, let my prayer come before thee, incline thine ear to my cry. Lord, hear my prayer . . .*"

Daisy the waitress stuck her head out the glass doors. "Hey, gals," she called, "anytime now. Your food's getting cold."

Gina and I, both groping through the car, stopped. "How much's the check?"

"How much is the *check?*" Daisy repeated slowly, looking in her apron pocket. "Thirty bucks. What, too much?"

We stared at each other. Then we straightened up and glared at Candy. "You got thirty bucks in your pocket, Cand?" I asked coldly.

"I have twelve. And don't give *me* your attitude. It's hard enough. I have enough to pay for what we ate."

"I have seven," I said, a notch milder.

"I have eight," said Gina, "but I'll be damned before I spend the last money I have in the world on you."

"Not on me," said Candy. "On food. For you."

"Shut up. I'm not speaking to you. You don't exist anymore. La-la-la."

"Gina, all right, you know what? I know you're . . ."

"You have no idea what I am." She was head in the trunk, searching.

"I know how you feel, because I feel it, too! But we need to stick together. We have no money. We have nothing." My eyes were swollen from crying, from salt. "Can't bail on us now, Gina."

"Watch me."

"Well, what are you going to do? Where are you going to go on your eight dollars?"

"Don't you worry your little heads about me," Gina said, "I'll be better off anywhere than with you. God, do you regret it now?" she said to me. "Every single bit of it, every stupid decision you ever made, you regret it now?"

I didn't answer. I locked up my car, locked that barn after the Russian horse had bolted, even though the car had nothing in it except my Maybelline mascara thrown in the glove compartment. We went back inside. "Daisy, listen," I said to the waitress. "We don't know what to do. That woman and her son, they just robbed us, and took all our money."

"What woman and her son?" She shrugged and gestured for me to stay quiet. "Do I look to you like I give a shit?" she said. "What am I, a genie? Here to fix all your problems? I got plenty of my own, missy. I'm trying to get custody of my kids while their dad is God knows where. All I need you to do is not be my shrink, just pay the bill."

"Am I boring you?" I said.

"You're not boring me, I just don't care. I gotta pay the rent, too."

"Well, we can't pay your rent," I said. "We have seven dollars to pay for our Cokes."

"What about the soup?"

"Give me a break," I said quietly. "You're ready to close, you scraped that clam chowder from the bottom of a burnt pot. Help us a little bit. Let it go."

"You know how often I hear your little likely sob story?" Daisy said, harshly. "About twice a day, honeybunch. You're in *Reno*. The things I hear would make God lose faith in man, would make Jesus drink whiskey straight from the dog bowl. I've heard it all. Your tale? About five times a week. I was robbed. Someone took my money. I looked and it was gone. I don't know what happened to it."

"Well, I hate to be so commonplace." I glanced over to Candy, standing at one corner of the booth, and Gina at the other, both eyeing their cold food. "Still, though. We ordered the food when we thought we had cash, and now we have none."

Daisy rolled her eyes and snorted; she shook her big frame, even her jiggly triceps shook. "What are you going to do now?" she asked. "Call the police? Oh, officer, they robbed me, and then they went and disappeared with all my money, and we got nothin', can you help us? You gonna file a report? That'll work. You go on and do that now. Because the police, they never heard that one in Reno."

"But it's the truth. That's what happened."

She lowered her voice. "So the fuck what? Who gives a shit? What's the police gonna do? Your money walked, baby, and you go ahead and spend the next four hours at a precinct, getting poked and interrogated. Four hours and a quarter won't even get you a ride back to your hotel."

I stepped away from her. I was sorry Gina and Candy were close enough to hear. "Just what I need," I said. "Down on her luck waitress dispensing advice while the ex-con cooks the short order."

"Just what *I* need," said Daisy. "Sass from a no-pay. Go on," she said. "Go finish your food, pay me what you have, and get the hell on out of here. I love to work for free, you know. I don't need to pay my nut, or feed my kids. You just go ahead and eat."

"Take our few bucks," said Candy, coming over. "Stiff him on the check."

"Do you even *see* the guy at the grill? You want to mess with him? Have me lose my job? I'll have your twenty bucks, whoop-de-doo, and then what?"

Candy lowered her voice. "I won't stiff you," she said. "Tomorrow I'll come back and pay the bill. I promise."

Daisy pointed to her face. "Yes, and I have sucker stamped on my forehead. Just eat, go, and stop botherin' me."

We sat down to our soggy onion rings, bread moist with mayo, wilted lettuce. "How much did she take?" I asked weakly. "She took about $600 from me." How in the world did I think I'd get back home on $600? Oh, would to have those problems now—how to pinch pennies on 600 bucks.

"She took about $300 from me," said Gina. "Maybe $350. Last time I counted before Salt Lake, that's what I had."

"She took Floyd's $1000 from me," said Candy.

Gina and I both emitted a groan of compassion. We remembered too well what it took to get that money.

"I'd take an atheist over this kind of Christian any day," said Gina, her hands in a knot, her mouth so tight she couldn't chew properly, and kept choking and coughing. "I'd take a Mormon, a Muslim . . ."

"A Mennonite," I finished in agreement.

"Anything!"

"What does this have to do with being a Christian?" asked Candy. "Why do you always keep harping on that? What do you think, she read the Gospel of St. Matthew and said, I know what I'm going to do, I'm going to rob three girls who are helping me out, because that's what the good Lord would have me do?"

"I really don't know, Candy," said Gina. "*You're* the one with all the answers."

"I guarantee you, this broad was not thinking about Jesus as she was stealing money from my bag."

"I'm beginning to understand," said Gina, "why the Romans fed the Christians to the lions. They were losing their empire through embezzlement. They needed to do something to save themselves."

"Didn't do such a good job saving themselves," retorted Candy. "Despite the lion feedings."

"Stop it," I said. "Those two must have planned it well ahead. Maybe back in Ely. Where else? They were always with us otherwise. The kid was told to go to the bathroom and stay there. Mother pulled a little wool over my eyes. Dropped her purse,

442

rooted around. When her son came out of the bathroom, he went outside, and they disappeared. Must have caught a cab right away. They worked this out good."

"We got to talking about faith at the bar," Candy said, "and she heard the thing in my voice, the thing that told her I would help her. She knew I'd be easy." The cold fry fell out of her hands.

"Candy," I said, "they could've planned this thing back in Salt Lake. When they knew they'd be coming with us."

"No, don't say that." Candy put her head in her hands. The blonde of it bobbed up and down. I wanted to comfort her, but who was going to comfort me?

"Maybe the cops will catch them," said Gina, putting her own head down. We were defeated; felt it, and looked it. "I don't care what the fat waitress thinks. Let's call them, Shel. File a report."

"They took cash, not Traveler's checks," said Candy, looking up at us. "The cops are going to have to catch them in another state. Because I'm sure they took our money and split good and proper. Caught a cab, went to the bus depot, are probably halfway to Seattle by now."

"So the police will catch them in Seattle," said Gina.

"And in Seattle, that Russian slag will say, what money, officer? I ain't got a penny. I'm a single mother with a small frail child and I'm broke. Dear God, I'd never take from young girls, what do you take me for?"

I shook my head. "I think they went back to Salt Lake. I bet you they were Mormons."

Candy disagreed. "When I met her, she was serving drinks wearing a cross. In Salt Lake. She didn't know a loser like me was coming. You don't wear a cross in Salt Lake unless you're not one of them."

"Well, for all the things she said about the Mormons—*they* didn't rob us."

"No." Candy took one last mealy bite of her burger. "She didn't rob us because she was a Christian, Gina. She robbed us because she was a bad woman."

443

"So you say. I thought your Christ was supposed to make bad people good?"

Candy almost laughed. "How little you understand," she said, taking her few dollars out. "Let's go. Let's find Jess at least."

We pooled our pennies together, counting out the quarters in the pockets of my jeans. We were young girls, we didn't carry purses. We had no wallets. We carried the combs to brush our hair in the back of our short denim shorts, and the dollar bills stuffed in our front pockets, with the peach lipgloss, in case we needed to touch up. We had no need for purses; we carried nothing; we lived as if we were still fifteen, about to go rollerblading and flirt with the boys.

After turning out our pockets, we scraped together $22.71. We left it on the table, casting an apologetic glance at Daisy. She just rolled her eyes and waved us off.

In the car, Gina said, "How much gas do we have?"

The tank was empty. Empty, empty, empty.

"Unbefuckinglievable," Gina exclaimed, as we pulled out and made a left on Virginia. One way or another we had to find this "Motel" or we'd be out of gas and sleeping in the car. We made a left under the neon sign for "Penthouse Dancers" behind a billboard that said, "Jesus: Acts 4:12."

Acts 4:12?

We were stopped at a light to allow ample time for perusal. Acts 4:12 and the Penthouse Dancers.

"Like a riddle," said Gina.

"Only for those who don't know," said Candy.

"Oh, like you know."

"Check out Gideon's Bible when we get to Motel, see for yourself."

"That would presuppose finding Motel. Which, as you well know, is not a given. So what does it mean, Miss Smarty Pants?" Gina appeared milder. Her stomach was fuller.

"*There is no other name under heaven, given among men,*" said Candy, "*whereby we must be saved.*"

444

"Huh." Gina tapped indifferently at her window. "Is that really true? And what a strange sign to hang in Reno of all places."

Light turned green; we rolled on down Virginia, which got seedier the farther it got away from the classy; gray, stringy, broke old men sitting waiting for the bus having spent their last penny. "You think your little fucking Lena that you invited for a joyride is going to be saved by Jesus?" asked Gina. Perhaps I had overstated the mild. "I wouldn't want her to. I'd want her to burn in hell. I want to learn voodoo so I can stick needles in her eyes. Tell me you don't. Tell me you want to turn the other cheek. Turn out your pockets, Candy, give her the film reel, too."

"Gina," I said. "Are you watching out for Motel? Because we're going to miss it with your unending bickering. You're like a married couple."

"An unhappily married couple," retorted Gina. Both of them looked away through the windows. "That fucking Lena," she said. "How did you find her? How could you not tell she was evil? How did you let a complete stranger into our car?"

"Who are you talking to?" I asked. "Me or Candy?"

Gina turned her head. "I don't know anymore," she said, mouth full of sorrow.

Candy's head beat against the window. "Sloane, don't drive so fast, we're going to miss it."

Why did we give all our money to Daisy? Again, we were making such bad decisions. We had thought with our stomachs, and now we desperately needed gas but had no money. "Did we save even a dollar?" I asked. "One lousy dollar for gas."

"We got nowhere to go until we get us some money," said Candy.

"Tomorrow, I'll call Emma."

"And I'll call my mother," said Gina. "What about you, Candy? Who are you going to call?"

"No one," said Candy. "But *you're* going to call your mother?"

"Yes. Why is that so surprising?"

"Well, until just now I wasn't sure you had a mother. You've never mentioned her. Certainly have never called her."

"Yeah? Why don't you call on your Jesus? Maybe he'll give you money."

"You know what," said Candy, "I'm going to get my money the old-fashioned way. I'm going to earn it."

"Good. Maybe money will *save* you."

We sat staring out the windows.

"Dear God," I prayed. "Give us a sign. Help us. Tell us what to do."

"There is no God in Reno," said Gina, banging on the window, as we passed by a billboard that said, "Do you know where you're going to? John 11:10."

The sign came first.

"Motel," it said. It was nearly three miles out from the main strip. "We're going to be pushing the car down Virginia tomorrow," I said. "We're out of gas."

"That's okay," said Gina. "We're out of money, too." Oh, *now* levity.

The Motel motel was a drab two-story building with a concrete courtyard, which is where we pulled in, sputtering to a stop. Candy had to knock five minutes before someone in reception opened the front door. After midnight, they figured anybody knocking was coming to rob them. Which right now didn't seem like the *most* awful idea in the world.

"Is Jess here?" Candy asked.

"Jess who?" yelled a crabby, barely awoken man.

Candy disappeared inside.

"I hope you understand that there is *no* walking away from this bonafide mess," Gina said.

Was there walking away before a mother and son robbed us of everything? I didn't think so. "I'm sorry, Gina."

"Too late. You can stuff your sorry in a sack, missy. How are we going to pay for this fine lodging establishment?"

Soon Candy came back. "Let's go," she said, her voice barely above a whisper. "My friend Jessica doesn't work here anymore. She doesn't live here anymore. Apparently she sold her car and

446

moved back east. Back to Huntington. That was three months ago, when I was still *in* Huntington. Maybe she was going to look me up at Jerry's Lounge where we used to hang out, but just hadn't gotten around to it yet." Candy dangled the keys. "I got us one night. We're up on the second floor. Sloane, what are you doing?" she said, when she saw me pulling into a beaut of a spot right near the stairs. "Park in the back." I groaned, I cursed, I banged the window. I parked in the back, in the dark near the bushes.

Room 528. It had two small beds and a sink outside the bath-room. It smelled moldy. Gina and I dropped our stuff and fell down on the beds. I felt my body giving out, surrendering. I kept doing the slow blink. "I'll call Emma tomorrow," I said, "but how much is Emma going to be able to send me? A hundred? Two?"

"We don't need much," Gina said, kicking off her shoes, trying to crawl under the covers without getting off the bed.

"No? We still have to get back to New York. Gas, food, lodging. A hundred is not going to cut it."

"It'll be okay, Sloane," said Candy. "Gina will be with you."

Gina shook her head. "Gina will not be with her. Gina is going to Bakersfield, and staying with Eddie. I'm not going back." She pulled the covers to her head. The AC was working poorly. I thought she'd be hot.

"Gina," I groaned. I didn't know how to say it. "Come on. What happened to I'm going to stick it out with you until the end?"

"This *is* the end, girlfriend," said Gina, throwing off the blanket. "What about all the things you told me? No hitchhikers. Once, twice. You told me many things. You promised me many things. We wouldn't be here with our life upside down if you'd kept to any of the things you told *me*."

"Emma can't send me enough money to make the trip alone," I whispered, too exhausted to cry.

"So, work," said Candy, sitting down on the corner of my bed. "Make a little money."

"I'm so tired," Gina said, her eyes closing. She rolled into a ball. "I'll register for community college in Bakersfield, instead of Geneseo State. We'll get married. I'll get my degree in California. I can teach anywhere. As long as I'm close to Eddie, I don't care what I do."

"And how am I supposed to make money, Candy?" I asked. "I've never waitressed. The only thing I've ever done is clean houses."

Candy laughed. "Perfect. So clean some houses. Go to the guy downstairs, his name is Taibo, and ask him if he needs a maid." Her eyes twinkled in the broken-bulb dark. "Ask him if he wants you to wear one of those cute little maid outfits. I bet he'll give you more money if you do."

That made me sit up on my elbows. "Candy, what are you talking about? How many rooms do you think I'll need to clean, maid outfit or no before I make enough to drive myself back home?"

Candy fell next to me on the bed, propped up on her side. Gina was drifting off. She had stopped speaking. "Sloane, you're supposed to be smart. A planner. Why didn't you bring enough money for the return trip?"

"I did, Candycane, oh, I did," I said, not fighting the bitterness in my voice. "I planned it all out beautifully. Except things happened I didn't count on. And, by the way, don't you think your criticism of me is a little misplaced, considering no matter how much money I'd have brought, it all would've been taken by the scavengers you let in my backseat?"

"Shel," cooed Candy, blinking warmth at me, "don't you know that a girl, no matter where she is, is never without means to make a buck?"

"What are you talking about?"

And then we were quiet.

I jumped up and went to the bathroom. When I came back, I had to turn away from her before I could lie down next to her, then she spoke again, close to my ear. "Shelby," she said softly. "You raise your skirt, you get a twenty. You give him a blowjob, thirty. A blowjob with an upskirt, fifty. Ten minutes, and you've got fifty bucks. That's 300 dollars an hour. Two hundred and fifty if you're dogging it. What else are you going to do in your young life to make $250 an hour?"

I nearly fell out of bed. "Are you crazy?" I hissed. "You are. You *are* crazy! What are you talking about? I'm not giving a blowjob— to who?"

"To the guy whose rooms you were about to clean for five bucks an hour, plus a dollar tip."

"Candy!"

"Shelby."

Oh my God. That's why she liked bars and grills and clubs, the dark places where men drank. She knew. She was drawn to them like a fly to a flame because she knew they were drawn to her like flies to a flame. They knew.

"Is that what you've been doing all along?"

"What did you think?"

"What did I *think*? I thought you were like us!"

She laughed softly. "The Jackson state trooper was off the clock. He was just a sweetie pie. But . . . you're so funny."

"No."

"You're in Reno now," Candy continued. "Where there's gambling, all other vices follow. *All* other vices. Where men gamble, they drink, and where they drink, there are women, ready to separate them from their money. Think of it this way—the house gets 51 percent. We get the other 49 percent. That's a lot of cash. Give yourself two days. Freelance. You'll make plenty."

"Candy, I'm not talking about this with you another second."

"Fine."

"Is that how much *you* make?"

"No. I make more. Because I give full service, I offer a larger menu."

"I will never do what you're suggesting. *Never*."

"Never's a long time, Sloane."

"Answer's still never. God!"

"Tell me," she said, "that little fun night in Indiana you and

Gina had when you gave it up to complete strangers, and all you got out of it was a free drink. You feel that was a fair exchange? You wouldn't have cared they didn't say hello to you in broad daylight if you'd taken their money."

"Candy, I'm not listening to this! Is that why *you* wouldn't have cared?"

"Right."

"I thought you said you've left all that far behind?"

"No. I said, I don't do it if I can help it."

"Oh, my God."

"I'm going to tell you a joke," she said, "and then I have to go. Because unlike you, lounging about, I have to go work. Someone's got to go out and earn a living. I can't just sit on my hands like you and your friend over there."

"Is that why you came to Reno?" I gasped.

"Why else?" She winked at me. "Now. A man comes up to a pretty girl and says, 'If I give you a million dollars, would you kiss me?' And the girl smiles and says of course. He says, 'All right, now kiss me for ten cents.' She slaps him, and says, 'What kind of a girl do you think I am?' and he replies, 'Oh, we've already established what kind of girl you are. Now we're just haggling about the price.'"

The joke took the heart out of me. But she leaned over, kissed me on the lips, laughed, and hopping off the bed, went to wash, change, get ready. I lay and waited for her to be done, gone. She was crazy. Lifting her skirt to her thighs, for everyone, oh God, what in the world was she thinking? I had been worried about her, but clearly, I had not been worried enough. I had thought Erv forced her into the worst of it, into impossible things, but there was no Erv here. What kind of life could she live with her baby anywhere, if this is how she was planning to conduct her days?

Candy came out of the bathroom. She looked so young and pretty. Her soft brown eyes were shining, her lips slicked with ruby-red gloss, and she'd teased her bleached hair into meringue-like spikes. A sexy mini-skirt skimmed the tops of her slender, smooth bare legs and her cheap, blue costume jewelry chimed with her every movement. She sat on the edge of the bed, smelling of soap and musk. "The last movie Erv made with me, he tied me to a tree in the woods upside down and tortured me. He was making a porn S&M underage video because that's where all the money was, and is. It sounds awful, I know, and it wasn't pleasant, but four hours and it was over. He paid me 3000 dollars for four hours of work, plus two re-shoots. I thought that wasn't a bad deal."

"Not a bad deal? And where's that money now?"

"Gone. But if I don't go and work, it will be gone forever. Come with me."

"No."

"If you come with me, you won't have to touch a man if you don't want to. You can just touch me. For this you and I will make more money in two hours than if you were giving six blowjobs an hour with upskirt for two days straight. We could make enough money in two nights for your ride back home in a limo and hire Jeeves to drive your 'Stang to Harvard. Your choice."

"Out of the question is what it is."

"Nothing is impossible. Only after death are things impossible in this world."

"What you're proposing is impossible."

"To touch a girl or to touch her for money?"

I moved slightly away from her on the bed. "To touch her for money," I whispered.

Candy smiled, reaching for me, her hands on my hips, on my ribs. "Come on, Sloane. Come with me." She hugged me, ruffled my hair.

I hugged her back. "Never in a million years."

"Have it your way." She got up, glancing over at Gina. "Bet she'd go if I asked."

"Wake her up and ask. I'd pay to see that."

"See—even *you'd* pay to see that."

451

"Stop it. Go."

"I'm not giving you any of my money."

"Oh, yes, you are. You're the reason *I* have no money!"

Candy got up to go. When she was at the door, I called out to her. "Candy, give Erv back his movie. Save your life, give him what he wants and run. You know he's only chasing you because he's scared."

She shook her head. "He's chasing me because that movie is his dinner. But I'm running because that movie is my life. I just have to outrun him. But I can't do that without money. And this is the only thing I know how to do. Except make caskets."

"Is there much call for that in Reno?" I muttered. Yes, she said, people die, even in Reno, then she grinned and added, "But not as often as they want to get laid." She left me then, left me to my miserable midnight thoughts, my wretched reelings from her revelations, my shame at myself, my false pride. All of this was in the Motel motel with me, under the grimy bedspread in a room smelling of old wet towels, where Gina softly snored under the broken air conditioning. Candy closed the door behind her, but where was she going? The strip was miles south; how would she get there? I couldn't imagine how Lena and Yuri's mortal sin made Candy feel. I know how it made me feel. My arms were over my face.

I couldn't begin to deal with the stark reality of it—they had taken all our money, and I hadn't even gotten to California yet. I still had my car, but no money to put gas in it, no money for motels, or food, or Cokes. Gina had no money. She might not even have a quarter to call Eddie. She'd have to call him collect. I know how he felt about that.

I waited for Candy, but I could have gone to hell and back before she returned. I wanted it to be morning. I wanted this to be over. All of it. I wished I'd never left Larchmont. I would trade every moment on the road to be back there. There was nothing the road had shown me that I wanted to see.

Except for the empty tabernacle and the song of the monks. *Here, songs grew up around me like a jungle.*

Except for the trill of the voice of the laughing girl who had absolutely no reason in the world to skip, to feel joy, to laugh—and yet did.

I struggled to stay awake. I fought my exhaustion and insane anxiety. I scratched my chest from worry, and tried not to think the unthinkable: *That fucking woman took all my money. Oh God, what am I going to do?* I rolled around in bed, I put all the pillows over my head to deafen the noise, the calamitous hammering. I waited and waited for her, waited for dawn, to do something, to say something to someone and, while waiting like this, fell into unconsciousness.

When I opened my eyes, it was light. Gina was in the bathroom, and Candy was lying next to me, naked, damp from the shower, sleeping. The shower stopped; I pushed Candy until she woke up.

"How'd you do?"

She smiled, her eyes remaining closed. "Leave me alone, I came in like six."

"But it's 9:30."

"A girl's gotta sleep."

"How much?"

"A few hours."

"No. How *much*."

"Oh. Seven hundred bucks."

I tried to whistle.

"I knew you'd be impressed. It wasn't as easy as I expected. Lots of competition. Imagine—I wasn't the only one trying to work. Half of it came from a man who wanted me to sit next to him while he played poker."

"That's all?"

"That's all. Well, that is, until the end, when he made me give him a handjob in front of his wife who was wearing flannel pajamas and foil hair curlers." She giggled, and drifted off once more.

Gina came out of the bathroom, dressed, coldly eyeing us both.

453

"Are we checking out? Because I'm going to walk, try to find a Western Union office."

"Check out and go where? The Western Union office? Do they have beds there? A shower? Rides to Bakersfield? You can check out if you want," muttered Candy, sleepily. "I paid for one more night."

I got up. "Cand, you sleep. Gina, I'll come with you. I'll call Emma."

Candy turned away from us on her side. "Nothing works out as we plan it," she said. "Nothing."

She was so right, this could have been a premonition. At the first phone booth we found, half a mile down the road where the racket from the traffic was not too great, Gina called her mother. Turned out, her mother, father and sister were in Hawaii. Who knew—a vacation in the summer. Her grandmother, who told her this, had no money to give. Scottie's small social security check had been spent. I couldn't *believe* it. The billboard right above my head said, "BORED? I HAVE A BOOK FOR YOU."

I wished I could fall temporarily blind before I called Emma so I wouldn't see the reflection of myself dialing the phone. The only money the three of us had was Candy's, and I flushed hot from shame as I dialed, sharp-as-a-razor me finally realizing that all the burgers from Mickey D's, many of the hotel rooms, breakfast, gum, and a third of the gas, were bought on Candy's back. She traded her body for gas, and I closed my eyes as I pumped, didn't care, didn't want to think about it, and I certainly didn't want to think about it now.

Emma was hard, disappointed in me. She didn't know what to say except, "Shelby, I bought you a car. I gave you extra money for the road. Come fall, I will have to give you for college, no? Maybe for books, supplies? My income is static, I'm not getting extra tips because you're across the country. You're calling me from *Reno*? Did you gamble away your money, and that's why you now need more?"

"Emma . . ." I too didn't know what to say. "We were robbed."

"You picked up hitchhikers?"

"A mother and her son."

"What a ruse. What a con. I don't know what to do. Shel, I don't have enough to give you for all the way back home. Have you at least been to Mendocino?"

I didn't speak. I wanted to say I wouldn't go if that would make it easier, but didn't. Couldn't.

"Oh, Shelby. Where do I get that kind of money?"

"I'm sorry, Emma," I whispered.

She made low noises on the phone, helpless noises of an adult who wishes she can wash her hands, wishes it desperately and grinds her teeth raw with her desire. "Let me go to the bank," she finally said. "I'll see if they'll increase my overdraft. Mine's full. I'll give you whatever they give me."

"I'll pay you back," I said; a lame perspiring fool. "I promise."

"Oh, Shelby," said Emma, and I felt even more ashamed. Yes, in some distant future, one I couldn't imagine, and one she didn't care about, I might give her back a few hundred bucks. What was that to her when her overdraft was full now?

I hung up and couldn't face Gina.

"Is she going to wire you the money?"

"I don't know," I said. "She doesn't have any. Is your grandmother going to wire you the money?"

"No." Gina frowned. "She doesn't have any."

I raised my eyebrows.

"Come on!" She started walking toward the road. "My grandmother doesn't work."

"And my Emma works like an indentured servant," I said loudly. "Eighty hours a week."

She continued to walk without turning around. "Are you coming?" she called.

"In a minute. I'm going to make one more call."

"I'm gonna be at the pool," she said. "I've got no other plans."

I waited for five minutes until she was gone. Then another ten to get my courage up. When I realized no courage was forthcoming, and my heart was ready for a coronary, I picked up the phone and called Eddie collect.

2

Balefire

The operator said, "Will you accept a call from—Shelby Sloane?" You could almost hear the stunned exhale. "Yes," he said. His voice was just as I remembered and my heart hurt to hear it. "Hey," he said. "Is everything okay?"

"Yes, yes," I said. "Hey. Everything's fine. Well, actually, it's not really fine."

"Is Gina okay?" There was quick concern in his voice.

Mine became colder in response. The heart beat a little slower. "Yes, she's fine. But . . ." What was I thinking? "Eddie, we need your help. We were robbed."

"You was what?"

"Robbed. A woman took all our money, and now we're really broke."

"What woman?"

I told him. Reno is in a valley, and behind every gas station the snow peaks of the Sierra Madre mountains rise. I noticed how large they were, how good the air smelled. Dry. Clean. How could there be snow if the temperature was a hundred degrees? Dog days indeed.

"Where are you?" he asked.

"Reno."

"You're broke in Reno?" He softly laughed. "There is no justice in the world."

"None." If there was justice, I would not be standing here like an idiot at a dusty, rusted phone booth, calling him under all kinds of pretenses, wanting *nothing* but to hear his voice.

"So what's Gina gonna do?" He paused. "What are *you* going to do? Don't you two still have to drive twenty-five hundred miles back home?"

"Yeah. We're in a bit of a pickle."

"I'll say."

"Which is why I'm calling. Eddie . . ." I hemmed. "Can you help us?"

"I got no money, if that's what you mean," he said quickly. "I'm between jobs at the moment. Just got fired from Long John Silver."

"No, I understand." Money would've been nice. Is that what I was doing? Begging my old lover for a handout? "Maybe you could come here, meet Gina? She's come all this way to be with you, and now we're all out. If you came to get her, she'd feel a whole lot better. I'm calling for her, really."

"Is *that* why you're calling?"

I stammered. "Yes."

There was silence on the phone. "You see, Shel," said Eddie, "problem is, I ain't got insurance for my car, and until I get a job, I can't pay to have it reinstated. I don't got any gas. And Bakersfield to Reno, that's probably two, three hundred miles, no?"

A sigh of heartache left my chest. "More like four hundred."

"Four hundred!" he exclaimed. "How am I going to do that? I mean, if Gina could pay for the gas, then that might work."

"If Gina could pay for the gas," I said, "I'd just drive her to Bakersfield, like I planned."

"Right, of course." He had nothing to say after that.

"Can I put her on the bus, Eddie?" I asked. God will forgive me. I was only eighteen and I wasn't thinking with the utmost rational mind, but why would I, after asking this question, feel regret that I wasn't going with her so *I* could see him, even from a distance, for a few seconds? Hot truth is, I could not accept that

457

Eddie had left Larchmont for good, and if I put Gina on the bus, there was a betting chance I would never see Eddie again.

"The bus?" Eddie said. "To go where?"

"Well—to Bakersfield."

"Ugh—I don't know, Shel. You said she's got no money. How is she going to get back home? I thought you were coming with her. You come, visit for a while, then drive back. That's what Gina told me. I just—I don't—if she comes by bus, what's she going to do?"

"I don't know, Eddie," I said. "She was thinking of coming and staying."

"Staying *where*?" He sounded horrified. "I live with my mother."

"I know."

"Shel, I really don't think it's the best idea. Honest. I'd tell you if it was. Maybe if she got some money. Came with a round-trip ticket. She could stay for a day, maybe two, then ride back. What do you think? Can you get some money from somewhere? Maybe you can talk to her."

"Yeah, sure. I'll talk to her." I stared down at the desert sand under my feet. "Well, look. I better get going, all right? Thanks again, though."

"Yeah, nice to talk to you, Shelby. Hey, maybe you two can take the bus together? She'll have some company then." He paused. "And I could . . . see you. I'm sorry things turned out the way they did. I hope I didn't hurt you too bad."

Fame! . . . people will see me and cry . . .

I hugged the curb for half a numb mile down Virginia. It was noon, one, maybe, and stiflingly, agonizingly hot. Not a bird flew in the sky. They'd all gone north for the summer. I was honked at half a dozen times in ten minutes of walking. Maybe a dozen. A honk every half a minute, and believe me it wasn't because I was so striking and tanned, invitingly smiling. I wasn't painted a come-hither yellow like my Shelby 'Stang. Maybe it was the blonde hair.

The barely cleaned pool was in the middle of the courtyard, right off Virginia. Gina was lounging in a chair, her ample boobs spilling from the sides of a tiny black bikini. "How did it go?" she asked. "Your phone call?"

"Not great," I said, motioning to her. "Come with me." In the room, the shades were drawn, and Candy was still sleeping. We sat on the other bed, opened the shades, made some noise. Finally she woke up. "What did you give me, an hour?"

"You want more?"

"Go swim. Suntan. I can't function on an hour's sleep."

"Maybe if you slept like the rest of us, during the night," Gina snapped, "you wouldn't be sleeping now."

"Maybe," returned Candy, "but then we'd be completely penniless, wouldn't we? Who's going to earn some money? You?" She stretched. "Well, I'm awake now," she said, sitting up. "What are you two going to do? Sit here and look at me?" She didn't even bother covering her bare body. I was the one who threw a modest sheet over her.

"What do you think we should do?" Gina asked.

"You're in Reno." Candy paused, giving me a meaningful glance, then sighing. "There are 500 bars, 500 restaurants. Go work a week at the Village Inn. Make thirty bucks. That's enough for a bus ride to Bakersfield."

I coughed too loudly, and apologized.

"Oh, is that what you made last night?" Gina asked.

"No. I made more. But you don't want to do what I do, do you?"

"Oh, God!"

"That's right." Candy threw on her clothes, short shorts, a white top without a bra and high wedge sandals, and in the next breath she said, "Well, why are you standing here in what looks like my black bikini? I thought you were all set, checking out and going your own way. You better hop to it. Buses to Bakersfield don't run every hour on the hour."

Gina became quiet. The room was dark, but outside the Nevada sun burned like a bonfire. "I thought Shelby was going to drive me," she said.

459

"Shelby," said Candy, "has no money. She doesn't have a dollar for gas."

There we stood, the three of us. Gina said in the beseeching voice of a chastised child, "Maybe we can win a little at the tables. My luck was pretty good at the Argosy."

"Unless there's something I don't know," said Candy, "you don't have a dollar to gamble with."

Gina just stared at Candy. "Come on, Cand," she whispered. "I was just mad yesterday."

"And I," said Candy, "am going to Paradise to get my kid. That's my only goal. I have two more days to work, and then I'm out of here. I'm not sticking around while you win enough money to get back home, or to Bakersfield, a losing gamble if I ever heard one."

"Which one?" asked Gina. I pointedly said nothing, not even a cough, changing into my navy string bikini in reply.

Gina and I were by the pool when Candy came downstairs, dressed for the evening, though it was three in the afternoon. "Come, help me," Candy said. "Come work for your supper. It's just one night out of your whole life. The three of us could make so much money, and then we'd be done. We could leave tomorrow. You on your way. Me on mine."

There is nothing so trashy that gambling can't lower another small ladder-rung into the sweltering sewer. How was that possible? Perhaps it's just the places we'd been. Maybe Las Vegas is classier. I don't know, I've never been. All I know, is that from the boat on the Mississippi, to the Argosy, to Nevada Hotel, to Reno, I've watched hypnotized couples in polyester pants or joyless, glazed young men looking down at the felt tables, wondering all night whether to hit or stand, double or split, give their money away slowly or quickly.

Come to think of it, that pretty well summed up all of life, not just Reno.

But the voluntary surrender of hard-earned cash seemed to open

460

men up to every one of the seven deadly sins. *Avarice*: More, more. *Sloth*: Their shoes were never shined, their belts opened an extra notch, shirt buttons loosened to allow for the deep breaths needed after putting their remaining nickels on number 23, and hearing, "No more bets." Cigarette butts spilled by the dozen from ashtrays and they left their garbage behind, dropping empty buckets on the floor as they kept walking. *Gluttony*: They drank to excess for free, partook of buffets, and, in exchange for this feckless feast, gladly threw away their money. *Envy*: Everyone is winning more than me. I want that kind of night, those should've been my numbers. *Pride*: I can control my own fate. I'll just put down another hundred on number 17 and all my troubles will be over. *Wrath*: I can't believe number 17 failed me again. It's always been my lucky number. What do you mean, no more bets? What do you *mean*?! *Lust*: They flirted both with bankruptcy and the barely-clad waitresses. Why did the waitresses need to be so scantily dressed to bring money to the prisoners on bar stools? If they sashayed up fully clothed, would the drunk boys leave? They didn't have the look of people about to head for the exits. Many looked as if they were never leaving. And why did Madam Prostitution go hand in hand with drinking and gambling? Not easy women, but paid-for women? As if the men had any money left to spend on sex. They couldn't even afford a drink! Had the casinos been smarter they'd have hired the women themselves, provided the sex for free, like alcohol. The men wouldn't leave the casinos at all then, and Candy could have permanent employment.

Yes, indeedy, a real nice town, Reno, for Tara to grow up in.

And yet here was Candy, asking if we'd like to go with her tonight, get dolled-up, canvass, stroll, flirt with the straightjackets.

"No, thank you," I whispered in my smallest voice.

"You're crazy," said Gina, I hope directed at Candy, not me.

"You gave it to those boys for free," Candy said to Gina. "Give it up now, but for a few bucks."

"For a few bucks?" Gina exclaimed. "I'm going to have sex with strangers for a few bucks?"

"You had sex with strangers for free," repeated Candy.

"Yes! A world of difference. I can't believe you'd even ask me. Right, Shelby?"

I said nothing.

Casting me a meaningful glance from above her drugstore sunglasses, she said, "Ask Gina what she's willing to do for a million dollars, Sloane. I'll see ya."

I didn't ask Gina; it was going to remain one of those unanswered questions. But what I knew this afternoon was this. Had Gina not been sitting next to me suntanning, ready to judge me, though firmly encased in a glass-house herself, I would've gone with Candy. I would have rather gone with Candy than ever admit I had called Eddie and asked for money. I would have rather gone with Candy than have Emma go to the bank manager and ask for a miserable extension on her overdraft so she could wire me 300 bucks, which still would not be enough to get me home. I'd feel less humiliated parading down the Reno strip naked. But Gina was sitting right there, and the pull of conformity was great. How could I face the shame of high school reunions where Gina would forever be telling the story to anyone who would listen: "Guess what our little cross-country runner, Harvard Alum Shelby did in Reno?"

I didn't move, said nothing, and steadfastly (that was me, steadfast!) avoided catching Candy's eye. I furtively watched as she wobbled toward the strip in her short shorts and high heels. Cars honked in loud appreciation. One jostled to the curb and Candy disappeared inside. Gina and I were left alone.

"She's crazy," said Gina.

"Like a fox," I agreed.

"Yeah? Then why did we get robbed, if she's like a fox? And if she's so foxy clever, has she thought for a second where Erv Bruggeman is waiting? Does she think he's still searching for her on the Interstate? Doesn't she understand he's in Paradise now?"

462

3

Cave, Cave, Deus Videt

It was all well and good to lament Candy's gallivanting, to judge her, to moralize while sitting at a pool in a concrete courtyard on the Reno strip in too-small bikinis. But she left us no percentage of her earnings, we had no gas in the car, and hadn't eaten. What were we going to do?

I cursed myself, cursed Lena. I cursed the sun, and the pool, and Reno. I cursed it all. Gina just cursed not being able to go and gamble. She wished not for food money, not for gas money, not for bus money, but for gambling money. She wanted our seventeen-year-old money-making protector in white shorts to give her a small stipend so she could sit fully turned to the metal lever. "Maybe," said Gina, with a small chuckle, dipping her toes in the water, "I should've taken Candy up on her offer. Maybe she's right. I do it for free without a lookback. What's the difference between doing it and getting a little scratch for the slots, huh? Maybe we wouldn't even have to leave the pool? What do you think, Shelby?"

Shelby pretended to be asleep, so Gina wouldn't see my perverse little sideways gaze. Just so I was straight: not money for the bus to see her fiancé, or to get back home, but she was advocating becoming lot lizards so we could put money in a poker machine.

"Gina, yesterday you said you weren't going back to Larchmont with me. Are you going to help get Candy to Paradise?"

She shook her head. "I can't go to Paradise, Shel. Erv's in Paradise. I just can't."

"We don't know that for sure. *She* doesn't think so."

"She's a fool."

"So what's your plan, Stan? Where are you headed?"

"I guess as soon as my mom gets home in ten days and wires me some money, I'll take a bus to Bakersfield."

I didn't have the balls to tell her about Eddie.

At nine in the evening, Candy came back. She was like mercy. Like Jesus doling out healing to the lepers and the blind. "Look!" she said happily, throwing twenties on the bed. "Sloane, you must be starved. I found us a fantastic buffet. And Gina, you simply *have* to come with me to Circus, Circus. It has to be seen to be believed. Come on, get dressed quick, and let's go. I'm not taking no for an answer."

"About that . . ." I said.

Gina interrupted. "I'll be ready in fifteen. Thanks, Candycane. God, thanks a lot."

She disappeared into the bathroom, but I continued to sit on the bed, looking up at Candy. She smiled. "Say nothing. Come on, just get ready."

After hitching a ride in the back of a rowdy convertible Thunderbird full of raucously unsober men (oh, if Emma could see me now, getting into a car driven by drunk strangers), we got dropped off in front of the glittering Circus, Circus and made our way to the casino floor. I don't know how Candy faked being over eighteen. She looked like a baby even with all that black around her eyes, even in her tottering platform heels and mini-skirt as if she were a sixties throwback. All that was missing was the long straight hair. She looked so mod with her piercings and tattoos, the joy streaks of blonde and bleach. She crossed herself before stepping onto the casino floor, surreptitiously, as if she hoped no one would notice.

"What are you crossing yourself in secret for?" the tactless Gina asked. "Are you hoping God won't notice?"

"I was kind of hoping He'd be the only one who would."

I wondered what prayer one could possibly mumble under one's breath at the particular moment of entering a casino in the hope of getting a large quantity of men to have sex with you for money. A little later, during a moment of rare respite, I asked her. She smiled. "What else can you say? *O Lord Jesus Christ, son of God, have mercy on me, a sinner.* My father taught me to repeat that prayer to myself incessantly."

"Do you?"

She turned to the blackjack table and ordered another drink, saying, "I'll split these nines." To me she said, "A million times a day." And when she won the split, making eighty quick bucks, she said, "Sometimes, though, I think, God stays far away from casino pits like this. I figure He thinks that if you're getting off at Circus, Circus, you already know you're going to be absolutely up to no good, and so He leaves you to your petty corruptions and busies himself in hospitals, where the sick pleading for Him are at least hoping to get out." We both looked over at Gina, sitting two stools away, a joyous smile on her face, having lost fifty dollars of the hundred Candy had given her. "Who'd want to help her?" Candy said. "She wants to be here."

"Do *you* want to be here?"

"No," she said. "I want my Tara, that's all. This is just a means to an end."

It was smoky and loud, the sounds of roulette tables, people shouting, and dealers calling out, "Shuffle!" like the din of a thundering waterfall, and I said, my own smile fading, "Was I just a means to an end, too?"

Candy touched my hand, her smile fading also. "Forgive me, Shelby," she whispered.

I may have won some money with Candy's generous donation of a hundred dollars. I don't know. Gina eventually won. Lost, won, and lost again. Roulette, blackjack, slots, drinks, young men flirting like mad, falling over. At one point, Candy had three natural blackjacks in a row, and the dealer, a Filipino woman

465

named Min, said she'd never seen that in twenty years. Candy smiled. "I must be lucky," she said, raking another $75 for herself.

The men swarmed to her like bears to honey, as if they could smell her. Was it written all over her face, her body? Why didn't they push closer to me, inch their stools toward mine? I was made up and skinny, I was bleached and mini-skirted, too. What vibe didn't I have? I tried to remind myself of things, comforting things, like: this isn't love. This isn't even lust. It's just availability. She somehow projects an I'm available message and they flock like seagulls. Soon they'll go, and still there will be no love. But I watched with envy. I wished I could be cool like her, all smiles, her sweet friendly eyes lighting up, her laughter heard at all tables. Candy looked as if she hadn't a care in the world. Her hair was up, her lips wet, her eyes sparkling. She giggled like a schoolgirl (ironic), demurely lowering her eyes when a drunk football jock whispered something clearly inappropriate into her eager ear. Who could tell that behind this breezy air, stood a fanatic set on killing her for a stolen reel of film depicting things I couldn't think about, much less talk about, a father who prayed six hours a day for his only daughter's soul, a dead boyfriend, and an innocent child who waited for her mother to come. While she smiled I couldn't muster even a grimace. The farther away the smile, the more money I lost. "Shel," Candy finally said, "you gotta stop this. You gonna make us broke again. Go away, sit out a couple of rounds."

"Yeah, baby," said the linebacker, jocular and jowly. "Don't you know the rules of the game? When you're hot you gotta play like you're on fire, like your cute little friend over here. And when you're cold, stay away from the money, baby, 'cause it's sure gonna stay away from you." I took their advice, and walked away.

Candy grabbed her chips, blew a kiss to the quarterback and came after me.

"You okay?"

"I'm fine. What time is it?"

"I've no idea. Casinos have no clocks."

Slowly we pushed our way past one filled table after another.

Candy purposeful, like she was trawling. She came to a stop at a table with a dealer and two players. Table had a $500 minimum. Watch, Candy said.

We watched a business-suit-clad gray-haired gentleman lay down 500 bucks on an 18, and lose.

We watched him lay down another $500 on a 10, double, get 20 and lose to a dealer 21. Ouch.

"This is the time this guy needs to stop playing," Candy whispered to me. But she didn't walk away. Moving from straight behind him, she angled herself at his shoulders, patted his back when the dealer finally bust and he won. He turned his head and smiled. She smiled back. He lay down another $500 chip. "Good luck," she said, moving closer. "Have you been watching me?" he asked. "I'm gonna need it. What's with me tonight?" But with her by his side after a lucky bust and a double, the man had won 2500 dollars. In three minutes from start to finish, he had won the sort of money it had taken Emma and me years to save. I was guilty then of one of those deadly sins. *Envy.* I wanted what he had, although in this case, it wasn't his money I wanted, it was his steel balls. The man hollered and whooped, gave the dealer a $100 chip and Candy a big hug, saying she must have been his good luck muse. We watched him play another fifteen minutes, and in that time exchange 6000 dollars back and forth.

"Don't think for a second it's bravery," Candy whispered to me. "He bets because he doesn't care, because he has the money to lose. That's not bravery, it's indifference. He's reckless, and because of that he wins. Cards love reckless gamblers. Casinos love careful gamblers. They know, the more careful you are, the more you'll lose."

I felt better. "Hey, you want to get going?" I asked.

"No way. He's my blackjack."

"I should probably check on Gina." I wanted to avert my eyes. "We've left her alone too long."

"Shelby, Shelby, Shelby," Candy said, holding on to my arm. "You're so thick. Why do you think she hasn't left as she threatened to yesterday? If Gina could, she'd gamble alone in the closet.

467

The last thing she wants is to have you standing over her shoulder watching how she's blowing my money."

I took a step back.

"Stay with me," Candy said soothingly, one hand on the Reckless Man's back, the other on my hand. Reckless Man looked neat and sharp Wall Street, middle-aged trying to look late youth.

Candy couldn't play at a $500 table, but Reckless Man placed a chip in front of her and said, "I'll take a gamble on you. Go ahead. Bet. See how you do."

"Thanks," she said, and without blinking got a 10 and wanted to double. Amused, he gave her another chip. She won a thousand bucks. He told her to keep her thousand, and placed a chip in front of her again.

"You play until you lose my $500, okay?"

Candy got blackjack. The next hand she split two 9s (with his money) and won both hands. After eight straight winning hands, she finally lost one, and gave him back his chip, gave the dealer $10, and had earned three thousand dollars for herself!

"Cand, let's go. Quick," I whispered. "Look how awesome you did."

"Awesome for what?" she said, pushing me slightly away. "If you and I split that money, it'll be just enough for you to get back home, but what will it do for me? Go. Go, check on Gina. Come back in twenty minutes."

"How do I know when twenty minutes are up?" I said grumpily, watching as Reckless Man got her a premium drink, and they toasted, flirting a little. He looked besotted, so I bowed out and went to find Gina. Wasn't hard to find her—she was in exactly the same place we'd left her hours before.

"Money holding out?" I asked, sipping my drink, my fourth or fifth. I felt myself getting tipsy. *Gluttony. Avarice. Sloth. Pride.* I can handle it. I can have more. I deserve it. I haven't had any fun. I deserve some fun. I'm worthy of fun. I ordered another screwdriver.

"Barely holding out," said Gina. "What about you?"

"Got a few hundred and intend to hold on to it."

"I won $700," said Gina, "but I've lost almost all of it now. I'm waiting to get hot again. If I won that much, so quick, I could win again. And more. God, this is the best place. How's Candy doing?"

"Pretty good. She seems to have all the luck."

Gina laughed at the unintended irony of it. I didn't laugh because suddenly Candy was behind me, pulling me away, spilling my drink. "Listen to me," she said in a low voice. I could barely hear in the din of the casino floor, but she refused to speak louder. She was very close; her hair tickling my ear. "Listen, Reckless Man has offered you and me a thousand bucks each if he can watch," she said.

"If he can watch what?"

She just looked at me. How dense I must have appeared to her, thick to my ankles. How naïve. I even repeated my question. It was the look in her eye that eventually gave me my answer, but I would not have guessed on my own without her help.

My eyes widened. "Are you out of your mind?"

"Shelby. Are *you* out of your mind? A thousand bucks. Combined with the few hundred in your hands, that's enough to get you home, no? Come on. He pays up front. We close our eyes, we think of England. I promise you, it'll be the fastest 1000 bucks you'll ever make."

"You have gone mad," I said. "Absolutely not. Not in a million years. Never."

A million years is a long time.

Never is a long time.

"Just to point out," I said, when we were in the elevator, going up to his penthouse suite on the fourteenth floor of Circus, Circus, "he dropped more cash on two rectangular pieces of paper with pictures on them than on us. Just pointing out we rate less than paper."

"Laminated paper, but okay, your point noted. So?"

"Cand, you just won 3000 bucks. For God's sake, take the money, and run."

"I'm not doing it for me, Sloane," she said. "I'm doing it for you. So you can get home."

The green elevator doors opened. "Do we have a time limit?" I asked.

"I don't know what you mean."

"Well, with a guy and a girl, you know when you're done, when the guy is done, but with . . ." I couldn't say it. "How do you know you're done?"

"After fifteen minutes, fake it, Shel."

I went quiet, my heart beating frantically. I couldn't believe we were walking down the well-lit corridor. The carpet was gold-toned and plush. "What about Gina?" I asked. "We didn't even tell her where we were going. What if she goes looking for us?"

"Shelby, she hasn't moved off that stool for hours. Is she really going to move in the next fifteen minutes?"

Heart beating ever more wildly, "Fake what?" I ventured. "Being done?"

"Hey, girlfriend," said Candy, knocking cheerfully into my shoulder. "Ain'cha considered the possibility you might not have to fake it?" A throaty laugh. A big toothy smile.

Wildly, wildly, wildly.

Turned out, though, I didn't have to fake being done.

I wish I could say it went off without a hitch, without incident.

But the mild-mannered gentleman who would indifferently drop six grand in a few minutes was less mild mannered when it came to us. His suite was a luxury apartment, fancy linens, marble in the bathroom (where I spent way too long trying to get up my courage), and recessed mood lighting. There were three TVs and gold lamps, a shiny dining-room table, a sofa, big closets with mirrors. I thought I could live in a place like that the rest of my life. Have the maid turn down my bed every evening. Have champagne brought up. Fresh towels. And outside the floor-to-ceiling windows Reno twinkled down below. If it weren't for the fact this place was in Reno, it would've been smashing. Candy knocked on the bathroom door for five minutes. Come out, Shelby. Come on. Stop hiding. He's waiting.

We agreed on terms, he paid us, I asked for the overhead lights to be turned off, and we lay down together on his swanky sheets. Somehow, though I don't know how, I managed to overcome my trembling embarrassment and mortification enough to forget his presence in the nearby chair. I don't know how much time passed, perhaps fifteen minutes, perhaps the blink of an eye, when suddenly he announced he wanted more; he wanted to participate. Panicked, I sat up, trying to remember where I'd left my clothes, my shoes, all the while stammering, No! No, no, no. Candy placed a calming hand on my shoulder, and told him she was willing. He shook his head, said it was me he wanted, that I had no choice. I refused and stood up. The man loomed menacingly near. I was naked and scared, and began to cry. Candy stepped between us, took his hand, while pushing me aside. "Come, honey," she said to him. "I know what I'm doing. She don't know how. She don't know nothing."

He laughed, mocked me—"There are four things that should never flatter men," he said. "I don't know what the other three are, but I know number one. The caresses of women."—but his mockery allowed me to dress and split, leaving her behind. I asked if she was going to be all right, but she didn't even turn to me as she shut the bedroom door with the back of her foot. "Go!" was all she said.

I waited for her on a bench right outside the elevator bank, fidgeting, biting my nails, my fingers unsteady, my knees. I was struggling not to think of her, and not to worry about her. Failure on both counts. She came downstairs half an hour later, looking roughed up. Her eye was swollen, her mouth pulpy. I jumped up. "Are you okay?"

471

"That guy was something else. Did you take your money?" She was slightly lisping as if she'd lost a tooth.

I nodded. "I'm fine." I could barely look at her. "You got yours? What happened?"

Without looking at me, she told me Reckless Man had taken her money, taken the thousands she'd won at his table. Told her it was his. Threw her a chip as she was leaving. She showed me. Five hundred dollars.

"Oh, Candy." My voice trembled, I wanted to cry. "You're going to have a black eye."

"Oh, Shelby. That's not the important thing." She looked so despondent.

"I'll give you half my money."

"No, it's yours."

"No. I never would have it without you. I'll give you half."

"You can't get back home on half."

That was true. I didn't know what to do. "Oh, God, Candy."

"Don't worry," she said. "Easy come, easy go. Let's find Gina."

And I wanted to say, *that* was easy? "Where do you think she is?"

"Exactly where we left her."

And she was. She had half a drink left, and about the same number of small chips strewn in front of her. Her gaze was glassy.

"Hey, Gina," said Candy, taking my arm, holding on to me, because her legs were buckling, as if she were about to break. "Ready to go?"

"Is it time?"

"Well, I don't know. Do you feel you've played enough?"

"What time is it?"

"Must be close to sun up."

"*What?*" That made her inflect upward, almost in surprise. "Just one more hand," she said. "I'm feeling lucky."

She lost. She played one more. She lost. She played until only the black, $100 chip was left. If she broke into that, she would play until it was gone. Candy pulled her off the stool. "One chip left," said Candy, dragging her away from the table. "A hundred bucks. Your bus ticket to Bakersfield."

I shoved Candy. I wished she wouldn't keep bringing up Bakersfield. I hadn't had a chance to tell her about Eddie yet. We had been too busy sucking up to Reckless Man.

On the way out, I asked Candy if she had looked for Lena in the casino. "No," she replied. "When I have a gnawing need to search for her, I say, Dear God, please help me forget and not think about her ever again. Please."

"Does it work?"

"No," Candy admitted. "But my father would say it's because I'm aiming too high. He says when you want to try your hand at forgiveness, don't start with the Nazis."

Gina was in a little world of her own, counting, recounting, muttering formulas under her breath. She hadn't even noticed what had happened to Candy's face. She said she had had 200 dollars on two face cards, split them, and lost.

"Gina, don't you know the cardinal rule of gambling?" said Candy. "Never split a winning hand."

"Yes, but I wanted to double my money!"

"And instead of winning $200, you lost $200. So you're actually $400 in the hole."

"That's stupid math," Gina said. "Did you win?"

Candy flashed her $500 chip. "Lena, my ass. Like we need her." She gave me a look I did not return, my face burning hot.

"You told that man my name was Bunny," I said to Candy back at the motel. Gina was in the bathroom, and we had two seconds to ourselves.

"I changed your name not for the man, but for Jesus."

"You think your charade can fool Jesus?"

"Yes. Bunny did it, not you. I thought you'd be more comfortable with that."

Burning hot, I couldn't look at her. I was very scared still, and so tired my eyes felt full of burning sandpaper. So this is what a glimpse of life on the other side was like. You give it to them, they give it to you, then beat you with one hand as they take it away with the other. Unwashed and fully clothed, I sank on the bed and fell asleep.

When I opened my eyes, it was 5:00 p.m. I felt bloated, disgusting and disgusted, like a sinner who'd been up all night, and now couldn't face day. That was me. I couldn't face day.

While the girls went to the pool, I walked half a mile to my phone booth and called Emma, telling her not to wire the money; I didn't need it.

"Now you tell me. After I've just debased myself to that man."

You and me both, Emma.

"So where'd you get money from?"

I told her we won it at the casino. I tried to stick to at least a partial truth, as if *lying* were just too undignified. Back at the hotel, the girls were out in the parking lot lounging on rusted chaises. They'd been in the water and their bodies were wet. We hadn't moved the car in three days. It was still in the back by the bushes.

We should have been spending our time figuring out what we planned to do, but it was far easier just to put on string bikinis and lie out in the parking lot at six in the evening under the 100-degree desert sun and turn our faces to the sky. Thanks to Candy we had about 2000 dollars between us, and could put Lena and her thieving skankiness behind us. We wanted desperately to put Erv behind us, too, to forget his menacing presence, and that made us reluctant to talk about tomorrow's plans.

We planned instead for today. Where should we go to eat? We should eat well, we hadn't had a good meal in so long. Maybe we should go shopping. Buy a few new things. We should definitely buy a present for Tara. What would she like? What did five-year-olds like? No one knew. No one had any idea.

"What did you like, Candy?" Gina asked, pleasant and subdued. Hostility had been replaced by affability. Her bathing suit was riding up—she had gained weight on our journey, she was spilling out of the top, and the bikini-bottom strings were digging into the flesh of her hips. "When you were a five-year-old?"

"I dunno," said Candy without opening her eyes, her face still up to the sky, the cheek under the left eye bruised and swollen. "Perhaps I colored, or made cups out of clay. Possibly I planed pine. Made glass mobiles to hang over cribs. I made wooden crosses." She smiled. "With my nubby little hands I made beautiful wooden crosses. One of them still hangs in my father's room. He prays underneath it."

"Okay, then," said Gina. "Perhaps we'll get Tara some rough-hewn wood. Here, honey. Your mommy has some lumber for you. Careful not to get a splinter."

Candy smiled. She hadn't gained any weight on our journey, she was still skinny, and her body had little pieces scraped away, at the torso, on the arms, around the knees, little bits of body that would never tan, places where life and Erv had crashed against her.

"All girls like to paint. We'll get her some markers. Some coloring books. She'd like that."

"She would," said Candy. "Maybe a doll?"

"What about a puppy?" asked Gina.

"A real puppy? You're mad."

We chuckled, soaked our skin under the Reno sun, then dunked our bodies in the bath-warm water. Suddenly, we all agreed we were starved. And had nothing to wear. So we threw on some rags, left the 'Stang in the lot at Candy's insistence and took a cab to the mall. We spent a blissful hour buying jeans and black dresses, and sandals with wrap-around straps. We bought new mascara, red lipstick, and hair mousse. Candy bought nothing for herself, only a large, blue rubber ball decorated with yellow flowers for Tara—"So we'll have something to do together," she said— and a pink lace dress fit for a princess, white shoes with silver buckles and a gold buckle for her hair. "She's not brown-haired like I once was," she said. "She's gold blonde like her daddy."

We changed in the public bathroom, slapped some powder on

475

our sunburned faces and with our loot in shopping bags, took a cab to Glory Hole on Virginia, stumbling in our high-heeled sandals, while the men ogled and the ladies glared—at the men! We asked for a quiet table in the back. I chose to sit next to Candy with Gina across from us, but only because I didn't want to keep looking at her. For some reason looking at her filled my chest with an emotion so thick and wordless that I was afraid one small glance would reveal my inner commotion. So I sat next to her, where I was close, but didn't have to see her. While she talked, I smiled into my salad, into my steak, into my glass of red wine. I could smell her Jovan Musk. We got some cheap Cabernet Sauvignon from Sonoma, and it tasted good to me but I wouldn't know—I was not a red wine drinker. But we were having steak, and it felt mature and grown-up to order red wine with our red meat.

Gina and I had to drink down two bottles of wine before we were able to broach the unspeakable with Candy. We had to figure out what to do next, what to do tomorrow. We couldn't just sit in the parking-lot pool until the manager got tired of Candy's offerings and threw us out.

Candy listened to us cough and splutter, glass in hand. I was worried she'd throw it at us.

"You can't go to Paradise, Candy," Gina finally blurted. "You can't show up there, looking for your daughter."

Candy did not understand.

"Where do you think Erv is?" That was hard to say, even on wine.

"Why would he be there?"

"Why wouldn't he be?"

"Why *would* he be? How does he know where I'm headed?"

"He doesn't know you had a baby?"

"Duh. Of course he knows that," she said. "But he doesn't know where Mike's family moved to."

"No?"

"No!"

"One Western Union receipt to Paradise," said Gina. "Or perhaps your mother. Does your mother know where your baby had gone to?"

"I don't think I ever told her. I didn't trust her with much."

"You were right not to," I said. "But, Cand, is Erv really the kind of guy who's just going to give up, having followed you for 3500 miles?"

Candy said nothing. She stopped drinking. "I don't know what you want me to do," she said. "Did you take me to a fifty-dollar restaurant to tell me this? So what if you're right? I still have to get her."

"But what if he's there waiting for you, waiting for you to take her? What if he hurts you both?"

She shook her head. "He won't hurt her."

I had seen his eyes, his ragged-out rage. "Candy, please."

"What are you worried about?" she said, mock-dismissively. "She'll be safe."

"*You're* not safe," I said. "How can she be safe with you?"

An agreeable and unperturbed Gina nodded. "Let's sleep on it another night. Let's think on it. Perhaps," she said, with a flushed smile, "we should go back to Circus, Circus. To get our minds off things. For just an hour. No use dwelling on unpleasant things."

I shook my head.

"For an hour."

"There is no such thing. We either go and stay or we don't go."

"So?" So affable. "We have nowhere to be. Let's go."

I tried not to show my disapproval. I wasn't thinking clearly myself. "Gina, we have to figure out about Candy first. We just have to."

"There's nothing to figure out," said Candy.

"There is," I said. "Gina and I were thinking that you should stay here and we'll go and get Tara for you."

A cloud passed over Gina's face. Her long, straight hair shook in refusal. "Shelby, are you crazy?"

"Don't you remember? This is what we talked about."

477

"We never did!"

"We did."

She didn't remember, and now she thought it was a *terrible* idea. But I couldn't quite tell why: was it because of the dangerous foolishness of it, or because of Circus, Circus?

"Shelby," Gina said, vehemently shaking her head. "I really have to get to Eddie."

"That's true," I said. "Gina's got a wedding to prepare for. And I've got Harvard to get to. I'm nearly out of time. I can't lounge about in Reno. This thing's not going to fix itself. And Candy has to get her baby. We all have big plans." I liked plans so much. "One thing is certain—we can't be sitting by the side of the road, looking forward to Circus, Circus."

"I agree," said Candy. "Take me to Paradise."

"Okay," I said.

"Interesting," said Gina from across the table, pouring herself another glass of Cabernet. "So how come *she* gets a ride to Paradise, but *I* get a bus to Bakersfield? How come I don't rate door-to-door service?"

"And Shelby, what about *your* mother?" said Candy. "Where's she in the mix?"

Yes, what about me? What had happened to my plans, my dreams? I was going to make my way to the Pacific and find her in Mendocino, sit with her for a few days, maybe in an outdoor café, if they had such a thing in her small town. I was going to invite her to come back east with me. I was going to—

"Clearly, I'm out of time for myself," I said, my sober words sobering me up. "Paradise, Bakersfield." I sighed. "You're right. I should drive you, Gina. Tomorrow morning we'll all go to Paradise, we'll get Tara, I'll take Gina to Bakersfield, then I head on to Mendocino."

Candy stared at me blankly, as if I were shooting down all her dreams single-handedly. I couldn't meet her eyes. Reaching out, she took my hand. I tried not to jump, not to pull away. "Sloane," she said softly. "Look at me."

My flushed eyes darted this way, that, finally resting on her face, softening, too.

"I know you're trying to help," she said. She didn't let go of me. "You're always thinking up big ideas. I *love* that about you. But you're forgetting one important detail. If *I* can't go to Paradise, you certainly can't go to Paradise. If Erv is there, what else would he be looking for, but your yellow Mustang? However you're going to help me, you can't help me in your car. I've said all along, the car is a menace. It's your worst quality. It's more true now than ever."

"Don't be ridi—"

"What do you think, we'll waltz into Paradise in your little yellow canary and snap up my kid?"

We studied the remains of the wine.

"Shelby, Candy's right," Gina said. "You may be able to change your hair, and your makeup, and wear different clothes, but the yellow Mustang parked next to the swings, you don't think that'll tip Erv off?" She looked pleased with herself—as if thwarting us was beneficial to her!

"Gina, you'll say anything," I said, "because you don't want to go, you don't want to help me."

"I want to get to Bakersfield!"

Another half-hour passed. Another sixty half-hours could have passed, because it was I who had become blind to the truth of what Candy and Gina were saying. In my car, we could not go to Paradise. And yet without my car, I was headed nowhere. *Nowhere.*

We sat and eyed each other grimly through wine-drenched eyes.

"I'll take a bus," suggested Candy.

"Yes, you take a bus," Gina instantly agreed.

"You're going to take a bus to Paradise?" I said. "And once you get there, then what? Is it a small town? Will you get around on foot? Is it Larchmont with sidewalks everywhere?"

"I don't know. It's a town. Clearly it will have some sidewalks. Huntington did. Rapid City did. Salt Lake did."

"I'll go instead," I suddenly said. "*I* will take a bus to Paradise."

After a gasp of incredulity, Candy laughed. "You want to take my five-year-old baby and say, come on, honey, we'll go and see your mama, but first you gotta come on the *bus* with me?"

"Why not? Bus or car, Candy. What, you think she'll more likely get into a yellow car with me? I guarantee you the rule applies to getting inside all kinds of transportation with strangers."

Candy placed her hands flat on the table. "Exactly," she said. "Just think about what you're proposing."

I was slow and on wine drip. I wasn't used to thinking, wasn't used to drinking. I wasn't used to living. Candy was used to a certain kind of living, but this? Figuring out the smart thing, the responsible thing? This is the girl who was going to take her child on a plane to a place ten thousand miles away without a passport.

"My child will never go with you anywhere. You think a five-year-old is just going to hop on a bus, into a Mustang, on a bike with you? Never. She knows *me*. She's my kid. How in the world do you think she's going to come with *you*?"

"What do you want me to do?" I said, downing (or drowning in) my glass of wine. "I want to help you. But I don't know how to."

"I told you this all along, Shelby," said Gina.

"Yes, you told me and told me!"

"I don't need your help, guys," said Candy, skeptical about the threat to her life. I felt overwrought. Gina had checked out. She had ordered a cheesecake and was relishing it. I wasn't looking at Candy or at Gina. I just stared at my two hands.

All three of us sat in that restaurant, trying to work out the stirrings of our souls, trying to meander through the fog. For a moment Gina looked pensive, thoughtful, as if close to an idea. Then she said, like a lightbulb had gone on, "Let's go to Circus, Circus and think about it. They have free drinks there. Yesterday's dealer, Raul, told me to come by tonight, said he'd be working the ten to six shift. Let's just go and think about it." She smiled as if we hadn't a care in the world, as if her fiancé had not refused to drive four hundred miles to help his future wife.

"Let her go," Candy said to me.

"No. Let her go and then what? We'll be pulling her out of there at dawn. Then she sleeps all day, and it all starts again. How long am I going to be sitting in Reno figuring out your life, Candy?"

"Not just my life, Shelby," she said.

"Please. Both of you. Stop." I got up. "I need to do something to clear my head," I said. "But all we're doing is driving, and getting robbed, and gambling. I can't think straight about anything. I can't remember a single thing I've learned. I've lost control of myself, of my life, of this trip, and of everything I wanted to do. I don't know how to help you, Candy. I don't know how to help you, Gina. Tomorrow morning, I need to get in my car and drive back home. I can't go to Mendocino anymore, do you understand? I can't go! You tell me what you want me to do. Otherwise, Gina, you make your own way to Eddie. And you, Candy, make your way to Tara."

"I can take a bus," said Candy. "That was my plan. Then she and I will head out."

"Head out where?"

"I still don't know," she said. "I haven't got that part figured out yet."

"He's waiting for you," I said. "What don't you understand about that? He's there, and he is waiting for you to show up. He knows you're coming." I was standing. I may have been talking too loud. "You can't show your face in Paradise, and the girl won't come with me. How do you want me to help you with this? I don't know what to do to help you." I was wrung dry of answers, of solutions, of ideas. Miserably, I started to cry. It was the wine crying.

Gina came to me. "I told you this, Sloane," she said, putting her arms around my neck. "All along I told you. Let her go. There is nothing you can do. You cannot help her. It's not your problem."

"Well, it's my problem now, isn't it?" I said, through my wet hands, stepping away from her.

"No, honey," said Gina. "It isn't. It's hers."

Candy got up. "Let's go back," she said. "We're all exhausted."

"How can we be?" I exclaimed. "We slept till five in the evening!"

"I'm not exhausted," said Gina, shaking her hips with a gurgle. "I'm ready to rumble."

We paid the bill, split it two ways between me and Candy. Gina had very little money. "You go rumble," Candy said. "Take a taxi to Circus, Circus. Have fun." To me, she said, "It's okay. Let her have a few hours. You know when she meets up with Eddie and they get married, she won't be able to sit at the blackjack table until 7 a.m. Let her do it now, while she still can."

"Bye, guys. Raul is waiting," said Gina, hurrying out the door.

"Yes, Gina. Raul is waiting." Candy waved.

The cab took Gina to Circus, Circus and us back to Motel motel. We told Gina to call the room if she needed rescue, but she didn't listen, was far too intent on getting out of the cab. By the way she hurried toward those gilded, casino doors twinkling invitingly open, I didn't think we'd be getting an emergency call from her any time soon. On the way back to our room, I told Candy about my conversation with Eddie. "Why did you call him?" was the first thing she asked, as if preemptively suspicious of my motives.

I suggested to her that if we used some of the money we had made the night before to pay for Eddie's insurance and gas, he could come to Reno, and the three of us, sans Candy, could go to Paradise together to retrieve Tara. We'd have Eddie for protection, we'd be in a different car, we'd be hidden, and we would help out Gina by reuniting her with the love of her life.

Candy listened like she always listened—intently. "It's interesting what you say, Sloane. There are a couple of minor flaws with your plan. Though I can see why you'd think it was a good one." She had her skeptical face on again. "For one," she continued, "you have to get it out of your head that my child would set foot into a car with a man and two chicks, none of whom she knows. It cannot happen, and it won't happen."

"Maybe you can call her, prepare her," I said.

"Call her. Last time I talked to Tara was a few weeks before Mike died. After that, I called the house, but that bitch hung up on me, then her repulsive husband hung up on me. I called back, and said, 'I'm the baby's mother,' and she screamed something into the phone to the effect that if the baby knew what kind of mother she had, she'd be ruined for life. So—no. Hard for me to call Tara and let her know what's happening. I told you, Mike knew this gal called Nancy, who had a bookshop, but Nancy is not a family friend. She can't herself call Mike's mother, ask to leave a message for a five-year-old."

I tried not to sigh like I couldn't breathe.

"And the second thing," Candy said quietly, "and this is something you obviously have not understood in all the years you've spent with Gina, and all the hours you've spent with her in your car, is this." The lights outside were rushing by. There was traffic. People crossing the street in front of us, laughing, well-dressed. "Gina is not going to Bakersfield. I'm not sure she ever intended to."

"What?"

"Shelby, Gina didn't come with you on your journey because of Eddie. She came with you because of you. She came to escape her life. Think how many times she didn't mind staying longer, lingering a few days here, a few days there. She got in the car with you, into the covered wagon to go west, because she too was looking for the summer, all the while hoping it was not with Eddie. Despite what you think, when that thing happened with you and him, it showed her what kind of boy Eddie was, what kind of husband he'd make. Her faith in him was gone. He was just an excuse to leave. As it was, you told me her mother barely let her go, even with you. How many times has Gina called her mother?" Candy paused. "Once, by my count, to ask for money. And she wasn't even there." She shook her head. "The worst thing that can happen to Gina is if we pay Eddie to come to Reno to help us. Unless," the girl said—and this is where her skepticism kicked in again—"unless you already suspect all this, and the idea was always for you and Eddie to go to Paradise together—and alone." She raised her eyebrows, in the darkened cab.

Rolling my eyes, I told her how silly she was, and turned away to the window, my heart aching with longing, briefly but viscerally imagining the sunny days in California, just me and Eddie in his beat-up truck with bare rims, no AC, just the hot wind from the orange groves, us together, me and him, going to find Tara, to save Tara's mother.

In the room, Candy drew the shades. I had a shower to rinse the wine from my pores. It didn't help. We got into bed, turned off the lights. I lay facing the window, thinking about Gina, while she lay facing the wall, her back to me. She said, "Shelby, I'm sorry. Gina is not going to help you help me. She is not going to leave here."

"What do you mean?"

"Now, you have a choice, Shelby. You can help me get my baby. Or you can leave tomorrow morning and drive to Mendocino. You have a thousand dollars. That's what you're up against. Or you can forget your mother, for the time being; there will be another time to find her. Go back home, and pack for Harvard. I hear it's a good school. You don't have much time. Summer is soon over."

"I'm not leaving here without Gina," I said firmly. "Her mother will *kill* me. She only let her go because she thought her baby girl would be safe with me."

"She *was* safe with you. But she's not a child. She's not my Tara. She was safe until she found her life. Now she's got to work to put it all together. And you have to work to put your things together."

"I don't have my things," I said into the pillow. "I have *your* things. I have Gina's things. That's what I got."

"Shelby Sloane," Candy whispered, "I have been abandoned by all the people I thought were my friends. I have surrounded

484

myself with those who hate me, who want to hurt me, who have betrayed me. My father is my rock, but unless I become a man and a monk, he cannot help me with my life. You are the only one who has not abandoned me. Please. Don't leave me now. All I want is my girl," she said in a bare tingle of a voice. "She's all I got. Her and you."

"God, Candy, don't say that."

"It's true."

"How can I help you?" I said. "Look what we just went through. You have a black eye; the guy who gave you money took it away, and then beat you up."

"I know. It's not always easy, living."

"I wish it were *sometimes* easy. Just once. Because I'm out of tricks."

She turned to me, sidled up behind me. Her hand caressed my shoulder, her breath was in my neck. She kissed the back of my damp head. "Shelby . . . please. Help me."

I closed my eyes. "What do you want me to do?" I said.

"Go get my baby."

"We talked about this . . ."

"Not you and Eddie. Just you."

"Without Gina?" Why did I say it so shocked?

"Sloane, Gina is not leaving Reno. Get it through your head. It took her a whole country, and a hundred towns, but she's found her life. Reno is calling to her. She's not leaving."

"You want me to go to Paradise *alone*?" I gasped, seeing nothing but Erv's wild eyes across the Roy Rogers table, telling me *I will not stop until I find her. You get what I'm saying to you?*

"I'll wait for you two right here," she said.

"Candy, no."

"I'll give you a picture of me and a letter to give to her."

"Does a five-year-old read?"

Her arm went around me. "Mike said she learned to read when she was four. She's very smart, Tara. Much smarter than me or Mike. Show her my picture. Give her my letter. Tell her I'm waiting for her. Tell her we're going to start a new life together. I've been telling her that I would come for her. Tell her I've come, the time is now."

"And I'm supposed to get there how?"

"We'll rent you a car."

First I laughed. Then I cried. She was so earnest, so serious. She had lived much, was old before her time, yet she didn't know the first thing about the practical world, about how it worked. She was like me, asking Emma if the motels gave you towels and shampoo. Her hand still caressed me. "Candy," I said. "I'm eighteen years old. *Eighteen.* No one rents cars to eighteen-year-olds. I don't have a credit card. No one rents cars to eighteen-year-olds without a credit card. You're just . . . I can't speak about this. I'm telling you, this is doomed."

"Don't say that. If this is doomed, then I'm doomed."

I swallowed. "Let's go in my car."

"We can't."

I turned to her. In the dark room, I felt all alone, overwhelmed by both fear and longing.

"Ours is a God who does wonders," Candy whispered. "All you have to do is ask Him in faith."

"Is that all?"

"Yes," she said. "He does not always give you what you want, but He always hears your prayer."

"Does he?"

"Yes. Did I ever tell you the story of the miracle at the fourteenth station?"

"No."

"No prayer asked at the fourteenth station ever goes unanswered," she said.

"What is this fourteenth station? I've never heard of it."

"You've never heard of Christ's fourteen stations?"

"No."

"And you make fun of me for not having watched 'The Brady Bunch.'" She smiled disbelievingly. "You'll have to learn the first thirteen, otherwise what's the point?"

"I don't know. What *is* the point?"

Reaching out she touched the strands of blighted hair in front of my blighted eyes. "Help me," she whispered.

"Help *me*," I whispered.

"He's not here," she said, "the man to give you a thousand dollars for touching me. There's no one watching this time," said Candy.

"I know," I said, drawing her near, drawing myself nearer to her. My hands intertwined on her back. Her soft skin pressed in the night against my skin. She was so warm. We lay on our sides, face to face, breasts to breasts.

In the deep of night, the lights out, her smell on me, her hands on me, her bleached hair rubbing against my arm, I thought she was asleep. I was staring at her intensely, trying to catch the contours of her shoulder, her elbow, her mouth, and then I saw her doe eyes blink at me.

I didn't know what to say. She spoke first.

"So," she said, "do you know any lullabies?"

"What? Oh. I don't know. Maybe one or two."

"Can you sing me one? Any one."

I thought of what I knew. Admittedly, not many but I knew one for sure. "Hush Little Baby," I said

"How does it go?"

"Hush little baby don't you cry . . ."

When I finished, she said it was pretty. "How do you know it?"

"I think," I whispered, "Emma sang it to me . . ."

We lay in the bed, a breath apart. Everything was dark and quiet. The air conditioner creaked and hummed.

"Shelby," she whispered, "you're a lovely girl."

"Candy," I whispered back, "*you're* a lovely girl."

"You know," she said, "my whole life, when I've been with another person, I've thought of other things. I count, or knit in my head. Mostly I sing Psalm 69; want to hear it?"

487

"Yeah, sure."

"*Save me, O God; for the waters are come in unto my soul . . .*" she began to sing, and broke off. "But I don't feel much like it tonight. When I was with Mike, I was so young. We were just fumbling through it, and then I got knocked up, and was sent away for a while till I had my baby. Being with someone, it's never been that good. Has it been for you?"

"Well, I haven't had your wealth of experience," I said. "But Eddie was good."

"Really?"

"Really." So sad and sick to think now, how the waters of him had flooded into my soul.

"Maybe that's what it is, then," Candy said. "Maybe that's why you can't let him go."

"I *can* let him go," I lied, I denied. "Don't have much choice, do I?"

She ran her hand along my stomach. "You're sweet," she whispered. "Soft."

"You, too." I closed my eyes.

"Oh, Shel," I heard her say. "What are we going to do?"

When I turned to her she was staring profoundly at me in the dark. "Nothing. What can we do?" I paused. "What are you talking about?"

"Ahh." She waved her hand away and fell quiet. "Talking 'bout everything, I guess."

I waited. I couldn't get my breath back to reply, this close, sealed up, locked like this into another human being. I was on my back, she on her side next to me.

"I'll do anything to help you," I said. Finally. One true thing.

"You know," she said, "when I first came to Huntington, I used to hang out by the river with my friends, but sometimes I'd go there alone, sit in the sand and look across. The Ohio is so wide in Huntington, it's like a sea, and beyond the river is another state, another life. I used to sit and dream of what that other life might be like, would be like. If I crossed the river, and went far

488

away, where would I go? I dreamed of Australia, because it was across the banks of the Ohio."

"Most things are across the river," I pointed out. "But why Australia?"

"It was the farthest in the world I could go and still be on this earth," she replied. "It had an ocean, sun, exotic fish."

"Yeah, sharks."

"I dreamed of nothing else, because it was so impossible, yet so desperately desired. In pity for myself, I'd sit and sing . . . *I asked my love, to take a walk, to take a walk, a little walk, down by the sides, where waters flow, down by the banks of the Ohio . . .*" Her lips kissed my arm, my shoulder. "Except for my dad, no one ever cared for me like you," she whispered.

"I told you, I'll do what you want," I said, my voice breaking. "What do you want me to do?"

"Go get my girl," she pleaded. "And then the three of us will find a place. We'll find a place to live. You know I need you to take care of things. And you need me to make money. We'll get jobs, a little apartment. And my baby will be with us. We'll go someplace where the houses have flowers in every yard and a church on every corner. We'll take her away from her horrible life, and me from my horrible life. We'll putter, and work, go to the bookstores, out to eat, and to church on Sunday. And I won't be alone. Nor Tara. Nor you."

For a long time I didn't speak. Couldn't speak. Her fingers continued to caress my stomach.

"Candy, are you . . . serious?"

"Guess not," she replied, her voice fallen. Her hand fell too, lay flat on me.

But there was a moment between her dream and my question, in that silence of space, in the dark of night, before thought or reason, where I caught a fleeting glimpse of the flowers and the spires and the white-washed houses, maybe a little blue water in the distance, where far away across the banks of the Ohio there was a hill, live oaks, and tall pines, where perhaps wine was served in small cafés, and in the school playground, on the swings, sat a small girl in braids and a floral dress, swinging, singing. It was like the scent of a coral rose, the canticle of bliss.

In the morning—at least I hoped it was morning—Gina was still not in the room, and my head felt thirty pounds full of fermented grapes. Candy laughed at me, stretched, jumped up, got into her old clothes. It was eleven in the morning.

"I can't believe Gina's not here," I said, putting on my shorts, my tank top.

"I told you—she's not coming. You want her, you'll have to go and get her."

"Don't tell me you think she's still at that table. With Raul."

"Oh, yes." Candy grinned. "When you ask her, she'll say, Eddie? Eddie who?"

"Funny."

I was self-conscious; she without reservations. I was ashamed of myself, that I could only look at her surreptitiously while she was bouncing around smiling openly at me.

"What am I going to do, Candy?" I said. "I can't leave her in Reno, can I? Just lose her in the casino. Oh, sorry, Mrs. Reed, is she not in the car? Oops. Must have left her at the blackjack table. So silly of me."

"Sloane, you've got more important fish to fry right now. Don't worry, when you come back with Tara, I guarantee, Gina will not have yet left the casino." She laughed at her own humor. "Me, I'm going to wait right here. Me and your car will be waiting for you and the baby girl."

Why did she mention my car like that? "How am I supposed to get there?"

"Take a bus."

"By myself? I'm going to take the bus by myself?"

"It's a bus, not the wheel of an airplane! But fine, let's go to

490

Circus, Circus, see if we can pry Gina's hot hands off the chips. Maybe she'll come with you."

"I wonder why she didn't come back," I mused. "Perhaps she won last night."

Candy nodded. "Don't you see? She's never going to leave either way. You're right, who'd ever leave a winning table? And if she's losing, she's just riding out the wave until she gets hot again. No one leaves, Shel. The trap door of Reno is above her head."

We couldn't find Gina. Raul had long ended his shift, and she was nowhere to be found. Candy told me not to worry. "She knows where we're staying. If she needs us, she'll call. Or she'll come. She'll be fine."

Back at the room, we moussed down my hair to make me look subdued and ordinary. We bought me a dress, and I *never* wear a dress. Especially one like this: long in the knees, with large purple flowers, ruffles at the hem and neckline. I looked ridiculous. "No, you don't, you look forty," Candy said, adjusting my buttons. "You look motherly and warm, like you're about to bake cookies."

"Splendid."

I left her my money, for safekeeping, taking with me a hundred dollars for a motel and a burger.

There were no buses going to Paradise from Reno, but there was one bus a day leaving for Chico at 3:25 p.m., the cashier told us, getting in at 11:15 p.m. I had questions for the cashier. Where was Chico, and how would I get from Chico to Paradise?

"What am I, an information booth?" she squawked. "I sell tickets. You want one or not?"

How in the world would I get a room that late, and where? I couldn't get a map of Chico in Reno, I couldn't . . . "Let me just take my car," I pleaded to Candy. "I'll take my car, I'll park in Chico."

"No," she said. "You can see that damn car for miles. It's like a beacon."

"Paradise is not Nevada. It's not flat desert."

"How do you know? You've never been there. California has desert. Isn't Death Valley in California?"

"Is Paradise in Death Valley?"

"Could be. Might be. I don't know. Do *you* know? I'm not ruling anything out, the way Mike described it. No car."

Time was ticking. Just ninety minutes till the only bus of the day left. "I'll come with you," Candy said.

"You can't. One glimpse of you, and—you're worse than my yellow car."

"I'll wear a wig."

"Forget it. You're already like Twiggy."

"Who?"

"Forget it. Wait here. Besides you have to wait for Gina. I don't want her to get frantic when she comes back to the room and finds us both gone."

Candy sighed. "Babysit the car, babysit Gina."

I fixed her hair, pulled it away from her face, wiped yesterday's mascara from under her eyes, touched her cheek briefly. "You think you have it tough?" I said. "I'm going to be in Chico at 11:30 at night without a room."

"Hang on," she said. "If there's only one bus to Chico, maybe we should find out how many buses there are *from* Chico."

Apparently there was also one. Leaving Chico at 11:25 in the morning, when Tara would still be in school.

"You'll have to stay one extra day," said Candy, giving me another fifty dollars out of the depleted stash of money. "You'll have to stay with her in your hotel, then take the bus back the next morning." She shook her head. "I don't like this at all. Tara's going to get scared. Instead of just driving, or riding, she'll have to spend a night in a motel. I don't think she's ever been in a motel."

"I could just take my car," I offered again.

"Cut it out," she said. "We could sell the car. Buy another one. Heck, with the money we'd get from it, we could buy three."

"No! I told you already. I'm not selling the car. I can't talk about this again." Why couldn't she understand?

"Okay, okay. What are we going to do?"

"What *can* we do? Tara is going to have to spend a night in a motel."

Tears came to Candy's eyes. "She'll get scared without me."

"I'll call you on the phone. Stay in the room. As soon as school is out, I'll bring her to the motel and we'll call you. You'll talk to her, she knows your voice, she won't be scared then. She knows your voice, right? You spoke to her a lot?"

Candy hung her head. "When Mike was alive, I should have called more often," she said. "But my life was so yukky. And the time difference . . . every time I thought of calling it was too late in California."

"But it's three hours earlier."

"I guess. But I was always busy in the evenings."

"What about Sundays?"

"She was with his parents."

One more hour till the bus. I left most of my things in the room, just took one change of underwear and a toothbrush in a little bag with Tara's things in it. We sat in the Greyhound station on a long wooden bench. The inside of the terminal smelled of people who had come into town with luggage and jewelry, perfume and money, and having lost it all, having sold it all, having pawned it all, were now sitting twenty-four hours in a depot waiting for the next bus to nowhere, because they had nothing.

Candy and I sat close, looking down at the floor. She took my hand. "Remember the two men in the Andes?"

"God, please no. Not that again."

"They did what they had to do. And they made it."

"The worst thing I ever heard. Don't remind me. So did Lena and Yuri, you know. They did what they had to."

"They were not those two men."

"I can't help thinking that perhaps I'm one of the twenty-nine unlucky ones. Whose flesh is about to be ripped off."

493

Candy smiled. "I'm going to tell you something about Judas," she said. "To make you feel better."

"I've never heard that sentence before today. But please, God, not that, either. How about a joke? A joke would be good right about now."

"Judas is not the worst story. It's the best story."

I was puzzled. "Judas in the pit of remorse for eternity is the best story?"

"Yes. When Jesus was dead on the cross and in the tomb, his disciples scattered, because they thought all was lost, all was hopeless, and around them was nothing but black despair. They thought they were defeated, that the world was right and they had been wrong. They thought they were doomed. But the truth was, God would not abandon his creation. The story wasn't over, Sloane. It was just beginning."

"Ah," I said, staring at her. Perhaps she was right. Some things required *more* contemplation, not less. You needed to think harder about the things that were the most difficult to figure out, until your puzzler was sore. You could not abandon the Question, though when you were eighteen, how desperately you wanted to. It was the prerogative of youth, to think of nothing as you blared the music with the windows wide open. The spiritual pressures didn't go hand in hand with Blondie and the Bee Gees. To hear your inner voice, to search for the Answer, you had to turn down the music. And who wanted to?

I brought with me a bag full of things for Tara: her ball, her dolly, and her markers. I brought her a dress, some underpants, a brush, a mirror, a picture of her mother, a letter from her mother. "Don't open the letter," she said. "Just give it to her."

"Of course."

"Tell her I'm waiting."

"That's the point."

"Tell her you're going to have an adventure. Tell her you're my best friend."

I blinked.

494

She gave me Mike's parents' address. "But don't go to the house. Just in case that's where Erv might be. Go to her school." Her school's name was written on a piece of paper. All the Pomeranians, Chihuahuas, and Taras, from Glen Burnie to Three Oaks to De Soto to Paradise, on scraps of paper in my hand.

"You have to stay put," I said. "Gina will be back."

"Of course she will." Candy smiled. "And you, come right back, okay?"

"Of course I will. Paradise sounds worse than the well of eternal sorrows."

"Exactly." She shuddered. "That's what Mike said. Just go get my baby. Tell her Mama's waiting for her."

I had seen the girl's small scribblings. "*Hapy Valentin, Mama, wen u com, I giv u chokolats and roses. From Tara.*"

"I don't want to do this alone," I said.

"I know."

"I can't do it alone."

"You can. You will."

I shook my head. "Even in your stupid story, *two* men schlepped together up the Andes. Who's going to watch my back?"

"God will watch over you, Shall Be."

Twenty-five minutes till the bus left. We got in line. Tara's bag was in my hand. Did I bring even a spot of lipstick for myself? What if I had to stay an extra night? Did I bring my running trophy T-shirt, my spiral notebook, the things of my other life? "I don't want to do this," I repeated in a whisper.

"Then, I'll go," Candy said. "Let me go. I'll be fine. You'll see. You've always been a worrier. You wait for Gina here, wait for me. Give me your dress."

This *is* where I rolled my eyes.

Twenty minutes.

Ten.

My turn. Before I climbed the steps, she kissed me. Around her neck my arm went. "*He shall give the angels charge over you,*" she said. "*And keep you in all your ways.*"

At my seat, I opened the window, and she stood underneath. "Be good, Grace," I said. "Do as we discussed. Please. Promise? Your Jesus commands you to be good."

She smiled back and waved. "Christ didn't come to earth to make bad men good," she said. "He came to earth to make dead men live." She blew me a kiss. The Greyhound hissed a shot of steam into the atrium well.

THIRTEEN
YOU ARE ASCENDING INTO PARADISE

1

Endless Skyway

The bus ride was interminable. Two hundred miles seemed to take longer than the last three thousand.

I slept some of the way, my head bouncing against the glass. When I opened my eyes, it was raining. I closed them again. Pretty. Wet fields. The sky was gray. The bus passed through snowy mountains. It got colder, strangely, for it was summer, but it *was* cold, and raining—decidedly *not* like my dreams of what California might be. The mountains and trees were the color of storm. We drove through the Tahoe National Forest where the trunks of trees were the size of cars; it looked man-made, movie-effect unreal.

The rain cleared, the sun shone, glinted through the wet; it got warmer; we opened the upper windows, and the air smelled of damp orange blooms. It was a long way on the winding two-lane highway, through fields of orange groves, past distant mountains, grass, green, the tangerine sun, the summer air, it smelled of familiar, happy things. California looked to be a paradise. But Candy had described it as the worst place on earth, full of hicks and narrow minds, ugly and oppressive. Maybe I was in the wrong place. She said Paradise was on Route 70, but clearly it wasn't, for we left Route 70 far behind, and were now somewhere else, between here and there.

When I opened my eyes again, the afternoon sun was shining

on wet strawberry fields. The bus was stopped at a farm stand. Did anyone want some strawberries? I clutched Tara's bag and didn't move. We bounced along again. I asked where we were.

"In California," said the unfriendly woman next to me, clutching her own bags. The strawberry fields looked so pretty, stretching deep into valleys, the orange groves blooming all around. The sun ... I don't know. It looked different in California. And in the distance were mountains. It was warm with the windows ajar, but not boiling like Reno. I touched the glass with my hands. Did a five-year-old need a ticket? I had never even *talked* to a five-year-old. Why hadn't I babysat? I was always helping Emma, never had the time. Like Candy. But different. Was Paradise here, in these strawberry sun-kissed valleys? Maybe Mike hadn't told Candy the truth because this sure didn't look awful. I closed my eyes again to try to keep my heart from pounding. I couldn't think of tomorrow, tomorrow was too frightening, even in this sun, and I didn't want to see Erv's face again—ever. What if he was waiting for Tara as she got out of school? And what if Mike's parents were there? Who picked a child up from school? I decided I would wait for her at recess. But I couldn't take her out of school, could I? Just like that, in the middle of the day? Who was I? How would I explain myself? If only Candy could have come with me. Or Gina. That Gina!

The sun was setting. It was nearly eight, or nine, late, and the fields were burnt sienna and golden green. It looked peaceful, and I was scared.

We're making good time, the driver said. We'll be in Chico early. We'll drive through Paradise first. We should be there in thirty minutes.

The road narrowed and wound far uphill, trees overhung the road, mountain vistas peeking through, strawberry fields glimmering in the valleys below. The bus chugged up the sloping hill, and didn't stop. The hill never plateaued, just spiraled up and up, through pines, groves and fields. Finally, just the embers of the sun remained in the blue and purple sky, on flat land at a mountain pass, under

Ponderosa pine full of sunset light, I saw a wooden sign adorned with blooming pink flowers: YOU'RE ASCENDING INTO PARADISE, it read. POP. 13,000, ELEV. 2400. Not as high as the Great Divide that we left long ago, but high enough.

You're ascending into Paradise. We were twenty-four hundred feet above sea level. Dusk had set; the bus had stopped at a light. I jumped up, pushed my way past the unfriendly woman, rushed to the front. "Do you think you can let me off here instead of Chico?" I panted. "Please?"

"I'm not supposed to," the driver said. "I'm responsible for each and every person on this bus. What if something happens to you?"

"Something's happening all the time," I said. This gruff man thought he was responsible for me?

"You got luggage?"

"Just this bag."

The light turned green. He pulled the lever and the doors hissed open. "Watch your step," he said. "*Comé con Dio.*" What did that mean? I took French in high school; a lot of good it did me.

I walked down a Main Street called Skyway with my bag (wondering why they called it Skyway) until I found a cabin in a place called Ponderosa Pines. I slept like the dead with all the doors chained and locked. The next morning was like one I'd never seen before. The sun was shining, filtering through the soaring spires of pine. The slight, southern breeze gently tossed the needled branches and danced the heads of the pink and white flowers that bloomed everywhere. There was no one else in the cabins, except for the one, of course, right next to mine. An old blue Lincoln was parked in front with a worn-out bumper sticker: "God is my co-Pilot." I waited for the people to come in or out, just to talk to someone, but everything was quiet. It was still early, and I had to find Tara's school, and Tara's house perhaps, to see where she lived. Candy had told me that they lived in a trailer park. I could get a cab there, but did cabs go inside trailer parks? Maybe I could just look at it from the outside. The girl attended Pearson Elementary; how far was that from here? A map would've been helpful. I told the woman in reception I'd be keeping the room for another night. She in turn gave me a map, told me Pearson was just off the Skyway, and that the Paradise Trailer Park was right behind Skyway, too, and nowhere near Tara's street, Lovely Lane, which apparently had no trailer parks on it, only small private homes. On the bad local map of the town, I found Lovely Lane.

2

Lovely Lane

A cab came and drove me around town at my request. When the ten bucks ran out, I got out, but I freely admitted I liked seeing things from the passenger window. What a novel way to see the road—out of the side window! Paradise is laid out in an upside down V on a flat butte in the high of the Sierra foothills, so if you drive just a few streets east or west, you'd go right off the cliff that overhung the stretched-out canyons and the valley below. Green-covered mountains ranged as far as my eye could see.

I had the cab pass quickly by 24 Lovely Lane. Tara lived in a little freshly-painted white house, nested in high old pines, and surrounded entirely by red and yellow flowers. It had a white fence, and a dog barked in the back.

I saw supermarkets and a library, a chamber of commerce. There were restaurants and drugstores, and a place called "Nancy's Books." That must have been the place Mike had called Candy from. There was a Paradise Recreation Center, set on pine needles with a playground; the center had pool and picnic tables, and everything was shaded from the California sun by the 200-foot Ponderosas.

Paradise had a church on four corners of every street. Catholic, Episcopalian, Baptist, Methodist, two Assembly of Gods. Why did they need two? There was a Safeway, an Albertson's and a Longs Drugs.

There was stuff. There was everything.

The cabbie dropped me off on Pearson, just as school was letting out. I watched four older girls, maybe nine or ten, with their books on their backs, walking home, gabbing with each other in the sunlight.

And farther on, in the school playground, on the swings, were three small girls. One of them, sparkly and golden, her feet up in the air, kicking high, swinging mightily, was a child that could've been Tara.

I placed my hands on the chain-link fence and pressed my face to the diamond opening, gaping, my mouth quivering.

Sometimes, no matter how hard you try, you cannot escape your life.

And sometimes, no matter how hard you try, you cannot keep it.

Which of those was this moment in time for me? For Candy?

It was as if my life had two realities. One in front of me, in which mothers walked their children to school on sidewalks under pines, and girls in pigtails ambled home cracking gum and jokes, the sun in their hair, in a town high up in heaven where cars stopped at school crossings, and there was a church on every corner, sometimes two, and where a boy said, here, let me help you take that out to your car, and where there was a book fair in October, and a ten-mile run from Paradise to Chico, and a winter festival and a dog festival, and where they now used the town's money to put up complimentary telescopes over the valley so that anyone who wanted to could study the sky in search of Aurora borealis.

And then there was Candy's world, where a strung-out man took small girls, dressed them in pigtails and school clothes, and hung them from trees, made them do unspeakable things and did unspeakable things to them. And, as if that weren't enough, he filmed his depredations and sold them to other men who paid

504

very good money to watch privately in the dark. This pitiless man took his lover's child, fresh from the monastery and sold her young body for smokes, gifts and icy cash to his friends at the local bar, he pimped her and kept the money she earned. He had a menu of her services typed up which he discussed and negotiated while she stood silent nearby. He plied her with alcohol and drugs to make her more pliant, put red lipstick on her thirteen-year-old mouth, black mascara on her lashes, bought her mini-skirts and told her not to wear underwear. He bought her tube tops and halters and told her not to wear a bra. He did all this, then brought the money he made off her to the girl's mother and said, here's your new washing machine, your TV, the truck you wanted. He traded her young body in stinking alleys and in adult bars at night, then used the money she made to buy Christmas gifts for her mother and his family. And the mother said to the child, why are you doing so bad in school? They keep calling me every day saying you're cutting eighth period and fifth period. What are you doing?

Erv Bruggeman's world was the only world that Candy knew, and all the people she had met were those who were turning their backs on her now. A universe of sewers separated the sun-drenched avenues of Paradise from the foul alleys of Huntington, but every once in a while a blighted soul tried to escape through the manholes. But all Candy did, every day of her bleak and lonely life, was look for the manholes to crawl back into.

All roads are parched and barren that lead to God, she said to me.

I watched the girls on the swings with a sadness so profound, I couldn't stand up anymore. I sank to the ground on my haunches, hoping the nice Paradise cop wouldn't arrest me for loitering, and put my face in my hands. I couldn't watch them anymore, I couldn't sit anymore. I didn't know what to do.

Like this I sat, shaking to the depths of my soul with sorrow, sat in the mess I could not claw out of. I didn't know how to turn away from the girls, or how to come close. I didn't know how to begin to right myself. Please help me, was what was on my breath. Please, please *please* help me. Help me.

A voice said, "Hey, Miss, you okay?"

I looked up into the face of a blonde angel in a pink dress, who handed me a tissue of dubious pedigree and said, "Here."

Her friends were at the monkey bars, looking at her and me, and giggling.

"Thank you," I said, or thought I said. What a sight I must have been. I wiped my face, blew my nose. I felt red and swollen, absurd, like a salt-sprinkled snail. I tried to get up, but my legs were noodles. The girl stretched out her hand.

I took her little hand, but pushed myself off the pavement. I crawled, half-standing, to the chain-link fence and sat down on the ground against it. She came and stood by me. "I'd sit with you," she said, "but I don't want to get my dress dirty."

"You're so right not to," I said. "Your dress is too beautiful to sit in the dirt."

"Thank you. My nana got it for me."

"Oh yeah? And what's your name?"

"Tara. I'm five. I just turned five on July fifteen." She smiled. "I'm a Yankee Doodle baby, I'm going to a big girl school now. I just started kindergarten. Are you in school?"

"I was," I said.

"Oh, you must be big."

"Do I look big to you?" The tissue was wet. It was disintegrating in my hands.

"Yes," she said with a giggle. "Big and sad."

"Well, I am sad."

"Why are you crying?"

"Honestly, I don't know. I just . . . felt blue all of a sudden. Does that ever happen to you?"

She nodded solemnly. "Last year I cried because my dolly's head came off, but I was a baby then, and my daddy fixed it." She

506

paused, for the briefest second. "My daddy died. Nana was sad. She cried. My daddy was her son, but she has two more sons, my uncles. Sometimes I cry when I miss my mama. Do you want to come play with us?"

I glanced behind her. "Those your friends?"

"Yes."

"You girls here all by yourselves?" I don't know what I was thinking. I wasn't really thinking, just crying.

"No. Megan's mama is over there, eating ice cream." She waved into the distance, too far for me to see clearly, where on a bench, under a pine, a woman sat wholly oblivious to little Tara in the street talking to a sobbing stranger.

"Where's *your* mama?"

"She's coming to get me," said Tara. "She writes me letters. I'm a big girl now, I can read them all by myself. Nana used to read them to me when I was a baby."

"Your nana reads you your mama's letters?"

"Uh-huh. She used to. Not anymore, because I'm big now. I keep them in my box where they're safe. I have seventeen dollars in there, and almost four dollars in quarters. Nana says that when Mama comes she can live with us and Popup."

"Your nana says that, does she?" I said. "Well, lucky you." I struggled to my unsteady feet at this point remembering that my sole purpose in being here was to introduce myself to this child and say, *I am Shelby. I am your mama's good friend, and she is waiting for you, here is her picture, and here is a letter she wrote to you, and if you come with me, we will catch a bus to where your mama is waiting. I have some toys for you, and a dress. Coming, Tara?* Why couldn't I even begin?

"What's your name?" the girl said.

"Shelby."

"Shall be?" And she giggled.

"I don't know, Tara," I said. "I may never know." I felt in my pocket for Candy's picture, for her letter. "Do you know your mama's name?"

507

"Yes. It's Grace Rio. I am Tara Rio. Well, Tara Rio Cordelli."

"Tara!" A woman's voice sounded from under the trees. A white-haired, extremely concerned woman was hurrying across the sand to us. "Tara! Come here now, young lady!"

"I gotta go," the girl said. "I'm not supposed to talk to strangers. Please can I play with your ball for just a little while?"

"It's yours. I brought it for you."

The girl's brow furrowed, her round face scrunched up. "For *me?*"

"Tara!"

She grabbed the ball and started to run. "Bye!"

"Bye . . ." I called after her, clutching the chain-link and her mother's picture, her mother's letter, while she skipped to a woman who scooped the girl up into her arms, admonishing her with her voice while caressing her with her hand; stern words but gentle kisses. She carried her all the way to the parking lot, to a tan station wagon, carried her and her bag, her little stones, her blue ball, and then put her in the backseat, strapped her in and kissed her. I watched the girl's hands wrap around the woman's neck as they hugged. She then got behind the wheel and drove away. On the bench, under the trees, Megan's mother finished her ice cream, and took the two other girls into her own car. The playground was quiet. Not even my hand rattled the chains.

It was early afternoon, and I had missed my bus back to Reno. I was supposed to call the room to tell Candy we'd be coming, but now I couldn't call and didn't know what to do. I had all these things in my bag for Tara that I forgot to give her, a dolly, a new dress. She looked so much like her mother. She had the same eyes, calm and deep, too wise for a five-year-old. There was no one walking on the street, but maybe in one of the parked cars, Erv sat stalking, waiting.

I didn't feel his eyes on me. But then I didn't feel anything. I walked the three miles back to my room, sat outside my little cabin under the pines, called no one and did nothing. At night

I watched TV. I didn't eat. I didn't drink. I didn't have a shower. In the early morning, I put my stupid matronly dress back on, and packed my few things—Tara's one bag.

I walked three miles along the Skyway back to the school. The buses were pulling in for the morning session. It was crowded. I felt conspicuous. I wished I had a camera. Well, why should I have had a camera? I was supposed to be bringing the real thing! Not a Polaroid. Oh, Candy. If only you could see her. Everyone was that small girl. Candy. Me.

I thought Tara might take the bus in the mornings, but not two feet in front of the coffee shop where I sat, the tan wagon pulled up, and the same silver-haired woman got out. She wasn't old and she wasn't ugly. Her clothes were decent and ironed. Just her hair was white. Maybe it had gone white after she lost her son; whose wouldn't? She opened the rear door and unbuckled the girl, helping her with her backpack. Tara had pink ribbons in her hair, and ladybug barrettes holding the front wisps away from her face, that's how close she was, that's how clearly I could see her. My nose to the glass, my hand fanned out, as if waving. Goodbye, Tara. She was wearing overalls and a yellow shirt with ruffles, ballet slippers for shoes and pink socks. The woman straightened her collar, wiped her mouth, bent to her head. Tara ran to school, waving. "Bye, Nana!" The woman watched her until she disappeared through the school doors. Then she drove away.

My hands remained flat on the glass. I wished I had my car. I wished I had it, so I could get in, and drive to Mendocino, or back home, never go back to Reno, never face Candy again, because I couldn't. I couldn't face anything.

It was nine in the morning. I called a cab company number tacked onto the public phone outside the coffee shop, and rode the ten miles to Chico, not seeing the canyon below, or the mountains, or the slight bright morning haze of a late summer sun. At 11:25 my bus came, and I got on, me, my dolly, and the pink dress with yellow flowers. The doors hissed closed.

509

On the bus back to Reno, I opened Candy's letter to Tara.

Dear Tara:

It has been so long since my heart has been with yours. Please—for me—above all things, be glad and young.

For, if you're young, whatever life you wear, it will become you.

Know that I am always with you. Wherever you are, wherever I am, where my treasure is, my heart is also. And my only Heart is with you.

Mama

It's as if she knew I wouldn't be bringing her baby back. It's as if she thought I was leaving and never coming back.

The eight hours on the rattling bus back to Reno were the longest eight hours of my life.

3

Four Last Things

The longest, that is, until the three days I spent in Motel motel, pacing, and cursing, helpless and alone, without Gina, without my car, without Candy, my hands fully emptied. The money left with Candy was gone. She must have taken it. I began to suspect that she, knowing I would not do what I told her I'd do, and not having any other way to be rid of me, sent me on a fool's errand, while she packed her things, took the money, sold my car, and was now headed to Paradise herself, to do what I could not do. I drank water out of the tap, and read Gideon's Bible.

Lift up thy hands that hang down, and thy feeble knees.

The longest three days, that is, until the five-hour ride in the back of the police car to Paradise. No strawberry fields for me, this time, no sunsets, hills or blue skies, no ascensions. Distinctly, I felt like Judas, desperately clawing his way back up to the small light.

By the time we reached Paradise it was late and dark. Yeomans and Johnson asked if I needed anything, and I said no. Like what? Look, Detective Johnson said, you look real beat up and scared, but this is the thing. You reported your car missing in Reno. You said your friend might have taken it. The guy at Moran's junkyard confirmed that a young gal brought the car to him. It was in good condition, he saw the dollar signs and didn't think of anything else. He gave her a thousand dollars for it. The girl fit the description of your friend.

"Okay," I said. A *thousand* dollars for my car! Well, it's only right. That's the money Reckless Man gave her and took away. "Why are we here, then?"

Yeomans and Johnson glanced at each other. "Early this morning, the body of a young woman was found at Neal's Sanitary Landfill off Neal Road. She had no identification on her. We think it may be the girl who took your car. She had some identifying, similar markings. You think you'll be okay to come take a look?"

My hearing left me. Mutely, I started to cry. "No, I'm not going to be okay," I said. It was like I crawled into my eardrum to hide and left no room for sound. "Where?" I whispered, but no one heard. "I'm not going to the town dump." I shook my head. "No."

"No, no. She's been taken to the morgue. If it's her, maybe we can notify her family. Does she . . . have family?" Yeomans asked with hope.

"It's not her," I said. "She's not here." I was nearly inaudible. Johnson patted me on the back.

"I hope you're right," he said. "But that's not what you said when you called to report your car missing. You told us she'd be heading to Paradise in your yellow Mustang."

I never looked up. "She didn't know how to drive." I kept staring at my feet, at the ground. "Why would you seek me out for this?" I asked. "Why would you come get me all the way in Reno?"

"This sort of thing doesn't happen often in these parts," said Yeomans. "The Reno cops were in touch with the Paradise PD. When we found her, we thought maybe the two were connected." He paused. "And she's been three days unidentified," he added.

They brought me to Enloe Medical Center in Chico, and took me down to the sub-basement, possibly even beneath even the sewer pipes, where all was cold steel and fluorescents. A man in a soiled white overcoat and black glasses, a man who didn't look at us, the living, even once, as if he had no interest in the still-breathing, took us to a room full of metal drawers, slid out one of the lower ones, number 518, and pulled a white sheet away from a small thin body. I didn't have to look at anything more than the tattoo on her bare left shoulder and the matted bloodied blonde of her sheared hair. Accidentally, I noticed the parted frozen mouth, the half-open eyes; the yellowing black-and-blue underneath one of them. I wanted to touch her dear head, to fall to my knees and kiss her hands and feet, but I could do none of these things. They told me she'd been bludgeoned, and my legs gave way. As they helped me up, the drawer slid shut with a metallic thud. I should have touched her, and will regret that I didn't for the rest of my life.

I don't remember how I got upstairs, but Yeomans sat me at a table in the hospital cafeteria. Johnson got me a hot tea.

"Tell me," he said. "Do you know anything about how this might have happened?"

"I know absolutely nothing," I said. "But I do know the man who killed her."

I told them everything. The man who killed her was Erv Bruggeman. He had been following us since Indiana. She had something of his, and he wanted it back. We told her not to come here, we told her he'd be waiting for her. She didn't want to believe us.

"Who's us?"

I blanched. Did I say us? God, what happened to Gina? Where was she?

"Why would she come here?" asked Johnson.

"Her little girl lives here," I replied.

Johnson asked where the film was.

"With her father."

Johnson looked notably relieved. "I'm so glad she has family," he said. "After the worst happens, all you want is for them to be properly buried. I can't tell you how many times in Reno these sorts of things happen, unfortunately, and the bodies remain unclaimed and unidentified, cremated in the end on the taxpayers'

513

dime as John Doe or Jane Doe. You want them to have a name in death. As in life. What was her name?"

"Her name was Grace Rio."

And so it came to be that Estevan Rio left the monastery in Melleray, Iowa, and came to Paradise, looking twenty years older than the last bright time I saw him, bringing the film his daughter left with him and a genuine monk-made, Trappist pine casket.

"Merciful Father, by your Son's suffering, death, and rising from the dead, we are freed from death and promised a share in your divine life. By the hands of monks, each day raised in praise of your goodness, this casket was fashioned for your child who died in faith. We ask you now to bless it. Receive the soul of our departed sister who is laid in this humble bed as in a cradle, safe in your care. As the thief who had confessed, Remember her, O Lord, when you come into your kingdom."

She was buried on a dazzling Friday in Paradise Cemetery, under a tree close to the overlook where Chico Valley lay as far as the eye could see to the hazy horizon, Estevan, the funeral director and me at the graveside. Tara didn't come, but she gave me back the dolly to be placed with her mother in the pine box, a picture of herself wearing the dress Candy had bought for her, and a Valentine's Day card. She kept the ball. After the burial, Estevan and I went to the Paradise stone and cement company to order a simple, black granite headstone. It was going to take eight to ten weeks to arrive. Estevan paid in full.

GRACE RIO
1963–1981
"She skated on noisy wheels of joy."

After the funeral, we met Tara and her grandmother Nora at the Paradise Recreation Center. I introduced Estevan to his grand-daughter, and he sat for a few minutes with her and me on a bench under the Ponderosas, showing us the pictures he had brought with him of a very young Grace. We agreed mother and daughter looked very much alike. "I wish you could have seen your mother," said Estevan. "She was beautiful like you."

"Oh, I did see my mother," Tara told Estevan.

"When did you see her, child?"

"A few days ago." She thought a moment. "Maybe seventeen days last Thursday. She came to the school, kind of like you did, Shall Be. We sat together, we talked."

"Did she cry like me?" I asked. So Candy did see her baby girl, after all.

"No." Tara giggled. "She said she was happy to see me, and happy to see me happy. She said she really liked my life. She bought me ice cream, and cotton candy, and a white clip for my hair. See?" She showed us the little white flower that held back her bangs. "She said she would come see me again someday."

Estevan briefly held the child on his lap as she talked, his hand patting her kindly. We were high in the hills, it was warm, and the smell of pine and fading summer was strong.

Nora called for Tara from the shadow of the mighty trees, the safety of the station wagon.

"Nana!" Tara called. "Come here."

"No, Tara, you come here!"

An open, loving child, Tara hugged Estevan. She even hugged me. Then ran to Nora, joyously skipping the whole way.

"That's how Grace was, too," said Estevan as we watched her, my heart so liquid with sorrow, I thought it would weep itself out of my chest. I clasped my arms around my stomach. "She was just like that, skipping through the abbey the first seven years of her life. She couldn't walk without bouncing. She ran and jumped and played hide-and-seek with the squirrels. She had to force herself to walk, but even after, she was like a spring, up, down, up, down, so full of joy."

I turned away as he spoke, faced the pines and the yellow gardenias. "She was still like that, Brother Estevan," I said. "She never lost that."

515

"You couldn't help it," he said. "Watching her roll around, pick flowers brought smiles to our faces."

"Maybe that's just what all children do," I said, not really knowing, watching Nora's face watching the animated Tara, talking, gesturing to us, folding her arms on her chest.

He nodded, wistfully. "Maybe. She was the only child I'd ever known."

The woman took Tara's hand, and together they slowly walked toward us.

"You see, Shelby, just when you don't know how," Estevan whispered to me, "a mystery happens." He stood up tall, dignified even in grief, stoic in his white cassock and black tunic, his hands ever ready for a blessing, a prayer.

"Estevan," said Tara, "I wanted my nana to meet you. She still doesn't believe me that you are my mama's daddy."

"I am," said Estevan. "I was."

Stopping in front of us, Nora nodded to Estevan, eyed me warily, but spoke only to him. "Ah," she said, her brown eyes widening. "*That* girl had a monk for a father? Well, well. The mysteries just don't end."

"You're so right about that," Estevan replied.

"So why didn't you want to take her, bury her somewhere close to you?"

"I think she would have preferred to be close to Tara."

I knew this to be true.

Nora stood awkwardly. She didn't know what to say, what to do. Did she shake his hand? Did she bow her head? He made it easier by making the sign of the cross on her, which gave her permission to retreat, step by step, as if she didn't want to turn her back on him. "Would you, um, like to come to the house with us?" she said, trying not to stammer. "Maybe have a bite to eat?"

"You are so kind," said Estevan. "Too kind. Thank you. But I must be going."

"Of course, of course," she said hurriedly, notably relieved. "But do come and see the girl, won't you? Any time you want. It'll make her happy, and that's all that matters. She'll be glad to know her mama's daddy. I want her to be happy."

"I can see that," said Estevan. "I live in a monastery in Iowa. This is the first time I've left New Melleray in eighteen years. I will try to come again for a few days, when I can get a little time. But you are always welcome to visit me with Tara. We offer hospitality to all guests. You can stay as long as you like. I live in a sanctuary. It's very peaceful."

Tara clapped with delight. Nora said they would try to come when they could. Before she left she said, "We received a package from her a few days ago. She enclosed some personal things of hers." Nora coughed. "There was a considerable amount of money. A few thousand dollars. I—I feel uncomfortable with it. Perhaps I can make an offering to your church?"

Lightly smiling, Estevan shook his head. "My abbey won't need it. Leave it for Tara, please. I know that's what Grace would've wished. Had she wanted me to have it, she would have sent it to me."

Pulling on her grandmother's hand, Tara was jumping up and down, squealing. "Nana, nana, nana . . ."

"What, Tara?"

"Maybe I can get that pony now? You said I could. Please?" She put her hands together as if in fervent prayer.

Apologetically, Nora shushed the girl, with an expression of *kids these days*. They said goodbye to us and walked back to their car, Tara holding Nora's hand, chatting to her, looking up at her. Something in Nora's stance, her hair, the shape of her face, I couldn't quite grasp or place it, reminded me of Emma. That ever-patient, slightly exasperated expression, that kindly, always-leaning-down tilt of the head, as if ever ready to listen, to hear anything. That proffered hand. Nothing too demonstrative. Except . . . I had seen the way Nora had kissed Tara as she strapped her into the station wagon. As if her entire heart held only Tara in it.

We watched them disappear from view, then Estevan turned

to me. "I really do have to be going," he said. "I have a long ride back."

"Don't I know it."

He took a breath. "What are *you* going to do?"

"You know," I said, "I have absolutely no idea. *God pity me*."

"*Whom God distinctly has*," he said in reply. We shared a cab to the Chico bus station. His to Dubuque wasn't until tonight. Mine to Mendocino was in forty-five minutes. We sat on a bench in the waiting room, the way his daughter and I had sat, in Reno, a lifetime ago. We didn't speak for a while.

"The last time I saw her, she said to me that no prayer was ever denied at the fourteenth station."

"Yes," the monk said. "In faith."

"She never told me what the station was."

He nodded ruefully. "Did she tell you to go learn the other thirteen? Just like her." He folded his hands. "The fourteenth station is Jesus dead in the tomb."

I turned to walk away, but at the last minute turned back to him and said, "Make it as secure as you can."

A light came into his eyes, and a small smile to his sad mouth that quivered slightly when he said, "Yes. Be not afraid, Shelby."

Nothing to be afraid of now. I had nothing left. I thought of calling Emma, but, considering I lost her twenty-thousand-dollar present, couldn't. I thought of calling Gina's mother, but, considering I lost her daughter, I couldn't do that, either. I didn't know what to do about losing Gina.

Johnson had said they would need me to testify in Bruggeman's murder trial. He'd been found, arrested, held without bail. Stay close, Johnson instructed. I asked for his card, promised I would get in touch as soon as I knew where I was.

One place I clearly wasn't: Cambridge, Massachusetts. Another place: Larchmont, New York. Neither was I in Reno. Or Paradise. I was on a bus—to Mendocino. We passed lake Geneva as the sun was setting behind the circling blue mountains. Night fell and gradually thickened with a dense, swirling fog blown in from the bottomless Pacific. The narrow, darkened lane was overhung on all sides by looming sequoias the size of skyscrapers, and the top-heavy bus lurched alarmingly, filling me with terror as it made those blind, ninety-degree turns. Behind me a woman began to pray. Slowly, slowly, on we went, winding through that seemingly unending black nightmare road. There was no light outside and the bus lights dimmed. I closed my eyes. Blind turns and then—nothing.

Hours later, terrors later, the bus finally dropped me off in Mendocino. I flew off that bus. I had with me nothing but the bag holding the remains of Tara's things. The cops didn't tell me to go back to my room in Reno, they didn't tell me to take my stuff, and I had left all I had brought with me in Motel. I left my books and my makeup, my clothes and my music tapes. I left my toothbrush, my underwear, my mini-skirts. I left my maps, and my spiral notebook.

In the pocket of my jeans I had a mint, twenty dollars and my license. This is what I took with me, this is what I had with me as I jumped off the Greyhound onto Lansing Street.

"This is Mendocino?"

"This is Mendocino." The doors were closing, the driver already pulling away.

I stood in the middle of the street, looked up the hill, looked down the hill. The town was quiet. It was nearing eleven in the evening. Matins? Vespers? Compline? How could it be compline? It meant after supper prayer, and I had not eaten anything but stale potato chips for two days. Far in the black distance was the sound of hard-breaking waves. It wasn't windy, and it wasn't warm. It just was. Across the street was an Irish bar, Patterson's, and from the bar came noise, the happy hubbub of drinking friends. I didn't go there, I shuffled down the hill. I looked down one street—darkness. I looked down another, darkness—but with a yellow light shining. The street was called Albion and the yellow light

519

shone in front of a white, multi-story house with steep steps and a glassed-in porch. A sign outside said, "MacCallum House." I walked up the steps, knocked. A voice from inside said, "Come in."

I came in, in my worn jeans, with my worn life around me, I came in, barely lifting my head, and said to the two men and a woman sitting at the small bar, "Can you tell me please if there's somewhere to grab a bite around here?"

"What, at this time of night?" One of the men jumped off his stool and came toward me. He stood right in front of me, but I couldn't look up. Not at him, them, the house, or another human being.

"Just something quick."

"This is Mendocino," he said as if that explained everything. "Closed by ten."

"Patterson's might be open," said the guy at the bar. "I don't know if they're still serving food."

"Yeah, they're open," I said. "Is there a bed and breakfast around here?"

"Um, *this* is a bed and breakfast," said the man in front of me.

"Oh. Do you have a room?"

"Yeah, we got a room." He paused. "Hey," he said.

I didn't know what that meant. Hey. I was looking at my dumb shoes. They were so beat up and the strap was broken. No wonder I was limping. I hadn't even noticed. I scraped the mud off one heel. "How much for a room?"

"A hundred and thirty dollars," he said.

I was quiet. "For a *bed and breakfast?*"

He said nothing.

"Anywhere else to stay? A little cheaper?"

"How much cheaper?"

I didn't know. I didn't say.

"Hey," he said again, but quieter, tilting his head down to peer into my face.

Finally I lifted my eyes. In front of me stood a dark, perfectly groomed, curly-haired young man in a white shirt and jeans. He had an open face, clear eyes.

"How much you got?" He smiled, appraising my bleached cropped hair.

"Twenty bucks."

Whistling, he grunted. "You'll have to wash dishes tomorrow. You'll have to barter for your room at the inn."

"I'll do what I have to."

"Hmm. So will you be needing *two* keys?" he asked, squinting lightly, his mouth quirking.

My gaze focused on him. "No."

He stuck out his hand. I took it.

"I'm Noah," he said.

"I'm Shall Be."

EPILOGUE
MacCALLUM HOUSE

One April, when the weather was dry and crisp and the azaleas were in yellow bloom on the bluffs of the Pacific, I was behind the bar, opening the books for the day, when a voice, a ghastly voice from the past, said "*Shelby?*"

I almost didn't want to look up. I'm good at that, looking at my feet when I need to lift my eyes. But I had already gone to morning Mass, I didn't need to lift my eyes again, the heavy lifting was already done. But maybe not. Eventually, profoundly reluctantly, I raised my eyes.

In front of me stood Gina Reed.

Gina, with her hair kinky permed and short, heavier, thicker from the eyes down, her chin, her neck, everything on her looking like she lived a life filled with many intense petty comforts, a life in which she denied her body nothing. She was wearing something indeterminately paisley and carried a bag from Nine West.

"*Shelby?*" she repeated incredulously.

It was April, but it could have been December, at night it got to the mid-forties in California, but the days were warm and the flowers fresh, so wherever you stepped in Mendocino, the Pacific Ocean was always seen through a prism of yellows, pinks and lavenders.

Funny how things get you.

Shelby?

Well, that *is* my name. I shouldn't have jumped or been startled.

It was the question mark at the end of it that was startling. The question mark at the end of my name carried with it years of uncertainty. In other words: Shelby, is that you? Because you've grown and you don't look like yourself, but weren't we friends? You don't look like that girl anymore. You're wearing a smart Armani skirt, you're pressed, your hair is straight and short, though you've kept it blonde, I see. You've gained or lost weight, the heels make you taller, the lines of life on your face make you nearly unrecognizable, and so I put the question mark at the end of your name, because I'm not sure it's you, and if it isn't, I will just apologize in embarrassment and walk on. The lilt at the end gives you permission to smile thinly and say, nope, not me. You got the wrong girl.

The years could have been kinder to Gina, for when she was young she had been so pretty. I could still hear through the haze of decades the boys calling out to her, "Oh, Geeeeena . . ."

This always happens to me—the world goes on mute for a few moments. Almost like I press pause on life and then mull whether to rewind, or get up off the couch, and go watch another show, or just instant-replay back to make sure I heard correctly, felt correctly, reacted as I should have to what was in front of me. I felt that the whole glassed-in porch with the Georgian windows fell on mute, too, and even the Australian travelers, who had been chatting animatedly about Coral Reefs and floods and cane toads, were holding their breath for what was next. We stood still, she and I. I looked at her, she looked at me, and we stood, and we said nothing. In my periphery, a woman stepped forward supported with her cane, thanked me for breakfast, and limped outside. For a few moments in time, a tick here, a tock there, one year, two—

"Oh my God!"

Sound came back. I slowly put down my tray, slowly; it clanged loudly against the glass countertop of the buffet. I came around the bar. We hugged. She was thick, and smelled of cigarettes. "It's good to see you. How long has it been? Twenty years?" Note my own hopeful question mark!

"Twenty!"

"Yes, yes, you're right. Twenty-five, more like."

"Twenty-seven years, Shelby," Gina said.

"Of course."

Awkwardly we stood.

"So, what are you doing here?"

"What are *you* doing here?"

"I'm having breakfast. We're staying at the Seacove Inn, down the road."

"Yes, I know it. Nice place."

"Not as nice as this. And you?"

"Well, I'm here. The MacCallum House is mine. Mine and Noah's."

"Who is Noah?"

Noah came downstairs, in his booming boots and indigo Cherokee stonewashed jeans. He was helping build a new garage and was not dressed for guests. I took care of the mornings. He labored outside. Tonight we were having a wedding, white tie, and everything had to be just right. There was a lot to do. Noah shook Gina's hand. "You're married?" She assessed him. "How long?"

"Too long," Noah said, pinching me. "I'll have Gracie come help you. I gotta go. They're waiting."

"Yes."

"Grace? He knows about *Candy*?" said Gina, with surprise.

"Who?" asked my husband.

"Grace is our daughter," I said.

"Oh, my God, you called her *Grace*?"

Once again I lowered my eyes to my shoes under her gaze. "Why is that so surprising?" Noah whispered to me. I pushed him gently away. Finally he bounded down the porch steps and was gone.

Gina stood by the bar. "What the hell happened to the both of you?"

"Us? What happened to *you?*"

Gina shrugged. Clearly the events of back then had grown fuzzy in her memory. She couldn't recall the sequence of things. She said she tried to find us, only to find us gone.

"I don't know how that could be," I said. "We looked for you for days. For all I know, my stuff is still at Motel motel. I never took it."

"Don't I know it. That weird creep had thrown all our things in the trash. I had to dig through a dumpster to find my duffel."

"Where did you go, Gina?"

"What?" She waved her hand. "I really don't remember. So what are you doing now?"

"Living here," I said, wishing I could take a step back.

"When did you make it back?"

"Back where?"

"Larchmont."

"I never did make it back. You?"

Gina shook her head. "I'm still in Reno." She rolled her eyes and laughed.

"Really?" I said. "Candy suspected as much. I hadn't believed her. You married?"

"Married, divorced, married again. Separated. I'm seeing somebody new now, trying to save up money for a quickie."

"A quickie what? Divorce or marriage?"

She paused, then chuckled. "I guess both. My boyfriend's real nice. He's a dealer."

"Not Raul?"

"Who?"

"Nobody, nobody. So whatcha been up to in Reno?"

"I have a dealer license," Gina told me. "Suspended. Can't practice at the moment. A little trouble with the casino. They accused me of embezzling, but I wasn't. I didn't. Case didn't go to court, I pled down, but lost my license in the process. But I'm bartending, so it's all good. Just a little probation."

"Whatever happened to Eddie?"

"Who?"

I was silent.

With a shrug, Gina said, "I don't know what happened to him. I never called him. For all I know he's still in Bakersfield."

"Yeah, maybe."

"Married to Casey." Gina laughed. "To think there was once a time when that mattered so much. More than anything in the world."

"To think." There was once a time when many things mattered more than anything else in the world.

"But what about you? What about Harvard?"

"Didn't go," I said. "I came here. Got a job, worked here, behind the bar." I smiled to even things out. "I was bartending, too. Took accounting classes. Noah and I got married a few years later."

"So you never left?" Gina looked through the front doors to the outside. MacCallum House is on a small hill, and beyond the rooftops you can see Mendocino Bay morning and night. "And now you own this?"

"Yeah, we bought it three years ago. Noah is a carpenter, a construction worker. But his friend Jed made a lot of money on dot coms. We went in on this together. Bought it from the old owners."

"Wow." She shuffled her feet. A fleeting cold wave passed across her face. "Well, I really have to be going."

She didn't ask about Grace Rio, about her little girl, what had happened to either of them. Didn't ask, didn't care, didn't want to know. Quietly Gina said, "I read in the paper about that guy. I'm glad he went down. Years later, I know. But still."

"Yes. After fifteen years of appeals." So she did know. Knew something, read the paper enough to know about it, a murder trial in another state, followed by a conviction, years later an execution. She knew. Just didn't ask. Well, what was there to ask, really. What was there to say? I told you so?

My hands have been muddied my whole life by not ever knowing what the right thing had been. To open my car? To go in the first place? To send her on her own? To never leave her side? Except . . . I hope that Candy's Tara has had a different life. That's the only thing. Candy must have hoped for that, too. Because, she, too, left Tara be, to her swings and her blue ball.

"It was good to see you," Gina said.

"Yeah, you, too."

"You mind treating me to breakfast? Bill was kind of steep."

"No, no, 'course not. Breakfast's on me."

"Thanks." She smiled. "Hey, aren't you gonna ask if I have any kids?"

"Do you," I asked neutrally, "have any kids?"

"Yeah, a girl." She giggled. "Can you believe it, me, a girl."

"I believe it. I have a girl." And two sons—for Noah.

"Mine's eighteen. What an age, huh?"

"Sure is. Mine, too." She's a senior at Mendocino high school that overlooks the ocean. She works with me on Saturdays, and goes up to Fort Bragg with her friends, calls me every five minutes asking for advice prefacing every query with a plaintive "Mommy . . ."

We were both looking at the wooden floor under our feet. Some things are just easier not faced. Unfaced, but not unwept. "What's *your* girl's name?" I asked.

"Tiffany."

"Ah. Where's her dad?"

"Out on parole in '09," she replied, slightly sheepish. But only slightly. "Tiff and my new boyfriend get along real well."

"Oh. Good for you. That's important."

As she was heading out the door, she turned around. "I almost forgot," she said. "Did you ever find your mother?"

"No." No trace of Lorna Moor anywhere. It wasn't as if I hadn't tried.

"Huh. Sorry about that. I know how much that had meant to you. You know, I stopped by your aunt's house in Larchmont many years ago. I must have been twenty, twenty-one. They said she'd gone. No one knew where."

"She came out west. I brought Emma with me when I knew I'd be staying."

"Really? You did that? Well, that's great."

"Yes," I said. "It is."

"How's she doing?"

"Good. She's our office manager. She walks the headlands every day."

"Oh, man, those headlands," said Gina. "Too windy for me."

"Yes. Emma likes that. Needs the extra shot of oxygen. The sun brings the tides and the tides bring the wind. When the sun goes down, the wind dies. She's always there at sunset. Tries to get Grace to go, who'll have none of it. Emma forces her to go on Fridays. Like penance."

"Penance indeed. Great. Well. Tell her I said hi."

"I will."

I turned away from the door, so I wouldn't see her clomping down my stairs and out of the gate. I heard her, though. Clop, clop. Then she was gone. The gate creaked. Carefully I washed out the glasses I needed to dry and stack for tonight. There was so much preparation for a wedding. No time to waste. I kept my mind here, on the glasses, and the oysters, and the crates of Cristal arriving any minute. Noah came back inside, all hammers, plywood and ripped apart jeans but a white shirt and designer stubble. He laid his dirty tools right on the bar counter despite my vocal protest, and said, taking the glasses from my hands and stacking them on the tray, "Okay, I'll bite—who in the world was that? And who is Candy?"

The story of Judas and the eternal sorrows had been far away until Gina clambered up into my room full of memories. I never forget. I never stop thinking of Grace Rio, because the roads that led me here, to the only place I ever want to be, haven't all been paved in gold. And yet, just when I thought it was over, my life was only beginning.

531

Not hers, though.

Lines from a poem came from long ago, one she had read to me in that other life I call youth.

> i walked the boulevard
> i saw a dirty child
> skating on noisy wheels of joy
> pathetic dress fluttering . . .
> while nearby the father
> joked to a girlish whore . . .
> of how she was with child

To Noah's questioning eyes, I waved my hand dismissively. *You know what I have been thinking,* she whispered to me our last night in Reno, *traveling with you through every mile of this country? What if there is no place in the world for me?*

That's what I was afraid you were thinking, I thought, but to her I said, *Don't say that. Look around you. The world is so big, so beautiful.* I tried to convince her. *There is a place for everyone. We just have to find it.*

Mendocino Bay was in front of me through the yellow-painted houses. To the right were the ocean headlands, and morning. Emma was out there somewhere communing with the divine. My own house was here, where I stood, with the glass porch, the Georgian windows, and the parquet floors.

You cannot save your life until you lose it utterly.

Well, no use loitering. There was still so much left to do.

"Are you going to tell me or no?" said Noah. "Who is she?"

"Oh no one," I replied, so casual, picking up the tray and spiral accounting books, catching my reflection for a moment in the mirrored surface of the bar. "She was just someone I used to know."

She was just someone I used to love.

A note to my readers

After I had written the first act of this story—my Shelby getting ready to go cross country—I said to my husband that I didn't think I could write the rest effectively unless I went cross country also. He was unconvinced. Me traveling by myself across the width and breadth of the entire continental United States did not appeal to him as the family's self-appointed Director of Security. He wondered why I couldn't write about a paper towel factory in New Jersey, safe and close to home. Or just make the whole thing up. "You always do."

Spending two weeks by myself in a car through the wilds of Wyoming didn't seem practical for a mother of four, like trying to be young again. He brought up another book I had once thought of writing, part of which was set in Barrow, Alaska, and wanted to know if I would've needed to go to Barrow to write it. Yes, I said, and perhaps this is why, after fourteen years of being a published author, I have no book about Barrow, Alaska. I've lived in Topeka, I've visited Dartmouth College, I was pregnant in Texas, and returned to the Russia of my birth; I've lived in New York City and been to Hawaii.

Now I had to see the Badlands. I had to see the Great Divide. I had to see Mendocino. This was also a journey I had to take, and I had to do it alone. If hubby were in the car with me, we'd be talking about the kids, arguing about directions, feeling hungry, listening to Counting Crows instead of the Bee Gees; it would be a different book, not this book: three girls on a quest for life and meaning.

I tried to rent an SUV. When I got to Baltimore, Avis didn't have my car; they were out of cars; would I mind waiting? I waited an hour. They offered me a Jeep, and a Chrysler sedan, but the Jeep was too open in the back and the sedan could've belonged to my grandparents. Suddenly the Avis man said, "I don't know if it will work for you, but a Mustang just came in. Wanna take a look?"

The rest is history. The Mustang was yellow, and it barely fit my stuff, but I was in the most audacious, fantastic, conspicuous car on the road, and renting it changed my travels and my fiction.

The other thing that changed my story was a conversation with my mother-in-law, Elaine, who said, "What are you going to write about driving on the Interstate? There's nothing to see." And she was right. I got off the Interstate. To her I owe the digressive paths that expanded my trip to 4000 miles and made this book what it is. To her I owe a lot.

Also to Susan Opie, my new lovely editor, who shared with me a magical afternoon on a balcony overlooking the seven hills of Rome, complete with champagne and strawberries, which, come to think of it, probably would've made the New Jersey Turnpike look attractive. She has proven to be a wonderful, smart, patient, indulgent editor. I'm lucky to have her.

To Linda Joyce, who, with her sharp eye and every deletion, comma, a well-placed expletive, made the book better.

To Amanda Ridout, because every time we drink a-merry and a-plenty at the Algonquin, a new project-idea-cover-title-contract springs forth. Clearly the Algonquin has remarkable drinks.

To Robert Gottlieb, for making the last seven years of my life possible, and to Claire Roberts, my new foreign rights director, for grown-up books and cookbooks and children's books (special thanks to Lara Allen for that one) and the Trek Madone—I'm biking all the way to your house in Jersey to thank you for that one!

To my high school friend Kathie. Like that Baz Luhrmann song that advised me to keep my old friends, sometimes I wish I had.

To the hubby who looked after the mass of children while I was away and to Pavla Salacova O'Rourke (I can't keep track of her last names, so fast and furious did she marry) who helped him and helps me every day, no grace and gratitude are enough.